Clarrie Hancock

by Evelyn C. Rizzo

G.W. Zouck Publishing
Beckleysville, Maryland

G.W. Zouck Publishing LLC
Beckleysville, Maryland
www.gwzouck.com

This book was set in Baskerville by Matrix Publishing Services, York, PA.
Book design by Bianca Bingaman, Kendall Ludwig.
Cover design by Kimberley Nichols.

Library of Congress Cataloging-in-Publication Data

Rizzo, Evelyn C., 1925-
Clarrie Hancock / by Evelyn C. Rizzo.
p. cm.
ISBN 978-0-9817315-1-3
1. Working class—England—Fiction. 2. Poor—England—Fiction. 3. Salford (England)—Fiction. I. Title.
PS3618.I95C63 2009
813′.6—dc22

2009006074

Printed in the United States
10 9 8 7 6 5 4 3 2 1

Dedication

Dedicated to the memory of my beloved parents,
Richard and Florence Crawford.

Acknowledgements

Many thanks and much gratitude to my teacher, mentor, and friend, Laurel Goldman, for her keen insight and guidance during the creation of this book. Thanks also to the members and former members of Laurel's Thursday morning writers' group for their astute comments and helpful suggestions. Thanks particularly to Anna Jean Mayhew, Lucinda Paris, Carolyn Muehlhause, Christina Askounis, Phaedra Greenwood, Charles Gates, James Ingram, Maureen Sladen, Jackie Ariel, Fabienne Worth, Joan Ritty, and the late Wilton Mason and Knut Schmidt-Nielsen. I also want to thank Emerson John Probst of Zouck Publishing for his enthusiastic appreciation and understanding of this work.

Thanks and gratitude to my husband, Ralph, for his unfailing support and encouragement, and to my children, Judith Gardo, Pamela Woodward, Christopher Rizzo, and Deborah Reid for theirs. And thanks also to the rest of my family, especially my grandchildren—Brendan, Amanda, Katie and Tim Stephens, Isabelle Gardo, Sarah, Graham and Evan Woodward, Benjamin and Gabriel Rizzo, and to my dear great-grandchildren, Mia and Vincent Stephens, Garrett Stephens, and Evelyn Lily Stephens de Jong, for enriching our family with their beauty, and their many-faceted talents.

Chapter One

A light flickered in the upper window of a blackened brick row house on Thurlow Street. Minutes later, the front door opened and a man emerged, recoiling as a gust of wind cut through his threadbare coat and pelted his face with sleet. With one hand holding the brim of his bowler, the other clutching the iron railing that separated his house from the one next door, he made his way down the slippery path and out the gate. The gas-lit streets of Salford were deserted. Earlier in the evening an icy gale, vicious even for February, had come howling through the town, ripping slates from roofs, slicking cobblestones, sending people scurrying home to their firesides. He paused under a street lamp to take off his spectacles, already coated with sleet. His bad eye felt like a ball of ice in its socket. And he'd rushed out without his gloves.

"Sod it!" he muttered, "Sod every bloody thing." Even the stray cats that prowled the backyard walls and chimney pots had more sense than to venture out in this lot. Pulling up his collar, he plodded, head down against the buffeting wind until he reached the midwife's house, where he found the brass doorknocker locked stiff from the cold. He hammered the door with his fist.

"Hold your horses!" The door opened a crack. The midwife raised a candle, squinting up at him. "Mr. Hancock? Good God, man, you look perished. Come in."

"Sorry to drag you out of bed at this hour, Nurse." He stamped his boots and removed his hat to shake off the sleet. The nurse pulled her scruffy flannel dressing gown closed, and pressed against the wall of the lobby to let him pass. "Is it Sally? She's not due for another six weeks."

"Aye. The pains are coming fast; we thought it best to get you right away."

"You're sure she's in labor?"

"She'd not send me out in weather like this for nothing."

The midwife set the candle down on the hall table while she fastened the cord of her dressing gown. "You better get back to her, then. I'll come on my bike, soon as I'm dressed."

"You'll never make it on your bike, love. The roads are slick as butter, and the wind's enough to bowl you over. I'll walk you back."

Nurse Walmsley took the candle and lit the gas-mantles on the wall, lighting up a large, oval-framed photograph of a bride. "Me, thirty years ago," she said.

William nodded. "Very nice."

"You'll have to give me a minute." She headed for the stairs.

William studied the photograph. Poor old girl was plain as a suet pudding even then, in spite of the bridal getup. Sally had turned up at the registry office lovely enough to take your breath away, her black curls pushed under her cap and just a bunch of violets pinned to her WAAC uniform. She was lovely still, after eight years and three children. There'd be four when he got back home at the rate it was taking that midwife to get dressed.

He paced the lobby blowing on his hands. A grandfather clock in a nook by the stairs read quarter to two. He caught a glimpse of his reflection in the hall stand mirror: he looked a bloody sight—soaking wet, unshaven, blue in the face. He rummaged in his waistcoat pocket for a comb, but before he could make himself presentable, Nurse Walmsley reappeared. She'd donned a navy blue uniform, and pinned back her grey hair in a neat bun. She thrust a bundle of papers into his hands.

"Shove these under your coat, Mr. Hancock, love, while I fetch my bag o' tricks."

"Newspapers?"

"The mattress—you don't want it ruined, do you?" She darted through a doorway and came back with a black bag and a bottle of red liquid. "Rose-hip syrup—best thing for the mother's blood. Have you a drop of gin or whiskey in the house?"

"No. Sally doesn't drink. She signed the pledge when she was just a lass."

"We'll have to manage without it then." Nurse Walmsley lifted a dark wool cape from the hall stand and fitted it around her shoulders. "Is anyone with her?"

"Just the youngsters. They've been down with scarlet fever, as you know. They're better now, except the little 'un. Sally wants you to take a look at her, if you will."

"I delivered twins over at the Rourkes's a couple of weeks ago. The poor devils lost three of theirs to scarlet fever just before Christmas." She stepped closer to the mirror and adjusted the dark veil of her nurse cap.

"Terrible business," William said. "I don't believe I know them." Why was this woman wasting time fiddling with her damned headdress?

"Irish lot . . . too many mouths to feed." She pulled a pair of knitted gloves from the hall stand drawer and wriggled her fingers into them. "A terrible year, 1925—pneumonia, diphtheria, scarlet fever, galloping consumption. Let's hope this year will be better."

William picked up his hat. "I think we'd best get a move on."

The nurse handed William her bag, turned the gas flame low and cocked a woolly grey thumb towards the front door. "Lead on, MacDuff."

Sally Hancock pulled a blanket around her shoulders, picked up a lighted candle and padded along the landing to the children's bedroom. The linoleum felt like ice under her bare feet; she must have kicked her shoes under the bed last night, but she didn't want to get on her knees to look. This baby was coming at the worst possible time. For weeks she'd been running up and down nursing three sick children, dashing out to the shops for food, and doing other folk's wash. There'd been no time to clean her own house or do her own wash. When it came to housework, Will was about as much help as a headache.

The three children slept together in a double-sized bed that had once been painted green. Now the paint was blistered and peeling, exposing the rusty metal bars underneath, and the springs sagged so badly they almost touched the floor. The children were tumbled together, Annie on her stomach, with an arm and a leg flung across Janet. Arthur was curled up at the other end of the bed, one grubby little foot touching Annie's face. It was a pity to disturb them, but she needed their help. She wasn't sure she could make it safely up two flights of stairs with a bucket load of coal.

"Wake up, love," she whispered, shaking Annie.

Annie turned, moving her arm and leg from around Janet. Sally lifted the damp strands of hair from Janet's cheek and kissed her forehead. She was burning up.

During the night a thin crust of ice had formed on top of the cup of water by the bedside. Sally broke the ice with her thumb, dipped the hem of her petticoat in the cup and wiped Janet's face. The child's breathing was labored. Sally propped her into an upright position and tapped her on the back.

"Bring it up," she whispered. "There's a good girl." Janet burst into a fit of coughing. "That's right, that's my love, bring it up."

A glob of rust-colored phlegm dropped onto the sheet. Sally poured a teaspoon of viscous black syrup from a bottle on the dresser and forced the tip of the spoon through Janet's teeth. Perhaps Nurse Walmsley would have something to loosen the phlegm. The medicine the doctor had left didn't seem to be doing much good. Janet sank back on the pillow. Sally kissed her hot cheek. She shook Annie again. "Annie!"

"Shut up," Annie muttered.

Sally gave a snort of laughter. This one grew more like Will's mother every day. "Open your eyes," she said.

Arthur stirred in his sleep. Near his hand lay a screw of newspaper. Sally picked it up and a small tooth fell out. The first of his front teeth. She wrapped the tooth back in the paper—she had nothing to leave under the pillow. Perhaps Will would have a ha'penny on him.

Annie sat up. "Why are you yelling at me?"

"I want you to help me get ready for the new baby."

"Where is it?"

"It's not here yet. Put your coat on. Try not to wake Janet."

"She keeps coughing. Arthur and me couldn't get to sleep."

"She's very poorly." Sally shook Arthur. "Come on, Arthur, get your coat on, put something on your feet."

Arthur reached for the scrap of paper. "Did the tooth fairy come?"

"Not yet." Sally sat down abruptly, doubling over as a fierce pain struck. Something hard hit her tailbone. She rummaged under the covers and removed the iron oven-plate. She'd wrapped it in newspaper and slipped it in the covers to warm the bed, but it had grown cold and the newspaper was in tatters. Annie and Arthur sat on the floor, fumbling with their bootlaces.

"Where are we going?" Arthur asked.

"Nowhere. I need to light a fire in the bedroom grate so the new baby won't freeze to death." She made a double bow in his shoelaces. "I've already brought up the firewood and paper. I want you and Annie to go down the cellar for the coal." She held out a dented bucket to Arthur. "Don't fill it or it'll be too heavy for you. Annie will hold the candle."

"I'm in charge, aren't I, Mam?" Annie said. "I'm seven, he's only six."

"Hold on to the banister. If the bucket gets too heavy, Annie will help you carry it up." She handed the candle to Annie. "Keep the flame away from your hair."

Arthur looked at her with big grey eyes. "What if we see a ghost?"

"Nonsense. There's nothing in the cellar to be afraid of."

She walked back along the landing and pulled the flannel sheets from the bed. They were a bit dingy, but they would have to do. She bent over the flattened mattress, kneading it to loosen the flocks. Her belly was in the way; it would be easier to turn the whole thing over. As she dragged the mattress half off the bed, a bedbug scuttled for cover. Sally squashed it between her thumb and forefinger—nasty, stinking thing. She tore a scrap of newspaper and wiped the smelly blood from her fingers.

She'd been fighting bedbugs ever since she and William moved here from Broughton three months ago. She'd scrubbed everything with turpentine—bedsprings, skirting boards, floorboards—but the children still woke up spotted with red bites and she sometimes found a bedbug floating in her bedside water-glass. Will said that when these old houses were built they'd mixed horsehair in with the plaster. The bedbugs loved it. All Salford was plagued with them.

They'd been lucky, though, to get a house like this—three rooms up and three down, a private back yard with a flush lavatory at the far end, a cellar with a boiler for washing clothes, and a separate cubbyhole for coal. The council people were even talking about running a gas line in. They'd got the house because Will's Great Aunt Nelly had fallen down the stairs and broken her neck. Sally felt guilty about rushing over to the Council offices the minute she'd heard about the accident, but if she hadn't, someone else might have the house, and they'd still be stuck in those two cramped rooms above that shop in Broughton.

Another pain! She lowered herself onto the bed until the pain subsided, then put the sheets back, turning them head to foot in the hope they'd look fresher.

A gust of wind shrieked through the chimney, sending a shower of ice and soot into the hearth. She went to the window and pulled aside the lace curtain. Particles of snow and sleet whirled out of the night into the yellow glow of the streetlight then sped back into darkness. A feeling of foreboding gripped her. She'd had a bad time when the others were born—what if she were to die in childbirth? William wouldn't have any notion how to manage with a new baby. What if he hadn't even made it to the midwife's? He might have been hit by a falling slate, or slipped on the ice, or—half blind as he was—slammed into a lamppost.

She turned from the window. The children were bumping upstairs with the bucket, stopping on every step.

"Let go—you'll make me spill it!" Annie yelled.

Sally went to relieve them. "Stop your squabbling."

Annie, red-faced, was holding the candle askew. The flame flared, dripping hot wax onto the floor. Sally carried the bucket and the candle into the bedroom. She threw the coal on top of the firewood then pushed the lighted candle between the bars of the grate. The fire blazed. Flame shadows leapt across the room.

"I'm going downstairs to get washed," she told the children. "Stay by the fire and keep warm. I'll bring you up some hot cocoa."

Annie and Arthur beamed at each other. Hot cocoa! In the middle of the night in front of the fire! It was unheard of.

Sally was halfway down when she remembered the chamber pots. She couldn't have Nurse Walmsley walking into a smelly house. She hauled herself back upstairs, pulled the chamber pot out from under her bed and poured the contents into the empty coal bucket. She rinsed the pot with the water from a cup by the bedside, then carried the bucket into the children's room.

Janet was on her back, arms flung out, cheeks flushed, her pale gold hair tangled on the pillow. She looked like some exquisite china doll that had been carelessly tossed aside. Sally touched the child's forehead. Still feverish. This one was so delicate—she would never get used to having such a faery child. She ought to take her into the other room, near the fire, but Janet was so timid; if she woke up during the childbirth she'd be terrified. And it was better not to expose the new baby to Janet's germs.

Sally tucked a small white sheepskin rug around Janet's shoulders. One corner was damp and matted together. When Janet was born, William's brother, Jack, who worked as a hide-classer for an abattoir, had given them the rug to put on the pram. They didn't own a pram, so she'd used it on the children's bed. Recently, Janet had taken to sucking on the thing. She'd tried several times to take it away, but Janet had cried so pitifully, she'd given it back.

The kitchen fire was low. She filled the iron kettle and a large saucepan at the scullery sink, carried them, one at a time, back to the kitchen and put them on the grid to boil.

The pains were coming nonstop and she was drenched with sweat. Better not wait for the water to heat; there wouldn't be time for a proper bath. At the scullery sink, she stripped to the waist, rubbed a flannel rag on a sliver of carbolic soap and washed her face, her breasts and her underarms. She lifted up her petticoat, washed between her legs then splashed herself with icy water to get the soap off. She sat on the three-legged stool to wash her feet.

William had left his old shoes under the scullery sink until he could afford to buy leather to mend them. His feet were longer, narrower than hers, but the shoes would do to get her back upstairs. She'd have to get Janet's old baby clothes out of the trunk. Thank God she hadn't given them away. They'd smell of mothballs, but they were clean—put away properly, the way Aunt Kate had taught her.

On her way through the kitchen she found the kettle bubbling over into the fire. The cocoa! She spooned cocoa powder and condensed milk into the cups, poured in the boiling water, and carried them upstairs. The children ran to claim their cocoa.

"I want to stay up until the new baby comes," Annie said.

"Me, too," Arthur said.

"When you've finished your cocoa, you can help me take some things out of your dad's trunk, then you must go to bed."

"I want to see Dad's costumes," Annie said.

In the alcove on the landing Sally knelt to open a wicker trunk, grimy from years of being hauled in and out of railway stations in strange cities, and dragged up and down the stairs of seedy boarding houses. She lifted out two brown-paper parcels of baby clothes. Under them, between layers of yellowing tissue paper, were William's costumes, and under those, his roller skates and a leather case full of greasepaint.

As long as he had his costumes and his skates, he could delude himself that his skating days were not over. It was a pity he'd had to leave, right in the middle of the tour, but his eyesight was getting worse every day, and nobody was interested in roller-skating anymore.

Sally closed her eyes. William, in his black and red satin Cossack costume, whirled behind her eyelids. She winced and dropped the costumes back in the trunk. This pain could no longer be ignored. "What's the matter, Mam?" Annie asked.

"Help me up."

A flood of water gushed out from under her petticoat as she got to her feet. She grabbed the parcels of baby clothes and flung them into the bedroom. The children gaped, wide-eyed, as water splashed onto the linoleum.

"It's not what you think," Sally said. "Run downstairs and fetch me some rags—the mop—anything. Hurry!"

She was wringing the mop into a chamber pot when she heard the key turning in the door. "Thank God!" She leaned over the banister. William was hanging up his coat. He took the midwife's cape. "You go right up, love," he said to her. The children were peeping down through the railings. "What are you two doing out of bed?"

"We're helping our mam get ready for the new baby," Annie said.

"Don't scold them, Will," Sally said. "They've been a big help, and they've kept me company."

"Go back to bed," William said. "We'll let you know when the baby comes."

Nurse Walmsley placed her gloves on the hall stand and went upstairs. "Now then, Sally, what are you doing?"

"The water broke while I was getting the baby things out of the trunk." Nurse Walmsley took the mop out of her hand. "Get into bed, right away."

"Give that mop to me," William said. He picked up the chamber pot. "I'll take this down, too."

"We need more coal," Sally said. Nurse Walmsley pushed her into the bedroom. "The bucket's by the scullery door." She called to William, "You'll have to empty it." Nurse Walmsley pulled back the bed covers. "Get in."

"Can you look in on our Janet, love? I'm worried about her. I gave her some medicine, but . . ."

"All in good time. First I've got to scrub up and take a look at you."

She followed William downstairs, lifted the kettle from the fire and carried it to the scullery. "I want you to scrub up, too, Mr. Hancock," she said. "I'll need your help."

"Right you are." What would she expect him to do, he wondered. When the other children were born there'd been women around to help. They'd shoved him out of the house, telling him to go to the pub for a pint. If it weren't such an ungodly hour, he'd try to get Mrs. Phipps in. She was a decent old body, and she lived just across the back street.

Nurse Walmsley came in from the scullery wiping her hands on her apron. "Go now and scrub your hands," she said. "I'm going to make some rose-hip tea. I'll call you when I need you."

He was puffing on his last cigarette stub when Nurse Walmsley called down the stairwell for him to come up.

Sally was lying on the bed, her knees flexed, her petticoat up around her chest. Her belly was standing up in a pale pyramid. A thin, purplish line ran from her navel to her pubic hair. William looked away. What a business! You'd think the Almighty—if there was an Almighty—could have found a better way of doing things.

Nurse Walmsley had set out cotton swabs and scissors on the washstand. "I'll need you to hold her leg." She pulled away a layer of newspaper from under Sally's backside where a brown stain was trickling down, crumpled it and threw it into the fire. Sally groaned softly and reached for the brass bed rod above her head. The nurse placed a hand on Sally's belly.

"Don't start pushing yet."

William stroked Sally's hair away from her face. "You all right, love? Can I get you anything?"

"Give her some of that rose-hip tea," the midwife said. William held out the cup. Sally took a sip, then waved it away.

"Here we go," Nurse Walmsley said. "Come over here, Mr. Hancock, and hold her leg. Push, Sally, that's the girl, bear down. Push, love, push! That's right. You're doing fine."

William held Sally's leg. His spectacles had slipped sideways on his nose and he could hardly see.

"You can stop for a minute now," Nurse Walmsley said. "Take a little breather, Mr. Hancock." A gust of wind howled in the chimney, rattling the windowpane.

"Will you listen to that," the nurse said. "This child picked a fine time to make an entrance. Good thing it's Sunday. You'll be able to stay home, catch up on your sleep. What kind of work do you do, Mr. Hancock, if I'm not being too nosy?"

William hesitated. "Well, right now I'm . . ."

"Oh, here it comes. Grab that leg again!"

Relieved to be spared explanations, William gripped Sally's leg.

"Push! Push! Push! Push!" Nurse Walmsley had her hands between Sally's legs. "Push love—that's the ticket, now you're doing it—push hard!"

Sally groaned. She clutched the brass bars of the bed with white knuckles; her face was crimson.

"What's taking so long?" William asked. "Can't you do something?"

"It's harder with a dry birth. She'll be all right."

Sally gave a shriek.

"This one should do it," Nurse Walmsley said. She called again for Sally to push. "Here comes the head," she cried. "Whoa! Whoa! Here it comes!"

Through a blur of tears, William saw the baby slip out into Nurse Walmsley's hands, and watched as she thrust two fingers into the baby's mouth and drew out a string of mucus.

"Is everything all right?" Sally asked.

"She's fine. A fine healthy lass," the nurse said.

"Can't you stop the bleeding?" William said.

"We have to wait for the afterbirth."

Beneath a coating of slime and blood, the baby was turning blue. The nurse lifted her by the heels and slapped the tiny buttocks. She slapped again. The shrill, pulsating cry of a newborn child filled the room. "Atta girl, let it rip!" the nurse said. The baby's skin was rapidly turning pink. "Good size, too," she said. "If it wasn't for the nails, you'd never know she wasn't full term."

"What's the matter with her nails?" Sally raised her head to see.

"They've not quite finished growing. It happens sometimes." Nurse Walmsley laid the baby on a towel at the foot of the bed while she tied and cut the umbilical cord. William was surprised by its thick, livid strength. He'd expected something more like the curled and blackened bits he had seen clinging to the navels of his other children.

Nurse Walmsley bound the infant with a bellyband then wrapped it in a blanket and handed it to William. "Here,

Daddy, take your baby. You get top marks for not passing out on me."

William lifted the baby gingerly and put her in Sally's arms. "What do you want to name her?"

"I think Caroline Eliza, after the two grandmothers." Sally took the tiny hand in her own. "I hope she won't have to go through life with no nails."

"Uh oh!" Nurse Walmsley cocked her head towards the door.

Annie and Arthur stood shivering in the doorway; Annie's face was ashen, her dark eyes enormous. Nurse Walmsley threw a sheet over Sally's legs. William moved quickly to block their view. "What's the matter?" he said. "Why are you out of bed?"

"It's our Janet," Annie whimpered. "There's summat wrong with her. Her hands are dead cold. She won't talk to us. She won't wake up."

Chapter Two

While Sally tried to feed the baby, William went downstairs to look again at Janet's body. The door to the parlor was slightly ajar. He distinctly remembered shutting that door and telling the children to stay out.

A hoarse, boozy whisper came from inside the room: "I heard that the mother laid her out herself—got right up out of childbed. I could never do that, could you?"

The second voice was younger. "She's not from 'round here, is she? She's from down south, one of them what y'callum's—Cockneys. Nowt seems to bother them."

"Not much of a coffin, is it?"

"I think the bad-tempered bugger's out of work. He sits in t'pub for an hour at a time, nursing 'alf a pint of bitter—won't even give you the time of day."

"Who's forking out for the funeral, then?"

William pushed open the door. "Not you two at any rate."

The women, both bent over the coffin, turned around. A sly fox face, button-eyed, stared at him boldly. Her cheeks were smeared with rouge, her brassy hair pressed into stiff Marcel waves under a dirty white beret—one of the floozies who hung around the pub cadging free drinks. The other—an old drab with brown snuff stains running from nose to mouth—dabbed her eyes with the corner of her shawl.

"Poor little angel. She was too good for this world."

William gestured toward the door. "Clear off, the pair of you."

"Well, I never!" The older woman clutched her shawl, squeezed past him, and hurried down the lobby.

The younger woman flared her nostrils. "That's no way to treat folks. Your neighbor told us about the little girl. We come 'ere out of the goodness of our hearts, to pay our respects."

"Clear off," William said. "Take your respects with you."

She sniffed as she passed William. "A right bloody tartar, you are, mister, and no mistake. I feel sorry for your poor wife."

Sally had come halfway down the stairs. Her hair was uncombed; her cardigan bunched up where she'd buttoned it wrong. "What was all that about? Who were those women?"

"Nobody, love—just a couple of trollops nosing around. Go back to bed." He took a step towards her, wanting to put his arms around her, to comfort her. He was stopped by the expression on her face. Janet's death had opened a rift between them. He had no idea how to bridge it.

From upstairs came the wail of the newborn baby.

"I'm dry as a bone," Sally said. "We'll have to give her a bottle . . . boil some cow's milk."

"I'll see to it, love." He went into the kitchen where the children were sitting at the table eating fish and chips out of a newspaper.

"Who let those women in?"

"Mrs. Phipps did," Annie said. "She brought us this dinner."

"Where is she?"

Mrs. Phipps poked her goblin face through the scullery doorway. "I'm right here, Mr. Hancock, love." She rubbed her hands on her apron and stepped into the room. Her legs, partially concealed beneath a voluminous black skirt, were severely bowed. "I tried to stop them women, but they shoved theirsels through t'scullery door, bold as brass. The young 'un—the suicide blonde—said she was a friend of yours from the pub."

"She's no friend of mine."

Mrs. Phipps clucked her tongue. "I should've known better."

"No harm done. I showed them the door. They'll not be back in a hurry."

"I've put some fish and chips on the oven shelf for you and the missus. Would you like me to mind the baby for you, while you're at the cemetery tomorrow?"

"Thanks, but there's no need. Maud, next door, is taking her to the church to be christened."

"Christened? So soon? Is the baby poorly, then?"

"The baby's fine, but they're having their own youngster christened, and they've offered to take ours at the same time. We never got around to it with our . . ." His voice broke and he turned away.

"You need summat to eat, love." Mrs. Phipps brought a plate of fish and chips out of the oven and set it on the table. "Who'll be the godparents, then?"

"They will; and Maud's sister, Clara, as the other godmother. The funeral's at the same time—one o'clock. Weaste cemetery chapel. You're welcome to come."

"Nay, I'd sooner make meself useful here—have a bit of tea ready when you come back." Mrs. Phipps pulled her shawl over her head. "I gave the young 'uns the last of the bread. Shall I get some for you when I do my errands?"

"Thanks, love." He slipped two half-crowns into her hand. "Get Hovis, it's better for the youngsters—we'll need milk, too."

Mrs. Phipps patted his hand. "It's the least a body can do."

He fished another shilling out of his pocket. "And we'll need a few sausage rolls—my brother and his wife are coming from Oldham. Let me know if that's not enough money and I'll see you straight tomorrow."

"Right you are." She thrust the money into the folds of her skirt.

William opened the door to a blast of cold air. "Watch out for those icy patches."

The day of the funeral was swathed in fog. Sally was fussing with the new baby—feeding her, getting her dressed for the christening, packing a canvas bag with several clean nappies.

"Can we come in?" Without waiting for an answer, Maud came through into the kitchen; her sister, Clara, behind her. Both women wore fur-trimmed coats and felt hats that covered their heads like helmets.

William nodded. "Much obliged to you for this."

Maud sat on a kitchen chair watching Sally swaddle the baby in a blanket. Clara, her younger sister, produced a compact from her handbag and contemplated her face in the mirror.

"I look like death warmed over," she said. Maud nudged her and shot a glance at Sally who didn't seem to have heard.

"Sorry," Clara said, "I wasn't thinking."

William excused himself and led Annie and Arthur into the parlor. "Go and look out of the window, Annie. Let me know if you see the horses coming."

Sally handed the baby over to Maud and the bag of nappies to Clara. "There's a bottle of boiled milk and a rubber teat under the nappies. Just pop the bottle in warm water."

In the parlor Sally found William gazing into the coffin. His shoulders heaved, and she moved swiftly across the room to take his hand. He gave a queer, strangled sob.

Arthur watched, wide-eyed, as Sally brought a pair of nail scissors out of her pocket and snipped off a lock of Janet's hair. "We haven't even got a photo of her," she said. A gold crescent fell into her hand. She placed it in a small saucer on the mantelpiece.

William rummaged in his pocket for a handkerchief. "I keep seeing her little face peeping out from behind those plush curtains in Broughton . . ."

Annie, who had gone to the window and moved aside the curtain, shouted, "They're coming!"

Stuffing his handkerchief back in his pocket, William walked to the window. Shadowy horses, their black plumes waving, emerged through the fog. A glass-sided hearse came to a halt in front of the house. The driver, wearing a top hat, climbed down from his perch.

"Open the door for him," William told Annie.

"'Morning, mister, missus." The man touched the brim of his top hat as he stepped into the room. "Are we all set, then?"

"Give us a minute," William said. "You can wait in the lobby."

With a quick last look into the coffin, Sally ushered the children out of the parlor. "Get your coats on," she said.

William's sister-in-law, Dora, pushed open the front door. She was dressed in a brown astrakhan coat and matching hat. "We're outside in a taxi, Sally love. We didn't bring our kiddies, so if you don't want them riding in the hearse, there's room for yours with us."

Sally finished buttoning Arthur's coat. "Thanks, Dora, we'd appreciate it,"

"Make way. I'm coming through." William backed into the lobby with the small coffin in his arms.

The undertaker stepped forward, "Let me take that."

"I can manage," William said gruffly.

The children stepped back on the stairs to make room.

A group of neighbors had gathered around the gate. A murmur went up as William came out with the coffin in his arms. Sally followed, holding a bunch of limp blue flowers, pushing the children ahead of her. One of the women onlookers wiped her eyes with the corner of her shawl. The men doffed their caps.

The undertaker opened the back panel of the glass hearse and helped William slide the coffin into place. He held out his hand to help Sally up the step. "Easy does it, love," he said. One of the horses whinnied, tossing its plumes.

Arthur tugged at his mother's sleeve. "Can I ride with you, Mam?"

Sally absently straightened the cap on his head. "Well . . . I suppose . . ."

Aunt Dora bore down on them. "You kids are coming in the taxi with Uncle Jack and me." She steered the children towards a black car with its engine running.

"That's it, then," the hearse driver said. He closed the back doors and climbed into the driver's seat.

Shortly after twelve-thirty, the funeral party converged in the Hancock kitchen where Mrs. Phipps had set out sausage rolls, mustard pickles, and a loaf of thinly sliced brown bread. She went to lift her shawl from the hook behind the door.

William took the shawl out of her hand. "Stay and have a bite with us." He introduced her to his brother, Jack, and his sister-in-law, Dora. "Mrs. Phipps has been a great help to us," he said, hanging the shawl back on the hook.

Dora pushed aside the sausage rolls to make room for a white bakery box. "I brought you a jam sponge and a few Eccles cakes." She spoke with a broad Oldham accent. "If you'll find me a nice cake plate, Mrs. Phipps, I'll put them out."

Mrs. Phipps handed Dora a plate. Dora ran a finger over a chip on the rim. Annie and Arthur squeezed behind the table to watch her arrange the Eccles cakes in a pyramid. "Don't touch them," Aunt Dora said. "Children must wait 'til the grownups are served."

Johnny and Maud Halliwell walked in, followed by Clara Shaw, carrying the new baby. "She's fast asleep," Clara said. "Where do you want me to put her?"

Mrs. Phipps pointed to the drawer William had removed from the bottom of the kitchen cupboard.

Clara Shaw laid the baby down. "Watch you don't step on your little sister," she said to Annie.

"It's too crowded in here," Dora said. "You'd have done better to set things out in the parlor, Mrs. Phipps."

"There's no fire in there," William said brusquely. "That's where our Janet was laid out."

The kettle bubbled over into the fire. "Where's Sally, then?" Mrs. Phipps asked.

"She's out in the lavatory, trying to pull herself together."

Mrs. Phipps poured the boiling water into the teapot. Dora took the teapot out of her hands. "Thank you, I'll pour."

Mrs. Phipps reached again for her shawl. "If there's nowt else then, Mr. Hancock, I'll be getting on back. My old fella has a fit if I'm not there to see to him."

William got to his feet. Maud, who was telling him about the christening, put out a hand to detain him. "Not a peep out of either of them—like two little angels," she said. She selected a second sausage roll. Annie and Arthur exchanged glances.

Sally came in from the lavatory and sat on the edge of a chair near the bookcase, as though she were a visitor. Dora handed her a cup of tea.

"She's taking it very well, isn't she?" Maud said in a stage whisper. "If it were me, I'd have jumped in the grave after her."

Sally looked up sharply. "Jumping in the grave wouldn't bring her back, would it? I've three others to think about." She put the tea down untouched. "Where's the baby?"

"Down there in the drawer," Maud said. "She's been an angel. You'd swear she knew summat."

Clara Shaw opened her bag and handed Sally a small scroll of parchment illuminated with colored inks.

"Here's the christening certificate."

"They've given you the wrong one," Sally said. "This is for a Clara Maud."

Clara Shaw darted a glance at her sister. "It's the right one, love. We got all the way to church when it dawned on us you hadn't told us what to name her. 'Well,' I said, to our Maud, 'We're the godmothers. I bet Sally wants us to name her after ourselves." She giggled. "So that's what we did—Clara Maud—after Maud and me." The babble of voices subsided. Clara leaned towards Sally, smiling. "You do like the names, don't you?"

Sally passed the parchment to William. He glanced at it and handed it back. "She was supposed to be named Caroline Eliza, after her two grandmothers."

"Doesn't matter," Sally dropped the parchment scroll on the bookcase table. The baby whimpered. Sally took a baby bottle from the mantelpiece and put it in a pan of water.

"You're not breastfeeding, then," Dora said.

"I've no milk." Sally picked up the baby.

Arthur fiddled with the fringe on the baby's shawl. "When is our Janet coming back?"

"Stop pestering your mam," William said. "Be a good boy. Get yourself summat to eat."

"Our Janet's dead, isn't she, Dad?" Annie said. William didn't answer.

Johnny Halliwell drank the last of his tea and pushed back his chair. "I need a fag. I'll step outside." Jack followed suit, muttering something about getting a breath of air. He paused in the doorway. "How about you, Will?"

"Not right now, thanks."

"A breath of air?" Dora said. "They're off to the pub more like it. I could do with a drink, myself."

"I've a bottle of gin next door," Maud said. "You're welcome to a drop. I'd like to show you our Gladys in her christening frock. Her Gran's over there, minding her. Is it all right, Sal, if I take her a bit o' that cake?"

"Help yourself," Sally said.

Maud cut a generous portion of sponge cake.

Dora got up, brushing crumbs from her lap. "We'll leave you and Will in peace, then."

When the visitors had gone, Annie and Arthur drew their chairs up to the table and began dividing the last of the sausage rolls.

"Leave one for your mam," William said.

Sally loosened the baby's clothes. "This child's soaked to the skin. I don't believe she's been changed all morning." She dropped the wet cloth onto the hearth-plate. "Pass me a clean nappie, Annie."

"Will that be her name, then—Clara Maud?" Annie asked.

"I suppose so. What do you think, Will?"

William unrolled the christening certificate and studied it. "There's nowt to be done about it, now. It'll have to suffice."

Chapter Three

The baby squirmed in her mother's arms. She could feel the wet places her mother had missed while drying her.

"What is it, then?" Sally said. "What are you fussing about?"

Cradled on her mother's shoulder, her face pressed against a coil of sweet-smelling dark hair, Clarrie was borne in the wake of the dancing flame across the draughty scullery. Shadows slid along the walls, glanced across the ceiling. She saw a shelf lined with newspaper cut into little points. Candlelight gleamed on a stack of chipped plates and saucers, on teacups hanging from hooks, and on a face—a rosy, jolly little man's face. The baby arched backwards, wanting to touch the red cheeks, the round black hat, but her arms were held by a confining blanket.

They turned a corner and passed through a doorway into another room, where a fire crackled in the grate. The jolly face had vanished—hope of touching it was lost. Clarrie began to cry.

"What is it?" Her mother lit an oil-lamp and blew out the candle. "I don't know what you want, child." She laid Clarrie on the table, unwrapped the blanket, and dusted her with soft sweet powder. Taking a cloth from the oven door, she held it for a moment against her face before pinning it around Clarrie's bottom.

William came in with the evening newspaper. "What's she fussing about?"

"Here, Will, you take her," Sally said. " I don't know what's the matter with her. She's usually good as gold—watching and listening, taking everything in. I'll be glad when she can tell us what she wants."

Her father pressed her tightly against his bony chest. "What are you skriking about, then, eh?" he asked. He had a smoky smell, but Clarrie liked it when he held her.

He ran a finger over her gums, then moistened a dummy teat with tea from his cup, and dipped it in the sugar bowl. "Here," he said, "let your meat stop your mouth." Clarrie closed her eyes, savoring the gritty sweetness, before lapsing again into sleep.

Clarrie was a big girl, now, her mother said—two years old—old enough to let her know when she had to go to the lavatory. But when she told her mam she had to go, her mam was high up on top of the ladder doing something with the kitchen curtains. She told Clarrie to take the three-legged stool out and climb on by herself. "I'll be there to help you in a minute."

Clarrie ran through the scullery into the yard, carrying the stool upside-down on her head. The legs of the stool hit something as she ran by the windowsill. Annie's china doll fell with a crash onto the flags.

"Clarrie!" her mother cried. "What broke—what did you do?"

Clarrie, afraid of messing herself, didn't stop to answer. She ran into the lavatory, climbed on the stool, pulled down her knickers, and slid gingerly onto the wooden lavatory seat. She sat very still so the crack in the seat wouldn't pinch her bottom.

From an opening in the wall, high above her head, a ribbon of light widened slantwise across the flags, shining on a trail of small, dirty footprints leading from the door to the bowl. Clarrie's feet dangled high off the floor, half hidden beneath the matted wool knickers bunched around her ankles. She couldn't see the soles of her sandals, only the curling tips of the leather straps, but she knew the dirty footprints were hers. She'd done something naughty again.

Out in the back street the dustmen were clanging the bins and shouting to each other. There was a smell of ashes, and suddenly, the ribbon of light was alive with dancing dust motes. Clarrie would have tried to catch them, but she was afraid to let go of the seat.

She'd watched the dustmen through the cracks in the backyard door—watched them hoist the bins onto their shoulders and empty them in a big lorry. They wore caps and leather waistcoats and smelled of ashes; their hands, clothes, and faces were always dirty.

Her friend, Gladys, who lived next door, told her there were bogeymen who waited in the dark entries to catch naughty children and carry them down into their cellars to live with the black beetles. Gladys's granny had said so, so it must be true. Clarrie thought it must be the dustmen who turned into bogeymen at night.

Her mother pushed open the lavatory door and stepped inside. "You should watch where you're going, love. You've broken Annie's doll!"

"We can mend it back."

"No, we can't. The head is smashed to pieces. Annie'll have a fit when she sees it." Her mother folded her arms across the damp front of her apron. "Let me know when you're finished."

Clarrie strained and something plopped into the water. A rich, familiar smell rose from the bowl. Clarrie strained again.

"Is that it? Are you finished? I can't stand here all day. I have beds to make."

Clarrie nodded.

"You're sure now? I don't want another mess like we had the other day."

Clarrie considered the matter. How could she be sure it was all gone? Did her mam expect her to look up her own bottom?

"I asked you if you'd finished. Why don't you answer me?"

"I'm saving some for tomorrow," Clarrie said.

Miraculously, her mother's frown vanished; her eyes, teeth, and dimples flashed, her belly shook with laughter.

"You're a comic cuts if ever there was one. Whatever will you come out with next?"

Her mother tore a square of newspaper that hung from a string on the lavatory door. "Here, wipe yourself, properly." She helped Clarrie with her knickers, then lifted her up so she could pull the chain and watch everything swirl around and disappear.

Later, while they were in the kitchen, waiting for their tea, Annie showed her father the broken doll. "Look, Dad, look what our Clarrie did! And I told her never to touch it. Granny Hancock gave me this doll."

William glanced at the doll and returned to his reading. "Perhaps it'll teach you not to leave your things lying about."

Sally got up to fetch the teapot from the hob. "She knocked it down accidentally while she was running to the lav. You never played with it, anyway."

"I climbed on the lavatory seat by myself," Clarrie said.

Her mother told them what Clarrie had said about saving some for tomorrow.

"Must be the Scotch blood coming out," her father said. "My Uncle Angus never liked to part with anything, either."

They were all laughing. Annie and Arthur pointed at her and held their noses.

Clarrie crawled under the table where it was dark and they couldn't see her crying.

The green bobbles at the border of the tablecloth almost touched the floor. She lifted a corner of the cloth to wipe the tears from her cheeks. Flame-shadows rippled along the fender and on her mother's shoes as she trotted from the table to the fire, carrying a frying pan and a bowl. When she threw a handful of potato chips into the frying pan, the fat crackled and sputtered. Her father, who was smoking a cigarette, broke into a fit of coughing. He cleared his throat and spat into the fire.

"Watch out for my chips!" her mother cried. "I do wish you wouldn't do that, Will, especially when I'm cooking."

"I was nowhere near the damn chips. What do you expect me to do? I'm all bunged up with this bloody phlegm."

"You'd feel better if you'd stop smoking."

"Don't start that again."

"Bunged," Clarrie whispered, "Phlegm." Bunged had a fat, grey sound. Phlegm sounded grey and nasty, too, which it was. She'd stepped in a glob of it once in the back street. Or perhaps that was snot. She didn't like the word snot, either.

Her mother's shoes came to rest near the table. They were badly worn and the toes turned up at the tips. Clarrie heard water bubbling into the teapot and smelled the tea. Her father came to the table and pulled out his chair. "Where's our Clarrie got to, then?"

"I think she must have run away," her mother said. "We'll have to have our tea without her."

"She's probably been stolen by Gypsies," Arthur said. "I might as well eat her egg."

"No!" Clarrie cried, "I'm here, under the table."

The edge of the cloth moved and her father peered at her. "What are you doing down there?"

"Listening."

"Listeners seldom hear any good about themselves." He dropped the cloth back into place.

The cloth stirred again and her mother's hand appeared, holding a slice of bread and butter. "If you want anything more to eat, you must come and sit at the table with the rest of us." Clarrie stuffed the bread into her mouth and crawled out. Her mother lifted her into a chair, cracked a boiled egg, scooped it over a heap of chips, and placed it in front of her.

"She likes to be in a little cave all by herself, don't you love?"

Clarrie nodded. Her mam knew what she liked. She gulped her sweet tea and sputtered. "I swallowed teavaleaves."

"Tea leaves." Her father brought his face so close she could see his milky, quivering eyeball moving to the side and back behind his specs.

"Teavaleaves," Clarrie said.

He pulled her plate out of reach. "Say it right."

"Don't tease her, Will."

"Well . . . she talks like a bloody Italian organ-grinder—matchabox, saltapot, coalahole, teavaleaves . . ."

Arthur pretended to wind a barrel organ. "You mama like-a-da music?"

Sally wiped Clarrie's face with the corner of her apron. "Say tea, love, then stop, take a deep breath, and say, leaves."

"Tea," Clarrie swallowed a mouthful of air, "—leaves." From now on, she'd have to say it their way, but she still thought her way sounded better.

Her father pushed her plate back. "You see, you can say it as well as anyone when you try."

Clarrie teetered on the edge of the bottom stair. She pulled her hand away from her mother's grasp. "I want to do it myself."

"Hold on to the banister then, as we go up. Your dad's Aunt Nellie broke her neck falling down these stairs."

But the banister was too high and too wide for Clarrie's small hand to grasp; her fingers slid off the polished wood. "I can't hold it."

"Hold onto the step in front, then. I'll be right behind you in case you fall."

Clarrie brought up one leg, then the other, stopping on each step to grasp the one above. Her mother stayed close behind, bumping up a wicker basket full of clean bedclothes. They crossed the landing to the middle room.

"Look out the window," her mother said. "Tell me what you see, while I make the bed."

Clarrie's nose reached only to the windowsill. If she stood on tiptoe, she could see into her yard and the neighbor's yard, too. In her yard there was nothing to see—only a few clothes flapping on the line—but in the next yard, one of the Morrow ladies was throwing a red ball to a little black and white dog. The dog ran fast, jumped up, caught the ball in his mouth, and dropped it at Miss Morrow's feet. When she bent to pick it up, the dog wagged his tail, waiting for her to throw it again.

Clarrie turned to tell her mother about the dog. She was bent over the mattress, wrestling with something, and the mattress, which normally stayed hard and flat, had risen up in the middle. Her mam was punching and pummeling it; trying to shove back down whatever was trying to get out.

Higher and higher it rose, until it suddenly burst open and a dark figure leapt out and came hurtling through the air towards her.

Clarrie screamed, and bolted through the door and across the landing.

The floor vanished abruptly under her feet. She was falling, tumbling helter-skelter down the steep stairs. She cried out in pain as her arm scraped against the curling edge of the carpet. And then, miraculously, she was drifting softly down, cradled by invisible arms. Puffs of feathery dust rose from behind the brass stair rods. The carpet's faded red and blue flowers spread their petals as she floated past. She came to rest at the foot of the stairs.

"Clarrie!" Her mother's voice, panicky and shrill, reached her from the landing. Her mother came running down to kneel beside her. "Are you all right? You're not hurt?"

Clarrie looked around, dazed. The shadowy, loving presence had vanished. And her arm was burning where she'd scraped it. Clarrie whimpered and held it up for her mother to kiss and make better.

"Why did you scream like that?" her mother asked. "What frightened you?"

"I saw a bogeyman."

"What bogeyman? There's no such thing as a bogeyman."

"He jumped out of the mattress at me."

"Nonsense. You're imagining things." She carried Clarrie back up to the bedroom and plopped her on a chair. "Wait here. I'll be right back."

Clarrie sat rigid, her eyes on the lump in the middle of the bed. If there was no such thing as a bogeyman, what had come flying out of the mattress? And who was the lady—it must have been a lady—who'd carried her safely downstairs? She wanted that lady to come back and stay with her forever.

Her mother returned with a pair of small scissors. She snipped the stitches from a patch in the mattress and slid her hand through the opening. "Hold out your hands." She dropped several gritty, egg-shaped wads into Clarrie's palms. "That's what's in the mattress—flocks—bits of pressed cotton and stuff, nothing else."

"I don't like them."

"Let's put them back in the hole, then." She took Clarrie's cupped hands in hers and thrust them through the rip. "What a silly girl you are—scared of an old mattress!"

Clarrie shut her eyes and snuggled into her mother's soft, warm shoulder. She'd like to tell her about the lady who'd carried her downstairs, but what if her mam got upset and thought she loved that other lady more than she loved her own mam?

Chapter Four

As soon as the tea things were cleared away, William brought in the zinc barrel from the back yard and set it in front of the fire for the children's Saturday-night baths. Sally filled the tub, alternating pans of hot and cold water, swirling them together until the temperature was right. Clarrie always went first because she was the baby and had to get to bed early.

Her mother slipped off Clarrie's petticoat and knickers and lifted her into the barrel. She was obliged to stand—if she tried to sit, the water would come up over her head.

After rubbing carbolic soap and borax into Clarrie's hair, and washing her all over, her mother handed Clarrie the flannel and told her to wash between her legs. Clarrie thought her mother didn't like to touch her down there because that's where the pee and the ca-ca came out.

"Keep your eyes closed." Water gushed over Clarrie's head. She screamed and grabbed for something to rub her eyes with. "I told you to keep your eyes shut!" Her mother doused her again, and then twisted her hair to wring out the water. She lifted her, dripping, from the tub. "Here, go to your daddy."

Her father wrapped her loosely in a flannel sheet and began to rub her dry, "Rub a dub, dub," he said, "three men in a tub . . ."

Sally opened the oven door to baste the roast and shrank back from the blast of heat. She cooked the Sunday meat on Saturday night, so it would only need to be warmed up when they came back from chapel.

The smell of roast beef filled the room, mingling with the smell of carbolic soap. Drops of moisture ran down the misted windowpanes, merging into tiny rivulets. Sally basted the meat, then cut a bit of the crispy brown crust from the top and popped it into Clarrie's mouth.

"Me, too. I want some, too!" Annie cried.

"Me, too," echoed Arthur.

"This is supposed to be for Sunday dinner," Sally said, but she gave them some anyway.

When Clarrie was dressed for bed in her clean vest and knickers, her father trimmed her nails, letting the parings drop on to his trouser legs. He played "this little piggy" with her toes, then bounced her on his knees, and sang:

Oh there was a little nigger and he grew no bigger,
So they put him in the wild beast show.
He cried for his Mammy and he cried for his Daddy,
And he cried for his old banjo.

"Don't sing that song, Will," Sally said. "Black folk don't like it when you call them that. The proper word is Negro."

Arthur started capering around the kitchen singing, "Oh there was a little Negro, and he grew no begrow."

"That's enough out of you, young man," William said. "Sit down and behave yourself."

Arthur took down the cigar box where they kept the tiddlewinks, and he and Annie settled themselves for a game at the kitchen table.

"It's an old music hall song," William said. "I didn't make the bloody words up. Anyway there aren't any blacks within miles of here. I bet they have a few choice words for us when we're not around. You wouldn't find me getting upset about it."

"You're an Englishman. It doesn't matter what folks say when you're top dog."

"Top dog? If I'm top dog, I pity the poor bugger on the bottom."

"But why did that little boy's mammy and daddy put him in a wild beast show?" Clarrie asked.

"Perhaps they needed the money to buy summat to eat," her father said.

Clarrie frowned. Her mam and dad were hard up for money, too—her mam sometimes said she didn't know where the next meal was coming from. Clarrie didn't think they would ever put her in a wild beast show. She was sorry for the little black boy. His mammy and daddy must have loved him, though, because they'd bought him a nice banjo.

She had never seen a real black boy, but she'd seen a picture of one on the shoe-polish tin. He had frizzy hair like Arthur's old golliwog, and fat red lips. And at Sunday-school there was an iron missionary box shaped like a head, with a face like the one on the shoe-polish tin. When you lifted the handle in the back, he stuck out a red iron tongue with a round flat place where you could put your penny. When you pressed the handle down, his tongue went back in and he swallowed the penny.

Her Sunday school teacher said the pennies went to Africa for the missionaries to feed the poor heathens.

"That boy's mammy and daddy can go to the missionaries if they're hungry," Clarrie said.

"Missionaries?" William winked at Sally. "Poor devils probably wanted summat more appetizing than missionaries for dinner."

"Will!"

William grinned. "I've never tasted missionary myself—I imagine it'd be a bit on the stringy side—but I did eat the parson's nose one Christmas."

Clarrie stared at her father. "You ate his nose?"

"Your daddy's teasing you," her mother said.

Clarrie leaned back against her father's chest. "Sing me another song." He jiggled her on his knee as he sang:

I had a little pony,
His name was Dapple Grey,
I lent him to a lady,
Who rode him far away.
She whipped him, she lashed him,
She rode him through the mire.
I wouldn't lend my pony now,
For any lady's hire.

"Why did the lady whip the pony?" Clarrie asked.

"She wanted him to get a move on," her father said.

Sally set the roast on the shelf above the range, then took the oven plate out and propped it against the fender to cool. "I'm not sure these old nursery rhymes and fairy tales are good for children," she said. "They're all about cruelty. People must have been very cruel in those days."

"Sing me another," Clarrie said. Her father sang a song about a little girl who had a little curl right in the middle of her forehead. It reminded Clarrie of the golden curl pressed between the pages of the Bible.

"That's our Janet's hair," Annie had told her. "And those blue flowers are forget-me-nots. They're to remind us never to forget her."

"Was that little girl our Janet?" Clarrie asked her father. "Is that the curl that's in the Bible?"

"You ask too many questions." He set her on her feet and lit a cigarette. "It's past your bedtime." He walked over to the window, where he stood smoking and staring out into the dark yard.

Clarrie shivered. The room suddenly felt cold, as though a door had blown open.

Sunday morning was wet, cold, and dreary. The children were not allowed to play in the street after they came home from Sunday school because Sunday was a day of rest, and their father said their noise would disturb the neighbors. They mustn't make noise in the house, either, because that would disturb their father. If the weather permitted, they could walk to the park, but when it rained, as it was doing today, they were trapped indoors with nothing to do.

Annie didn't want to read a book, or play draughts, or do anything else her mother suggested. She kept snatching *The Hotspur* magazine out of Arthur's hands until it finally ripped. Arthur made a fist and shook it under her nose and threatened to knock her clean through the window into the middle of next week.

William put down his newspaper and glared at Annie. "Keep it up, young woman, I'm warning you, just keep it up."

Sally was sifting flour into a blue-ringed basin. The sieve shook in her hand, spilling a cloud of flour onto the table.

"For heaven's sake Will, let them go out!" she said. "It's not raining hard. I'm trying to make a birthday cake for this child, but my heart isn't in it. And you're not helping matters."

"They can go for a walk then, until teatime," their father said, "but they'd better behave."

"See that you bundle up well, and take good care of our Clarrie," Sally said.

"We're going to the cemetery," Annie announced, as the back door closed behind them. "It's three years today since our Janet died. We ought to put some flowers on her grave."

"It's too far for our Clarrie to walk," Arthur said.

"She's not a baby anymore. Anyway, I'm the eldest, so I'm in charge, and I say we go to the cemetery."

"You can carry her home, then."

"She can walk. She's not paralyzed."

"We've got no money to buy flowers," Arthur said as they walked along Eccles New Road.

"You leave that to me," Annie said.

Outside the wrought-iron gates of the cemetery, they passed a flower seller huddled under a dripping oilcloth. She held out a bunch of purple flowers. "I'll let you have the whole bunch for tuppence."

"We don't need any flowers, thank you," Annie said. When they were safely through the gates and out of earshot of the flower seller, she told them they could pick flowers out of the rubbish bins. "People sometimes throw them away before they're dead."

She led the way past two small chapels. "That's the Catholic side over there; this side is for Protestants."

"Does God care which side people are buried on?" Arthur asked.

"How should I know? Maud next door says they separate us because the Catholics have to go to purgatory. She says you should never set foot in a Catholic church, because once you step inside the priests never let you go, and you're stuck for life."

Clarrie looked back over her shoulder at the little stone chapel. The priests must put glue on the floor. She imagined how it would feel to became stuck to the floor forever, like a fly on a strip of flypaper. If it happened to her, she would take off her shoes and climb over the seats to get out.

"Don't step on any graves," Annie warned Clarrie. "It's bad luck." They walked down a long gravel road, past flower beds, past graves covered in white pebbles and bordered with black marble. Annie read out the names and dates on the headstones as they passed—"Butterworth, Jackson, Wilson, and look here—this man buried four wives and seven babies, and he's still going strong." At the corner where they turned off the main path stood a white marble statue—a woman holding a bouquet of stone lilies.

"Here's the statue of the bride," Annie said. "She dropped dead on the church steps as she was going in to be married, so they buried her in her wedding dress." Standing off by itself was a black marble mausoleum with a spiked fence around it and the single name "Bardsley" over the doorway.

"They must be rich," Arthur said.

"Could be our relations," Annie said. "Dad has cousins named Bardsley—they own a pub in Eccles. Our grave's down there, near that tree."

There was no marker of any kind to show where Granny Hancock and Janet were buried. The grave was nothing but a grassy mound squeezed between the backs of headstones belonging to other people. On top of the mound, a pickle jar lay on its side, holding some withered stalks. Annie picked it up and led the way to a water spigot. "You two look in that rubbish bin for some decent flowers, while I fill this jar."

Among the discarded flowers in the big green wire bin, they selected a few that looked almost fresh. Annie arranged them in the jar and set it on Janet's grave. She took a handful of white stones off a nearby grave to keep the jar from falling over. "They've got plenty," she said, "they won't miss these."

Halfway home, Clarrie's legs gave out. Annie kept on walking as though she didn't care whether Clarrie was following or not, but Arthur turned back for her. "Hop on my back, love. I'll give you a donkey ride." He squatted down so she could wrap her arms around his neck.

"You're spoiling her rotten," Annie said when they jogged up to her. "This is the last time I'm bringing her with us."

"Mam will take me then," Clarrie said.

"She never will," Annie said. "Mam can't abide the cemetery."

"Why not?"

"She can't bear the thought of our Janet being there in that cold grave."

"I thought our Janet was up in heaven."

"So she is," Arthur said quickly. "It's only her body that's in the ground, but Mam doesn't like to be reminded about it."

Clarrie was about to ask how Janet could be up in heaven if her body was in the ground, but Annie slapped her on the leg and told her to stop asking questions.

Chapter Five

William, immaculately dressed in a dark serge suit, starched shirt, and white celluloid collar, his grey suede spats neatly buttoned over the tops of well-polished boots, paced back and forth across the kitchen puffing on a cigarette. "Aren't you lot ready yet?" he asked Sally.

"I've been up since five o'clock baking mince pies and getting these children ready—what have you done?" She moistened a corner of her handkerchief with her tongue and wiped a smear of chocolate from Clarrie's face.

Clarrie swerved her head away. "I don't like spit."

Sally gave her the handkerchief. "Wet it yourself, then."

"I polished everyone's shoes, didn't I?" William said, "I brought up the coal, I pressed my own trousers."

Sally handed a brown paper parcel to Arthur. "You carry the mince pies, love. Keep them away from our Annie, or there'll be nothing left by the time we get to Oldham."

"You blame me for everything," Annie said.

"Are we going or not?" William put on his bowler hat. "We've got to leave right now, or we'll miss the flaming bus." He picked up his umbrella and held the door until everyone was out of the house. They waited by the gate while he locked the door, and trooped after him down the street to the tram stop.

A man approached them, pushing himself along with his knuckles on a little wooden platform. He wore a dirty army jacket. The stubs of his missing legs were concealed by a blanket. He held out a beaker full of pencils. Through the holes in his grey mittens, Clarrie could see his knuckles smeared with dirt and blood. Sally rummaged in her purse.

"We've no time for that," William said.

"It'll only take a second." Her mother dropped a penny in a moneybox nailed to the platform.

"Take a pencil, Mam," Annie whispered. Her mother shook her head and moved on.

They climbed aboard the tram and mounted the curved staircase to the upper level. Clarrie sat by the outer railing looking down at the street. A cold breeze whipped her scarf back. There were only a few people out. All the shops were closed. The tram rattled and shook and squealed and sent out sparks where the pole touched the wire overhead. Her father pointed out the Victoria Arch and the Peel Park Museum.

"Some grand parks, has Salford. You can't take that away from us. Down Eccles Old Road there are houses fine as any in the country—millionaire's mile, they used to call it. I lived in one of those big houses myself when I was a lad, before my . . ." He broke off as the tram jolted to a halt. "Come on, this is where we get off."

He helped them off the tram and charged ahead again, striding rapidly down the street, calling over his shoulder for them to get a move on.

Her mother swooped Clarrie up in her arms and trotted after him. "That man!" she muttered. Clarrie's head was bobbing up and down, and she had to hold her head back to keep the drooping green feather in her mother's hat from tickling her nose. "Wait, Will!" her mother shouted. "This child's too heavy for me."

Her father threw down the stub of his cigarette and hoisted Clarrie onto his shoulders.

"Are you sure we're going right?" Sally asked. "I don't remember coming this way last time."

William strode on without answering until they came in sight of the bus depot. "There's the Oldham bus now," he shouted. "Run! Run!"

They scrambled aboard just as the bus started moving. It took them down an endless road lined with small shops. Somewhere along the way, Clarrie fell asleep, and when she woke up they were in Oldham.

Uncle Jack's house stood alone at one end of a narrow, walled street. The only other building was a pub with a swinging, weathered sign of a bull's head above the door. They went through a gate into a huge cobbled yard, passing a set of enormous scales with iron weights big as coalhole covers. In the back of the yard stood a row of open sheds stacked with sheepskins and cowhides. Three bicycles leaned against the house.

"They're not short of anything by the looks of it," Sally said.

William nodded. "Aye. He's top hide-classer. He gets this house rent free."

"It wouldn't hurt to ask him to put in a good word for you."

"It wouldn't do any good. They've just laid off half their men."

Two fat white rabbits, their pink noses twitching, looked at them through the wires of a large cage set on a trestle near the back door.

"Bunny rabbits!" Clarrie cried. She picked up a lettuce leaf lying on the ground in front of the hutch and was trying to push it through the wire holes when her father told her to go in the house.

Auntie Dora greeted them at the kitchen doorway. "Come in, come in. Jack'll be back in a minute—he's across the road getting brandy for the pudding." She patted her wavy red hair with manicured hands as she ushered them into a large kitchen fragrant with warm, delicious smells. A dark-haired young man was bent over the fire, stirring something in a saucepan. He raised his head and smiled shyly.

"Our Clifford's doing the custard," Aunt Dora said. "He's already made the stuffing. He's a champion cook is our Cliff. And here's Beryl and Norman." A girl and a boy who looked the same age as Annie and Arthur came in from another room. They each had wavy red hair and long chins like their mother's. Clarrie couldn't remember having seen them before.

Cousin Clifford left what he was doing to collect their coats and hats and carry them away somewhere.

"Turkey's in t'oven." Aunt Dora opened the oven door and lifted up a strip of brown cheesecloth to show them the sizzling, well-browned bird.

Clarrie tugged at her mother's skirt and asked why the people in Oldham talked so funny. Her mother frowned and raised a finger to her lips. "Smells lovely! Give me an apron, Dora, love, tell me what you want me to do."

Annie and Arthur had disappeared with the cousins, but there was nobody the right age for Clarrie to play with. She spied a doll on the window seat and ran to pick it up.

"Better not touch that doll," Aunt Dora said. "Our Beryl doesn't like anyone touching her things."

Clarrie went to the sideboard to look at the Christmas cake. The icing was sparkling white, the whole top covered by a miniature snow scene—a tiny snowman, children on toboggans, carollers under a lamppost—and wrapped around the sides of the cake, a ruffle of red, green, and silver paper. Clarrie reached out a finger to touch the snowman.

"No, no!" Aunt Dora said. "You'll get germs all over it."

Clarrie went over to the stove to watch Cousin Clifford stirring the custard. "Don't stand too close, love," he said, "you'll get splashed."

Her mother was washing pots in the scullery. Clarrie asked if she could go outside and feed the rabbits.

"I suppose it'll be all right," her mother said, "but don't open the cage."

The rabbits were sitting quietly twitching their pink noses. One of them was dropping small dark pellets on the floor of the hutch. It reminded Clarrie that she had to go to the lavatory. There was no latch on the lavatory door, and the door was too far away to keep it closed with her foot. There was nobody else in the yard, so she thought it safe to pull down her knickers and climb on the seat. The door slowly opened. Norman's long-chinned face appeared. Clarrie screamed at him to go away. Norman just grinned, then stuck out his tongue. Clarrie slid down, pulled up her knickers, and ran crying into the house.

Her father was in the kitchen talking to Uncle Jack and Aunt Dora. "What's the matter with you now?" he said.

Clarrie told him. "He's only having a bit of fun with you," Aunt Dora said.

To Sally, who had come in from the scullery, she said, "She cries if you look at her, this one, doesn't she?"

Sally wiped Clarrie's tears away with her apron. "Our Clarrie's shy about things like that. She won't sit on the chamber pot if anyone's in the room. Little Miss Prim, Will calls her."

"Takes after the Kentish side," William said. "Sally's Aunt Pearl is so refined she doesn't pee at all—isn't that right, Sal?"

Sally didn't answer. "If you have to go again," she said to Clarrie, "use the upstairs bathroom."

"It doesn't do to baby her, Sal," Aunt Dora said. "She's too mard if you ask me."

Clarrie thought Auntie Dora should be scolding Norman for spying on her in the lavatory instead of picking on her. She went into the parlor and sat on the carpet looking through some ladies magazines until her mother called to her to wash her hands; dinner was almost ready.

She joined the others at a long table filled with all sorts of delicious looking food—turkey with stuffing, roast pork, chestnuts, buttered carrots, Brussels sprouts, roast potatoes, giblet gravy.

"Our Clifford's a born chef; he did most of the veggies himself."

"Aunt Sal helped me," Clifford said.

"Our Beryl ought to lend a hand," Uncle Jack said. "She never lifts a finger if she can help it." He picked up the carving knife. "Who wants the parson's nose?"

"I do, I do!" Clarrie cried. Everyone laughed. Uncle Jack put a small triangle of meat on Clarrie's plate and passed it to her.

"It's the turkey's bum," Annie said. "That's what you get for being greedy."

Clarrie was about to cry again, but Uncle Jack told her to pass her plate back so he could give her a proper helping. When the main part of the dinner was over, Clifford took away the dinner plates and brought out a bowl of custard and a Christmas pudding with a sprig of holly in it. He went into the scullery for the mince pies and came back with his mouth full. "I've got to hand it to you, Auntie Sal," he said. "Your pastry is light as a feather."

Sally said she didn't think the pies were quite as good this year. Uncle Jack poured brandy over the pudding and set fire to it. The holly caught fire with a crackling and sparking.

Uncle Jack waited until the blue flames went out, then cut the pudding. He told them all to chew slowly because Father Christmas might have put some presents in. Clarrie searched every morsel of hers, but she couldn't find any present.

"You haven't looked properly," her father said. "I'm sure I saw something. Pass me your plate."

Clarrie didn't hold out much hope, but she passed it to him anyway.

"Look!" her father pointed to the window. "There's a bird on the windowsill."

Clarrie looked, but the bird had gone.

"Never mind," her father said. "Look what I found!" He passed the plate back to her, and there was a threepenny bit sticking up out of the pudding. Clarrie was sure her dad had put it there, but she didn't let on.

After dinner, she ran upstairs and into the lavatory. Cousin Beryl was sitting on the edge of the bathtub smoking a cigarette. She had bold black eyes like Annie's and an even bigger chin than Aunt Dora's. "Shut the damn door!" she snapped, "I thought I'd locked it."

Clarrie shrank back. "I have to go to the lav."

"Go in the yard then. And send your Annie up. I want to talk to her."

"Auntie Dora said I could come up here." Her attention was caught by another doll, larger and prettier than the first one, sitting on a shelf near some towels. "Is that your dolly too?" she asked.

"Yes, it's mine. You keep your hands off it." Beryl threw the cigarette into the lavatory bowl. As she was leaving, she turned in the doorway. "If you tell anyone you caught me smoking, I'll murder you!"

Clarrie locked the door after her. When she'd finished on the bowl, she walked over and gazed for a long time at the doll. She was tempted to pick it up, but afraid Beryl would know somehow. As she walked along the landing she peeped into the bedrooms. The beds were all made with neat bedspreads. In one of the rooms there was yet another doll propped against the pillows, but she didn't dare go in to look at it.

Downstairs, she found her mother in the scullery, doing the washing up.

"Where's everybody gone?"

"Your dad's gone to the pub with Uncle Jack and Aunt Dora. The others are around somewhere. Did you find the bathroom all right?"

Clarrie nodded. "Why doesn't your auntie have to go to the lav?" she asked.

"What?"

"Dad said your auntie doesn't have to wee . . ."

"He was joking. Everyone has to go to the lav."

"Even Princess Elizabeth and Princess Margaret Rose?"

"Yes. Queen Mary, too, I suppose, although I admit that's hard to imagine."

"They must have a gold lavatory seat."

"I wouldn't be surprised."

"There's a dolly upstairs on the windowsill," Clarrie said, "and one on the bed. Will you ask Auntie Dora if I can have one?"

"No. It's very bad manners to ask for presents. You've just had a lovely dinner. You found threepence in your pudding. Be satisfied."

Clarrie went into the parlor, lifted the lid of the piano, and tried to pick out the notes to "Twinkle, Twinkle, Little Star."

Uncle Jack, Aunt Dora, and her father came in the front way. Uncle Jack and Aunt Dora were arguing in loud voices. As Dora went past the parlor, she stuck her head in and told Clarrie sharply to stop that racket and close the piano lid—she had a headache. Beryl and Annie came in the back way with their heads together, whispering and laughing. Uncle Jack asked them where they had been, and Cousin Beryl said something that Clarrie couldn't hear. Whatever it was, it made Uncle Jack jump out of his chair and slap Beryl hard across the face.

"I've had about enough of your bloody lip!" he shouted, raising his hand to hit her again.

"Don't you dare hit my daughter, you bully!" Aunt Dora lunged at him, pummeling his chest with her clenched fists. Uncle Jack pushed her away. She tripped over the fender and fell against the oven door. William rushed over to help her back on her feet.

"Stop it, right now," he said to Uncle Jack, "before you do summat you'll really be sorry for."

Uncle Jack's face was purple. "You stay out of it," he said. "This is between me and my wife. I'm master in this house."

Sally came in from the scullery with a tea towel in her hand. "What happened?"

"Your brother-in-law hit our Beryl," Aunt Dora said. She was rubbing her arm. "And he knocked me into the fire!"

Norman and Arthur appeared in the doorway, each holding an angora rabbit.

"What's all the commotion?" Arthur asked. "Did someone fall?"

"I think we've overstayed our welcome," William said. "Fetch our coats, please, Norman."

"You see what I have to put up with?" Aunt Dora said.

While they were getting into their coats, Uncle Jack came over and slipped a silver coin into Clarrie's hand. He winked at her. "You're a nice little girl. Don't you grow up cheeky like our Beryl, will you?"

"It's the drinking that spoils everything," Sally said as they walked to the bus stop. "I can't for the life of me understand why you have to go out boozing in order to enjoy yourselves."

Her father stopped to light a cigarette. "Don't start."

"You leave me stuck in the kitchen like muggins. I'm supposed to do the washing up and take care of the kiddies while you all traipse off to the pub."

"You could have come with us. Our Annie's big enough to mind Clarrie."

"That's not my idea of a good time. The pub's not even supposed to be open on Christmas day."

William blew out a cloud of smoke. "They live on the premises, the Smithers do, and they've every right to entertain friends in their own house."

"I'll bet you paid for your drinks though, friends or no friends."

"Let it drop, will you."

Clarrie could see her dad's eye jiggling. She kept her fingers crossed so her mother would not say any more about the pub.

"My father sometimes slipped into The Wheatsheaf for a pint of ale after working in the fields, but he knew when to stop. I should think after what the booze did to your parents . . ."

"I told you to let it drop." They had reached the bus stop.

"Did you remember to ask Jack about that job?"

"I did not. You heard him carrying on. Master of his house, indeed. It's the bloody abattoir that's master if you ask me." Her father rummaged through his pockets "I'm out of fags." He turned to Clarrie. "Where's the threepenny bit from your pudding?"

"I must have left it on the table."

"I shook out the tablecloth in the yard," her mother said. "I didn't hear anything drop."

"Uncle Jack gave me a shilling, though."

"He didn't give me anything," Annie said.

"Me neither," Arthur said.

Her father held out his hand. "Better let me have it before you lose that, too." Clarrie rummaged in her pockets and produced the shilling. As she went to hand it over, the coin slipped through her mittened fingers, rolled down the pavement, off the curb, and through a grating in the gutter. Clarrie squatted, peering into the grid.

"We'll need a pole with soap on the end," Arthur said.

Clarrie's mother picked her up in her arms. "Never mind that now," she said. "The bus is coming."

"Clumsy little bugger," her father said.

"That's right, Will. Take it out on the children. It always ends the same way whenever you and your brother get together."

"Right, we'll stay home from now on."

"And a good time was had by all," Arthur said as they climbed aboard the bus.

Chapter Six

William threw a handful of coins on the table. "That's the lot. No more dole. They've cut us off."

"I've been expecting it." Sally scooped up the coins and slipped them into her apron pocket. She handed a duster to Clarrie and told her to dust the table legs. "Maud was here a few minutes ago, all upset. They've cut Johnny off, too. He signed on about the same time as you. You'd better try again down at the docks."

"I just came from there. Nothing doing. What the hell do we do now?"

"I might be able to take that job at the butcher's shop," Sally said. "I went to the infants' school this morning to see if Clarrie could start school early."

Clarrie poked her head out from under the table. "Yes. I want to go to school."

"Miss Littleton says she can start tomorrow. She'll give her a few days on trial, and see if she behaves herself."

"I'll behave myself," Clarrie said as she crawled out.

"Yes, love, I know you will."

"I'd be working in Trafford Park right now if it wasn't for this bloody eye," William said.

"The army should have given you a pension. You were on active duty when that accident happened. What difference should it make whether or not you were hurt in a battle?"

"Tell that to the buggers in London."

"In the meantime, we'll have to pawn something." Sally took a swift inventory of the room. She picked up a glass-domed arrangement of wax lilies from the sideboard. "This thing can go for a start."

"That belonged to my aunt," William said. "She kept it in the middle of her kitchen table and wouldn't let anyone touch it."

"Well, it's time we got rid of it. It's nothing but a dust gatherer."

William removed his pocket watch from its chain and slid it across the table. "You might as well take this, too."

Sally pushed the watch back to him. "I don't need that just yet." The watch was gold. William had won it in a skating race with a cyclist. It meant a lot to him.

He reattached the watch to its chain. "I'll hold on to it then, for now."

Sally lifted the heavy green cloth from the table. "I washed this yesterday. I soaked that ink stain in milk, but it wouldn't come out." She told Clarrie to take hold of one edge of the tablecloth while she folded it. "Bring your corner over to the middle so the stain doesn't show. That's the girl. Now run upstairs, and fetch your Sunday frock out of the wardrobe."

The frock had originally belonged to Phyllis, the niece of the Morrow sisters, next door on the left. For several weeks, the sisters had been tossing little bundles of clothes over the wall that separated the two back yards. One day on his way back from the lavatory, William had caught one of the bundles as it sailed over.

"What's this, then?" he'd demanded, shaking the bundle under Sally's nose. "Why are those old maids next door chucking their rags at us? What do they take us for?"

"They know you're out of work. They're trying to help us." Sally untied the bundle and began sorting through the clothes. "This cardigan just needs a couple of buttons."

"Tell 'em to give it to the Salvation Army."

She held up a dark jacket. "Just look at this lovely material—I believe it's West Riding cloth. If I take it in a little . . ."

William grabbed the jacket. "Give it here, I'll throw the bloody things back myself."

"Don't do that, Will. You'll hurt their feelings."

"What about my feelings?"

"Let me deal with them—I'll think up some excuse."

"Tell 'em thanks, but no thanks. We don't need anything."

She glared at him. "We need plenty. And if I left it to you, I'd have nobody to talk to."

"Why don't they have the decency to come to the door?"

"I imagine they've heard you bellowing through the walls."

He shook open the newspaper. "Let 'em stay home then, where they belong."

The following day Clarrie had gone with her mother to speak to the Morrow ladies. Her mam told the sisters that Mr. Hancock was a proud and stubborn man who found it difficult to accept gifts unless he could reciprocate. She'd given them a homemade apple pie. "As a small token of our appreciation." Since then, there'd been no more bundles sailing over the wall.

"Be a good girl, now." Clarrie's father gave her shoes a final swipe of the brush. "Don't you go mithering the teacher with a lot of questions, and whatever you do, don't start blubbering."

"She'll be good, won't you love?" her mother said. "She knows how important it is." Clarrie nodded emphatically.

"Why are they taking her?" Annie asked. She was squatting by the grate toasting a slice of bread, her face crimson from the heat. "You're supposed to be five. She's not quite four."

William glared at her. "Keep your mouth shut about that. The teacher's doing us a favor so your mam can take the job at the butcher's shop."

Sally was forcing a shrunken blue jumper over Clarrie's head. Clarrie pushed her mother's hands away. "You're squashing me, Mam. The hole's too little."

"You mean your head's too big," Annie said.

"Keep still." Her mother jammed the jumper over Clarrie's nose.

Annie spread her toast with beef dripping. "If you need to go to the lav, you're supposed to put your hand up like this." She waved the knife in the air. "Please, Miss, may I leave the room?"

Arthur came in from the scullery, drying his face on a torn towel. "And be careful not to fall in the hole. You don't want to plop down in all that muck and end up in Australia."

William released a cloud of cigarette smoke. "That's enough out of you, my lad."

Sally pinned a clean handkerchief to Clarrie's jumper. "Remember your manners, and don't unpin this hankie and lose it like you did in Sunday school."

Clarrie looked down at the handkerchief. "What if I have to blow my nose?"

Annie cast a critical eye over Clarrie. "Her hair's straight as a poker." She patted her own thick, golden brown curls. "You should've put it up in rags, Mam."

"It's all right as it is."

Her father perched Clarrie on the sideboard and pushed her feet into her shoes. For the past few days he had been teaching her to tie her own laces, but when she tried, the laces came undone again.

"Never mind," he said, "I'll do it."

Her mother held out a brown coat with a black velvet collar. It had originally belonged to one of the Kentish cousins and was already too short and too tight. "Take hold of your cardigan sleeve."

Clarrie grasped the sleeve, but it slipped from her fingers and got crumpled in the coat-sleeve. They tried again. This time her hand got hung up in the coat lining.

"Oh, for heaven's sake!" Her mother yanked off the coat, straightened the lining, and stuffed Clarrie's arms back inside. She told Annie and Arthur to put on their own coats and run on ahead or they'd be late for school. She handed Clarrie a lunch bag and picked up the parcel of things she'd prepared for the pawnshop. The coalman, bent under a bulging sack, was coming up the front path as they opened the door.

"Mornin' Missus!" He put the sack down and lifted the iron lid of the coalhole.

She handed the parcel to Clarrie while she rummaged in her handbag. "I hope you're not giving me a load of slag, like the last lot."

The coalman's eyes flashed blue and white in his sooty face. "It's good-size lumps, Missus, look for yourself if y'dunna believe me." The coalman's horse was eating from a nosebag—snorting and tossing the bag in the air, showering himself with oats. Clarrie asked the coalman why his horse wore blinkers.

He winked. "So 'e don't see no more'n's good for 'im."

Sally counted money into his sooty palm.

"You're a tanner short, love," he said. "T'gaffer won't let me bring any more 'less you pay up."

"That's all I've got to my name right now. I'll go by the coal shed on my way back." She picked up the parcel, grasped Clarrie's hand. "Walk as fast as you can. I want to stop at the pawnshop before it gets too busy. We'll go the back way—less chance of running into anyone we know."

They crossed the street and turned down a long entry, squeezing past a row of horses and carts. They had to walk single file, stepping aside now and again to avoid the horse manure, and to steer clear of the carters who were lounging against the back walls, smoking and talking and laughing, while they waited for their horses to be shod. The blacksmith, covered from chest to knees by a black leather apron, crouched over his forge, poking about with long fire tongs. Clarrie pulled away from her mother and lingered to watch him. He grasped a bar of white-hot iron from the forge, swung around, dropped it onto the anvil, and picked up a hammer. Sparks flew out as he beat and twisted the hot metal into shape. Clarrie heard a splashing sound. She looked back. A thick pipe had descended from one of the waiting horses, and a yellow stream was gushing out, foaming over the cobbles. Her mother pulled her away. "Yes, yes, I see it. We've no time to dawdle."

Several shawled women holding cloth bundles and paper-wrapped parcels were queuing up outside the back door of the pawnshop. A woman with wrinkled stockings and a torn lining hanging down beneath her coat stepped out of the queue and hammered on the backyard door.

"Open up, we haven't got all day! What yer doing in there, Chuck, polishing yer brass balls?"

The pawnbroker's helper came out and slid back the bolt, saying "Keep your shirt on, Missus."

The crowd surged through the yard into a back room that smelled of mothballs. Clarrie's mother lifted her onto the polished counter while the pawnbroker unwrapped their bundle. He set the glass dome and the lilies to one side, and examined the Sunday frock. He unfolded the tablecloth and pointed without comment to the ink stain. With his round glasses and his sharp nose, he looked, Clarrie thought, like the stuffed owl at Buille Hill museum.

"Six and a tanner."

"Can you make it seven and six? I'll redeem them next Friday when I get paid."

"Sorry." He gathered their things together and shoved them back to her across the counter.

"You're holding us up, love," the woman behind them whispered. "Take it, it's better than nowt."

"I'll take it," Clarrie's mother said.

The pawnbroker counted out the money, tore a ticket from a strip, placed a sticker on the glass-domed flowers and put them on a display shelf; he put another sticker on the bundle and dropped it in a basket. "Next!"

As they stepped into the street a stout woman with a wicker shopping basket over her arm hailed them.

"Been to Uncle's again, 'ave you, Sal, pawnin' the family heirlooms?"

"Just the silver candlesticks. I get fed up with polishing them." The two women laughed.

"Nosy devil," her mother said when the woman was out of earshot.

"Where were the silver candlesticks?" Clarrie asked.

"It was a joke, love. You know we have no silver candlesticks."

The walled schoolyard was empty. "We're late. They've all gone inside," her mother said. She helped Clarrie up a flight of steps and through a doorway into a room where several children sat in a semicircle around a small fire.

They turned to stare at Clarrie and her mother. A thin grey-haired lady rose from her desk, smiling. She took Clarrie by the hand.

"This must be Clara."

"We usually call her Clarrie," her mother said. She steered Clarrie forward. "Say good-morning to Miss Littleton."

Her mother removed Clarrie's coat. "Be a good girl and don't forget to eat your butty," she said.

Miss Littleton whispered something in Sally's ear, then said, "I'll show Clarrie where we hang our coats." She told the other children to be quiet and led Clarrie into a room filled with coat hooks and coats. When they returned to the classroom, her mother had gone.

Clarrie sat on a little wooden chair with the other children, while Miss Littleton opened a big book. The children raised their hands and answered, "Present, Miss" as their names were called. At the Sunday school Christmas party, the presents had been hidden in a barrel of sawdust. Clarrie had pulled out a big box, but her present was disappointing—only a thin wire with a hook on the end and some paper fish.

Miss Littleton finished calling the names and closed the book.

Clarrie, worried about getting her present, stood up. "Please Miss, you forgot to call my name."

Miss Littleton smiled. "Sit down, Clarrie. We don't get out of our seats without permission. Your name has not been entered in the register yet; I'm not sure you'll be staying with us."

The door opened and a man entered, followed by a pale boy with a high, bulging forehead and black hair parted in the middle. He wore a stiff-looking black suit and black knee socks. Miss Littleton went over to them. The man whispered something in her ear, then patted the boy on the head and left. The pale boy suddenly broke away from Miss Littleton, and ran to the door, calling "Daddy, Daddy!"

Miss Littleton brought the boy back and squatted in front of him, drying his tears and wiping his nose with a handkerchief she took from her sleeve. The children started giggling. Miss Littleton shook her head at them over the boy's shoulder.

"Behave yourselves, children. Malcolm's mummy has gone away to heaven, and Malcolm is very sad." She led Malcolm to his seat.

Clarrie wanted to comfort him, but the teacher had said she was not to get up. She waved across the room to get his attention and called out "Don't cry, little boy."

Miss Littleton produced a box of red and brown clay from her desk drawer, and gave each child a ball of clay. She demonstrated how to make a cat by placing a small piece of clay on top of a larger one, then rolling bits in the palm of her hand to make whiskers and a tail.

Clarrie's clay was dry. It wouldn't roll properly and it wouldn't soften up. She looked around the room. Malcolm had his head on the desk and seemed to be asleep. Clarrie felt sleepy, too. She'd been in school for such a long time and she hadn't eaten her butty yet. Her mam had told her not to forget. She opened her paper bag.

"Look, Miss!" A plump girl with a blue bow in her dark hair pointed to Clarrie. "The new girl is eating her butty."

Miss Littleton, who had been going from desk to desk admiring the clay cats, scurried over.

"Put that away, Clara. It isn't time for our snacks yet. Oh, dear, look at the mess you're making." She sent the dark-haired girl to fetch a brush and dustpan out of the cupboard, and told Clarrie to sweep up the crumbs. Miss Littleton showed the rest of the class the right way to fold paper to make a lantern. When Clarrie finished sweeping she tried to make her lantern, but she folded it the wrong way.

Miss Littleton told them to sing, "Polly put the kettle on," while she warmed the milk to have with their snacks. She poured each child a beaker of sweet, fragrant Horlicks, and sat with her arm around Malcolm while he drank his. Then they all trooped into the schoolyard and everyone, except Malcolm, played "Ring Around the Roses" and "Farmer in the Dell." After that, it was time for everyone to go to the lavatory.

The lavatory was a long, low brick building with a door at either end. Clarrie went in the first door and into one of the cubicles. There was a hole cut in a slab of wood, and deep in the hole, white stuff swirled around that smelled like the sheep dip her mother used to clean the bedsprings and chamber pots. Clarrie slid her bottom over the hole, gripping the edge so she wouldn't fall in. The boys were yelling, and through the cracks around the sides of the door, she watched them having a contest to see who could pee farthest. A big boy with bristly hair and cross-eyes was chasing another boy with his john-willie. Clarrie looked down to where hers ought to be, but between her legs there was only a tight fold, like a date stone.

Miss Littleton called through the door. "Everybody out, playtime is over."

Clarrie pulled up her knickers and came out into the yard. The big boy with bristly hair pointed at her.

"That girl was in the boys' lav, Miss."

"I was not." Clarrie blinked hard. Her dad had warned her not to cry.

"Yes, you was."

"Be quiet, Ernie Cruikshank." Miss Littleton took Clarrie by the hand. "Next time, Clara, use the girls' lavatory—the door is at the other end."

Back in the classroom, Miss Littleton picked up a wooden pointer and went along the ABC pictures on the walls, asking each child to name the right letters. Clarrie named them all without hesitation. Miss Littleton patted her on the head. "Splendid, Clarrie. Well done, indeed! Tell your mother you may stay. And tomorrow, we'll add your name to the register."

Clarrie smiled. School wasn't so bad after all. When the bell rang, she could hardly believe it was time to go home.

Her mother was waiting in the schoolyard as she'd promised. When she caught sight of Clarrie, her white teeth flashed, the dimples deepened in her cheeks. Clarrie ran across the yard and buried her face in her mother's rough, mothball-smelling coat. "I didn't cry, Mam," she said, "but Malcolm did."

Chapter Seven

On the days when their mother worked at the butcher's, Annie was to walk Clarrie to the infants' school and pick her up afterwards. Clarrie's school day ended at three, Annie's at half-past four, so arrangements were made for Annie to run over to fetch her sister back to her own classroom, where Clarrie must sit quietly until Annie's school day ended. After school, Annie and Arthur sometimes took Clarrie to play on the tip at the bottom of the street.

Once a public midden, the tip was a steep, downward slope, overgrown with dandelions and silverspoon grass. They had to be careful where they walked, because it also served as a graveyard for dead cats, rusty bedsprings, and buckled bicycle wheels. At the bottom lay a wide stretch of gritty wasteland that ended at a wall, from the top of which they could look down into a sawmill, and watch the huge buzz-saws slicing through logs as if they were loaves of bread. Plumes of sweet-smelling white dust flew out on either side and settled into little hillocks. Sometimes, when the workmen were not there, they jumped down into the sawmill yard, and the three of them rolled around in the sawdust.

Once, they even ventured across a vast web of railway lines to the docks to watch the stevedores unload a big ship. There was a loud cry from the stevedores as a crate of oranges slipped from the metal teeth of the crane and shattered to splinters on the cobbles. One of the men who ran to pick up the rolling fruit, shouted, "Catch!" and tossed the children each an orange wrapped in tissue paper stamped with the word, Seville.

"That's in Spain," Arthur told them. "When I grow up, I'm going to be a seafaring man and sail all over the world on a big ship like that."

"I want to go, too," Clarrie said.

"You can't." Annie said. "They don't allow girls to be sailors."

Arthur squeezed Clarrie's hand. "Never mind, love. I'll sneak you into one of the lifeboats." He pointed to the lifeboats, suspended by ropes alongside the ship. "I'll hide you under a tarpaulin so you won't get rained on."

"What if I get hungry?" Clarrie asked. She imagined herself huddled under one of those dark, stiff tarpaulins, cold and hungry, afraid to stick her head out.

"I'll sneak you some dinner in my pocket when nobody's looking."

"Sailors don't have pockets," Annie said.

"I'll hide it under my hat, then," Arthur said.

Summer brought a spell of unusually dry, hot weather. The sun blazed down on slates and bricks and cobblestones, transforming the grimy warren of streets into an oven. Flies buzzed through open doors and windows, and struggled to free themselves from the curling strips of flypaper hanging from every kitchen gas bracket. Swarms of vendors roamed the streets—fruit and vegetable peddlers, pan and kettle menders, knife sharpeners, and a man who sold ice-cream wafers and cornets sprinkled with sweet raspberry vinegar.

The heat wave coincided with the school holidays. Children, numerous as the flies, ran in and out of their houses all the day long for drinks of water and jam butties. The streets echoed with their shouts, and with the crack of bat against ball. Small girls strolled about in moth-eaten bathing costumes twirling Japanese paper sunshades—faded souvenirs of long past charabanc excursions to Blackpool or Southport. Out in the back street, workmen were repairing the water pipes, tearing up the cobbles, digging deep into the red-brown clay beneath, heaping it high.

Clarrie and Gladys, her friend from next door, clambered among the mounds of clay, looking for the softest pieces, and after they found them, they took refuge from the sun in a tent that Arthur fashioned by nailing one side of a threadbare blanket to the backyard wall and securing the other to the dirt edge along the pavement. In the dim shelter of the tent, Gladys and Clarrie sat on grimy cushions, fashioning clay cats and baskets of clay eggs. When she was home, Clarrie's mother brought out lemonade and jam butties for them, and for the workmen.

"I hope it's not sewage that makes the clay smell so sour," she said to one of the workmen when Clarrie showed her a clay cat she'd made.

The workman's red face and brown arms glistened with sweat. He mopped his forehead with a handkerchief.

"Nay, Missus—a bit o' clay'll never 'arm 'em," he said. "We 'andles it the live-long day."

"She's nice, isn't she, your mam?" Gladys said, champing happily on a jam butty.

"Yes," Clarrie hesitated. "Your mam's nice, too," she added politely.

On the days when their mother was at work, Annie and Arthur were charged with minding Clarrie. Annie soon grew bored with the back street and began venturing farther and farther afield. Early in the morning she would gather together a band of whatever children were playing in the street, and laden with blankets, butties, and bottles of sarsaparilla, they'd set off for they knew not where. If Arthur questioned Annie about their destination, she would turn on him, her dark eyes glittering behind her wire-rimmed glasses.

"You'll know where we're going when we get there."

"You don't even know where you're going, yourself, do you?" Arthur said.

After walking for miles to Bluebell Woods, the Three Sisters pond, or Barton Aerodrome, Annie would choose a spot to rest and partake of their refreshments. At the end of the day, the ragtag band would straggle back exhausted, having abandoned along the road the wilted wild flowers they had gathered and the jam jars filled with tiddlers and slimy frogspawn. After a few of these grueling safaris, one by one the children dropped out. Finally, Arthur, too, rebelled.

"I'm not going with you anymore, Annie. I told you last time when you dragged our Clarrie all the way to Heaton Park. Mam and Dad would have a fit if they knew how you cadged strangers for carfare to get home—lying, telling people at the bus stop our Clarrie had sprained her ankle."

"It worked, didn't it? They gave us the money. And you loved Heaton Park. You thought it was smashing when that peacock opened its tail."

"Well, from now on, you can count me out."

In the end, Annie's best friend, Jessie, was the only friend who remained loyal. Clarrie had no choice; where Annie went, she was obliged to follow.

The big girls walked with their arms around each other's waists, and their heads together—Annie's thick, golden brown curls next to Jessie's dark bob. Clarrie scurried after them, up Langworthy Road, toward the park. They passed a shop with a sign outside the entrance advertising refreshments and mineral waters. It reminded Clarrie that Annie had a bottle of dandelion-and-burdock in the lunch bag. "I'm thirsty," she said.

"You'll have to wait."

At the crossroads, Clarrie rested on a heavy iron chain looped across the corner, while she shook gravel out of her sandals. Annie and Jessie forged ahead. "Wait for me!" Clarrie shouted, running after them.

"When you're out with me, you rest when I say so," Annie said. "Have you got that?"

They had reached the park gate. On one side was a trough for horses, on the other, a huge iron bowl shaped like a shell. An iron cup hung from a thick chain attached to the waterspout.

"Drink this," Annie said. "I'm giving your share of pop to Jessie." She held the cup while Jessie pumped.

Clarrie shook her head. "Mam said we shouldn't drink out of that cup."

"I rinsed it out. Drink it—she won't know if you don't tell her."

Clarrie made a wry mouth. The iron made her teeth ache.

"We'll be in the lav." Annie called over her shoulder when she and Jessie were halfway up the path.

Clarrie let the cup fall with a clang against the side of the bowl. "Wait for me, I don't know where to go!"

"Follow your nose."

Clarrie ran after them, but by the time she reached the crest of the hill, the girls had disappeared. A sign shaped like a pointing hand said "Ladies." There was indeed a strong lavatory smell. Clarrie followed the curving downward path to a green wooden door. She lifted the latch and pushed.

Swarms of flies—black flies, giant bluebottles, shiny green flies—buzzed over the stinking messes and puddles on the floor.

Annie was opening the doors of the stalls. "Putrid . . . every one of them." She tried the last door. "This one's nailed shut."

Jessie pushed her knickers down around her ankles and squatted. "The lady what used to clean these lavs committed suicide in there." Her voice sank to a whisper. "My mam said she was in the family way."

Annie cocked a thumb towards Clarrie. "Little pitchers . . ."

Clarrie asked what "committed suicide" meant.

"Don't ask so many questions," Annie said. She told Clarrie to stop wriggling and pee on the floor before she wet herself.

"It's too dirty."

"She's right, for once," Annie said. She shoved Clarrie towards the exit. "Go behind the bushes. I'll stand guard."

Clarrie, desperate to go, but fearful of being seen, squatted on the grass behind the rhododendron bushes. Annie handed her a furry dock leaf and told her to wipe herself. They went over a grassy hill, past the bandstand and the tennis courts to the museum. They were gazing at a dusty, stuffed elephant, when a man in a blue uniform came out the side door. "Clear off you lot. You can't come in here without a grownup."

"I'm almost fourteen," Annie said.

"But . . ." Clarrie was about to remind Annie that she was only twelve.

"Shut up, you," Annie hissed, pinching Clarrie's arm.

The museum guard raised his hand and took a step toward Annie. "How would you like a clout across the ear'ole?"

The girls scurried down the steps.

On the way to the playground, they stopped by the greenhouse—a steamy, glassed-in world of strange plants and hot, earthy odors. The man who looked after the greenhouse was watering the plants and picking off dead leaves. He looked nice, Clarrie thought—a bit like Arthur, only older.

"Is it all right if we look around, mister?" Annie asked.

"That's what it's here for."

They lingered for a while by the Venus flytrap, hoping to see it catch a fly. Clarrie, curious though she was, was relieved when they gave up and moved on. Annie lifted her up to show her a plant that quivered and shrank away as she reached out a finger to touch it. "It's called a sensitive plant," Annie said, reading from the label. "It's afraid of its own shadow, just like our Clarrie."

"She's not like you, then, is she?" Jessie said. "You're bold as brass, that's what my mam said."

"I believe in sticking up for myself. I take after my Granny Hancock."

The playground was crowded, and all the swings taken. Clarrie followed the big girls over to the glider, a long, thick plank, suspended at either end by iron bars attached to horizontal bars overhead. Several children sat astride the plank, holding onto metal hoops. At either end of the plank, a girl stood holding the suspension bars, waiting the signal to set the ride in motion.

Annie pointed to one of the support poles as she and Jessie climbed aboard. "Stand there, our Clarrie, and don't move. You're too little to go on this one."

The girls who were facing each other at the ends of the plank bent their knees and pushed with all their might, shouting, "Ready, set, go!" The plank glided slowly forward, then back, swinging out higher as it gathered speed, shaking and banging as it moved forward and back. The children astride the plank began to scream. Annie shrieked louder than everyone else. She gripped her iron hoop with both hands, holding on for dear life. Her honey-colored curls blew out in all directions; her glasses slipped, hanging from one ear. She was sliding sideways, about to fall.

"Annie!" Clarrie shouted.

"Get back!" Annie shrieked.

Clarrie dashed forward to save her.

With a powerful thud, the plank smashed Clarrie back into the support pole. There was a blinding flash of pain and everything went dark. When she opened her eyes, Annie was kneeling over her, her face stricken. "Get up our Clarrie, come on. You're not really hurt." She grabbed Clarrie's arm and pulled.

Clarrie screamed and Annie let go. "You can't stay here. You've got to get up." She took Clarrie by the other arm and dragged her to her feet. "I told you to stay near the pole, and not to move." She held Clarrie's hand and set off down the wide downward-sloping path, with Jessie running after.

"Stop crying," Annie said, "I'll pick you some nice flowers." She tore a handful of purple blossoms and dark shiny leaves off one of the bushes.

"Run!" Jessie cried. "The parkie's after you. He saw you pick them flowers!"

Annie shoved the blossoms into Clarrie's hand, then picked her up and ran. Clarrie screamed as the pain ripped through her arm.

"Shut up!" Annie shouted. "Stop your skriking." Over Annie's shoulder Clarrie could see the parkie falling behind. He was shouting something and shaking his fist. When they were safely out of the park, Annie set Clarrie down. "Stop crying, or Mam'll know something's happened, and you'll get Jessie and me in trouble."

"It's nowt to do wi' me," Jessie said. "She's your sister."

Chapter Eight

Clarrie knelt in the patch of sooty soil they called the garden, planting an apple seed. She was obliged to work with only one hand because the other was in a sling, the arm caked with plaster of Paris. She had planted apple seeds once or twice before, but nothing had ever come up. She was sure, if she kept trying, someday a small green shoot would come poking through the black earth.

Her mother's sweet voice drifted up through the cellar grid. "I know a bank whereon the wild thyme grows . . ."

It must be in Kent, that bank, Clarrie thought. It was easy to grow things there. Not like here. Too many chimneys here, her mam said, and not enough sunshine. Clarrie was smoothing the black soil over the seeds when she heard her name called.

Gladys was waving from the other side of the wall. "Come and see what I'm doing."

Clarrie climbed onto the wrought-iron gate. Gladys was jabbing a twig into the cracks between the bricks.

"I'm poking out spiders. There's millions of them. They try to get away, but I stop them. They're scared of me. Look!"

A pale spider with a tiny round body and long legs scrambled out. "Get a stick. You can do it, too."

"I'm not supposed to go past the gate."

"Your mam's in the cellar. She can't see you."

Clarrie hesitated, then climbed down to open the gate. With her trowel she probed the crumbling cement between the bricks until a long leg, thin as a hair, emerged. Out came another leg, then another. The spider ran for its life along the wall.

"Stop it!" Gladys screamed. "It's getting away!"

Clarrie barred the way with her trowel. The spider paused, ran to the edge of the wall and dropped to the pavement.

"Kill it!" Gladys's normally pale cheeks were red. She was breathing hard. She pushed Clarrie. "Get out of the way, let me do it!" She pressed the stick down on the spider. One of the delicate legs had come off, and was waving about as though it had a life of its own.

Clarrie threw her trowel back in the soil. "My mam's calling me" she said.

"I didn't hear anything."

Clarrie ran to squat by the cellar grid. The bars of the grid were spaced wide enough to let light and air—and also dirt and spiders—into the cellar. Through a cloud of steam she could see her mother bent over the copper boiler.

"Did you call me, Mam?" Clarrie shouted. "Is it time for the dolly blue?" Her mother always let her put the dolly bag into the final rinse water. As soon as the bag touched the water, a stream of blue ran out. If you swirled the bag around a few times, the water turned a dark, lovely, color.

"Not yet," her mother called back. "I'll let you know when."

"I have to go in, now," Clarrie said, running back to Gladys. "I've got to help my mam."

"Come out when you've finished. We'll catch more spiders."

Clarrie was scrubbing the dirt from her hands when her mother staggered up the cellar steps with a basket piled high with wet washing. Clarrie followed her into the back yard and helped turn the wheel of the mangle while her mother fed sheets and blankets through the big wooden rollers.

The clotheslines in the back yard were full, so her mother ducked under the wet sheets, and carried the basket out into the back street where more clotheslines were strung. Clarrie picked up the bag of pegs, and passed them to her mother, one by one, while her mother demonstrated the right way to hang up the washing. The clothesline must first be wiped clean. Sheets and blankets should be folded double but pegged loose enough for the breeze to blow through them; shirts were to be turned inside out and hung upside down. When everything was hung, her mother pushed a long prop between the sagging lines and jammed the other end of the prop between the cobbles. The clothes swayed, as though they were about to topple, then righted themselves.

"Why do you prop them up so high?" Clarrie asked.

"So the dogs won't chew them, and you children won't slap at them with dirty hands as you run by." Her mother stepped back to admire her work. "That blanket turned out lovely," she said. "I wish we could afford bedding like that." Even as she spoke, a black cloud poured from one of the tall mill chimneys across Eccles New Road, and a shower of soot descended like a swarm of flies on the clean washing.

"Oh, Lord!" her mother said. "Nothing stays clean for five seconds in this place." She picked up her basket. "Well, I'm not doing them over. I've got another boiler full downstairs."

Clarrie followed her into the cellar. "Where does the dirt come from?"

"Everywhere; chimneys, cotton mills, trains, buses, coal yards . . ." Her mother lifted the lid of the copper boiler and, using both hands, swished the clothes with the posser. The muscles on her arms bulged from the effort.

"How did the dirt get here?"

"It's part of the earth."

Clarrie stepped onto a wooden box to watch the rinse tub fill. "But how did the earth get here?"

"God made it."

"What out of?"

"I don't know. He must have made it out of nothing." She pressed one end of the stick down, straining to lift a sopping flannel sheet out of the water. She dropped the sheet and put the lid back on the boiler. "It's still black as the hobs of hell! That man must go to bed in his overalls."

"How could God make the earth out of nothing?"

"If you're God, I suppose you can do anything."

"Where did God come from, then?"

Her mother leaned over and turned off the tap. "I don't know, love. I've never thought about it."

"Why can't we see God and ask Him?"

"Perhaps He doesn't want us to." With the back of her hand, her mother wiped away a trickle of water coursing down her face. "Don't worry your head about things you don't understand. Just be a good girl and you won't go far wrong."

"But . . ."

"What is it now, child?"

"Nothing," Clarrie said. She wondered why people didn't like it when she asked questions. It wasn't fair. Grownups had been here in the world a lot longer than she had—long enough to have the answers. If her mam and dad didn't know the answers, who did? Her Sunday school teacher had said that you had to be christened in order to go to heaven. Janet hadn't been christened. How could they be sure God had taken Janet to heaven?

At night, before Arthur and Annie came up and disturbed her, she liked to lie in bed and think about God. She pictured Him up in heaven with His angels, watching over everyone. She wanted to see God for herself, to hear Him speak. If she tried hard enough, perhaps she'd hear Him calling her, the way He'd called to Samuel in the Bible.

"Clara," He'd say, "Wake up, Clara."
She'd sit up in bed. "Yes, Lord, I hear you."
"I have a task for you."

"Oh, my God!" her mother cried.

Something was happening to the copper; it was tilting sideways, splashing water. Suddenly, the supporting brickwork gave way with a loud crunching noise. Bricks flew out in all directions and the copper boiler tipped over and flooded the cellar with boiling sudsy water. Her mother dropped the posser, scooped Clarrie up, and ran with her through the archway, past the coal pile and up the steps. At the top, her mother set her down. Through a cloud of steam, they watched a swirling tide drag the wet washing around the cellar floor.

The washhouse was down Hodge Lane, on the other side of the railway bridge. Sally was pushing an old pram Mrs. Phipps had lent them. It was filled with the gritty sheets she had gathered up from the cellar floor. When they reached the bridge, she had to turn the pram around and drag it up a flight of stone steps. At the top, she leaned against the wall to catch her breath before bumping the pram down the other side.

Halfway along Hodge Lane, they were enveloped by a cloud of steam that billowed from the open door of the washhouse. The whole lane smelled of soap and washing soda. Sally gave the woman at the gate some money, and the woman handed her a beige ticket torn from a roll.

"Stalls are all in use, but there's eighty of 'em, so you won't have long to wait."

They pushed the pram up and down the long aisles of the steam-filled room, looking for an empty cubicle. Rows of women bent over the tubs, scrubbing, rinsing, and wringing out washing. The sinks and scrubbing boards were set so that each woman must face somebody else's backside. The women were shouting to one another, but what they were saying could hardly be heard above the running water and the banging pipes. A lone man, his trousers covered by a long apron, stood at one of the boards scrubbing a shirt collar.

"There's Malcolm's daddy," Clarrie said.

Her mother glanced at him as they passed by. "Poor fellow—he ought to get married again."

There were no sinks free, so they found a seat on a wooden bench by the wall and watched a woman with black curly hair, doing her washing.

"Sure and you can have this stall in a minute," the woman said. "My washing's about done."

"Let me give you a hand." Clarrie's mother slipped off her coat, hung it across the handle of the pram, and helped the woman wring out a pair of dripping overalls.

"How old is your little girl?" the woman asked.

"She turned five last February. She's my youngest."

"And what did she do to her arm, then?"

"Broke her wrist and collar bone in the park."

"Always getting hurted, the young 'uns is. I had eight, so I did. Three was took by the diphtheria, and last year, didn't the police come knocking at me door telling me they'd found me boy, Patrick, drownded in the reservoir."

Clarrie's mother stopped what she was doing. "You wouldn't be Mrs. Rourke by any chance?"

"Do I know you, then, Missus?"

"I'm Sally Hancock. I heard about you through Nurse Walmsley. I was in labor with this one when my other little girl died of pneumonia."

Mrs. Rourke made the sign of the cross. "Nothing worse than having young 'uns took before their time." She pulled the plug to let the rinse water drain. "Yous can take my place now. I'm all done."

At the far end of one of the aisles, shrill, excited voices cut through the steam. Two women were having a tug-o-war with a sopping sheet. A fat woman, her face purple, was screaming that the other had stolen her sheet.

"Your sheet? You took it out of the tub, the minute my back was turned, you thieving bugger!" The second woman lunged and in the struggle lost the pins from her hair. Grey hair fell in greasy strings around her face.

"Run quick and fetch the ticket lady," said a woman standing nearby. Clarrie ran down the aisle to the entrance.

"There're two ladies fighting," she said, breathlessly.

"Good lord, not again!" The woman bundled up her knitting. "Show me where they are."

She followed Clarrie, then pushed her way through the crowd. "All right, all right, back to your tubs everyone. We don't want any trouble." The women went on fighting as if they hadn't heard her. Malcolm's daddy was standing at the back of the crowd.

"You're a man," the door-lady said. "Can't you do summat?"

"I'll try." He stepped forward and the group of women parted.

The woman with the greasy hair raised her fist, preparing to swing at the fat one. Malcolm's father grabbed her wrist. "Ladies, ladies, please!"

The woman jerked her arm away. "Stay out of this, you little pansy." The two women went down, rolling over and over on the wet floor.

Malcolm's father shrugged and turned away. "I tried."

A hunchbacked old woman, bent almost double, cackled: "They're like two cats on a backyard wall, someone ought to chuck a bucket of water over 'em."

Clarrie ran to ask her mother where she could find a bucket. "They're rolling about on the floor," she said. "You can see their knickers."

Her mother's face was wet from the steam. "Stay here. Let them sort it out for themselves."

"But what if the wrong lady got the sheet?" Clarrie asked as her mother trundled the pram full of washing home.

"It's better to lose a sheet than roll about on the floor, fighting like alley cats."

Clarrie frowned. She'd expected her mother to be on the side of justice. "That's not fair," she said.

"Lot's of things aren't fair in this world, love."

"Well, they ought to be," Clarrie said.

Chapter Nine

To mark the annual harvest festival at the Methodist Chapel, the Sunday School children were putting on a stage production, and Annie was to play the woman who lived in a shoe.

"I can't imagine what all this dressing up has to do with bringing in a harvest," Sally said, holding out her old skirt for Annie to try on. "Those children don't even know what a harvest is; they have no idea what they're supposed to be celebrating."

"What can I wear?" Clarrie asked. Her class had rehearsed a dance to "Wee Willie Winkie," and Miss Larkin had said each child must wear a nightie or pajamas. Clarrie had no nightie or pajamas; she slept in her vest and knickers.

Sally took a pin from between her teeth and marked the place for the button on Annie's skirt. "Mrs. Wardle has offered to lend you a pair of Herbert's pajamas."

"But Herbert's a boy."

"Pajamas are pajamas. Nobody will know they're not yours."

"Herbert will know. Everyone will laugh at me."

Her father looked at her sternly. "Do you want to be in this pageant or not?"

Clarrie nodded.

"Climb in the tub then and stop whining."

"In Kent we decorated the church with sheaves of wheat," Sally said. "I don't suppose there's any chance of finding a sheaf of wheat in Salford?"

"We can barely afford a loaf of bread, let alone a flaming sheaf of wheat," William said. He spread a sheet of newspaper on the floor and arranged the shoe polish, rags, and brushes on the paper.

"There's a notice on the Chapel bulletin board," Annie said. "They're asking people to bring fruit and vegetables to decorate the chapel for Sunday."

Sally marked the skirt with chalk. "I bought a nice vegetable marrow yesterday, we can donate that."

"We're giving them a plate of jam tarts, aren't we?" William said. "Let that suffice."

"Those are for my skit," Arthur said. He was to be the knave of hearts, who stole a plate of tarts. His teacher had suggested he cut out circles of cardboard and color them red to resemble jam, but Sally had baked a batch of real tarts for him to steal. "Mam says I can share them with the class after it's over," he added.

"I believe there's a spoonful of jam left in the pot," William said. "Why not give that away, too? We can't have bloody great piles of food cluttering up the kitchen."

"You can take the skirt off now," Sally said to Annie. "It'll have to do." She lifted Clarrie from the tub and rubbed her dry with a rough towel. She told Arthur to wrap the oven plate in newspaper and take it upstairs to warm the bed. "Stay with Clarrie—read her a story while Annie has her bath."

"What about my candle?" Clarrie asked.

"For heaven's sake stop worrying. You'll have your candle—we'll put it in that green tin candlestick you like so much."

Arthur slipped the oven plate among the covers and sat on the edge of the bed to read Clarrie a story about Aladdin and his magic lamp.

"When Mam takes you to the rummage sale at the festival tomorrow, keep your eyes skinned for a magic lamp like this." He held up the book to show her the picture. "It looks a bit like the old oil can Dad uses on the door hinges, but don't let that fool you. It might be made of gold or silver and have a genie inside, like this chap." He showed her a picture of a large man with a turban on his head. "If the genie asks you to let him out, you first have to make him promise to bring you whatever you want."

"Can he bring me a doll?"

"He can do that with one hand tied behind his back. Ask him to bring a three-speed bike for your brother while he's at it."

Her mother called up that it was time for Arthur's bath. Arthur closed the book. "Go to sleep now."

"I haven't said my prayers yet."

"The floor's too cold," Arthur said. "Say them in bed."

Clarrie closed her eyes; "God bless Mammy, God bless Daddy, God bless Annie, God bless Arthur . . ."

"You're taking too long." Arthur blew out the candle. "Just ask him to bless everyone in the whole world and get it over with."

Clarrie lay under the covers, unable to sleep. She was supposed to kneel to say her prayers, and to name everyone separately. She'd not be able fall asleep until she'd done it right. She pushed back the covers, and knelt shivering by the bed. The room was cold indeed—the floorboards hard against her bare knees. From the bed came the warm, inviting smell of faintly scorched newspaper. She clasped her hands in prayer and began the litany again.

She had just snuggled back under the covers, when Annie came up smelling of carbolic soap and crawled in beside her. "Shift your bony bum," she said, "and stop breathing through your mouth." She kicked Clarrie's feet off the oven plate.

Clarrie rolled to the edge of the mattress. She'd tried many times to keep her mouth closed, but in the end, she always had to open it and gulp in air. She wished she didn't have to sleep with Annie; she wished she could have a bed all to herself.

In a little while, Arthur came back upstairs and climbed in at the foot of the bed. He and Annie started a feet fight over the oven plate.

Down in the kitchen, their parents were arguing. Clarrie pulled the sheet and coat over her head to block out the sound. A complaining edge had crept into her mother's voice. Her father answered in an angry rumble.

"Just listen to them!" Annie said. "Chunner, chunner, chunner. How do they expect us to get any sleep?"

"You're the one keeping me awake," Arthur said.

Annie climbed out of bed, pulling the coat off Clarrie and wrapping it around her own shoulders. "I'm going to listen on the landing—see what they're nattering about."

Clarrie rolled back into the middle of the mattress. By and by, the voices stopped. She heard the front door slam shut.

Annie ran into the room, and climbed into bed, shivering. "Dad's gone out blazing mad," she said. "Mam wants him to ask Uncle Jack for a job at the abattoir. Dad says he'd sooner starve than ask Jack for anything."

"Dad hasn't forgiven him for running away from home when they were lads," Arthur said, "and I heard Dad tell some bloke that he couldn't stand the stink of an abattoir."

Clarrie stuck her head out of the covers to ask why Uncle Jack had run away.

"None of your business," Annie said. "Go to sleep."

"Leave her alone," Arthur said. "How can she go to sleep when we're talking?"

"Dad was on again about that sheepskin rug Uncle Jack gave us. He said Mam should never have let our Janet suck on it. He thinks she got sheep hair in her lungs."

"What sheepskin rug? Where is it?" Clarrie asked.

"Gone," Arthur said. "Dad threw it in the dustbin. He blames that rug for Janet dying."

"He blames me, too," Annie said.

"Don't be so daft."

"Yes, he does. I heard him tell Mam that I should have come to get them sooner. You were there, too. I don't know why he blames me."

"Where was I then?" Clarrie asked.

"You were just born." Annie said. "You were yelling your head off in the front room."

"What was I yelling about?"

"How do I know?" Annie poked her in the back. "Just shut up and move over."

"I can't, I'm already on the wires." The mattress was too narrow for the bed, and she was clinging by her fingertips to the bare springs to keep from falling onto the floor.

Perhaps, if she found a magic lamp at the festival tomorrow, she'd ask the genie for a bed as well as a doll. A nice brass bed, like Gladys had. Gladys wasn't sleeping in hers now though, because she was back in the sanatorium. Clarrie wanted her to hurry up and get better. With Gladys gone she had nobody to play with.

There were no magic lamps on the jumble sale counter—nothing but a heap of old clothes, one or two rusty mesh handbags, and a few dusty felt hats. Clarrie was disappointed but not surprised. Salford wasn't the sort of place where people found magic lamps—even so, it was worth a try.

It was time for the five-year-olds to get ready for the show. Clarrie's pajama trousers were baggy around the waist, so her mother tied a double knot in the cord.

"That should hold it," she said, "I'm going now to find a seat."

Miss Larkin gave the children a last check to make sure that all was in order. With an exasperated clucking sound, she pounced on Clarrie. "This will never do!" She unfastened the thickly knotted drawstring on Clarrie's pajamas and tied it in a neat bow. "That's better!"

Miss Larkin reminded the children to do the dance exactly as she'd taught them—candle in right hand, left hand on the shoulder of the person in front—one, two, three, then hop—everybody with the same foot at the same time. "I will be at the piano," she said. "When you hear the first note it is time to come out." She put her finger to her lips and led them down the hall and through an open green baize door to what she called "the wings."

The people in the audience were chattering and coughing. Clarrie's stomach fluttered. She could hardly breathe. Suddenly, there was a rattle of curtain rings, and a wine-colored plush curtain swung back. She knew the people were out there, watching, but she couldn't see them because the shell-shaped lights at the foot of the stage were dazzling her eyes. Miss Larkin struck the opening chords of Wee Willie Winkie, and the children, dressed in an assortment of nightwear and holding aloft their unlit candles, shuffled onto the stage.

Clarrie counted under her breath; one, two, three, hop; one, two, three, hop. Her right hand clutched a candle, her left hand rested on the shoulder of the boy in front. She could feel the drawstring loosening on her pajamas. Without losing count, she took her hand from the shoulder of the boy in front long enough to hoist them up. Someone in the audience giggled. The boy in front was hopping when he should be skipping. Clarrie looked at her feet and tried to match her steps to his. Another boy pushed her from behind. "You're out of step," he hissed. Clarrie stumbled.

"I am not," she said.

A ripple of laughter ran through the audience. Everything was going wrong. Half the children were hopping when they should be skipping, and now her trousers were coming down. She came to a halt, the way Miss Larkin told them to do if anyone made a mistake.

She turned to the boy behind her. "Stop! We're getting all mixed up. We have to start over."

A roar of laughter rose from the darkened hall. Miss Larkin had stopped playing and was waving from the piano, mouthing something. Clarrie struggled with one hand to secure her pajamas, but her candle fell out of the candlestick and rolled across the stage. The laughter subsided. The people fell silent, waiting to see what she would do. She turned to face them and was blinded by the footlights.

"It wasn't me!" She spoke as loudly as she could. "It wasn't me who got out of step. I was counting."

There was a burst of applause. Chairs scraped, shadowy figures rose from their seats, and a tidal wave of laughter came crashing over her. She turned in a panic, bumped into a large cardboard panel, painted to resemble a house. The panel swayed, then toppled and fell.

"Over here!" Her mother was below the stage, at the back, beckoning to her. "Come on, jump! I'll catch you."

She fell into her mother's outstretched arms. "They're laughing at me!" she wailed.

Her mother held out a handkerchief. "Stop crying, now. You should be pleased; it's not everyone who can make folks laugh."

"But it wasn't my fault. I was counting."

Her mother shrugged at Miss Larkin, then took Clarrie's hand and led her down the hall to Arthur's classroom. "Give our Clarrie one of your tarts, Arthur, love," her mother said.

Clarrie turned her head away.

"What was everyone laughing at?" Arthur asked. His friends, dressed like playing cards, were capering about, pushing each other.

"Our Clarrie stopped the show." Her mother winked at Arthur's teacher. "She told the audience that everyone was out of step but her."

Another burst of laughter. Clarrie looked down at the scuffed floorboards. Nobody believed her. Nobody cared to know the truth, not even her mother.

"Quiet down, everyone," Arthur's teacher said. "It's time to go on stage."

Clarrie's mother set her on her feet. "We've got to go. We don't want to miss our Arthur stealing the tarts."

Clarrie pulled away, shaking her head. "They're still laughing at me."

"Oh, for heaven's sake! Wait here in the classroom then, until I come back. Find some crayons or something." She hurried out, closing the door behind her.

Clarrie pressed her face to the glass panel. Her mother, distorted by the ripples in the glass, moved swiftly down the hall and disappeared behind the green baize door.

Chapter Ten

October had come and gone with little to mark its passage but drizzling rain. From time to time, a pale sun broke through the clouds to dance briefly over the wet slates and cobblestones. Sally was at her wit's end trying to dry the washing indoors. Wet towels steamed over the oven door, lines of shirts and underwear crisscrossed the kitchen, and damp sheets hung for days over the rails of the landing.

"Autumn was never like this in the country," Sally said. "When I was a child, it was my favorite time of the year. We played conkers with chestnuts, bobbed for apples, gathered nuts along the lanes . . ." Her voice grew dreamy as she described a lost Eden of falling leaves, gentle morning mists drifting over the fields, the scent of wood-smoke rising from cottage chimneys. Clarrie imagined a "gentle morning mist drifting over the fields" would look like the lacy curtain she'd once seen blowing away from a clothesline.

There were no gentle morning mists in Salford. November brought fog, and the November fog was nothing to be trifled with. Within minutes, an impenetrable, murky vapor would descend upon the town, bringing traffic to a standstill. Coalmen, swinging lanterns, walked holding the reins of their horses, and men riding home from work on bicycles slammed into bridge abutments. Children got lost on the way home from school, and in a picture show the fog could quickly obliterate the screen, leaving the hapless cinema managers no choice but to give everyone in the audience their money back.

It was getting close to teatime. Sally came bustling in with a loaded shopping bag. "Hurry everyone, get the boards up, we're in for a right pea-souper!"

Everyone sprang into action. Clarrie went upstairs with Annie to jam rags around the doors and windows. Arthur did the same downstairs. Her father pulled out the sheets of cardboard kept alongside the bookcase to barricade the unused chimneys. Arthur closed the wooden shutters across the kitchen window, returning to the kitchen table where he'd been cutting newspaper into strips.

"Put that stuff away now," Sally said. "We'll have an early tea, while we can still see what we're doing."

"Just let me finish the Guy's head."

"Move over," William said. He crumbled sheets of wet newspaper into a ball and handed it to Arthur. "Start molding and pasting with the strips you've cut. I'll shape the nose."

"That's quite a schnoz you're giving him, Dad," Arthur said.

"That's a Napoleonic nose. The French are famous for their big noses."

"It's almost as big as yours. Are you sure you're not French, Dad?"

Clarrie leaned over the table to watch. "Was Guy Fawkes a Frenchman, then?"

"He must have been, with a name like that. Whatever he was, he was a crafty bugger—he managed to smuggle twenty barrels of gunpowder into parliament."

"Remember, remember," Arthur sang, "the fifth of November—gunpowder, treason, and plot . . ."

"Put some specs on him, Dad," Annie said, "and he'll be the spitting image of you."

William snipped a strip of thin wire from around a bundle of firewood and shaped it into spectacles.

"Make some for me, too," Clarrie said.

He fashioned another pair of glasses and set them on Clarrie's nose.

"Did they have bonfires when you were little?" she asked.

"Aye, they did indeed. I can remember being woken up by my father to see the bonfires celebrating the relief of Mafeking. That had nothing to do with Guy Fawkes, of course, but there were bonfires everywhere. Everyone was singing and laughing and dancing in the streets, and the whole town seemed to be on fire. It's one of the few good memories I have of those days. My father told me all about the Boer War and the terrible long siege that had left a whole Garrison starving. He told me never to forget that night. I never have, and I never will."

Clarrie said she would never forget it, either.

"You weren't even there, you daft nit," Annie said.

Clarrie said she was too. She had gone there in her mind while her dad was talking.

"You must be barmy, then," Annie said.

Arthur was setting the Guy's head in the hearth to dry when Sally came in from the scullery. "That's a fine looking head you've given him," she said.

"Dad did most of it," Arthur said. "Harry and me—I—are taking the Guy 'round in Harry's wheelbarrow to-morrow. I hope the fog's gone by then—nobody will give us any money if they can't see him. We want to buy pinwheels for the eyes."

"We used to call them Catherine wheels in Kent," Sally said. Clarrie asked why, but her mother said she didn't know. She set out some meat and potato pies she'd bought at the bakery for a special treat. By the time they'd finished the meal, thick fog had shrouded the corners of the room, and the gaslight overhead was lost in an orange haze. William reached up and turned off the light. "It's a waste of gas," he said.

They picked up their chairs and seated themselves in a semicircle round the fire for a sing-song.

In a clear, strong voice, Arthur opened the singing with, "Marta, Rambling Rose of the Wildwood." Everyone applauded. They all joined in singing "Lily of Laguna," "It's a Long Way to Tipperary," and "Nellie Dean." Someone suggested "On Ilkley Moor B'aht 'at"; Clarrie wanted to know what "B'aht 'at" meant. Her father said it was old Lancashire dialect for "without a hat." Annie began the first verse mimicking an angry mother accusing her son of courting his girl "On Ilkley Moor B'aht 'at" on such a dark, cold night. Everyone joined in the chorus, repeating "On Ilkley Moor B'aht 'at" at the end of each verse.

Sally asked William to sing "The Spaniard Who Blighted my Life," and the children cried, "Yes, yes, do it, Dad!" William picked up the poker, and brandishing his imaginary sword at an imaginary Spaniard, he sang: "He shall die! He shall die! I'll raise a bunion on his Spanish onion, he's the Spaniard who blighted my life." The children applauded wildly.

"Do your clog dance, Will," Sally said.

He put on his shoes, and then lifted the enameled hearth plate onto the mat. "I haven't danced since . . . I can't remember when. Sing 'Lassie from Lancashire,' and blow on a paper and comb. I'll see what I can do."

Arthur tore a strip of paper, wrapped it around a comb, and blew. The others sang and clapped, keeping time to the tap-tap of William's feet on the enameled hearth plate.

Clarrie was sitting on the floor, her head resting against her mother's knees. "I never knew my dad could dance," she said.

Her mother stroked her hair. "You should see him skate. Perhaps he'll take you to the rink and show you sometime."

"Yes. I want to see him skate," Clarrie murmured sleepily. She wished they could stay like this forever.

On Guy Fawkes' night, Clarrie, wrapped in an old coat, sat on her three-legged stool outside the back door to watch the building of the bonfire. Arthur and his friends glided like shadows through the fog, carrying out the junk they'd stored in the yard, and stacking it in the middle of the street. The Barlow family had come out in force to help. Mr. and Mrs. Barlow brought out kitchen chairs, and kept scolding various younger members of their brood, who were running in and out of the house to get thick slabs of bread and dripping. Gladys, from next door, had brought out her own small stool and parked it next to Clarrie's. Several neighbors huddled together, clutching their shawls against the damp November dusk as they chatted. The men hung about in small groups, smoking and calling out warnings and advice to the lads who were stacking the bonfire.

"Not too high, now," William cautioned. "We don't want anyone getting burned."

Arthur and Harry Barlow brought out the Guy, tied to a broken chair. Harry shone a flashlight on its face to show the pinwheel eyes, and everyone agreed that it was the best Guy they'd ever seen. It took a few minutes to settle the Guy securely in place, then William told everyone to stand back as he held a lighted paper brand to the base of the pyramid. With a loud crackling noise the flames caught, licking their way through the carefully structured pyramid and casting an orange glow over the foggy street.

The grownups moved their chairs back from the heat and pulled the smaller children out of reach of the flying sparks. Some of the older boys threw rick-rack fireworks that jumped about the ground with a series of sharp explosions. One of these went off under Mrs. Sidebotham's chair, startling her so much, she went back into her house for a little something to calm her nerves.

Sally, who had spent the morning preparing buttery treacle toffee and moist, spicy parkin, sent Annie in to fetch the trays, and told her to offer them first to the children, and then to the grownups.

"You've got it wrong way 'round, lass," Mrs. Sidebotham said, helping herself to a large slab of parkin. "You're supposed to serve grownups first."

"My mam's funny that way," Annie said. "She's got this daft idea that children are just as important."

Arthur lit two sparklers, handed one to Clarrie and the other to Gladys. Clarrie, fearful of the sparks that were burning her hand, promptly dropped hers and began to cry.

"I think you've had enough excitement for one night," her mother said. Ignoring Clarrie's protests, she sent her off to bed, telling her she'd be up in a few minutes to tuck her in.

Standing at the back bedroom window, Clarrie watched the scene below. Sky Rockets, Golden Fountains, Prince-of-Wales Feathers burst and shimmered through the amber fog. Cries of wonder rose from the crowd as a shower of sparks fell like golden rain. Shrieks of laughter mingled with the crackle of the bonfire. But the room was cold, and Clarrie was afraid her mother might come up and find her still not in bed. She ran back, said some hasty prayers, and climbed between the covers. Drifting off to sleep she heard Arthur's voice chanting, "Remember, remember . . ."

Chapter Eleven

Sally stared into the tin tea caddy, wondering if it would fetch anything at the pawnshop. It was a nice tin. There was a portrait of King George the Fifth on one side, and a portrait of Queen Mary on the other, taken on the occasion of their coronation. She didn't really need a caddy, and right now there was hardly enough tea in it to make a decent pot.

"Guess what Maud next door told me," Annie said. "The Rourkes did a midnight flit last Sunday night. They left six weeks rent owing and the gas meter broken into."

Clarrie asked what a midnight flit was.

"It means someone moved in the middle of the night, without paying their rent."

"If that's true, the poor things must be desperate." Sally emptied the contents of the caddy into the teapot, poured in boiling water and set the tea to steep under a green-striped cozy.

"Maud says they're shanty Irish, straight out of the bog; she says their name is really O'Rourke, but they knocked the O off so people would take them for English."

"I'd love to know where that woman gets her information. Mrs. Rourke seems a decent enough sort to me. Her children look as if they get a square meal once in a while—which is more than you can say for Gladys. A cup of Oxo for a growing girl's dinner! I hope they'll do better now that she's out of hospital."

"Maud was giving her pobs for her tea," Annie said.

"Pobs? What on earth is that, pray?"

William looked up from his newspaper. "It's stale bread soaked in hot water, with a spoonful of condensed milk," he said. "My mother sometimes gave it to me, after she—after we left the Hancock house. I was glad to get it, too."

"They can't have gone too far," Arthur said. "Just yesterday my pal, Harry, saw the Rourkes busking outside the Hippodrome. Old man Rourke was playing 'Phil the Fluter's Ball' on a tin whistle; the rest of the kids were doing the Irish jig. Mrs. Rourke was nowhere in sight."

Sally handed William his tea. "She was probably home taking care of her new baby."

William took a sip then pushed the cup and saucer away. "What in hell's name did you do to this tea?" he asked. "It's weak as water."

"That's all the tea we have until Mr. Hutchins pays me. Leave it if you don't like it."

"We could go out busking, too," Arthur said. "I could sing "Marta," Dad could wear his Cossack outfit . . ."

"We're not reduced to that, yet, thank God," William said.

Sally took two flatirons from the cupboard. "Clear the table, Annie."

"Why can't our Clarrie do it?"

"Do as your mother tells you, and no back chat," William said. "You can wash the pots later. I'll take what's in the kettle. I want to shave."

Annie gathered up the plates and carried them into the scullery. Arthur settled himself in his father's chair with a dog-eared copy of *The Hotspur*. Sally spread a flannel sheet across one side of the table, stepping over Arthur's legs to set a flatiron on the grid.

Clarrie followed her father into the scullery to watch him shave. He honed his razor on a leather strop. "Be a good girl," he said. "Run upstairs and fetch me my collar studs off the dresser, and my maroon tie."

Clarrie ran off, happy to be of help. She wasn't sure what color maroon was, so she picked the only tie that was neither blue, nor striped. His studs were not on the dresser, but she rummaged under his pillow and found them.

Her father had finished shaving and was standing at the kitchen window staring out into the dark yard. He was still in his long drawers and undervest, a towel draped around his neck.

"It's raining." He turned and looked at the tie and studs. "Thanks, love. Put them on the sideboard."

"You've cut yourself, Dad," Clarrie said.

"Aye." He dabbed the cut with the towel. "I can't see a bloody thing in that cracked shaving glass."

Her mother lifted the iron from the fire. With a deft flick of the wrist she turned it downside up and spat on it; the spittle sizzled and flew off into the fire. She rubbed the bottom of the iron with a crumpled piece of brown paper. "What happened to that safety razor I bought you?"

"I couldn't get used to the bloody thing, so I pawned it." He glanced at the wrinkled shirt she picked from the laundry basket. "Is that my shirt you're ironing?"

"This is the Hutchins's stuff."

"I thought you were going to pack it in after the boiler broke."

"You've been out of work for months, now. I'm just trying to make ends meet."

"Is it my fault there's nowt doing? Read the paper, woman. Half the able-bodied men in England are out of work. It's even worse down Newcastle way."

"Did I say it was your fault? Makes no difference whose fault it is, we've still got to eat."

He walked over to the fire, thrust the poker between the bars and lit a cigarette with the red-hot end. "Can't you iron me a clean shirt, without a song and a dance? I've been wearing that other thing for three days now."

"Oh, for heaven's sake!" Sally threw down what she'd been ironing. She fished in the bottom drawer of the sideboard.

"Listen to that rain—it's coming down in bloody buckets."

"Why not stay home, then?"

"You know it's my Odd Fellows night."

"Why don't you ask them to give you something to tide you over?"

"You can get that idea out of your head right away."

"They helped out that acrobat fellow when we were on tour, didn't they?"

"He'd broken both his legs."

"And you've got a blind eye."

He walked over to the sideboard mirror, produced a comb from his pocket and parted his hair. "Clarrie love, fetch me the jar of Brilliantine from over the sink."

Clarrie ran into the scullery and came back with a small jar. "I think it's empty, Dad."

He unscrewed the lid, stared gloomily into the jar, ran two fingers around the inside, then rubbed his fingertips through his wispy hair and combed it a second time.

"If you get that parting any straighter," Sally said, "it'll look like the great North Road."

"In a snowstorm," Arthur said. Everybody laughed.

"It's you lot that are giving me grey hairs."

"Here's your shirt," Sally said.

"Ta." He buttoned the shirt, pulled the trousers over his long drawers and slipped the braces over his shoulders. The top of the trousers came up almost to his armpits. He sat down to lace his boots. The lace snapped. He fumbled with the broken pieces, trying to tie them together.

"Pass me my spats out of the bottom drawer, Annie."

"It's 1931, Dad," Annie said. "Nobody wears spats anymore."

"I wear them." He pressed a stud into his celluloid collar, knotted his tie, slipped a garter over each sleeve and fastened the buttons of his waistcoat. He took his watch chain off the mantelpiece and tucked one end in the waistcoat pocket, the other through the buttonhole, looping it across his chest.

Arthur looked up from his magazine. "Where's your watch, Dad?"

"In the pawnshop."

"So why are you wearing your watch chain?"

"If I wear the chain, nobody needs to know where my watch is."

"What if someone asks you for the right time?"

"I'll tell 'em my watch is not working."

"It's not the only thing that's not working," Sally said.

William put on his jacket, brushed his shoulders with a clothes brush, and stepped away from the glass, turning to view the back. "These trousers have had their day. I look as if I've been sitting in a tub of lard. Even the ammonia can't get rid of the shine . . ."

Sally put the iron down on an upturned saucer and looked at him. "What a dandy! Beau Brummell isn't the word for it."

William felt in his trouser pockets, in his jacket and waistcoat pockets. "I think it's starting to let up a bit."

"You know very well it's doing no such thing."

He went over to the fireplace, picked up the poker and jabbed at the coals.

"What's keeping you?" Sally asked. "You're all dressed in your nice clean shirt—why don't you go on your merry way—have a good time while you're young."

"Don't talk bloody rubbish, woman. I haven't even got shoe leather. I'm walking on the soles of my feet." He felt in his trouser pockets. "Haven't you got anything?"

"Such as?"

"You know what I mean. A shilling—sixpence—summat to jingle in my pocket."

"We're a week behind on the rent. We owe four shillings to Timson for groceries, and two and six to the coal-man."

"They'll get their money. Must you give me a flaming financial report every time I go out? I'm sick and tired of hearing about it."

"And I'm sick and tired of not knowing where our next meal is coming from."

He snatched his bowler hat off the sideboard. "You're driving me to drink, the bloody lot of you." He stormed out, slamming the door behind him. The sound hung for a moment in the silence.

"Dad forgot his umbrella," Arthur said.

With a sigh, Sally set down the iron. "Clarrie, run after your dad and take him his umbrella. His suit will be ruined." She fished in her apron pocket, withdrew her purse and took out a sixpence. "And give him this. I don't like him going out with nothing in his pocket." Clarrie scrambled to her feet.

Arthur turned the page of his magazine. "Better hurry. We can't have poor old Beau Brummell getting his suit wrinkled."

"That's quite enough out of you," Sally said. "Your dad's doing the best he can."

Clarrie ran down the lobby with the sixpence and the folded umbrella. In a few moments she was back in the kitchen. “Dad says thanks. He wasn’t wet—he was waiting for me on the front step.”

Chapter Twelve

Arthur lifted his jacket from its hook behind the door. "I promised Harry I'd help him deliver his papers, Mam. He said that next year, when he finds a proper job, I can take over his route."

"That'll be a help, love." Sally stopped rummaging through the kitchen cupboard long enough to turn and smile at him. "But it's not next year I'm worried about. Christmas will be here before we know it, and there's a new baby coming . . ."

Clarrie looked up from her book. "What new baby?"

"We're getting you a little brother or sister," her mother said. "Didn't I tell you?"

"I want a little sister," Clarrie said.

Annie paused in the act of clearing the table to scrape the last bits of mashed potato out of the bowl and lick the serving spoon. "Dad says when his ship comes in, he's going to buy us all new outfits," she said.

Arthur opened the door to a blast of cold air. "His ship must have sunk," he said. "It's down in Davy Jones's locker, covered in barnacles."

"Who's Davy Jones?" Clarrie asked. "What's a barnacle?" But Arthur had gone, closing the door behind him.

With a deep sigh, Sally slammed the cupboard door. "We're out of almost everything. I'll be damned if I'm going to stand here waiting for your father's ship to come in. I'm going down to that Odd Fellows Hall myself and see if Mr. Horne is in his office. I'm sure they'll be only too glad to help us."

"Better not let Dad catch you," Annie said. "He'll have a fit if he finds out."

"If you all keep your mouths shut, there'll be no need for him to know."

Clarrie ran over and flung her arms around her mother's bulging belly. "Don't go out, Mam, please! We don't need any money."

Her mother removed Clarrie's hands. "Don't be silly, child." She put on her coat and tied a scarf around her head. "I know what I'm doing. There's nothing for any of you to worry about."

When her mother had gone, Clarrie went into the back yard to play. After a few minutes Annie pushed open the window and stuck her head out.

"Get in here, our Clarrie. I want you to help me with this toffee."

The smell of burning sugar filled the kitchen. Annie, wrapped in her mother's flowered apron, was bent over the fire stirring something in a saucepan. The table was littered with pans, a pool of spilled syrup, and crumpled greaseproof paper sticky with margarine.

"Hurry up!" Annie yelled. "This toffee's almost done. Bring me a cup of cold water, quick!"

She grabbed the cup from Clarrie's hands. "Now while I'm testing, you grease the baking tin. Make sure it's clean."

Clarrie examined the tin, scraped some bits of black stuff out of the corners with her fingernail, then began smearing the tin with lard.

Annie trickled a ribbon of syrup into the jar. "Not quite ready." She put the pan back on the fire. "Promise to help me clean up this mess and I'll tell you a secret."

"I promise."

"You're getting a gorgeous doll for Christmas."

Clarrie studied Annie's face. Tendrils of hair were stuck to her flushed cheeks, and her wire-rimmed glasses were coated with steam, making it hard to see her eyes. "Did Mam tell you that?"

"Mam doesn't know about it. It's from my sewing class. We're not supposed to tell anyone. The church ladies are collecting used dolls and my class is making clothes for them." She took the pan from the fire and tested the syrup. "Pass me that tin."

"Are you giving me yours, then?"

"Yes. They're Christmas presents for the girls in Standard One. That means you lot. I grabbed the best one for you. She's got real hair and eyes that open and close."

"What color is her hair?"

"Black—long black ringlets. I'm making her a cape out of some red velvet, and I'll finish the outfit off with some felt shoes and a white fur muff. They're going to hand them out before school breaks up for the Christmas holidays. Miss Smallwood says she'll pin your name to the cape."

Annie poured a stream of boiling syrup into the tin. Clarrie's heart sank. Black grease was swirling out of all four corners, mingling with the golden toffee. Annie set down the pan, removed her glasses and cleared away the steam with her apron.

"What's all that black stuff ?"

"What black stuff?"

Annie's hand flew out as though of its own volition and slapped Clarrie across the face. "It's dirty old grease, that's what. You've ruined my toffee. All that work—all that syrup and butter gone to waste." Clarrie ducked as Annie went to hit her again. "You're hopeless," Annie yelled. "Can't you do anything right?"

"I thought I cleaned it."

"I'm sorry I picked out such a nice doll for you." Annie took off her apron. "You don't deserve it. You'll probably break it, like you did mine." She put on her coat. "I'm going out. You'd better have this mess cleaned up before Mam gets back if you want that doll."

Clarrie's heart sank. The spoiled toffee was already hardening on the spoon, the pan, and the baking tin. It would be impossible to clean. She filled the iron kettle and carried it to the fire, staggering under the weight, then sat down in her father's chair to wait for the water to boil.

She wished, for the thousandth time, that Janet were alive—someone to be her friend, to side with her against Annie. Arthur had always stuck up for her, but he wasn't around much these days. If she ever did get a baby sister, she'd be kind and gentle, not cruel like Annie.

It was wrong to think a thing like that about her only sister. She was supposed to love her. And Annie was nice sometimes—she told exciting stories, she knew all the best places to go for walks, and best of all, she'd picked out a wonderful doll for her. She'd call her doll Rosie. She'd dress her up, and tell her secrets, and take her with her wherever she went.

On the last day of school before the Christmas holidays, Clarrie rushed downstairs, washed hastily, threw on her clothes, bolted her porridge, and sped off to school. For once she was early.

"Have you seen any dolls?" she whispered to Gladys, as they marched into assembly. "Our Annie says we're getting those dolls today, the ones I told you about." Gladys shook her head.

After the usual morning routine of prayers and hymns, they went back to the classroom, where Miss Jones, the arithmetic teacher, set them to memorizing the two times table. What if it was a joke? Annie might have been teasing her.

At lunchtime she ran home, but she couldn't eat.

"Don't get so worked up, love," her mother said. "Annie wouldn't lie about a thing like that. They'll probably hand them out just before you leave."

Clarrie raced back to school, to be confronted by a spelling test. She finished quickly, waiting impatiently while the slower ones chewed their pens and stared at the wall. Finally the teacher collected the papers. "No more work today, children." She smiled down at them. "We are going back into the Assembly Hall, where the Standard Seven girls have a surprise for you."

A buzz of excitement ran through the room as the girls filed out.

The Standard Seven girls were already in their places. Miss Hughes, the headmistress, was standing behind a large barrel decorated with red and green crepe paper. On one side of the barrel, the Rector sat gazing at the assembly with his usual expression of kindly severity. Seated near him were two well-dressed ladies, neither of them known to Clarrie. Miss Smallwood, the sewing and cookery teacher, hovered in the background wringing her hands. She was wearing a red cardigan with a sprig of mistletoe pushed through one of the buttonholes, but there was an unhappy expression on her face.

The Rector rose and led them in the Lord's Prayer. He introduced the ladies, who smiled and bowed their heads graciously, like queens riding by in a coach. The Rector told the assembly that the ladies were responsible for collecting and donating a number of used dolls to the school, and that the dolls had been splendidly refurbished by the girls of Miss Smallwood's sewing class. He was sure that everyone was most grateful to the ladies for making this happy occasion possible. The Rector glanced at the headmistress. She nodded, and tapped her hands together to let the children know it was time to clap, then raised one hand when it was time to stop. She picked up a sheet of paper and told the girls of Standard One to come forward as their names were called.

Clarrie watched eagerly as each girl went forward to receive a doll. Some of the dolls were very small and scantily dressed. Violet Fawcet's was the worst, but Violet was smiling down at it, as though it were the loveliest doll in the world. None of the dolls seemed to have labels or nametags. What if Miss Smallwood had forgotten to put the names on? But she had given her promise to Annie. It would be all right. The "H's" would be coming up soon.

"Clara Hancock," the headmistress called, stretching out the first "a" in Clara. Clarrie stumbled from her seat, her heart pounding. The headmistress had her arm in the barrel. She rummaged about for a while, then brought out a small doll and thrust it into Clarrie's hand. The doll had a china head with painted staring eyes, and painted-on hair. There were no legs; the lower half was a stiffly padded pincushion.

The headmistress frowned. "Where are your manners, child?" she whispered. "Say thank you."

"This isn't mine," Clarrie said. "My doll has a white muff and a red velvet cape."

"Take what you have been given," the headmistress hissed, "and return to your seat at once." She looked down at her list of names. "Elsie Harvey . . ."

Clarrie looked wildly at Miss Smallwood, but Miss Smallwood's attention seemed to be focused on the wall at the other side of the room. Raising herself on tiptoe, Clarrie peered into the bran tub. A scrap of red velvet caught her eye. She plunged her hand down as far as it would go.

A gasp went up from the assembled students, and one of the church ladies made a loud, disapproving "tutting" noise. The headmistress grasped Clarrie's arm and removed it from the barrel. Miss Jones moved quickly to the front of the room and hustled Clarrie back to her seat. The Standard Seven girls turned to stare at her as she went by. Annie was gesturing, mouthing something.

Back in her seat, Clarrie saw the headmistress cover the side of her face with the sheet of paper and whisper something in the Rector's ear. The Rector nodded. Through a blur of tears Clarrie stared down at the scuffed floorboards. Annie had promised. Miss Smallwood had promised.

"Clarrie!" Gladys whispered from the row behind her. "Muriel Monk's got your doll."

Muriel Monk, who already owned several dolls and a brand new fairy bike, too, was walking down the aisle, her Shirley Temple curls bouncing against her white lace collar. In her arms she cradled a large doll. The doll wore a white fur hat and a red velvet cloak; its hands were tucked into a white fur muff.

Clarrie jumped to her feet and pushed past the row of girls to Muriel. "There it is! That's my doll," she cried. "That's Rosie!"

Muriel lifted the doll high above her head.

Miss Jones bore down on Clarrie, her eyes blazing. "Behave yourself!" She took hold of Clarrie's arm with an iron grip and escorted her, still struggling, from the room.

Chapter Thirteen

On Christmas Eve, the children strung the newspaper chains they had made across the kitchen ceiling. Sally fished a crumbled red paper bell out of the parlor cupboard and told Arthur to tie it to the gas bracket. Annie put the finishing touches to the decorations by sticking paper snowflakes on all the windows and writing "Merry Xmas" on the hall mirror with a piece of soap.

"That looks smashing," Arthur said.

Through the holes in the paper snowflakes on the kitchen window Clarrie watched real snow falling softly from a grey sky. Arthur came up behind her. "My teacher says that of all the snowflakes that have ever fallen, no two have ever been the same."

"How does he know that?" Annie asked. "Did he run around the world collecting them all?"

William came in shivering. He handed Annie a bulging paper bag. "Put this in the cupboard and don't open it."

"What is it?"

"Lay-holds for meddlers and crutches for lame ducks."

"It's tangerines," Annie said. "I can smell them."

He shook the snow off his hat and gave it to Clarrie. "Be a good girl and hang this up in the lobby for me."

Arthur put on his version of an upper class accent. "I say, Pater old bean, may I borrow one of your long black socks to leave out for Father Christmas? Mine could do with a bit of a wash."

William took a rolled-up pair of socks out of the sideboard drawer and handed one to Arthur and one to Annie.

"What about me?" Clarrie said. "My socks are too little." Her father fished out another sock, then sank back in his chair, untied his boots, and asked Clarrie to help pull them off.

"Did you and Uncle Jack hang socks up for Father Christmas when you were little?" she asked.

"Aye, we did that. One Christmas Eve, we hung up pillowslips for a joke. When we came downstairs on Christmas morning, we found the pillowslips filled with ashes and cinders."

"Why did Father Christmas do that?"

"It was just my dad trying to teach us a lesson. 'That's what you get for being greedy,' he said."

"I'm not greedy, am I, Mam?" Clarrie asked.

"You are when it comes to mashed potatoes. Otherwise, you're pretty good."

"Good?" Annie snorted. "After the way she carried on in school, she'll be lucky if she gets anything in her stocking."

"You shouldn't make promises if you can't keep them," her mother said.

"It wasn't my fault. Miss Hughes took the label off Clarrie's doll; she said she wanted no favoritism, and that the dolls must be given out at random."

There was a knock at the front door. "I wonder who that could be?" Sally said. "See who it is, Arthur."

Arthur went along the lobby to open the door. A gust of cold air swept into the kitchen. The door slammed shut again and Arthur staggered into the kitchen carrying a large wicker hamper.

"What the devil!" William rose from his chair.

"This was on the doorstep. It weighs a ton."

"Who left it, what did they say?"

"I didn't see anybody." Arthur put the hamper on the table. Clarrie climbed on a chair to get a closer look. Her mother lifted the lid. On top were several parcels wrapped in Christmas paper and underneath the parcels a fat raw turkey.

"Look at this lovely bird!" Sally put the turkey on the table, lifted out a jar of mincemeat, a bag of chestnuts, and a blue-ringed pudding basin covered with cheesecloth. The children lunged for the presents.

"Don't touch those," William said. "There's been a mistake."

"I knew it was too good to be true," Annie said.

Arthur handed his father a white envelope. William drew out a Christmas card showing a gift-laden stagecoach unloading a host of merrymakers in Victorian dress. He adjusted his spectacles to read. "To William Hancock and family, all the best for a Happy Christmas and a Prosperous New Year. Compliments of your local Odd Fellows." He put the card back in the envelope. His face had a strange expression. He looked at Sally. "Is this some of your doing?"

"No—well, I may have mentioned something to Bertie Horne about you being out of work . . ."

He picked up the turkey, piled everything back into the hamper, and slammed the lid. "We're taking it back. I'm not having any flaming charity."

"No, Dad!" the children wailed.

William glared at Sally. "You went behind my back, didn't you . . . showing me up?"

"I asked if anyone knew of any job openings, that's all. The hamper was their idea. They must mean it for a Christmas present."

"Aye, and I suppose everyone else got one, too?"

Sally opened the hamper and lifted out the turkey again. She bounced it up and down in her hands. "Feel the weight of this bird," she said. "It'll feed us for a week."

"It's going back, right now."

Sally clutched the turkey to her breast as though it were her child and he intent on murdering it.

"Don't be ridiculous, Will! It's Christmas Eve, there won't be anyone there."

William picked up the poker and savagely raked the ashes. "You've ruined it for me at the Odd Fellows," he said. "I won't be able to hold my head up again."

"Are we supposed to starve to death just so you can hold your head up?"

He swung around, the poker in his hand. "Doesn't it make any difference to you, then, what I want?"

"What you want?" Her mother's voice grew shrill. "What about your children, man? Look at the state they're in!" Clarrie glanced down at her undervest, where her mother was pointing. There were a few holes, but it was only to sleep in.

"We've already lost one child," Her mother cried. "Wasn't that enough for you?"

The color drained from her father's face, leaving it a sickly grey. He doubled over as though someone had stuck a knife in his chest. Clarrie's own chest hurt. Nothing this bad had ever happened before.

In *Little Women*, the library book her mother had been reading aloud to her, the March girls had given their Christmas dinner to the poor. "We could give that hamper to the poor," Clarrie said.

Annie jabbed her with an elbow. "Shut up you daft nit. What do you think we are?"

William threw the poker down in the hearth, yanked his coat from the hanger, jammed on his bowler. "Do as you bloody well please. I'm going out. You can expect me when you see me."

"You can stay out, for all I care," her mother said.

The front door slammed. Clarrie ran along the lobby after him. "Come back, Dad!" she shouted. "Mam was only kidding; she didn't mean it." But her father was already striding down the street, and he didn't turn around.

Clarrie's socks had come off in the night, and her feet were freezing. She sat up in bed and felt down among the rumpled covers for the missing socks. Annie was already up. From downstairs came a wonderful aroma. Clarrie jumped out of bed and scrambled into her clothes. Christmas Day! Father Christmas must have been by now. She sniffed the air, trying to sort out the different smells—tangerines, sausages, thyme, onions, mincemeat . . .

Suddenly the scene from the night before came rushing back. What if her dad never came home?

She walked to the window and scratched a clear space in the frost ferns. The ground, roofs, walls, windowsills, and lampposts were covered in snow. There was a ridge of snow along the clothesline. A black cat sprang from the roof and picked its way daintily along the top of the wall. Clarrie shivered. Gladys said a black cat was bad luck.

She dressed quickly and ran downstairs. The kitchen was warm, the fire roaring up the chimney. Her mother and Annie were clearing away the cooking mess, making room for breakfast.

"There you are," her mother said. "Merry Christmas, love."

"Merry Christmas."

Arthur looked up from the comic he was reading. "Ho, ho, ho!"

"Where's Dad?" Clarrie asked. She crossed her fingers behind her back.

"He's still sleeping."

Clarrie uncrossed her fingers and said a silent prayer of thanks. When breakfast was finished, she ran to the glass-covered bookcase and from a hiding place behind the books on the bottom shelf, she brought out a bundle of paper spills and a dried orange studded with cloves. She handed the orange to her mother. "I made this in school. It's for your dresser drawer—to make it smell nice."

"Lovely!" Her mother sniffed it. "I wondered what had happened to my cloves."

Clarrie laid the paper spills in the hearth. The black sock she had draped limply over the fender before going to bed, now leaned, bulging, knobby, and mysterious against the wall. She shook out a small pink celluloid doll, a tortoiseshell hair-clip, an apple, a tangerine, a handful of nuts, and a net bag filled with gold-wrapped chocolate coins. She ate the tangerine and one of the gold coins, then stuffed everything but the celluloid doll back.

Her mother handed her one of the packages from the hamper. "Here. You can open this, too."

"Did Dad say we could keep it, then?"

"Didn't I just say you could open it?"

They had given her a jigsaw puzzle—Cinderella climbing into her coach. Annie and Arthur had each got a pair of new woolen gloves. As soon as breakfast was over, they said they would put on the gloves and go into the back street to build a snowman. Clarrie couldn't go with them because she had no Wellies and her shoes needed mending.

She rummaged through her mother's ragbag for scraps to make a frock for the celluloid doll, and found a piece of pink and white gingham. She folded it, cut a circle for the neck, and sewed up the sides, leaving holes for the arms. She slipped the doll's head through the neck hole, but when she tried to push the arms through the armholes, one of the arms came off. She struggled for some time to reattach it, but she couldn't do it. She threw the doll on the floor and opened her puzzle.

Annie and Arthur, back inside after a snowball fight, were quarreling over which pieces of Clarrie's puzzle went where. William came downstairs in his long drawers and Sally started testing the potatoes with a fork, acting as though she hadn't noticed him.

"Merry Christmas, Dad," Clarrie said.

"Aye. Bloody humbug." He stepped past her to get to his chair. There was a crunching sound. "What the . . .!" He picked up the squashed remains of Clarrie's celluloid doll. "What was this doing on the floor?"

"It was already broken," Clarrie said.

"You don't deserve to have playthings if that's the way you take care of them." He tossed the crushed doll into the fire. Clarrie watched it shrivel and melt. It didn't matter. Celluloid dolls never lasted more than a day or two anyway. She handed her father the paper spills.

"What are these for then?"

"Spills to light your cigarettes. I made them myself."

"Good," he said. "Now all I need are the cigarettes."

Sally opened the cupboard, and threw him a large packet of Players. "Merry Christmas, you old misery."

"Thanks. I didn't get you anything."

"I'm satisfied. We're having a nice Christmas dinner."

William lit a cigarette with one of Clarrie's spills. After a while, he got up, put on his trousers, his coat, hat, and went out to shovel the steps.

"Should I go and help him?" Arthur asked.

"No, leave him alone. Put away the puzzle, Annie, and help me set the table."

William came in and sat by the fire, warming his hands.

Sally stood back with her arms folded, admiring the array of food. "This is what I call a real groaning board—turkey, chestnut stuffing, roast potatoes, Brussels sprouts, plum pudding, and custard. Have I forgotten anything?"

"What about the gravy?" Annie said.

"I've run out of basins. We'll have to dish that up from the pan."

William shook open his newspaper.

"Aren't you coming to the table, Will?"

"I'm not hungry."

She heaped food on a plate and handed it to Clarrie. "Pass this to your dad." Clarrie held out the plate to her father.

"Ask your mother if she's gone deaf," her father said. "I said I wasn't hungry."

"Suit yourself." Sally piled food on her plate. "I'm going to enjoy my dinner."

Arthur took a forkful of turkey. "It's scrumptious, Dad. You don't know what you're missing."

Clarrie waited by her father's chair, still holding the plate of food.

"Never mind," her mother said. "If your father doesn't want to eat, let him be. Come to the table before your dinner gets cold." She took the plate out of Clarrie's hands and put it on the top shelf of the range. Annie gave a strangled cry. She jumped from her chair and ran upstairs.

"I hope you're satisfied," Sally said.

William lowered his newspaper. "Are you talking to me?"

"You're ruining Christmas. You've gone and upset our Annie, and now you've got our Clarrie in tears, too."

Hot tears rolled down Clarrie's cheeks and splashed onto her Brussels sprouts.

With a sigh, her father folded his newspaper. "You're grinding me to a bloody powder, the lot of you." He took his plate from the warming shelf and put it on the table. "Stop blubbering," he said to Clarrie. "Run upstairs and tell our Annie to get down here on the double."

Annie was standing by the bedroom window, staring at the snow. "Go away," she said. "Leave me alone." She'd taken off her glasses, and Clarrie could see the sore red marks they'd made on the sides of her nose.

"Dad says you're to come down, on the double." Annie's shoulders heaved. Fresh tears flooded her eyes. Clarrie put her hand timidly on Annie's back. "Don't cry, Annie, love. Dad's not angry any more. He's even eating his dinner."

It was the custom on New Year's Day for the neighborhood children to make a tour of shops to wish the shopkeepers a happy New Year. Clarrie and Gladys were too young to go by themselves, and since Annie had promised to do some housework for Mrs. Sidebotham, Arthur was prevailed upon to take the girls around. They should start first thing in the morning, as soon as the shops opened, Arthur told them, because the shopkeepers stopped giving stuff away at the stroke of noon, and children who came after twelve got a smile and "Same to you, love," but no present. And they'd have to pack it in by half-past eleven, because he'd promised Harry to help clean out his uncle's cellar to use for a clubhouse.

Gladys knocked on the Hancock's door promptly at nine o'clock on New Year's Day. Her hair, the color of oatmeal and almost as straight as Clarrie's, was uncombed and her coat was buttoned wrong. She carried a large oilcloth shopping bag.

"You're a bit early, Gladys, love," Sally said, "Clarrie's not finished her breakfast."

"Arthur said we had to start early."

"Does your mother know you've left the house?"

"She's still in bed, but I told her I was going."

"Come in, then, out of the cold. Take off your coat while you're waiting."

Clarrie slid off her chair, anxious to be on her way.

Gladys stepped closer to the table, her pale blue eyes fixed on Clarrie's plate. "Are you going to throw out the rest of that porridge?"

"Can she have it, Mam?" Clarrie asked.

"Sit down and finish your breakfast. Gladys can have her own bowl." Sally passed Gladys a bowl of porridge and a steaming mug of cocoa.

"We'll start with the shops on Eccles New Road and work our way back home," Arthur said when they finally pulled Gladys away from the table.

They'd made successful visits to a couple of shops, when Gladys suddenly squatted against a wall.

"What's the matter?' Arthur asked. "Do you have to go to the lav?"

Gladys shook her head. She began licking the palms of her hands.

"She always does that," Clarrie said.

"It feels nice," Gladys said. She patted the flagstone on her right. "Sit here, Clarrie, try it. You'll see."

Clarrie squatted alongside her friend. She ran her tongue across her own palms.

Gladys nudged her. "Didn't I tell you?"

Clarrie nodded. In the face of Gladys's enthusiasm, it seemed rude to say what she really thought. Perhaps Gladys's hands tasted better than her own.

"Can't you lick 'em while you're walking?" Arthur asked. "It'd save time."

"It's not the same," Gladys said.

By eleven-thirty Arthur had them back home. They'd done well, he said, considering that Gladys had stopped at least four times to squat and lick. He examined the things the shopkeepers had given them: two blood oranges, a few dried locust pods, two yellow jute ropes for skipping, a new pencil, a metal frog that clicked when you pressed it, and two bags of kali powder, each with a lollipop dabber and a licorice sucker for sucking up the sweet powder that fizzed and tickled as it touched the tongue.

Arthur handed the bags back and took off, telling them to share everything and to stay near the house until it was time for lunch.

"Which of these do you want," Gladys asked Clarrie, "the pencil or the frog? I'd like the frog, myself."

"I'll take the pencil," Clarrie said.

Gladys's mother stuck her head out of the doorway and called her to come inside, her cup of Oxo was ready.

Clarrie set down her bag and tried to toss the jute rope over the crossbar of the lamppost to make a swing. She threw the rope with all the strength she could muster, but the crossbar was too high. A window cleaner passing by with his bucket and ladder stopped to watch. Again she threw the rope up and missed. The window cleaner put down his bucket.

"How old are you?" he asked.

"I'm five," Clarrie said.

He propped the ladder against the lamppost. "Are y' big enough to climb up me ladder and throw yer rope over?"

Clarrie nodded.

"Up you go, then. I'll hold on so's you don't fall."

Clarrie climbed up, dropped the rope over the crossbar, and began a shaky descent. She was halfway down when the window cleaner reached under her skirt and caught hold of her hips.

"I gotcher," he said.

"You can let go now, Mister," Clarrie said. The window cleaner seemed not to hear. He had his hands inside the elastic of her knickers, holding her so tightly she could hardly move.

There was a rattling on the cobbles. Clarrie swerved her head. The knife grinder was making his way down the street. He had his head down and was trundling his whetstone on a barrow. The window cleaner released his grip. Clarrie, who was not expecting it, fell down the last few steps, landing in the gutter on her hands and knees.

The window cleaner folded his ladder, grabbed his bucket, and hurried away, leaving her sprawled in the street. Clarrie examined her bloody knees, the scraped heels of her hands. Now, instead of trying out her swing, she'd have to go in and let her mam put that rotten stinging iodine on. There was something funny about that window cleaner. He'd been kind enough to let her climb his ladder—he'd held on to her very tightly to make sure she didn't fall—but after she'd fallen, anyway, he just rushed away without bothering to help her up, or even to ask if she was hurt.

Chapter Fourteen

All week long the tantalizing music of the roundabout drifted up from the tip where the Gypsies had set up the fair. Every time anyone opened the door the throb and jangle of the fair rushed in at Clarrie, who was confined to the house recovering from whooping cough.

Annie and Arthur had run down to the tip after school the very first day to watch the Gypsies assembling rides, setting up stalls. Arthur had even managed to find a job, selling Wigga Wagga toffee in the Death Rider's tent.

"What are they paying you?" his father asked.

"They didn't say. But they're letting me see the show for nothing."

"Oh, aye? I bet they're letting you work for nothing, too." Still, he hadn't stopped Arthur from taking the job, and he'd even given Annie spending money.

Clarrie, tucked up on the sofa, had been trying all week to persuade her mother to let her go. Today was Saturday. Tomorrow, the Gypsies would dismantle the fair and move on.

"Please Mam, everyone else has been."

"It's too cold out, love, and you're still coughing."

"Annie said Gladys was there yesterday. She's always coughing."

"I'm not Gladys's mother."

"I've never been to a fair in my whole life."

"Your whole life? You're six years old, child."

"But it's the last day."

"There'll be another fair next year."

"What if there isn't?"

"That's enough. I don't want to hear any more about it. I'll make you some hot lemon and honey, and then I have to go to work. I've missed enough days, and I promised Mr. Hutchins I'd have everything spic and span by Monday. Annie will stay with you."

Annie groaned. "Can't she stay by herself for once? I promised Jessie I'd meet her at the fair."

"Jessie will have to survive without you. You've been to the fair every day this week, that's more than enough. There's stew on the hob. If Dad comes home before me, you can warm it up."

"I'm fed up with you, our Clarrie," Annie said when their mother had gone. "I can never go anywhere because of you."

"It's not my fault."

Annie went into the front room to look out the window.

"Get your coat on," she said when she came back. "We're going out."

"But Mam said . . ."

Annie took down the tin where they kept money for the gas meter and slipped a coin into her pocket. "Do you want to see the fair or don't you?"

"Yes, but Mam said . . ."

"She doesn't have to know. She won't be back for a couple of hours."

Clarrie followed Annie down the street. She had that sick feeling in her stomach—a mixture of fear and excitement. This was the worst thing Annie had ever done.

The ump-a-pa of the roundabout music grew louder as they approached the tip. At the end of the street, where the houses ended and the downward slope of the tip began, Clarrie stopped. The black cinder croft at the bottom of the hill had vanished. In its place a gaudy city had sprung up—painted caravans, striped tents, colorful rides that whizzed and rattled. She could hear people shrieking.

Annie plunged into the deep grass, half running, half sliding down the hill. "Come on!" she shouted. "I have to find Jessie."

With Clarrie following, Annie elbowed through the crowds, down narrow paths covered ankle deep in sawdust and walled on either side with stalls laden with penny whistles, windmills on sticks, celluloid dolls with feather headdresses. Pungent smells filled the air—horse manure, pea soup, brandy snaps, and hot axle grease. A man with an ugly scar down the side of his face beckoned to them. He held out three rubber balls, urging them to try their luck at the coconut shy.

"You've got those coconuts stuck on with glue," Annie said. "Yesterday I slammed one really hard, but it never even wobbled."

"Bugger off," the man said, "before I slam you really hard."

"Rotten cheater!" Annie called over her shoulder. She grabbed Clarrie's hand and scuttled away before he could make good his threat. The back wall of the croft, where Annie and Arthur had often lifted her over to play in the sawdust, was lined with painted caravans. Steam blew from the nostrils of two mangy-looking horses tethered nearby.

"I want to take a gander inside one of those caravans," Annie said. "To see how the Gypsies live." She peered through a small window at the back. "There's nobody home. There's no furniture—just a mattress on the floor and some buckets of paper flowers and some skirts hanging up."

"Let me see," Clarrie said. Before Annie could lift her up, a half-starved Alsatian dog ran out from behind the caravans. The dog bared its teeth and growled. Clarrie backed away.

Annie took her hand. "It's chained up; it can't hurt you."

They stopped to play the penny roll downs. A man with a huge nose and a red neckerchief exchanged Annie's shilling for pennies. The higher the number, Annie told Clarrie, the more pennies you got back. If your penny landed on a blank space, or on a line between two squares, you'd lost it.

Annie slid one of the pennies into a little wooden slot. "Keep your fingers crossed."

Clarrie crossed her fingers. The penny fell on a square marked 2d. The man threw two pennies across the board. Annie gave one penny to Clarrie. She rolled down another penny, and told Clarrie to roll the other. The man raked both pennies towards him with a long stick and slipped them into his apron pocket.

"Those pennies hadn't stopped rolling," Annie said.

"They was on the line."

"Another rotten cheater," Annie muttered as they walked away. "I've a good mind to fetch a policeman."

They slipped between the tents and headed for the rides; everything seemed to be whirling around, chair-o-planes swung wide overhead, the people whizzing past on a dragon ride screamed as a green canvas cover descended, plunging them into darkness. A group of girls and boys, chattering like monkeys, were waiting at the big boats. Overhead, several huge, elaborately decorated boats swung out, creaking, rumbling, and kicking up a racket that almost drowned out the screams of the passengers, who, after swinging higher and higher, were suspended upside down for one breathtaking moment. Below them, the engines belched out evil-smelling black smoke.

"They're going to fall off!" Clarrie cried.

"They're strapped in," Annie said. "I'm going on there myself, as soon as I find Jessie."

"I don't want to," Clarrie said.

"Don't worry, they won't let you; you're too young."

At the roundabout a crowd of small children with their mothers and fathers were waiting in a straggly queue to get on board.

"Stay here." Annie pressed a penny into Clarrie's hand. "I'll be back in a minute, I've got to find Jessie."

When the ride rumbled to a stop, Clarrie moved forward with the others but was shoved aside before she could climb on. It happened every time the ride stopped. Annie was taking too long. Clarrie was about to step out of the queue to look for her when she reappeared.

"Haven't you been on yet?" She took Clarrie's penny, and pushing Clarrie ahead of her, elbowed her way to the front. "Pardon me, pardon me. My sister was here before you." She lifted Clarrie onto the platform and climbed on after her. "Get on, you gormless nit. What do you want, a tiger?"

"A horse," Clarrie said. The tigers and the other animals were fixed to the floor, but the horses moved up and down on twisted brass poles.

Annie hoisted her onto a red and gold horse with flaring nostrils and stood beside her. "Put your feet in the stirrups and hold on."

Clarrie clutched the pole. The music started, the roundabout began to revolve, and her horse rose majestically. A man wearing a dirty red apron came weaving between the animals, to collect money from the riders. He tore off a ticket and held out a soiled palm to Clarrie.

"I've got it." Annie handed him the penny. The man said something that was drowned out by the music. Annie cupped her hand to her ear.

"Another penny," he shouted.

"I'm only standing here so she won't fall off," Annie shouted back.

"Another penny. Don't matter whether you sit or stand."

"I'll get off then." Annie darted past him and leapt off the moving platform. The ticket man shook his fist at her. The ride picked up speed. At the center of the roundabout, a sort of mechanical one-man band was at work. Bells rang, drums banged, cymbals clashed, as the huge brass stoppers opened and closed. Clarrie's head hurt from the noise.

As the ride slowed, she saw Annie waving to her. "Get down," she shouted.

Clarrie slid sideways, her foot still in the stirrup, and fell on her knees. The man in the red apron came swaying through the maze of painted animals towards her.

"Are you barmy?" he yelled. "You're supposed to wait 'til it stops!"

Annie leapt onto the platform. "Leave my sister alone!" She released Clarrie's foot from the stirrup and grabbed her hand. "Jump," she hissed as the ride jolted to a halt. She jumped off the platform, pulling Clarrie with her.

A cold wind had sprung up, flapping the striped awnings, blowing over a painted sign outside the fortuneteller's stall.

"I don't feel well. I want to go home," Clarrie said.

"We'll go in a minute," Annie said. A Gypsy woman with small angry eyes and a weather-beaten face beckoned to them from the doorway of a small tent. "Black pea soup, penny a cup."

"We'll have some of that," Annie said. "It'll warm us up." They followed the woman inside the tent. The woman pointed to a splintery bench and told them to sit. She shouted something through a flap in the back of the tent, and a filthy barefoot girl, no older than Clarrie, ran in carrying a chipped bowl of steaming soup. It smelled of vinegar. Annie stirred it with a tin spoon, and a few hard black peas rose to the surface. She sipped from the spoon and wrinkled her nose.

"Tastes like washing-up water. God only knows what they put in it." She handed the bowl to Clarrie. "Don't ever tell Mam, she'd have a fit if she knew we drank this stuff."

They wandered through a maze of sawdust alleys, past stalls that sold brandy snaps and toffee apples.

"I want a toffee apple," Clarrie said.

"There's Jessie!" Annie shouted. Jessie was standing outside the freak show, talking to two cheeky looking lads wearing white paper sailor hats; on one was written "Kiss me quick," and on the other, "Oh you kid!"

Annie ran up to Jessie with a squeal of delight. "I thought I'd missed you!"

One of the boys had pimples all over his face and looked as though his hair had been cut with the help of a mixing bowl. The other, a nicer-looking boy, was smoking. He winked at his friend and then offered the cigarette to Clarrie. His hands were red and raw.

"You want a puff, love?" he asked her.

"I'm only six," she said scornfully and turned away.

Jessie showed Annie a handful of coins. "I almost got caught," she said, giggling.

Clarrie tugged at Annie's sleeve. "Mam might be looking for us. Let's go home."

"I'm going in the freak show with my friends," Annie said. "Wait here until we come out."

The lad who'd offered Clarrie a puff of his cigarette winked at Clarrie. "Don't do anything I wouldn't do."

Outside the freak show were posters showing Zelda, the bearded lady, an India rubber man with his legs wrapped around his neck, and a calf with two heads. She wondered if the people in the freak show minded people staring at them. She was glad there was nothing strange about her. She felt sorry for the calf, too. Which head would win, she wondered, if one head wanted to go in a different direction from the other?

She wished Annie and Jessie would hurry up. From time to time people entered the tent, but she'd seen nobody emerge.

"Can I go inside to look for my sister?" she asked the man in the ticket booth. "She's been in there a long time."

"Buy a ticket and you can look as long as you like." Clarrie told him she had no money.

"Go 'round the back, then," the man said. "She'll have to come out 'round back."

Annie had told her to stay where she was.

"Are you deaf ?" the man said. "I told you to go 'round back."

Clarrie walked in the direction the man was pointing. She turned left, where the back of the freak show ought to be, and found herself in a narrow alley, lined with booths. There was nothing that looked like the back of a tent, and she was feeling colder by the minute. She clutched the lapels of her coat together. In the distance, she could see the big boats swinging through the red sunset. Perhaps they'd gone back there. Keeping her eyes on the boats, Clarrie turned down another path. It was getting dark, and the Gypsies were lighting the oil lamps that hung, swaying in the wind, outside their stalls. The lamps cast eerie shadows on the faces of people passing by.

She came to a clearing. A poster in front of a huge tent showed a lion with its paw raised, about to attack a man on a motorcycle. A row of shiny motorcycles stood against the side of the tent. Nearby a man in a leather jacket sat on some wooden steps, eating a sandwich.

"Is this the death-riders tent, mister?" Clarrie asked.

"Aye, it is, love. But you can't go in without a grownup."

"I'm looking for my big brother, Arthur. He works here. He sells Wigga Wagga toffee."

The man stuffed the last of his sandwich into his mouth. "Wait here, I'll see if I can find him."

When Arthur came out of the tent, Clarrie ran to him in tears. "What's up, then?" Arthur asked. "Who's taking care of you?"

"Our Annie brought me. She went into the freak show with Jessie and some lads. I waited and waited, but they didn't come out."

"They make you come out the back so you can't tell the people in front what a gyp it is. She must be looking high and low for you." Arthur took her by the hand and they hurried to the freak show tent, but there was no sign of Annie.

"I've got to get back to work," Arthur said. "You come with me, and I'll tell my boss I have to take you home." He led the way up the wooden steps into the death-riders' tent. It smelled of raw wood and motorcycle fumes. Benches, arranged in tiers, were set around a deep drum-shaped pit. The pit was draped with nets where two lions were prowling. A man on a motorcycle was perched on a wooden platform at the top of the pit. He looked like the man who had gone in to fetch Arthur, but she couldn't be sure because he was wearing black goggles.

"He's the champion rider," Arthur said. "He's not afraid of anything. I might decide to be a death-rider, too, when I grow up." He left her to find his boss, and came back in a few minutes with a tray. He handed her a paper bag of toffee. "I'll take you home as soon as I've sold my tray. My boss said I could give this to you." He winked. "It tastes like a lot of nowt, but don't tell anyone." He walked away shouting, "Get your Wigga Wagga, twopence a bag."

With a loud roar, the motorcycle started up and zoomed out, riding horizontally around and around the pit. The lions growled, thrusting out their paws as the motorcycle whizzed past.

The show was almost over by the time Arthur was free to take her home. They joined the crowds of people climbing up the hill towards Thurlow Street; fathers dragged tired children by the hand, mothers tried to comfort their wailing infants with candy floss and celluloid windmills.

"There's Mam," Arthur said. Their mother, her coat flying open over her huge belly, hurried across the street towards them.

"Thank God!" She bent and fastened the buttons on Clarrie's coat. "Where's our Annie, then? Didn't I distinctly say you were not to go out?"

Arthur explained what had happened. "She's probably still there looking for our Clarrie." He handed a bag of toffee to his mother. "I have to get back to finish up so I can get paid."

"If you see Annie, send her straight home. And you can tell her from me she's in a lot of trouble."

"She did it for me, Mam." Clarrie's eyes filled with tears. "She felt sorry for me because I wanted to see the fair."

"She's old enough to know better than to leave you alone."

Clarrie was anxious to be asleep before Annie came home. Annie would never forgive her for getting her in trouble. Arthur now slept alone in the little back bedroom, and with him gone, there was nobody to stop Annie from slapping her and shoving her onto the wire springs. She said her prayers and got under the covers, but she couldn't fall asleep. She got out of bed and ran along the landing to her parent's room to look out the front window. There was no sign of Annie, but a scrawny little man was clinging to the lamppost outside their house, singing as if his heart would break.

Show me the way to go home,
I'm tired and I want to go to bed,
I had a little drink about an hour ago,

And it went right to my head.
Wherever I may roam,
Over land or sea and foam,
You will always hear me singing my song,
Show me the way to go home.

He must be really lost, Clarrie thought. Her heart overflowed with pity for him, for Annie, and for all the other poor souls trudging the dark streets. She knew how it felt to be cold, alone and lost.

She had just drifted off to sleep when she was awakened by the sound of a door slamming. Downstairs her parents were talking in low, urgent voices. She heard the front door open again, and then the creak of footsteps on the stairs. Her mother came into the room in her hat and coat. She held a guttering candle.

"Are you awake, Clarrie love?" she whispered.

"What's the matter?"

"Our Annie's not home yet. Do you have any idea where she might have gone? Do you know who those lads were that they went into the freak show with?"

"I never saw them before."

"Your dad and I are going out to look for her again. Arthur's in the kitchen. He'll listen for the door in case she comes back."

"Can I go downstairs, too?" Clarrie asked. She was suddenly afraid for Annie. What if something terrible had happened to her?

"All right. Put something on your feet and a coat over your shoulders."

Arthur followed his mother down the lobby. "She can't be still at the fair, Mam," he said. "Everything was closed when I left. She must have gone to Jessie's."

"That's the first place your father went. Jessie's asleep in her bed. She's being punished for stealing money out of her mother's purse. And it looks as though our Annie helped herself to the gas money. Nice goings on, I must say. Do you have any idea who these lads are that they were larking about with?"

"No. I didn't see them."

"We'll be back as soon as we can. Make some cocoa for yourself and Clarrie."

"What if they can't find her?" Clarrie asked Arthur when their mother had gone.

"They'll find her, never you fear."

"What if the Gypsies stole her?"

"Our Annie? They wouldn't dare. If they did, they'll be hammering at the door any minute now, begging us to take her back."

"Tell me a story," Clarrie said, when they were settled by the fire with their cocoa.

"Have I ever told you about Excalibur?" Clarrie shook her head. "Well, many years ago, before there were guns or motor cars, knights rode around on horseback saving ladies in distress. They all carried swords, but there was one smashing sword called Excalibur that was stuck in a big white stone . . ."

"He had the same name as you, that knight," she said when Arthur finished the story.

"So he did."

"You could have pulled the sword out of that stone, too."

"I'd have given it a good try," Arthur said. He picked up the coal bucket. "I'll fetch some more coal."

"Don't be long," Clarrie said. In the firelight, the room was filled with shadows. Evil faces leered at her from the folds of the curtains. One of them looked like the man on the roll downs at the fair. She heard the key in the front door. Her parents came down the lobby with Annie.

Annie had taken off her glasses. Her eyes and nose were swollen from crying, and her curls were tangled and windblown.

"Get up, Clarrie," her mother said. "Let our Annie sit near the fire. She's chilled to the bone." Clarrie could see Annie's shoulders heaving as she tried to stifle her sobs.

Arthur came in with the coal bucket. "You found her then," he said. "Where was she?"

"Chapel Street," William said. "She was trying to get to Auntie Ethel's."

"Your dad spotted her from the top of the tram," Sally said. "I was on my way to the police station when I saw them coming down Cross Lane."

"Why were you going to Auntie Ethel's?" Arthur asked Annie.

Fresh tears spilled down Annie's cheeks.

"She was afraid to come home, and I'm not surprised," Sally said. "She says she took Clarrie to the fair because she was sorry for her, but when Clarrie got lost she panicked. The silly girl's got it into her head that nobody loves her."

"We love her," Clarrie said, "don't we Mam?"

"Of course we do. Your dad and I have been worried sick."

William jabbed at the coals with the poker. "Aye, as if we don't already have enough to worry about!"

"She's just feeling sorry for herself," Arthur said.

Annie glared at him. "Shut up, you."

Clarrie looked at Annie's tearstained face. Why should Annie feel sorry for herself ? Wasn't it she, Clarrie, who got slapped and bossed around and made fun of? Wasn't Annie the one who did it?

"It's time our Clarrie went to bed," her mother said. "Take her up and tuck her in, Arthur."

"What will Mam and Dad do to her?" Clarrie asked Arthur when they got upstairs.

"Nothing. They'll be afraid to punish her in case she runs away again. She'll get away with it, scot free, just you wait."

Clarrie's sympathy vanished. What right had Annie to frighten her mam and dad like that, and take away their proper grownup power?

"Where is Auntie Ethel's? I didn't know we even had an Auntie Ethel." Clarrie said.

Arthur tucked the covers around Clarrie, and sat on the edge of the bed. "She's not our real auntie. She owns the shop in Broughton where we used to live. She let us play behind the counter with the balloons and pencils and stuff."

"Did you like Auntie Ethel?"

"She was all right. We had the two rooms upstairs. There were some dusty old green plush curtains hanging in the doorway. Our Janet liked to play hide and seek there with Dad. She'd pull the curtains over her face and he'd pretend he couldn't find her."

Arthur's face was sad. Clarrie had never seen him look like that before.

"What's the matter?" she asked him.

"Annie thinks Dad blames her for our Janet dying. She thinks Janet was Dad's favorite."

"Was she?"

"I don't know. He played with all of us, but he changed after Janet died."

"Did he play with me, too?"

"You weren't there, love. We moved here just before you were born." Arthur stood up. "No more questions now. I want to go to bed."

Clarrie couldn't fall asleep. Annie had been scared to come home. Did she truly believe that nobody loved her? She'd tried to go back to Broughton—to a time when Janet was still alive and they'd all been happy playing hide-and-seek among some dusty green curtains. They hadn't known anything about Clarrie in those days, so they'd never missed her. Why had God taken Janet away and sent her instead? And where was I, Clarrie wondered, before I was born?

Chapter Fifteen

Annie had gone out and left her alone in the house, telling her to finish her Saturday jobs and to listen for the sandbone man. Clarrie had just finished the dusting, when she heard the sandbone man's cry from the back street. She picked up the pennies her mother had left and ran outside to buy the donkey stones.

The sandbone man was occupied with another customer. Clarrie examined the contents of his barrow while she waited. Along the sides were glass jars with live gold fish in them, and in the front, a stack of donkey stones. The rest of the barrow was piled with old clothes and boots and broken toys. She moved closer to examine the toys, her attention riveted by a doll, half buried among a pile of rags. Its blue eyes, fringed with thick curling lashes, gazed up at her out of the rubbish.

Clarrie had put the pincushion doll that Annie had brought home for her into her mother's sewing basket. Much as she longed for a doll, she saw it as a pincushion only, and could never bring herself to play with it. The sandbone man was saying something to her.

"White or brown?"

"What?" Clarrie said. She could not tear herself away from the doll. Its face was dirty, its yellow hair torn and matted, but the eyes looked real . . . as real as those of a live girl. It seemed to be asking her to rescue it.

"You want donkey stones, don't yer?"

"Yes. Two brown, two white." She paid for the stones, and without much hope asked him how much he wanted for the doll.

The man lifted the doll from its bed among the rags and handed it to her. "Fourpence."

Clarrie's heart sank. The doll had no arms or legs—nothing but a head of yellow hair and a dirty pink torso. She smoothed the hair. This was not the doll she'd been longing for. Whoever had owned it had not taken care of it, but even armless and legless, it was better than that pincushion. She tilted the head back and the eyes closed obediently. If she cleaned it up and combed its hair and wrapped it in a little blanket, she could pretend it was all there. Reluctantly, Clarrie handed the doll back to him.

"Just for you, I'll knock a penny off—threepence." He held out a filthy hand.

"I haven't got any money, but I'll get my Saturday penny when my mam comes home."

The man cleared his throat, spat a glob of phlegm onto the cobblestones and mashed it with his boot. "Tell yer what. You go, see if you can find summat—a nice old coat or a jacket—if I like it, yer can 'ave this lovely dolly for nothing."

Clarrie sped back into the house, rummaged in the drawers, and finding nothing there, ran into the lobby where the coats were hanging. "Something nice," he'd said. Most of the coats were only used as extra blankets in cold weather—they had torn pockets, missing belts and buttons, drooping linings—the sandbone man wouldn't want those. Set off by itself on a separate hook was a man's blue jacket. It didn't look as bad as the others. She pulled the jacket from the peg, threw it over her arm and ran out, relieved to find him waiting.

He examined the jacket briefly. "It'll do," he said, handing her the doll. He shot out another glob of phlegm, and crying "Sandbone!" trundled his barrow down the street. Back in the house, Clarrie examined her prize and tried to ignore the sick feeling beginning to stir in her stomach. For some reason, that feeling always came after she had already done whatever it was that was wrong, never before.

"I can't call you Rosie," she said to the doll, "because that was going to be my other doll's name. I'll have to think of a new one. First I'm going to get you nice and clean, and then I'll see if we can take you to the doll hospital to get some new arms and legs put on."

She filled a bowl with warm water, slathered the doll with soap, and began to scrub. The doll's pink skin was turning greyish and sticky and soft. Dirty pink paint clung to her fingers, and chunks of grey cardboard stuff were breaking away and sinking to the bottom of the bowl.

Her thumb had gone right through the doll's belly button. She pulled her mother's apron from a hook behind the scullery door and tried to pat the doll dry. The mechanism that worked the eyelids had slipped sideways. Clarrie was poking her finger into the eye sockets, trying to pull the eyes back into place, when her mother walked in carrying a basket of groceries. Her mam's coat was open; she'd grown so fat around the tummy that she could no longer button it.

"Where's Annie?"

"She said she had to go out for a minute."

"Did she indeed. We'll see about that. She should know better than to leave you alone in the house." Her mother frowned at the glutinous grey mass disintegrating in Clarrie's hands.

"What on earth is that?"

"It's a dolly. I'm giving it a bath."

"It looks as though it needs more than a bath. Where did you get it?"

"The sandbone man gave it to me."

"Gave it to you? I've never known that man to give anything away. You didn't waste the donkey-stone money on it, did you?"

"I gave him one of Dad's old jackets."

Sally put her shopping basket on the table. "What old jacket? Show me where you got it."

Clarrie led the way into the lobby and pointed to the empty peg. The sick feeling in her stomach was getting worse.

"Oh, Lord!" Sally brought a hand up to her face. "You've given him your dad's suit jacket. He needs it for a job interview at the roller rink."

"I thought . . ."

"You didn't think, that's the trouble. And neither did our Annie. We've got to get it back before he finds out." She took a handkerchief from her pocket and wiped Clarrie's face. "Stop sniveling. Your dad asked me to take that jacket to the cleaners, but I tried to save money by doing it myself. Get your coat on. Which way did he go?"

"That way." Clarrie pointed down the back street towards the croft.

Her mother took Clarrie by the hand, and they walked up one street and down another. "I don't know what I'm going to do with you," she said. As they turned the corner, Clarrie spotted the barrow parked outside the pub.

"There he is!"

"Thank God!" Her mother ran over and began sorting through the heap of rags. A grubby little boy guarding the barrow asked them what they were looking for.

"It's not here," Sally said. She pushed open the door of the pub. "Come on, we're going in after him."

The sandbone man was at the bar drinking a glass of beer, the jacket draped over his arm. There was a smell of cigarette smoke. A fat blonde woman, polishing the brass handles behind the bar said, "Sorry, love. No children allowed."

"We'll only be a minute." Sally pushed Clarrie ahead of her. "That's my husband's jacket," she said to the sandbone man. "I'd like it back, if you don't mind."

He held the jacket out. "Two bob and it's yours."

The barmaid stopped what she was doing. "You're a cheeky bugger," she said to the sandbone man. She turned to Sally. "He wanted me to give him three bob for it. I told him to keep it. I'm a widow. What would I want with a man's jacket?"

"It's not for sale," Sally said. "He tricked this child into giving it to him. I've been all over Christendom looking for him."

"You shouldn't be running about like that, upsetting yourself in your condition," the barmaid said.

The sandbone man wiped his nose across the back of his hand. "I give 'er a nice doll for it, didn't I? Fair and square."

"You gave her rubbish! You took advantage of a child."

"One and six, then, that's my last offer."

Clarrie saw her mother's face turn crimson. "If I report you, it will be your last offer. You'll get your license taken away."

"I bet he hasn't even got a license," the barmaid said.

"No need to get yerself all aeriated, Missus." The man finished off his beer and slammed down the glass. "Gimme a tanner to pay for the doll and we'll call it quits."

"He said it cost fourpence," Clarrie said.

"He's lucky to get anything." Her mother pulled a threepenny bit from her purse. "Here, it's all I've got to my name."

The sandbone man took the coin and held out the jacket. "Take the bloody thing."

Clarrie's mother took her hand as they walked home. "Stop crying. We've got your Dad's jacket back, so there's no real harm done. I'm sure you've learned your lesson."

"I still haven't got a doll," Clarrie said.

"If your dad gets this job he's trying for at the rink, we might be able to get you a nice doll next year."

"I'll be too old by then," Clarrie said. "I won't want one anymore."

"Clarrie, wake up!"

Clarrie opened her eyes. Arthur was standing over her, holding a lighted candle. "Come and see our new baby brother."

"We haven't got a baby brother."

"Yes, we have. He's in Mam and Dad's room."

Clarrie searched his face; Arthur liked practical jokes—last April fool's day, he'd put fake soap in Dad's shaving cup and her dad had come storming out of the scullery with black stuff all over his face.

"I don't believe you," she said.

"See for yourself, then. I'm going to be late. Annie's already gone."

Could it be true? Clarrie climbed out of bed and ran to her parents' bedroom. The room looked different. There was a fire crackling in the grate, and a dresser drawer, padded with a flannel sheet, on the floor near the bed. Her mother was half raised up on her pillow. She had her arms around a blue blanket-wrapped bundle. She smiled when she saw Clarrie.

"Hello, love. Have you come to see your new baby brother?" Her mother moved the blanket to reveal a fat pink face nuzzling at her breast. She smiled down at it as though she had known and loved it forever.

"Where did it come from?"

"He, love, not it. God sent him."

Clarrie glanced around the room. The windows were tightly shut. There was a fire lit in the grate, and if the baby had come down the chimney, like Father Christmas, he'd have been burned. "Why is it so fat?"

"He's big for a newborn—a fine, healthy boy."

"How did he get in here?"

"I told you. God sent him."

Clarrie looked heavenward. The ceiling was smooth, white, unbroken. He couldn't have come through there. "Did God send the blanket, too?" she said.

Her mother laughed. "Leave it to you to ask a question like that. Better get ready for school. You're going to be late. Be quiet so you don't wake your dad.

"Where is he?"

"Sleeping in Arthur's bed. He started his new job at the roller rink last night, and he had to go out again in the wee hours to fetch Nurse Walmsley. She's downstairs getting your breakfast."

Clarrie ran downstairs.

Nurse Walmsley put two cups of tea, a plate of toast, and a jar of Marmite on a tray. "I couldn't find any oatmeal. I made you some toast."

"Thanks." Clarrie reached for the toast.

"That's your mam's." Nurse Walmsley pushed Clarrie's hand away. "Yours is over there." She nodded to a plate on the table. "Get yourself washed and dressed first."

"Where did that new baby come from?" Clarrie asked.

"I brought it in my black bag."

Clarrie looked at Nurse Walmsley's black bag on the dresser. "The baby's too big to fit in there."

Nurse Walmsley laughed. "Can't pull the wool over your eyes, eh?" She picked up the tray and went up the stairs.

Clarrie frowned. What wool? Was she talking about the baby blanket? She felt a surge of anger. They were lying to her—keeping something from her—some secret about the new baby. And they were laughing at her because she didn't understand.

In the scullery, she washed quickly and put on the clothes she had worn the day before. She went back into the kitchen to eat her toast. It was cold and hard, and the butter didn't taste right. The teapot was still warm, but when she lifted the lid, there was no tea left—just a lot of tea leaves around the holes inside the spout. She went to the foot of the stairs. "I'm going now, Mam," she called.

There was no answer. Nurse Walmsley and her mother were talking and laughing. She wanted to run upstairs and see her mother again, but she was already late for school. She felt in her coat pockets for her gloves. They weren't there and she couldn't remember where she'd left them. "I'm going now!" she shouted again.

The cold air took away her breath as she stepped out of the house. There was a pain in her chest, as though a piece of toast had got stuck halfway down. She looked back towards the house before she turned the corner, hoping to see her mother standing at the door, but there was only a light flickering in the bedroom window.

When Clarrie returned home from school, Nurse Walmsley had gone, and Mrs. Phipps was in the kitchen washing the baby's bottle.

"Your mam's asleep, love," Mrs. Phipps said. "The baby's sleeping, too. Your mam's very tired, so I don't think you should wake her."

"Where's everyone else?"

"I don't know where the others are."

Mrs. Phipps put the baby bottle in a pan with water and carried it into the kitchen. Clarrie followed her.

"Can I have something to eat, then?"

"Aye. Your mam told me you'd be hungry. I got a jam butty ready for you. When you've finished, you're to go next door and play with Gladys until teatime. I'll stay here with your mam until Annie gets back."

Gladys's house was dark, the lower half of the walls covered with ancient, slick, brown wallpaper smeared with greasy finger marks. The house smelled funny, too—a mixture of dirty clothes, stewed tea, and stale cigarette smoke. Clarrie's own house smelled of laundry soap, and of whatever her mam was cooking. Gladys's house was interesting though. The wall facing the window was taken up by a large, gloomy oil painting of a woman with swirling hair and wild, terrified eyes. She was clinging for dear life to a huge cross that stood on a rock in the middle of the ocean, while all around her a violent storm was raging. As if that weren't enough, the lady's large bosom seemed about to fall out of her flimsy nightie. On a small brass plate at the bottom of the frame was the title "The Old Rugged Cross." Clarrie wondered why the lady was out in a storm with nothing on but a nightie, and why someone had set a cross on a barren rock in the middle of the ocean.

"How's your mam doing with the new baby?" Gladys's mother asked. She was sitting by the fire, smoking a cigarette and reading a magazine. Her feet, clad in soiled pink slippers, were propped up on the steel shelf in front of the oven. Her legs, like the legs of many Salford women, were stained with brown rings. Clarrie had heard her mother say that such rings were the result of sitting for too long, too close to the fire.

"She was asleep when I came home."

"How do you like your baby brother?"

"He's all right."

Gladys shuffled a pack of cards and placed them face down on the table. "I'll tell you your fortune, but first you have to cross my palm with silver."

"I haven't got any silver." Clarrie said.

"Just pretend." With a swirling motion of her hands she moved the cards around, and selected one. "This is your first card. Turn it over."

Clarrie turned it over.

"That's the hanging man," Gladys said, "it's bad luck."

Gladys's mother blew a cloud of smoke. "You're not doing it right. That's how you tell your own fortune, not someone else's."

"It's the way my gran does it," Gladys said.

Mr. Halliwell walked in from the back yard adjusting his braces. He sat down at the head of the table, lifted the tea cozy, and stared gloomily into the pot. "No tea left?"

Gladys was busy spreading out the cards and arranging them in some sort of order. Clarrie glanced over at Mrs. Halliwell. It didn't look as though she was about to get up and make more tea.

Mr. Halliwell replaced the tea cosy. He fumbled in his pockets and brought out a cigarette case. "I'm out of fags."

Mrs. Halliwell flipped a page of her magazine, tapped her cigarette ash into the hearth, and blew a ring of smoke. "You're not getting any of mine," she said.

Mr. Halliwell rolled his eyes towards the ceiling. Clarrie followed his glance. The ceiling was almost as brown as the walls. A strip of curling flypaper dangled from the kitchen gas bracket. It had been there since last summer and was so thickly encrusted with dead flies there was scarcely room for one more. Nevertheless, another had managed to find a spot to land and was desperately struggling to escape.

Mr. Halliwell took a tobacco tin off the mantelpiece and opened it. "I need some butts."

"I thought you were going out," Mrs. Halliwell said.

"Not without some fags." He slammed the tin down in front of Gladys. "Fetch me some butts."

"I'm telling Clarrie's fortune."

Mrs. Halliwell glanced up from her magazine. "You heard him. Get going. Take Clarrie with you."

"Which shop?" Clarrie asked as they were leaving the house.

"No shop. My dad rolls his own. I find butts for him in the street."

They walked towards Eccles New Road. Outside the Waverly Hotel, Gladys spotted a longish cigarette butt tipped with red lipstick. "That's a good 'un," she said, holding it up for Clarrie to see. "You don't find many as long as that." She dropped her find into the tobacco tin.

A strange-looking man wearing a fantastic many-colored feather headdress and a cloak that swirled out behind him strode by on the other side of the street. His skin was a rich golden brown. He was like nobody Clarrie had ever seen before.

"That's Prince Monolulu," Gladys said. "He gives tips at the race track." She broke into a deep-voiced chant. "'I gotta horse, I gotta horse'—that's what he says." They ran across the street after him. Gladys cupped her hands to her mouth and shouted, "Give us a tip, Prince Monolulu."

The man stopped and turned around. "I don't give no tips to no cheeky kids on de street." His voice was thick and sweet as caramel.

"It's for my mam."

"You tell you mama go to de track. Tell her dat. I'll pick a horse for her dere." Prince Monolulu turned and walked on. Gladys skipped after him, singing: "I like coffee, I like tea." Clarrie picked it up the refrain. "I like sitting on a black man's knee."

Prince Monolulu swung around and fixed them with a baleful glare. "Can't a fella walk along de street minding his bizniss? How come you kids ain't in school?"

"We just came home."

"Well, go home again, and tell your mamas to learn you some manners."

"I don't know what he was getting so ratty about," Gladys said as they walked away. "I was only asking for a racing tip."

"It was that song," Clarrie said. "He didn't like it." Her face was burning.

"What's wrong with it? My mam sings that song, herself. She told my dad that if she had it to do over she'd marry a darkie, because a black man who marries a white woman worships the ground she walks on."

Clarrie had a vision of Gladys's mother, dressed like a bride, coming down the church steps on the arm of Prince Monolulu. At the bottom of the steps, the prince sank to his knees, his feather headdress brushing the flagstones.

It was hard to believe that anyone—particularly someone as grand as Prince Monolulu—would go to all that trouble for Gladys's mother. It'd wear holes in the knees of his trousers, too.

It was starting to rain. "We'd better go back," Clarrie said. "Your tin's almost full."

Gladys's father took the tin without looking at the girls. He tipped the butts onto the table and began to tear them apart, sprinkling shreds of tobacco onto cigarette papers, and rolling them into cigarettes. He licked the edges of the papers closed, arranged the cigarettes into a metal case and slipped the case into his pocket. "I'm off," he said. He took his cap from the hook behind the door and went out.

Gladys's mother put her magazine down. "You girls go and play in the parlor," she said. "I've got things to do."

Clarrie followed Gladys into the front room. In one corner was a mahogany gramophone with a big trumpet and a picture on the underside of the lid of a dog listening to the same sort of trumpet, with "His Master's Voice" written in gold letters. Except for that and a dusty aspidistra on a bamboo stand in front of the window, the room was empty. The last time Clarrie had played in Gladys's house she'd peeped into the parlor and seen a rumpled bed, a gate-legged table, and two chairs.

"Where's all the furniture?"

"It belonged to the lodger. My dad kicked him out."

Gladys took a small stack of records out of the cupboard. "I'll put them on myself so they don't get scratched, but you can start winding the gramophone."

Clarrie turned the handle. Tinny music, and a man's voice sang, like the voice of someone singing far away, "When it's springtime in the Rockies . . ." Clarrie knelt on the bare floorboards, ready to turn the handle whenever the music slowed.

"How do they get the music into the record and out again?" she asked. Gladys didn't know.

From the room above came a wild yelp. Clarrie stopped winding the gramophone. "What was that?"

Gladys shrugged. "Perhaps it was your new baby brother."

"Sounds like someone got hurt. Let's go and see."

"We can't. The door's locked."

Clarrie ran over and tried the door. She rattled the knob. "Why is it locked?"

Gladys shrugged. "Sometimes when my mam has visitors she locks me in."

"Call her. Tell her I have to go to the lav."

"She'll kill me if I do." Gladys opened the cupboard and brought out a battered enamel chamber pot. "You can go in there."

"I can't go if someone's with me."

"You'll have to hold it, then." Gladys removed "Springtime in the Rockies," and put on "Tiger Rag."

"I know how to do the quickstep and the black bottom," she said. "I'll teach you how to do them, too, if you like."

Clarrie giggled. "The black bottom?"

"It's what they call it."

Another yelp sounded from the room above.

"There it is again!" Clarrie said.

"Keep turning. The record's slowing down."

Clarrie turned. The music speeded up again.

"That's Harry Roy's band," Gladys wiggled her hips as she sang along with the record, "Hold that tiger . . ." Suddenly, she broke into a violent fit of coughing. She pulled out a crumpled handkerchief from her sleeve, spat in it, and held it out for Clarrie to see. "I can spit up blood. Can you do that?"

Clarrie said she didn't think so.

Gladys tucked the handkerchief into her sleeve. "Promise me you won't tell anyone. They'll send me back to the sanatorium if they find out."

"I promise."

"Cross your heart and hope to die."

Clarrie crossed her heart. "I thought you liked it there."

"It's all right, but I don't want to go back. You have to stay in bed without moving."

The key turned in the lock, and Mrs. Halliwell pushed open the door. "You can come out now," she said as she went back into the kitchen.

Clarrie jumped to her feet. "I've got to go home."

A young woman draped in a tattered shawl was fumbling with the front doorknob. Before letting herself out, the woman turned her deathly pale face to look for a fleeting moment into Clarrie's eyes. Shaken by the raw misery in the woman's face, Clarrie looked down at the cracked linoleum. A trail of red drops led from the stairs to the front door. It looked like fresh blood. It couldn't be Gladys's though, because Gladys was still standing in the doorway of the parlor.

"Ta-ra, love," she called to Clarrie. "I'll see you tomorrow."

Clarrie found her mother and father sitting by the fire. Her father was cuddling the new baby.

"What were you doing in there?" her mother asked. "It sounded as though you and Gladys were having a high old time."

"What was all that yelling about?" her father asked.

"That wasn't us. We were just playing records. Gladys's mam locked us in the parlor."

"Locked you in?" her mother sounded alarmed. "Why on earth would she do that?"

"Gladys said she always does that when she has company."

Her mother and father exchanged glances.

"I thought Johnny threw that lodger fella out," her father said.

"It wasn't the lodger," Clarrie said. "It was a lady. She looked as though she'd been crying, and . . ."

"And what?" her mother asked.

"Nothing," Clarrie said." She'd been about to tell her parents about the trail of blood in the lobby, but if it got back to Gladys's mam, she might think it was Gladys's blood and Gladys would have to go back to the sanatorium.

Chapter Sixteen

They named the baby William after his father, but everyone called him Billy, or simply, "the baby." Mrs. Hutchins, the butcher's wife, presented him with a splendid, high-riding perambulator; its navy blue body lined with cream-colored leather was decorated along the sides with a silver crest. Clarrie thought it a carriage fit for a prince. Mrs. Hutchins bought it for her own baby, but had never used it because the child died a few hours after it was born.

Clarrie pleaded to be allowed to wheel the baby in his new carriage, but it wasn't until the baby was two months old that her mother gave her permission. She showed Clarrie how to put the brake on and off, and how to raise the hood in case of rain.

"Leave it up, Mam, it looks nice like that," Clarrie said. "And dress him in those new clothes Aunt Dora sent." The white knitted hat, scarf, and cardigan set with red trim were not exactly new—they had been cousin Beryl's when she was a baby.

"We ought to keep those for Sundays," her mother said, but she put them on him anyway. When Billy was all bundled up, her mother lifted the carriage down the front step. She cautioned Clarrie to wheel the baby up and down the pavement, not to cross the street. Clarrie made sure to arrange the blanket so that the embroidered "B" on the baby's scarf could be clearly seen. With his plump rosy cheeks and wisps of silky blond hair, he was, she thought, the most beautiful baby in the world. It was hard to believe that just a few weeks ago, he had looked like a pink sugar pig.

"Clarrie!" Gladys cried to her from her doorway. "Wait for me!" She ran down the path and, after a brief glance at the baby, began stroking the hood and the chrome handle of the carriage. "This a smashing carriage. Let me wheel it for a bit."

Clarrie relinquished the handle and followed Gladys anxiously around the block. The back door of Gladys's house opened and Gladys's mother stuck her head out.

"Get in here, our Gladys, you've got work to do."

Clarrie wheeled the carriage around to the front. The baby was sound asleep, and with Gladys gone, there was nobody to talk to. She was about to unlatch the gate and go inside to tell her mother she'd had enough, when a woman came out of Gladys's house. She teetered down the path on high heels and stopped.

"Ooh!" she said. "Let's have a look at your baby."

The woman's hair was a slick, greenish yellow, like the rope the greengrocer gave out on New Years Day, but the black roots showed along the parting as she bent over the pram.

"I can hardly see it for all them covers." The woman's black eyes narrowed. "Are you one o' them Hancock kids?"

Clarrie nodded.

"I thought so. I used to live not far from here. Your neighbor, Maudie, she's an old friend of mine."

The woman looked towards the house. "That's where you live, isn't it? Me and me friend, Rita, went inside when that little girl passed away.

"Our Janet?"

"Janet. That's the one. Lovely gold curls, your sister had, just like an angel." She lifted a strand of Clarrie's hair. "You got left out in the cold in that department, didn't you, love?"

Clarrie straightened the baby's covers, hoping the woman would notice Billy's nice outfit.

"Funny thing, that—one being born while t'other was passing away!" The woman clucked her tongue. "We was just trying to pay our respects. We got no thanks for it, though. Me and Rita nearly broke our necks getting out of there. Your old fella's got a rotten temper, 'asn't he? If looks kill!"

Clarrie frowned. "My dad was probably upset."

"Aye. So how old are you?" the woman said.

"Six."

"You must be the one, then—the one as was being born when t'other died. She was too good for this world, I suppose, so the Lord took her back and sent you instead, ha-ha!" The woman winked and nudged Clarrie to let her know she was joking. "If you hadn't been in such a big hurry to get here, your sister might be alive today."

The woman was watching Clarrie closely, as though waiting to see the effect her words would have.

"You popped out before your mam was ready for you. Your sister died while she was flat on her back in labor."

Clarrie nodded politely. Labor meant working—but what sort of work could her mother do flat on her back? Out of the corner of her eye, Clarrie saw the curtain lift. Her mam's face appeared at the window.

"Perhaps I've spoke out of turn." The woman moved around to the other side of the carriage. "This is a fancy pram. Your dad must be working, now then? He was on t'dole when you were born. They didn't have two pennies to rub together."

Clarrie glanced toward the house. Her mam and dad would not like her talking to a stranger about her dad being out of work.

"Take the hood down so I can get a better look at the baby."

Clarrie fumbled with the metal rods of the pram hood.

"Here, let me." The woman pushed down on the steel rod.

"Ow!" Clarrie pulled her hand away.

"Tch! You have to be careful with them hinges."

Clarrie thrust the pinched finger into her mouth. The covers moved. Billy was waking up. The woman pulled aside the blanket.

"Looks like she had a boy this time. How old is he?"

"Eight weeks." Billy started to cry and thrash about. Clarrie jiggled the pram.

"He's a big lump for his age, isn't he?"

Clarrie glanced back at the window. Her mother's head moved out of view and the curtain dropped back into place. "I've got to take him in now."

"He's got a good pair of lungs, I'll say that for him." She nodded to Clarrie as she walked away. "Nice talking to you, love."

Her mother came out onto the front step and lifted Billy out of the pram. "Who was that woman you were talking to?"

"I don't know—she used to live around here. She said she came to our house when our Janet died."

"I don't remember her. Turn the pram round, it'll be easier to get it up the step."

"She said if it wasn't for me, our Janet would still be alive."

Her mother stopped, her eyes wide. "She said what?"

"That Janet died because I was born too soon."

"What nerve! To say a thing like that to a child!" Her mother's face had turned bright red. With her free hand she helped Clarrie steer the pram down the lobby. "She'd better not let me catch her talking to you again, or I'll give her a piece of my mind."

"But did she?"

"Did she what?"

"Did our Janet die because of me?"

"Don't be silly, child. Janet had scarlet fever, then she caught pneumonia on top of it."

"Our Annie thinks dad blames her."

"Nonsense." Her mother's voice sounded high and strange; her hands shook as she removed the baby's hat and jumper. "Your dad doesn't blame anyone. Janet was too delicate from the start. There was nothing in this world any of us could have done."

"This baby's sharp as a tack, Sal." William bent close to the baby and pointed a finger at the ceiling. "He understands everything. Watch this: up?" Billy's eyes followed the pointing finger. He raised his own chubby forefinger. William beamed. He tossed the baby in the air. Billy's silky hair flew out.

"He's too little to be jiggled about like that, Will," Sally said. "You'll frighten him."

"Not on your life. He loves it." William put the baby back in his carriage.

Clarrie turned her attention to the design she was chalking on her top. A few days ago, as if in obedience to some mysterious, unspoken command, the children in the back street had suddenly abandoned their balls and skipping ropes in favor of these small wooden tops and leather thong whips. Arthur had fished out an old top for her from the bottom of the cupboard and had taken her down to the croft, pointing out that its smooth macadam surface was best for spinning tops. He showed her how to wrap the thong around the rim of the top and jerk it away, making the top fly out and hit the ground whirling. With a flick of the whip, Arthur could keep the top spinning as long as he wanted.

"Look, see the design I made." She held the top out for her parents' admiration.

Her mother glanced up. "Very nice," she said. Her eyes went back to Billy.

Billy started to whimper, and William picked him up again. "I think this little feller m'lad wants his titty."

Clarrie squirmed. She hated the word "titty." She watched as her mother unbuttoned her cardigan, lifted out a swollen, blue-veined breast, and guided the baby's head to the nipple. Billy closed his eyes and sucked noisily. Her mother smiled down at him.

"I'm going to try out my new pattern." Clarrie said, jumping to her feet. The stool she'd been sitting on fell over with a clatter. The baby's head swiveled sharply in the direction of the noise and a rope of milky saliva hung suspended between his mouth and the wet, red nipple.

Clarrie righted the stool, picked up her whip and top, and went out. She paused on the step to button her coat. Through the back window she could see her parents' heads bent over the baby.

Raucous shouts and the crack of bat against ball told her that the big boys had already claimed the croft for a game of cricket, or rounders. She watched for a while, trying to get up the nerve to ask if she could join the game. A handsome lad in a grey and red striped jersey swung his stick and hit the ball with a sharp crack. The ball flew straight towards her. Clarrie dropped her whip and top and jumped to catch it.

"Out of the way you daft gawp!" another lad cried, shoving her aside. The others jeered, telling her to clear off.

"You don't own the street," Clarrie said haughtily, but she picked up her whip and top and ran home to throw them in the yard. She went next door to see if Gladys could come out to play. Mrs. Halliwell told her to wait outside. In a few minutes, Gladys appeared, buttoning her coat. The girls wrapped their arms around each other's waists and ran down to play on the tip.

"Look!" Gladys bent to examine a dead cat, half buried in the grass; she turned it over with her shoe, exposing a mass of white maggots. Clarrie took a step back. She told Gladys how Arthur had once found a wooden crate stamped "Currants" right here on the tip. He had dragged it all the way home, only to find, when he pried it open, that the currants, just like this dead cat, were swarming with maggots.

"What did he do with those currants?"

"My dad made him drag the crate back to the tip."

"You could've washed them currants off an' et 'em."

"You can't eat maggoty currants," Clarrie said. She remembered how her mother had once found Gladys standing at the sink eating rice pudding skin she'd scraped from the edge of a bowl soaking in soapy water.

"I swear that child doesn't get enough to eat," her mother said.

"Let's go and see if my granddad is at the allotments." Gladys was already squeezing through the opening in the timber yard gates. "He might give us a carrot or summat." Clarrie squeezed through after her, following the narrow path along the railway lines.

"See them bumpers?" Gladys pointed to the steel buffers at the end. "I saw Maisie Bowker lying across there with her knickers down." Her voice sank to a whisper. "Freddie Watkins was tickling her with a big feather, right on her privates. Would you ever let someone do that to you?"

Clarrie's face grew hot. She turned her eyes from the scene of the crime and said she would rather die.

"Me, too," Gladys said. "That's not all he did," she added, "he did the other thing, too."

"What other thing?"

"You know—what grownups do to make babies." She leaned over and whispered in Clarrie's ear. "Everybody does it," she said. "You have to if you want to have a baby."

Clarrie shook her head. Her heart was thumping in her chest. "No, they don't. My mam and dad would never do that."

"Mine neither, but that's what they say."

Clarrie jumped over a ditch and ran through a cluster of poker-like weeds. She grasped a fleshy stalk laden with dark red beads.

"Don't pick that!" Gladys shouted. "That's Motherdie. Woe betide you if you pick it. Your mother will die, and it'll be your fault."

Clarrie dropped her hand. The weeds stank like sour milk. She was almost certain she'd trodden on one when she jumped the ditch. "What if I accidentally stepped on one?"

"I'm not sure if that counts."

Clarrie fell silent as they walked along the rutted path in the gathering dusk. Would God really make someone's mother die, just because her little girl accidentally trod on a weed?

The allotment was deserted. Freshly turned soil lay in black clumps around the potting shed, but the door was shut. Gladys climbed on an upturned wheelbarrow and peered through the smeared window of the shed. "Oh, blimey! My granddad must have fainted; he's lying on the floor!"

They ran to the door and shook it. It wouldn't budge. Clarrie climbed on the wheelbarrow and pushed open the window, but it was too small to climb through. She could see Gladys's grandfather sprawled face-down, his white clay pipe lying broken near his hand. There was a smell of burning pipe tobacco mingled with the smell of earth and something that smelled like pee.

"We'd better tell someone," Clarrie said. They raced down the path and across the tip as the last streaks of red were fading from the sky. To her immense relief, Clarrie saw her mother standing on the back step with Billy in her arms, both of them very much alive.

"You're late," her mother said. "Where have you been?"

"Gladys's granddad's fainted!" Clarrie cried. "He's on the floor in the shed, but the door's locked and we can't get in."

Her mother handed Billy to Annie. "Hold the baby. I'll go for help."

"There was nothing they could do for him," her mother said when she returned. "The poor old chap was dead."

Clarrie lay in bed for a long time that night, unable to fall asleep. She could smell the sour water in the ditch, see the gleaming railway buffers and a shadowy Maisie Bowker stretched out, her legs spread apart. The thing in Freddie Watkins's hand kept changing from a feather to a stalk of purple Motherdie and back again to a feather.

She pulled the covers over her head. She would never, ever, as long as she lived, let anyone do that to her. She wouldn't go near the Motherdie weeds, either. Her mother was fine, but Gladys's granddad had died. He was an old man, though, and not even related to her. Perhaps it had nothing to do with the broken weed.

Gladys was wearing a new Teddy bear coat with a black diamond-shaped patch on one sleeve, when she came over to Clarrie's house a few days later.

"I'm going to me gran's to say good-bye to my granddad before they take him away. My mam says you can come with me if you want."

"Please give your granny our sympathy," Clarrie's mother said to Gladys. "Let me know if there's anything I can do."

Gladys's granny lived two streets away, near the croft. Her house was very small, but neat and cozy—not at all like Gladys's house. The kitchen floor was strewn with homemade rag rugs, and in one corner was a big stone jar where they kept the bread.

Gladys's granny led them through the hall into a tiny parlor that smelled like the wet plaster her father used to fill the holes in the walls. The parlor door had been taken down and balanced over two trestles. On this makeshift bier lay Gladys's granddad, dressed in a dark suit. Gladys bent and kissed him on the cheek. "Ta-ra, Granddad," she said.

Gladys's granny steered Clarrie towards the body. "You have to give him a kiss."

Clarrie looked at the still form, the grey face, the lifeless eyes covered by pennies. She took a step backwards, shaking her head.

Granny gave her a push. "There's nowt to be afraid of. Kiss the poor owd fella goodbye. There'll be bad dreams for you tonight if you don't."

Clarrie brushed the plaster-smelling forehead with her lips.

In the kitchen, Gladys's granny made them sit at the table. She lifted a tea towel off a plate of thick sandwiches. "There," she said. "Help yourselves to a nice mutton sandwich while I brew a spot of tea."

Gladys stretched out her hand to the plate. Her grandmother slapped the hand away, "Company first."

"No, thank you," Clarrie said.

Gladys's granny pressed half a sandwich into Clarrie's hand. "Eat up, lass, don't be shy."

Clarrie nibbled at the corner. The bread was musty, the meat grey and gristly. She struggled to choke down what was in her mouth. "I'm not very hungry."

"Not hungry?" Gladys's granny wagged her head in disbelief. "You youngsters today don't know when you're well off. I'd have give me right arm for a bit o' cold mutton when I was your age."

Gladys took the sandwich out of Clarrie's hand. "I'll eat it if you don't want it."

"You best take the lass home and eat it on the way," Granny said. "She must be coming down wi' summat if she can't find room for a nice mutton butty."

Chapter Seventeen

Clarrie was beginning to regret she'd ever begged to wheel the baby. Now, if it wasn't raining when Clarrie got home from school, her mother bundled Billy into his carriage and parked it outside the back door, telling Clarrie to keep an eye on him. On most days, Clarrie didn't mind, but today was Shrove Tuesday. The back street was swarming with children. Clarrie had suggested they play "There came three dukes a-riding," or "Poor Mary sat a-weeping"—games she could play while still keeping watch over the baby. But the boys had over-ruled her, saying they didn't want to play sissy games. They'd voted for "Run, Sheep, Run"—an exciting game that ranged over the whole neighborhood and required a great number of players.

"But what about me?" Clarrie cried. "I can't play then. I have to mind the baby."

Nobody was listening. They'd already formed a circle and were dipping up sides—dividing the group into sheep, wolves, and shepherds. Clarrie watched as Herbert Wardle, a shepherd, led his sheep away into hiding. As soon as Herbert came back, the wolves ran off in search of the sheep, with

Herbert, puffing along after them, ready to call out, "Run, sheep, run," if the wolves got too close to his sheep.

Clarrie propped Billy up on his pillow. "They've left us," she said, kissing his cold cheek. "They don't care about us." Billy was almost three months old now and much better-looking than Gladys's cousin, Elsie, who was said to have won a beautiful baby contest at Blackpool. Beautiful or not, Clarrie wished she didn't have to mind him this afternoon. She hardly ever got the chance to play "Run, Sheep, Run."

"Never mind, love," she said to him. "We'll play by ourselves." She ran along the pavement pushing the pram in front of her, let it go, then ran to catch it. Billy's eyes grew big as she let the carriage go, but when she ran to catch hold of the carriage handle, he chortled with glee. It was the first time she'd heard him laugh like that. She grew ever more daring, waiting until the very last second before running to grab the pram as it teetered on the very edge of the curb.

"Clarrie Hancock!" Mrs. Barlow had her head out of her back-bedroom window and was glaring down at her. "Stop that, this minute! You're going to break that poor baby's neck!"

"I always catch him in time." Clarrie said.

"I'm telling your mother."

A few minutes later her mother opened the back door. Her eyes flashed fire. "Mrs. Barlow's just knocked at the front door to tell me what you've been up to." She pushed Clarrie's hands away from the carriage. "Get in the house."

"But the baby liked it. He was laughing!"

"You might have killed him. I thought you had more sense."

Clarrie ran into the house, tears streaming down her face.

"Don't bother to take off your coat." Her mother pushed the carriage into the kitchen. "I need you to run an errand for me." She rummaged in her purse and handed Clarrie sixpence. "Timson's is out of lemons. Do you think you can manage to find your way to the greengrocer's without getting into any more mischief ?"

Clarrie nodded.

"It'll be getting dark soon. Don't go down the back street—stay where it's light, and remember to look both ways before you cross."

On the other side of the street, old Granny Witchy was picking her basket up off Timson's step and trying to shoo away a stray dog sniffing at the rags that trailed beneath her skirts. Clarrie felt she ought to go over and help her, but her mam had told her to hurry, and anyway, she was afraid of strange dogs.

She turned the corner, stopping to watch the lamplighter working his way along East Wynford Street. Stopping at each lamp, he pushed a hooked pole under the glass, but she couldn't see what he did to turn on the light. She was about to ask him, but he crossed the street before she reached him.

Outside the greengrocer's window, a row of dead rabbits dangled from a string. Clarrie reached up and stroked one of the soft paws for good luck. Mr. Elwood, at work over the potato bin, looked up when she went in. A small pyramid of rotten potatoes, oozing white stuff, lay on an upturned barrel beside him.

"Phew!" Clarrie held her nose.

Mr. Elwood raised his head. "Aye. Nothing stinks worse than a rotten potato, unless it's gangrene. I hope you never . . ."

He was about to tell her again how he lost his leg in the Great War. "I'm in a hurry, Mr. Elwood," she said. "My mam's got the pancake batter ready."

"I'm out of lemons, love. Plenty of oranges though—blood oranges. Orange juice goes very nice with pancakes; the froggies never use anything else on their crepe suzettes. I remember when I was in . . ."

Clarrie shook her head. "My mam wants lemons." The Shrove Tuesday pancake ritual was sacred. Nothing but lemons would do.

"That greengrocer down Regent Road—Pearson charges more, so he might have some left."

Clarrie thanked him.

"You'd better hurry," he called after her. "It's going to rain, and it's getting dark out."

It was drizzling by the time she found the other greengrocer, and there were several people ahead of her so she had to wait. The woman behind the counter took the sixpence Clarrie handed her and put four lemons in a paper bag.

Clarrie pointed to a chalked slate in the doorway. "Your sign says six for a tanner, Missus."

"That's for small lemons—they're all gone."

Clarrie took the bag. It was getting dark out. Her mam would wonder what was taking so long. It seemed silly to waste time going the long way round, when she could cut down the back entry. She recalled Gladys's story about Springheel Jack—a murderer who wore springs on his shoes and could leap out and stab you and cut your gizzard out and be miles away before the bobbies had time to blow their whistles. It was probably just another made-up story—like the bogeyman and Ginny Greenteeth—so she wasn't going to believe it. She wasn't going to run, either. Waving the bag of lemons, she sang loudly as she skipped along.

Pancake Tuesday's a very happy day,
If they don't give us a holiday, we'll all run away.
Where shall we run to? Up Cross Lane?

She was nearing the end of a dark entry, when she tripped over somebody's shoe, and fell sprawling across the wet flags.

A man stepped out of the shadows and hauled her up by the armpits. "Whoopsie Daisy!" He set her on her feet and made as if to brush her down. She backed away, looking down to see where she had dropped the bag. One of the lemons had rolled into the gutter. The man picked it up and rubbed the lemon against his trouser leg before putting it back in the bag.

"Somebody's having pancakes for tea!"

A light went on in a back bedroom and Clarrie recognized the man as the window cleaner who'd let her climb his ladder. He grinned, revealing black, crowded teeth.

Clarrie stretched out her hand. "Can I have my lemons back, please?"

He moved the bag out of reach. "You'll have to wrestle me for them."

"Please, mister, I'm in a hurry."

"You're a big girl, aren't you? How old are you?"

"I'm six."

"Have you got a sweetheart, then?"

Clarrie hated it when grownups said things like that. She reached for the lemons. "I have to go home."

He shoved the bag of lemons into his jacket and brought a small cardboard box from his trouser pocket. He opened the box and offered it to her. "Licorice Allsorts. Help yourself."

Clarrie hesitated, then took a piece and put it in her mouth. She wasn't supposed to take toffee from strangers, but the window cleaner wasn't really a stranger.

"More?"

Clarrie shook her head.

"Go on, there's plenty more where these came from."

She took another piece. "I've got to go home now, my mam's waiting for me."

He put the box back in his trouser pocket. "Don't worry, I'm not going to pinch your lemons." Leaning his face close to hers he gave a silly giggle. "I might pinch your little bum instead."

Clarrie stepped back and hit the corner of somebody's back door.

"If you'll take your knickers down for a minute," the window cleaner said softly, "you can have that whole box of Allsorts."

Clarrie was shaking. Wasn't he ashamed to say such a thing?

"I just want to see what you look like down there." He fumbled at his trousers. "You needn't be shy. I'm not shy, am I? I'll show you what I look like." He grabbed her head, pushing her face against his trousers. Beneath the smell of licorice there was a whiff of ammonia. "I'm not going to hurt you," he said. "You'll see . . . you'll like me once you get to know me."

Clarrie pulled at his hands, struggling to free herself. She felt his belt buckle scrape her face. "I already know you," she gasped. "You're the window cleaner."

He released her so quickly she almost fell again. He pulled the bag from his jacket. "I was just having a bit of fun with you. Here—take your lemons. There's no need to tell anyone about it."

Clarrie bolted out of the entry. The chapel clock was chiming six as she reached the house. She stopped to catch her breath. There was a sharp pain on her right side. Still shaking, she pushed open the back door and stepped into the yard.

The kitchen light was on. Clarrie rubbed her lips with her scarf to wipe away the licorice stains. Through the kitchen window, she could see the table set for tea, the plates warming on the hob. Her mam was bent over the fire, holding a frying pan. She would never be able to tell her or anyone else what had happened.

That night, Clarrie dreamt she was searching for something in her father's wicker trunk but found, instead of whatever it was she was looking for, the body of a yellow-faced mandarin in a red and gold dragon costume. It seemed to be a matter of some urgency that she lift the mandarin out of the trunk and bring him back to life.

She was struggling with the inert figure, when, to her horror, the blue flowers in the wallpaper started moving, breaking away from the wall, floating across the landing towards her. Fleshy leaves stroked her arms, her face; tendrils slid sinuously around her legs, her body, wound themselves about her throat, her wrists. Tearing free, she dragged the limp mandarin out of the trunk and along the landing to her parents' bedroom. She hauled him onto the bed and propped him in a sitting position. The mandarin's body slumped down. Along both edges of the bed, more bodies were slumping over. She ran frantically from one side to the other, propping them up, only to have them slump back down. The room started spinning. Faster and faster it flew. The open doorway whizzed by so quickly she was afraid to leap through to safety. She glimpsed her mother at the foot of the stairs, arms outstretched crying "Jump, Clarrie, jump!" She flung herself headlong through the open doorway, and awoke with a cry, unsure for a moment whether or not she had landed safely.

Chapter Eighteen

"Don't go to work tonight, Mam." Clarrie took hold of the hem of her mother's coat. "I want you to stay home." Her dad was working at the rink. Arthur was spending the night with one of his friends. She would be alone with Annie.

Her mother gently disengaged herself. "I can't stay home, love, there's too much to do at the shop. You'll be all right." She turned to Annie. "Make sure Clarrie and the baby get to bed on time, and don't forget those jobs I asked you to do."

Annie watched until her mother was out of sight before putting on her own coat. "I'm sick and tired of doing everything around here," she said. "You're big enough to wash the pots and put the baby to bed. Don't go hiding the pans to soak under the sink like you did last time, and remember to change Billy's nappie before you put him in, and clean out the pram properly, the way I showed you. I want it done perfect, so Mam will think it was me." She turned in the doorway. "Breathe one word of this to anyone, and I swear I'll murder you."

Clarrie filled the cast-iron kettle at the scullery sink and carried it to the kitchen fire. The kettle was so heavy she had to set it down twice before she reached the hearth. Billy was asleep in his carriage. Clarrie took her book of fairy tales off the dresser and sat by the fire to read until the water boiled. When the water began to bubble into the fire, she carried it to the scullery sink and poured it into the washing-up bowl. A sliver of soap, embedded with dried tea leaves and bits of rusty steel wool, was all there was to clean the pots with. She threw the soap into the water and slid in the plates. The water turned a greyish blue. Scraps of soggy beetroot rose to the surface. She scooped them into the perforated enamel scrap-dish hooked to the corner of the sink. It wasn't fair that she had to stand here in the cold scullery doing Annie's jobs. She was as bad off as Cinderella—worse. Cinderella had been allowed to sit by the fire.

She rinsed the plates and dried them and was scraping at a saucepan coated with burnt milk, when Billy began to cry. After setting a freshly filled kettle on the fire, she went to change him. He was sopping wet. She removed his nappie, washed and powdered his bottom, and dressed him in a clean nappie and nightshirt. "Time for beddy-byes, Billy boy."

Billy was ten months old now, and so heavy she was obliged to stop on every other stair to catch her breath and adjust his position. She carried him along the landing, tucked him into her parents' bed, kissed him, and sat on the edge of the mattress to sing him a lullaby.

Billy listened, drowsy eyed to "Rock-a-by-Baby" and "All Through the Night." Halfway through "Golden Slumbers" his eyes closed. Clarrie got to her feet and, still singing, tiptoed backwards to the door. Billy's eyes flew open. He set up a loud wailing.

"Shh! I'm still here, I haven't gone anywhere." She sat down to sing another chorus. Billy's eyes closed. Again she backed stealthily towards the door. Again he began to cry.

"Go to sleep, Billy, love," she begged, "Clarrie's tired. I still haven't cleaned the pram, yet, or done the pans. Our Annie will kill me." She wiped Billy's wet cheeks with her apron. She felt like crying herself.

By the time she made her escape, the kettle had boiled dry and the fire was almost out. She threw on more coal, forced twisted paper between the bars of the grate, then propped the shovel over the grate and spread a sheet of newspaper across it the way her mother did, to make the fire draw. She wheeled the pram into the scullery to be near the sink and lifted out the covers. Beneath the folding sections at the bottom of the pram, there was a smell of sour milk. She pulled out a dummy teat, and some mushy arrowroot biscuits. She had just started washing the pram when from the kitchen came a loud whooshing sound. She dropped the wet cloth and ran. The newspaper she had spread across the shovel was in flames. Scraps of burnt paper were flying about the room. Flames licked at the baby blanket hung over the oven door. She threw the blanket into the hearth and was stamping out the fire when Annie came running in. She pushed Clarrie out of the way and stamped on the smoldering blanket.

"What's going on?" she screamed. "What did you do?"

"I was trying to get the fire going with the shovel and paper, but the paper caught fire."

Annie shoved her away. "Get to bed—out of my sight before I do something I'll be sorry for."

Clarrie ran upstairs without even cleaning her teeth. She crawled into bed and pulled the covers over her head to shut out the sound of Annie slamming things about down in the kitchen. Her feet were like ice; her whole body ached. Tears rolled down her cheeks. She wanted her mam.

That night she dreamed she found a dead baby lying in a laundry basket under a heap of soiled clothes. She had a gun in her hand and knew that if anyone saw it she would be blamed for killing the baby. She must get rid of the body before anyone came in. She thrust the gun in the back of the cutlery drawer. She was forcing the baby's head down the drain hole in the scullery sink, when it changed into a raw potato that she was pushing through the chip-cutter at the fish and chip shop.

The next morning, the school was abuzz with a story of Violet Fawcet's mother. Gladys told her, in a horrified whisper, that Violet's mother, who was in the habit of walking in her sleep, had made her way downstairs during the night, lit the kitchen fire, boiled a kettle of water, and—still fast asleep—had carried the kettle back upstairs and poured the boiling water over her sleeping husband. Mr. Fawcet had run outside in his nightshirt, screaming bloody murder, waking up the neighbors. The police had come and an ambulance; Violet's mother was taken to the lunatic asylum and her husband to Salford Royal Hospital.

The skin prickled on the back of Clarrie's neck. What if she, like Violet's mother, were to get up out of bed and walk along the landing while she was asleep? What if she too were to do something evil before she could wake up and stop herself?

That evening Clarrie caught sight of her mother lifting a kettle of boiling water off the fire. She threw down her fork, bolted from the table, and fled to the lavatory.

"What's the matter with you?" her mother said when she returned. "It isn't like you to leave food on your plate."

Her father paused for a moment while spreading polish on his shoes. "Finish your dinner."

"My throat keeps closing up," Clarrie said, "I can't swallow."

Her mother frowned. "This afternoon, you told me you didn't want to go out to play because your legs hurt."

William set the shoe brush down and looked at Clarrie over his spectacles. "Growing pains," he said. "Your bones are stretching."

"This is more than growing pains." Sally put a hand on Clarrie's forehead. "Look at those dark circles under her eyes."

"She needs a good cleaning out," William said. "A dose of castor oil should do the trick."

"I think I'll keep her home from school tomorrow."

The next morning Clarrie's mother set Billy down on the bed next to Clarrie and told her to keep an eye on him while she went across the street to get the castor oil.

Clarrie buried her face in the damp silky curls at the nape of Billy's neck. He smelled of talcum powder. With her forefinger she scratched lightly at the flecks of dried porridge clinging to his cheek. She remembered her dream about the baby. Those evil thoughts had crept into her head while she was sleeping, unable to defend herself, but she loved her little brother and wouldn't hurt him in a million years.

Nevertheless, she was relieved to hear her mother's key in the door. That night she lay watching the shadows on the ceiling, waiting for the morning, beseeching her guardian angel to keep watch over her lest she should she happen to fall asleep.

The doctor removed the stethoscope from his ears. "No sign of consumption, but this wee lassie has a throat infection. And her legs are hurting because she has rheumatic fever. She needs complete bed rest—six to eight months and perhaps longer."

"Can I go to the sanatorium like Gladys?" Clarrie asked. She was hoping he'd say yes. If she were sent to the sanatorium, she'd be far away from home, which meant that Billy would be safe.

"You're better off at home, lassie." Doctor MacRae said. He wrote out a prescription and handed it to her mother. "Be sure to keep her warm and dry and free from draughts."

She awoke in her father's arms as he was carrying her upstairs. He put her down on the double bed in the big front bedroom.

"Am I going to sleep with you and Mam, then?"

"No. Your mam and I will sleep in the middle room with the baby. Annie's moving into the back bedroom. Arthur will have to make do downstairs on the sofa."

Her mother came in with a bucket of coal and a fire-lighter.

"Do we really need to have two fires going?" her father said.

"Doctor MacRae said she's got to stay warm." Her mother struck a match and put it to the papers. The fire flared up as it caught hold.

"We'll end up in the bloody workhouse at this rate."

"We can let the fire downstairs go out. I'll do the cooking up here until the weather gets warmer."

"Will you lock me in before you leave?" Clarrie asked her mother.

"Lock you in? Why on earth should I lock you in?"

"In case I walk in my sleep."

"You're not going to walk in your sleep, child. I couldn't lock you in even if I wanted to. There's no lock on the door."

"Stay with me then."

Her mother stroked her head. "I'll stay for a while if you promise to go to sleep." Clarrie closed her eyes. When she opened them again, she was alone. The fire was almost out—just a few red embers winking at her. A tramcar, grinding along Eccles New Road, sent a beam of light sliding slantwise across the ceiling, widening as it traveled down the far wall. Suddenly, her attention was riveted on two eyes glaring at her from the top of the wardrobe. The eyes protruded from a black face topped by a bush of frizzy hair. Clarrie screamed.

Her mother ran upstairs. "What is it, whatever's the matter?"

Clarrie pointed.

Her mother raised the candle she was carrying. "There's nothing there . . . did you see a mouse?"

"A black man's head! On top of the wardrobe."

Her mother placed her hand on Clarrie's forehead. "You've got a fever, love. There's nothing on the wardrobe."

"I can still see it."

"It's the fever talking. I tell you there's nothing there." With a sigh, her mother lifted Clarrie out of bed, held her high so she could touch the top of the wardrobe. Clarrie ran her hand over the place where the head had been—nothing but dust.

Her mother carried her back to bed and tucked her in. "Take this medicine and go back to sleep, love," she said. "Nobody's going to hurt you."

Clarrie lapsed into confused and feverish dreams, waking from time to time, aware of others moving about the room, of her mother raking coals from the fire, of voices urging her to open her mouth, take her medicine, swallow some water.

Days passed in an endless, feverish blur. But one day, awakened by the smell of soup bubbling on the fire and assailed by hunger pangs, she managed to sip a couple of spoons of soup before sinking back on her pillow. Gradually she was able to sit up and take part in the family meals.

Arthur brought in a stack of tattered boys' magazines and read to her the antics of Billy Bunter at boarding school.

"Look, you've made our Clarrie smile!" her mother said.

Clarrie wanted Arthur to read more, but it was time for him to deliver his papers. He promised to read Clarrie a story a day from his magazine collection, until they were all finished.

A few days later, her mother brought home a magazine for girls that featured similar stories about Bessie, Billy Bunter's chubby sister.

Boarding school sounded wonderful, Clarrie thought.

Her school would have grey stone towers covered with ivy, like the school in the magazine. There'd be a quadrangle, a common room, a hockey field, and a tuck shop. Along with her gymslip, she'd wear a striped school tie, a straw boater, and a blazer with the school emblem on the pocket. She'd sleep in a dormitory with a lot of jolly friends. They'd have marvelous adventures—exploring caves and gathering in the dorms for forbidden midnight feasts.

Through half-closed eyes she watched the pretty and popular Clarissa Hancock, hockey stick slung across her shoulder, stroll across the quad to the tuck shop. She had just scored the winning goal for her team, and her chums—Roberta, Cynthia, Penelope, and Jill—jostled for a place at her side. "I say," they cried, "top-hole, Clarissa old bean! Jolly good show! You're an absolute brick!" Clarissa tossed her perky red-gold curls. "It was nothing, really, any one of you could have done the same."

It would be the answer to her prayers—better by far than going to the sanatorium. She'd be out of Annie's clutches. And if by any chance she were to walk in her sleep,

Billy would be safe. Clarrie smiled. Yes. There could be no doubt, that was the place for her—boarding school!

"Boarding school?" Her father released a cloud of cigarette smoke. "Who do you think I am, Baron Rothschild?"

Her mother looked up from her darning and smiled. "Remember, Will, she's not well."

"Aye. She's in a bloody dream world." He frowned at Clarrie over his glasses. "Tom Brown's Schooldays—that's what you want to read, my girl. Those places aren't what they're cracked up to be."

"Boarding schools aren't for people like us, love," her mother said. "They cost too much."

"But now that Dad and you are both working, I thought . . ."

"You thought wrong," her father said.

Her mother nodded. "We barely make ends meet as it is, love."

Clarrie let the matter drop. She would read Tom Brown's Schooldays—her dad had promised to fetch it for her from the library, but she couldn't go anywhere until she was better. In the meantime, she had this bed all to herself and plenty of time to read. And she no longer had to stand in the cold scullery every night doing the washing up.

As soon as the weather grew warm enough to dispense with the bedroom fire, the family moved back into the kitchen, leaving Clarrie upstairs with a bell on the bedside table to summon help if the need arose. Through the open window came a jangle of noises from the street below—peddlers, street singers, children playing, and panic-stricken cows being herded along Eccles New Road to the abattoir.

She was not supposed to get out of bed except to use the chamber pot, but she didn't always obey. Every Saturday at teatime, two small men with black curly hair and black waxed moustaches, known locally as "the Italian brothers," came down the street trundling a barrel-organ which they parked in front of Clarrie's house. As soon as the music started, Clarrie got out of bed and went to the window. The barrel organ played the same three or four tunes over and over, but she never tired of them. After a while, her mother would come out of the house bearing a plate of sandwiches, or a slab of bread-pudding, which she set on the garden wall. The Italian brothers would smile and nod, but they always waited until she'd gone back into the house before wolfing down the food. One day, to Clarrie's delight, they showed up with a small monkey dressed in a glittery waistcoat and a red fez. The monkey perched on top of the organ gibbering excitedly when anyone passed by and snatching at the proffered coins.

At closing time, on Saturday nights, tipsy men and women spilled out of the pub on the corner to linger in little groups under the street lamp outside Clarrie's window, continuing some friendly argument started in the pub. Sometimes they formed a circle, their arms around each other's shoulders, and sang the old pub songs—"Nelly Dean" and "Two Lovely Black Eyes," and "Show me the Way to go Home."

And sometimes she caught sight of her father hurrying off to his waiter job at the roller rink in Manchester. He walked swiftly, his shoulders slightly hunched, a cigarette between his fingers. She always felt an urge to comfort him, to tell him she understood—but what it was she understood was not clear to her.

One evening, as she lay in bed listening to the bursts of laughter coming from the kitchen downstairs, she was deluged by a tidal wave of self-pity. Here she was, ill, alone, abandoned, forgotten, while the rest of the family were downstairs in the cosy kitchen, laughing and having a fine old time, not giving her a second thought. She picked up her bell and gave it a shake.

"I want some toast and tea, please," she shouted in answer to her mother's question from the foot of the stairs, ". . . three slices, with lots of butter."

A short time later, Annie stomped upstairs and slapped a plate of buttered toast on the bedside table. She had recently started work at Worrall's Mill, and being a working girl hadn't improved her temper. Her lips were clamped together in a grim line.

"I'm sick of running up and down these stairs every time you ring that damn bell."

"I didn't ask you to come, I wanted Mam to do it."

Annie's dark eyes flashed behind her steel-rimmed glasses. "You think Mam's got nothing better to do than wait on you? I don't believe you're ill at all any more. You're putting it on."

"Doctor MacCrae says I've got rheumatic fever." She cried. But she wondered if Annie could be right. Was she just imagining the pains in her arms and legs? In any case, she wasn't going to worry about it. She licked the butter from her fingers and reached for her new library book, *The Merry Madcaps of Hilltop Academy*.

Later that evening, her father came into the bedroom. "Put something around your shoulders, love, and bring your pillow," he said, "I've got a surprise for you." He carried her across the room, helped her out onto the roof of the bay window, then climbed out and sat beside her.

"What is it?" Clarrie asked. "Why are we sitting out here?"

"Keep your eyes left, towards Eccles New Road." Her father put out a protective arm. There was the familiar grinding and rattling. A tramcar went by. "That wasn't it," he said. A little later came another tram rattle. "Keep your eyes open, here it comes!"

Red, green and amber lights danced along the road. Her father gripped her tightly around the waist as she leaned forward.

The illuminated tramcar! She'd been hearing about it for as long as she could remember. It came by every year, but this was the first time she had been allowed to stay up late enough to see it.

"Where's Mam? Where is everyone?" she cried. "They're going to miss it!"

"They're not missing it. Your mam's gone with them down to Eccles New Road to get a better look."

Glittering and shimmering with hundreds of colored lights, the illuminated tramcar rolled majestically down the tracks and disappeared into the night.

"Where does it come from?" Clarrie asked.

"Ah! That's the mystery." Her father spoke in a deep sepulchral voice. "Every year it appears like that, out of nowhere. It rolls along the tracks towards Eccles, and then . . . poof . . . it vanishes!"

Eccles New Road was the longest, straightest road she had ever seen, or could imagine. She'd never been all the way to the end. What if it didn't bend with the curve of the earth but went careening off through the clouds, carrying the illuminated tramcar with it? Perhaps the tramcar switched to other rails at some point, and travelled around the world for a whole year before it came back to its starting point. Seeing the half-smile on her father's face, it seemed more likely that he'd made up the whole story to amuse her.

And then the long summer days were over. Once again the wind moaned in the bedroom chimney, and the room grew so cold Clarrie could barely hold her fork, or sit up in bed long enough to eat her dinner.

"I hate having to cart coal up two flights of steps again," her mother said, "Tomorrow, I'll ask the doctor to take a look at you. I think you're well enough now to come downstairs."

Doctor MacRae listened to Clarrie's heart and took her temperature "She's not out of the woods yet," he said. "But she can go down and sit by the fire for a while."

Her mother saw the doctor out, and came back into the room. "Put something around your shoulders, love. I'll get your shoes."

Clarrie's feet had grown during the months she had spent in bed, and the shoes no longer fit her. Leaning on her mother, she made her way downstairs to the kitchen in bed socks. It was not yet dark enough to light the gas, and in the gathering dusk the room seemed smaller and shabbier than she remembered. Her father had gone off to work at the rink. Arthur and Annie stared at her blankly as though trying to remember who she was.

"Blimey, look what the cat dragged in," Annie said.

"Arthur, help Annie move the table away from the wall," her mother said, "so our Clarrie can sit down."

Clarrie leaned against the sideboard. She was shaking and had broken into a sweat from the effort of walking down the stairs.

"The table looked better where it was," Annie said. "This way takes up too much room."

"We can't help that. She's got to sit somewhere."

Tears welled in Clarrie's eyes. She'd expected to create a little stir, to be greeted with smiles and exclamations of joy, but they'd got used to being without her, and now nobody cared if she came down or not.

"Oh, boy, the tragedy queen is back." Annie said. "Greta Garbo doesn't stand a chance."

Clarrie's tears spilled over. "I want to go back to bed," she said.

Chapter Nineteen

Clarrie was curled up in front of the fire, looking through the family photograph album while her mother ironed. "Why are Dad and Uncle Jack dressed so funny?" She held the album open to the large, sepia-tinted photograph of her father and his brother.

The brothers, posed in front of a rose-covered trellis, looked owlish in identical wire-rimmed spectacles. They wore stiff-collared shirts, striped ties, and heavy tweed jackets, their trousers tucked into high-buttoned boots. Her mother set the iron down on an upturned saucer.

"That's the way they dressed in those days. This must have been taken in the back garden of the Hancock house, where your dad was born."

"Were they rich?"

"They were comfortable, but that was before his parents separated."

"Why did they separate?"

"Your Granddad Hancock thought his wife had killed his pet birds."

"Did she?"

"I don't know. The birds were all dead in the attic. I suppose it was the only explanation he could think of. The house is still there on Sorrel Lane, but it's empty now."

"Why don't we live there, then?"

"It doesn't belong to us, and even if it did we couldn't afford to keep it up."

"Who does it belong to?"

"One of your dad's cousins. I'm not sure if he's still alive."

"I want to see it."

"It's a good long walk. Perhaps, when you're all better, Annie will take you there. But you won't be able to go inside the house."

"Were you rich when you were a little girl, Mam?" Clarrie already knew the answer, but Billy was taking a nap and she had her mother all to herself. She wanted to hear more about Kent.

"Rich?" Her mother laughed. "Far from it, love. My father was a farm worker. My mother died when your Aunt Ruth was born, leaving my poor dad with six children to support. The boys were useful on the farm; your Aunt Pearl was old enough to take care of the baby, but I was only three at the time, too young to be of much help."

"Who took care of you?"

"I went to live with my Aunt Kate—she had five children of her own, so it was very good of her to take me in. Look." She turned the page to show Clarrie a picture postcard of a strange, crooked tower. "That's what they call an oast house. They have them all over Kent. This one's at the farm where I used to live."

She spoke lovingly of places she had known as a child—Ide Hill, Toys Hill, Four Elms, Brasted, Chartwell, Westerham, Sevenoaks, Tunbridge Wells. At hop-picking time, she told Clarrie, Londoners swarmed out of the city to work in the hop fields, shocking the country folk with their crude manners and their ignorance. "Some of those poor Cockney children didn't know where milk came from, or what a handkerchief was for. I felt sorry for them, though. Picking hops is hard work."

It wasn't only hops that grew in Kent, her mother said. Everything grew in Kent. That was why it was called the garden of England. In summer the chestnut trees arched across the lanes, transforming them into leafy tunnels. Scarlet-runner beans, cabbages, and strawberries sprang up like weeds in all the cottage gardens. Blackberries grew fat and juicy along the hedgerows. Fish leapt out of the streams into the children's buckets. In the autumn, apple trees bent low, groaning under their burdens; nuts rattled down like hailstones, cider gushed like liquid gold from the cider presses.

"You were lucky, Mam," Clarrie said.

"Yes, but it wasn't all beer and skittles." Her mother took a fresh iron from the fire and wiped it clean. "There was never enough money. They were kind to me, but I knew I was a charity case, so I worked hard for my keep."

"When I grow up, I'll buy you a big house in the country."

"I have trouble enough keeping up with this one."

"You can have servants to do all the work."

Her mother laughed. "Well, in that case!" She shook out a wrinkled shirt. "Someday, when your dad's ship comes in, I'll show you where I grew up. You'd love it there. I'll take you down to the common to pick mushrooms." Her voice grew soft and dreamy. "You have to get up at dawn, while the dew is still on the ground, to find them . . ."

Clarrie had a vision of her mother—a child, with apple-red cheeks and untidy black curls, rising from her bed in the chill dawn to dress. The child tiptoed down the cottage stairs, slipped a dark wool cape over her shoulders, lifted a raffia basket from behind the kitchen door, and stepped out into the misty garden. Huge dew-spangled spider webs broke, and drifted wide as she made her way to the gate. She closed the gate behind her and ran down the lane to the village common to gather the pale mushrooms that had mysteriously sprung up overnight in the dewy grass.

Her mother set down the iron. ". . . and one morning, just as I got back to the cottage with my basket of mushrooms, guess what I heard?"

"What?"

"A hunting horn!" She made a fist and raised it to her lips, blowing her horn. "And then I saw the fox!"

Clarrie closed her eyes. A furry red-brown streak flashed across the cottage garden.

"The hounds were right on its heels." Her mother made a yapping sound. "The poor fox was terrified. He ran hell for leather, straight into the outhouse. And you'll never guess what I did."

"What?"

"I shut him in. Just in time. The hounds were on his trail, sniffing around the outhouse, running this way and that, yapping their heads off, and right behind the hounds came the huntsmen in their red coats—hunting pink, they call it, but it's really red." She stood up, making a galloping motion with her arms. "Tallyho!" she cried. "Yoicks! Tallyho!"

Clarrie could see the huntsmen, feel the earth shake under the horses' hooves.

"I stepped in front of the outhouse door and pretended I was just coming out. The leader of the hunt asked had I seen the fox, I shook my head, and . . . oh Lord!" Her mother slammed the iron down. Fox, hounds, huntsmen, and horses vanished. She held up a scorched shirt. "Now look what you made me do." She threw the shirt back in the basket. "I wish you wouldn't get me started talking about Kent when I'm ironing. Your dad's going to have a fit."

"How much farther?" Clarrie asked Annie. She had begged Annie to take her to the Hancock house, but her legs were weaker than she'd realized, and her new shoes were making blisters on her heels.

"You're the one who wanted to come. If you're going to start whining, we can turn right around and go back."

They'd been walking for what seemed hours down a wide road, seeing nothing but identical semi-detached houses set back behind identical well-trimmed hedges. The neighborhood was quiet as a graveyard—quieter—no children at play, no one at work in the gardens, and, with the exception of one lone cyclist and a green, single-decker bus, no traffic.

"I'm just asking."

"We're almost there," Annie said. They crossed the road and turned down a lane lined with trees. On the corner, a wooden signpost read "Sorrel Lane." Golden brown leaves drifted down on them as they walked; acorns crunched beneath their feet. It was hard to believe they were still in Salford. Clarrie picked up an acorn and held it in the palm of her hand, admiring the way the shiny nut fit so neatly into its rough little cup.

"You can't eat those," Annie said. "They're only good for pigs."

The lane grew narrower, shadier, the sound of their footsteps muffled by layers of damp leaves. They passed a prickly, overgrown hedge jutting through some spiked railings, and at last Annie came to a halt in front of a large, wrought-iron gate. "This is it."

The gate was locked and chained. Clarrie ran her fingers over an iron scroll spelling out the name "Hancock." Annie rattled the chain. "Look through those bushes. From here you can only see the roof and the chimneys." She boosted Clarrie up, waiting until she had climbed over the gate and dropped onto the gravel drive, before shoving the bag of refreshments through the bars of the gate and climbing over after her. As they walked around a curving path to the house, a fat black and white bird flew out of the bushes.

"That's a magpie," Annie said. "You never see them around our way because there's nowt to steal. They're thieves, are magpies. If they see a ring or a sixpence, or anything shiny, they'll fly off with it."

A large, square house came into view, its sooty bricks partially hidden by creeper vines. The steps leading up to the front door were green with moss, the front windows latched and shuttered. Annie pushed the brass letter slot and peered in. "Can't see much. It looks as though that big Chinese vase I told you about is still there at the bottom of the stairs." She moved aside so Clarrie could see. "I brought you here once before, when you were a toddler. You were a little misery. Our Arthur had to carry you all the way home . . . don't you remember?"

Clarrie shook her head. "Why doesn't anyone live here?"

"It belonged to our great-granddad, and he left it to his younger brother, great uncle Claude. Uncle Claude went to live in Germany. He had no children to leave it to, so our granddad took it over."

"But granddad's dead, now, so they ought to let us live here."

"We couldn't afford to heat it, and there's all sorts of back rates and taxes and stuff to pay. Uncle Jack's family would have first dibs anyway."

"They already have a nice house."

"Uncle Jack's the eldest son. He got all the furniture, too, when Granddad died."

"That's not fair," Clarrie said.

"You know what they say—them as 'as, gets, them as 'as nowt, gets nowt." Annie sat on the mossy steps, opened the bag of sandwiches, and passed one to Clarrie. "I don't care, anyway. This may be a posh neighborhood, but I wouldn't want to live here. You can't run out to the shops, or to the pictures. There's nothing to do but sit at the window and watch the grass grow."

Annie was right, Clarrie thought. Their own neighborhood, crowded and rundown though it was, was full of life. The streets echoed with the cries of barrow boys and the shouts of children playing. In the evenings when the street lamps went on, you could hear mothers calling their children in to supper.

"Tell me about the birds," Clarrie said.

"Granddad had turned the whole top floor of this house into an aviary. He had dozens of birds—budgies, canaries—all sorts. Granny Hancock hated them. She thought he cared more about those birds than he did about his own children. One day he came home and found his birds stone cold dead. He accused her of killing them out of spite, and he threw her and the lads out on the street without two pennies to rub together."

"I don't think she did it" Clarrie said.

"I wouldn't blame her if she did. He must have been a real tartar to throw them out like that. Granny had to pawn the few bits and bobs she owned and rent a room behind the Palace Theatre. They queued up at the workhouse every night for a free bowl of soup. She went to work for Worrall's, like I'm doing now." Annie took a swallow from the bottle of dandelion and burdock and passed the bottle to Clarrie. "What a come-down, eh? It's no wonder she took to drink. She was three sheets in the wind half the time."

"What happened to the lads?"

"Uncle Jack went back to granddad and got a job at the abattoir. Our dad was about seven or eight at the time—not much older than you—but he had to leave school and go to work."

"Poor dad," Clarrie said. Her heart ached for the child who became her father.

"He was all right. He got a job selling programs at the Palace Theatre and running errands for the actors. Marie Lloyd was one. She always wanted steak and kidney pudding and a bottle of stout."

They fell silent, watching a small brown bird splash in the bowl of a stone fountain. Here on the steps of the Hancock House, hearing these stories, Clarrie felt closer to Annie than she ever did at home. At home, she was always expecting Annie to fly into a rage, waiting for those angry sparks to flash from Annie's eyes, for the hand that was so quick to dart out and strike.

Annie stuffed the empty pop bottle and the sandwich papers back in the bag. "Never throw pop bottles away," she said. "You get a ha'penny when you take 'em back."

Clarrie said she was still thirsty.

"Let's try the fountain." The brown bird flew off as they approached. Annie put her finger in the spout. "It's sealed with cement or summat. That must be rainwater in the bowl." She brushed aside the tall grasses around the base. A naked stone baby with a stone leaf covering its privates was holding up the bowl.

They followed a crazy paving path to the back of the house. At the corner of the house was a rain barrel half-full of water and blackened leaves. The back windows had crossed wooden slats nailed over them.

Annie peered through the slats. "Can't see a thing. It's all dark."

Clarrie banged the iron knocker. "Is anybody there?" she shouted. "'Is anybody there,' said the Traveler knocking on the moonlit door . . ."

"What are you talking about?" Annie said.

"It's a poem." There was no moonlight at the moment, and no horse champing the grasses, but she was sure there were listeners—invisible listeners—ghosts waiting to be restored to life.

"Did you hear that?" she asked Annie.

"Hear what?"

"That fluttering noise."

"Must be bats."

They explored the neglected garden and found a patch of tall red rhubarb. They each broke a stalk to chew on. "We'll take the rest of that home," Annie said. "It's only going to waste."

Clarrie looked back at the house, at the sealed fountain, the neglected garden. "I wish we could live here and bring it back to life."

"I thought you'd like it," Annie said. They walked home in companionable silence, their arms laden with crisp pink stalks of rhubarb; the setting sun, ablaze in all the windows along Eccles Old Road, cast a ruby glow over everything they passed.

After tea Clarrie stood in the scullery doorway drying a plate, surveying the kitchen with a critical eye. She was familiar with every scratch on the furniture, every lump and blister in the painted woodwork. Her father, who had been so cruelly deprived of his rightful home, was sitting comfortably by the fire in his long drawers, smoking a cigarette and reading *The News of the World*, apparently unconcerned about his fate. The brown leatherette on his armchair had split in several places and the stuffing was sticking out. In spite of her mother's repeated efforts to pry them loose, blobs of spilled food and grease had become ground into the coconut matting in front of the fire. What would the rich people think, she wondered, if they should happen to look in the window as they were passing by? People like Princess Elizabeth and Princess Margaret Rose?

The young princesses, identically dressed in velvet-collared coats and matching bonnets, peeped in at the kitchen window. Clarrie opened the scullery door. "You can come in if you like, and have some tea," she said. The Princesses stepped daintily over the threshold.

"We don't want any tea, thank you," said Princess Elizabeth. "We were just curious to see how you poor people live."

Clarrie, overcome by a sudden fierce protective love for this home and this family, spoke up in their defense. "Your palace wouldn't look so posh if it wasn't for all those servants slaving their heads off," she said, hotly. "How would you like it if your mam was a servant—working her fingers to the bone—scrubbing floors and washing other people's dirty clothes?"

The room, small and shabby though it was, was warm and friendly, and there was beauty here. The cinders in the fire glowed red and grey between the bars of the grate. The flames leaping up the sooty chimney kept changing from red to gold and back to red again, and in the front, where her dad had just dumped fresh coal, tiny blue-green tongues were darting about, licking at the pitch bubbles. Loveliest of all was her mother sitting there lost in thought—the flame shadows dancing across her face made it look as though the fire was burning inside her.

Chapter Twenty

At the sound of the final bell, the girls of Tatton Memorial School flew like starlings through the schoolyard and out the gate. The sun had come out, shining on the wet roofs and cobbles. Shrill voices bounced and echoed through the street. Clarrie was struggling out of the coat she'd just put on, when someone tapped her on the shoulder and cried, "Tick, you're on!" Clarrie threw her coat against the wall and took off in pursuit. The other girls tossed their coats on top of hers and joined in the game. Clarrie, exhilarated, ran madly, tagging them one by one. Her heart was racing, and her legs threatened to give way, but she outran them all before collapsing, breathless, on the schoolyard step. "Have to stop," she whispered.

"Me, too," said the girl she'd just tagged. "I'm supposed to go straight home after school."

One by one, the girls picked up their coats and dispersed—running homeward, past the sooty little gardens, down the narrow entries, calling to each other as they ran, "Ta-ra, love, ta-ra—see you tomorrow!"

The street was suddenly quiet. Clarrie got to her feet and was putting on her coat when a boy stepped out from the corner. The boys hardly ever passed this way—their own schoolyard opened onto another street two blocks away. This lad's hair bristled like hedgehog quills on his oversized head, and he had such a bad squint, she couldn't tell if he was looking at her or not. Half the kids she knew were a bit cross-eyed, but that squint, combined with that bristly hair, could belong to only one person. He was bigger now, of course, and even uglier than she remembered, but there was no doubt it was the dreaded Ernie Cruikshank—the boy who'd tormented her in infants' school.

"Hey, Clarrie Hancock. Does yer mother know yer out?"

Clarrie kept her head down and walked quickly away, her heart pounding. Clogs sounded on the pavement behind her. Something whizzed past her ear and hit the ground. A stone. She glanced over her shoulder. Ernie was only a short distance behind her.

She broke into a run. Ernie Cruikshank clattered after her. "Yer can't get away from me. I'm goin' ter make mincemeat out of you."

Clarrie kept on running.

"I seen yer knickers when you was bending over," he shouted, "they're navy blue."

Clarrie sped down to Eccles New Road and burst into the butcher shop. Mr. Hutchins came around from behind the counter, wiping his hands on his blue-striped apron.

"Steady on, lass! What's the matter?"

"Where's my mam?" Clarrie gasped.

"She's not here. We weren't busy, so I sent her home."

"There's a boy chasing me. He's been chucking stones at me."

Mr. Hutchins pointed to the window, where Ernie Cruikshank's grinning face was pressed against the glass. "That him?"

Clarrie nodded. Mr. Hutchins moved swiftly to the door, and Ernie Cruikshank bolted. "I caught him tormenting a cat the other day." Mr. Hutchins stepped outside, looked up and down the road, then came in and closed the door. "He's gone."

"Can I stay here for a while to make sure?"

Mr. Hutchins smiled. "I'll be in the back. Let me know if any customers come in."

He disappeared into the storage room and returned with a wet, chamois leather. "Here, keep yourself busy. Wipe the finger marks off the glass for me."

She was cleaning the outside of the display cases when Mr. Hutchins staggered out of the back room with an animal carcass slung over his shoulder. Sweat rolled down his plump cheeks; his apron was stained with blood. With his round belly, pudgy face, little black moustache, and kiss curls stuck to his forehead, he looked, Clarrie thought, like the fat one in Laurel and Hardy. "Is that a fatted calf ?" she asked.

"Nay, lass. It's a side o' lamb."

Clarrie held the carcass steady for him while he struggled to hang it on a meat hook. Blood dripped onto the floor.

"Grab a scoop o' that sawdust and throw it down," Mr. Hutchins pointed to a wooden barrel behind the counter. Clarrie took a tin scoop and sprinkled sawdust over the blood. Mr. Hutchins cut away a chunk of creamy suet from the hollow belly, dropped it on a square of greaseproof paper, and threw in a few beef bones. He wrapped everything in newspaper. "Here, give this to your mam."

Clarrie thanked him. "Did you have to kill that lamb yourself, Mr. Hutchins?"

"Nay, lass. That's done at the abattoir. I just cut 'em up into chops and roasts. I never killed nothing in my life."

"A mad bull ran down our street the other day, while they were driving the cows down Eccles New Road to the abattoir," Clarrie said. "It ran right past our house."

"A mad bull? I doubt it. He was probably just scared because he knew his number was up." Mr. Hutchins walked over to the window. "I doubt that lad's coming back." He rang open the till and handed her a penny. "Here, buy yourself some gob-stoppers. If he bothers you again, tell your mam and dad."

Her mother was in the kitchen frying liver and onions. She lifted a floury hand to brush the hair from her face. "You're late. Where've you been?"

"Ernie Cruikshank was chasing me. I went in the butcher's because I thought you'd be at work. I waited there to make sure he'd gone." She put the parcel down. "Mr. Hutchins gave us some bones and suet."

Her mother opened the parcel. "Lovely. We can have soup tomorrow, and a roly-poly pudding. But you mustn't go bothering Mr. Hutchins—he's got enough on his mind. He's worried he may lose his shop if his customers don't start paying up."

"Ernie Cruikshank says he's going to make mincemeat out of me."

"Wash your hands, then set the table." Her mother dropped a piece of floured liver into the pan. Hot fat splashed out onto her hand. "Damn it!" The pan fell with a clang, splattering liver and onions across the hearth plate. She bent and picked up the liver. Tendrils of damp hair clung to the sides of her face.

"Can I give that to Champ?" Clarrie asked. Champ was the little dog who belonged to the Morrow ladies next door. He was old now, hardly able to walk. The Morrow ladies were old, too. Clarrie suspected that they sometimes forgot to feed him.

"We can't afford to go giving good liver to dogs. I can wash it off." She took her purse from her apron pocket. "Run across the street and get me some more onions."

Clarrie followed her into the scullery. "What if he's out there, waiting for me?"

Her mother was running cold water over her scalded hand. She turned off the tap. "What if who's out there?"

"Ernie Cruikshank—the boy I just told you about."

"Ask Gladys to go with you."

"Her mam says she's poorly again. She didn't go to school today. "

"Well, you'd better learn to stand up yourself. You can't stay in the house for the rest of your life."

Clarrie was on her way home from school the next day, when something sharp hit her between the shoulder blades. She whirled around. Ernie Cruikshank was grinning at her from behind a low wall. He held up a jagged piece of brick.

"Leave me alone, you bully!" she shouted.

"You'll be black and blue by the time I'm finished with you, Clarrie Hancock." He flung the brick. This time it missed its target.

Clarrie ran. She didn't stop until she reached the safety of her house.

The next Monday morning, Ernie Cruikshank jumped out at her with a yell as she was passing the coal shed and hit her on the back of the head with a large chunk of coal. She sped home and had to sit on the back step to catch her breath and wait for the stitch in her side to go away.

Her mam wanted her to learn to stick up for herself, but Ernie Cruikshank was twice her size. In the park, when the big kids pushed her off the swings, Annie or Arthur had always come to her rescue, but now Arthur had his papers to deliver, and Annie didn't get home from the mill until after six. If she had to defend herself against a big stupid lump like that, she'd need a weapon. The fireside poker would be good, but her mam would never let her take it out of the house.

While her mother was busy cooking breakfast, she ran down to the cellar to look for some weapon she could hide under her coat. The sticks of firewood were too short, but she found an old ax handle covered with coal dust. Perfect. She'd smuggle the ax handle out of the house in the sleeve of her coat and hide it behind a bush inside the schoolyard door.

All day long her heart was heavy at the prospect of confronting Ernie Cruikshank, but when school let out, and Ernie didn't show up, she began to hope he'd given up on her and found other prey.

She was walking home, rattling the ax handle across some railings, when he suddenly stepped out of a side street, to face her. He was holding a stone as big as a duck egg. Clarrie tightened her grip on the ax handle. "You better not throw that, Ernie Cruikshank." Her voice came out thin and quavery.

Ernie Cruikshank grinned. "Who's goin' ter stop me?"

"I am."

"You and whose army?" He drew back his arm and hurled the stone. Clarrie swung the ax handle wildly. There was a sharp crack as the wood made contact with the stone. With a howl, Ernie clutched his head and staggered back.

Clarrie's heart was thumping; had she really hurt him? But Ernie had already recovered and was running towards her, shaking his fist. "Now yer bloody well going ter get it!"

Clarrie waved the handle over her head. "Come on, then, come on. Let me knock your ugly block off!"

Ernie stopped in his tracks, his eyes on the ax handle.

"Come on, you yellow-belly!" Clarrie shouted.

Ernie looked down at his feet as though wondering what they intended to do.

"What are you waiting for?"

Ernie turned and ran. The iron studs on his clogs struck tiny sparks from the flags as he disappeared around the corner.

Had she actually scared him away? Clarrie couldn't believe it. What if this was another of his tricks? Gripping the ax handle, she ran to the side street, looked over walls, peered down the entries. Ernie was nowhere in sight.

The hedges along East-Wynford Street had thrust dainty white blossoms through the railings, filling the air with a sweet, powdery scent. Clarrie broke off a sprig, then another, twisting the two to form a crown. She started to sing the May Day song, but it wasn't May Day yet, and the occasion called for something more triumphant. Herbert always sang "Onward Christian Soldiers," on his way home from Boys Brigade, but, if she sang that, someone might think she was mocking him. Suddenly, the right song came to her. She marched home, crowned with privet blossoms, waving the ax handle over her head and singing "The British Grenadier," at the top of her lungs.

The backyard door was unlatched. Clarrie tossed the ax handle behind the dustbin and went through the scullery into the kitchen. Billy was in his carriage, fast asleep. Her mother was bent over the oven, stirring something in a brown earthenware casserole. A delicious smell of lamb, simmering with onions and potatoes, filled the room. The kitchen windows sparkled. The range gleamed, black and glossy, under a fresh layer of polish, its steel trim burnished mirror-bright with emery paper. The brass knick-knacks on the mantelpiece twinkled.

"Everything looks so clean and shiny," Clarrie said.

Her mother smiled. "I got off work early. Mr. Hutchins said he'd finish the cleaning up himself."

"I stood up for myself today, like you told me to."

"Was that boy bothering you again? He sounds like a nasty piece of work. Perhaps I should have a talk with his mother."

"No need. He threw a stone at me but I hit it back with my stick. He ran like a scared rabbit."

"Is that why you're so pleased with yourself ?" She touched Clarrie's privet crown. "You look like the Queen of the May."

Chapter Twenty-one

Arthur had transformed a broom handle into a maypole, wrapping it in strips of colored crepe paper and topping it with his old garf, one of the iron hoops he and his friends used to race through the streets. Annie had shown Clarrie how to cover the hoop with more strips of colored crepe paper and finish it off with ribbons that dangled from the ring to the ground. The maypole was supposed to be carried from house to house by a boy—assuming one could be found who was willing to do it—while the girls, each dressed in a paper frock and holding a ribbon, sang the maypole song.

Clarrie's mother helped her and Gladys make frocks out of crepe paper and ropes of tinsel. While she sewed, she told stories of the May Day celebrations of her childhood. In Toys Hill, she said, the men of the village always erected a huge maypole, tall as a ship's mast, on the common; later, the whole village turned out for the maypole dance and the crowning of the May queen. Clarrie, yearning for a time, a place, an England she had never known, tried to persuade Gladys and the other girls, that they, too, should dance around their maypole. Gladys was willing to give it a try, but the others would have none of it. People would think they'd gone barmy, they said; nobody in Salford had ever danced around a maypole.

The girls assembled outside Clarrie's back yard, dressed and ready to go, but they had found no lad willing to carry the maypole. Most of the neighborhood lads had their own May Day business to attend to. Dressed as pirates or cowboys or old washerwomen, they ran through the streets, shoving each other, banging on doors, and singing comic songs.

"We've got to find someone quick," Gladys cried. Her cheeks were blotched with feverish red patches. She shook the jar her mother had provided. "If the other maypoles get 'round before us, we won't get any money!"

"I'll ask Herbert," Clarrie said. "He never goes out with the other lads."

"I already asked him," Gladys said. "He wants a double share of the money."

"We'll have to give it to him, then," Clarrie said. She ran over to Herbert's house to make the offer.

"I'll do it," Herbert said, "but only as a favor to you." He told her to wait in the lobby while he got ready. A few minutes later he came downstairs dressed in his Boys' Brigade uniform.

By the time Clarrie returned with Herbert, Gladys was jumping up and down, beside herself with excitement.

"The others are getting a head start," she cried. "Come on, let's go!"

Panting and sweating in his hot uniform, Herbert took hold of the maypole, struggling to hold it straight, and with each girl clutching a ribbon, they set off down the street. From time to time, other maypoles passed them. The rivals eyed each other critically. Clarrie was confident that their own maypole was better than any other; their pole-bearer, in his uniform, with the leopard skin stretched across his chubby belly, gave them a touch of grandeur. When she remarked on this to Herbert, his pink, overheated face turned crimson, and his bored expression vanished.

They moved along the street knocking on doors and singing the maypole song.

We come to greet you here today,
And we hope you will not turn us away,
For we'll dance and sing, in a merry ring,
On Maypole Day.
For we're all, we're all,
Bright as the blossoms that bloom on the tree,
Free as the birds that fly in the air,
Happy as fishes that swim in the sea,
Yes, we're all as happy as happy can be . . .

The person who opened the door usually waited with a smile until the song was over then slipped a coin into the jam jar. Rarely, a door slammed in their faces before they had finished. When it did, they continued on their way, undiscouraged.

Herbert had been complaining for some time that his arms were getting tired. Margie Barlow was trailing a streamer of paper behind her and crying because she'd torn her skirt on a nail as they passed the coal yard. Gladys was gasping for breath and hardly able to sing for coughing.

"We'd better pack it in," Clarrie said. "It must be almost teatime, and the jam jar's nearly full.

"Not yet, not yet!" Gladys cried. "My granny's expecting us. I promised her we'd be coming."

"Just one more stop, then," Clarrie said. Along the way, they debated how best to spend the money. Herbert thought they should pool it and go to the pictures on Saturday afternoon. Gladys voted for a blowout at the fish and chip shop. When they reached her grandmother's house, she knocked on the door and shouted through the letterbox. "It's only us, Gran, open up!"

Her grandmother came to the door. "Well, now, don't you look a treat," she said, "a sight for sore eyes." She rummaged about among her dark, voluminous skirts and produced a black leather purse. They began the maypole song.

Gladys held out the jam jar to accept the coin. "Thanks, Gran." Suddenly she broke into a fit of violent coughing. Blood sprayed from her nose, gushed from her mouth. The jar fell from her hand and smashed on the pavement, coins rolled down to the curb. Gladys dropped to her knees, doubling over, losing her tinsel crown as her head hit the step.

"Oh, dear God in heaven!" her grandmother shrieked. "Run quick, somebody. Fetch our Maudie!"

Clarrie was standing in the front doorway, still in her paper frock, when an ambulance pulled up in front of the house. Two men got out and went up the Halliwell's path. A little while later they came out bearing Gladys on a stretcher.

"Mam!" Clarrie called. "They're taking Gladys away!" She ran down the path. Gladys's mother came out of the house wearing her fur-trimmed coat, and smoking a cigarette.

"Where are they taking her?" Clarrie asked.

Maud threw her cigarette down and stepped on it. "To Ladywell." She climbed into the ambulance. "You won't be seeing her for a while, love."

"I wonder why they didn't realize the consumption was back?" Sally said when Clarrie returned to the house. "There are usually signs . . . she'd have been coughing up blood for some time, I imagine."

"She was coughing up blood," Clarrie said. "She showed me her hankie."

Her mother stared at her. "You knew about it? Why didn't you say something?"

"Gladys made me promise not to." Clarrie started to cry. "She didn't want to go back to the sanatorium."

"It's no use crying. Gladys is very ill and you might have caught it yourself. You should have told me."

Shortly before teatime, Maud stopped by the Hancock's house. Her eyes were red from crying. Gladys was dead, she told them. She had not even made it to the hospital.

"Oh, my God!" Sally said. "Come inside, love. Sit for a minute. Let me make you a cup of tea."

Maud shook her head. "I can't stay. I haven't even told her granny yet."

Clarrie looked from one to the other. How could Gladys be dead? "We were going to go to the chip shop with our maypole money," she said.

Maud thrust a paper bag at Clarrie. "She was taking this to the hospital with her. The last thing she said was 'Give my doll to Clarrie.' She must have known something."

As soon as Maud left, Clarrie's mother took the bag out of Clarrie's hand. "I'm sorry, love," she said. "I know how much you want to keep it to remember Gladys by, but consumption's very catching. Her poor mam was in shock—she wasn't thinking straight."

Her mother's mouth was set in a grim line as she threw the bag into the fire. Clarrie's chest hurt. Clearly it would be no use trying to change her mother's mind.

The doll had already started to blacken. A smell of singed hair filled the room. Her mother grabbed the poker and jabbed at the doll, trying to force it under the coals, out of sight. Scraps of burning cloth fluttered like black moths up the chimney.

Chapter Twenty-two

Squatting on the damp steps of the schoolyard, Clarrie examined the contents of her paper bag: a salmon-paste sandwich, an apple, and a special treat—four of her favorite chocolate biscuits. Gladys would have loved these biscuits, but Gladys was gone, and she had nobody to share them with.

Because of her long absence from school, she'd been put back into a lower standard where, with the exception of Myra Tarrant, who was older than she and had been left back twice, she hardly knew anyone. There were a few girls—like Violet Fawcet and Elsie Harvey—who would be only too glad to be friends with her, but they were scruffs—the girls nobody wanted to be seen with. They had nits in their matted hair, tidemarks around their necks, and runny noses.

Violet Fawcet had come around once or twice after school, knocking on the Hancock's door, asking if Clarrie could come out to play. Clarrie always made excuses. She was afraid to be seen with Violet—afraid she might never be able to get rid of her. And then people would look down on her, too.

And there were others, older girls—like Lillian Porter, who kept to themselves. Everyone said they were stuck up.

Clarrie thought Lillian might make a good friend, but she didn't want to risk a rebuff by making the first move. She had finished her sandwich and was about to bite into one of the chocolate biscuits when she noticed Elsie Harvey eyeing it hungrily. Clarrie held out the bag.

Elsie thrust a grimy hand into the bag. "Thanks, love." Quickly, as though she were afraid Clarrie might change her mind, she ran to the other side of the yard. Within minutes, Clarrie was surrounded by girls clamoring for chocolate biscuits. She handed them out, reserving the last one for herself. She was about to pop it into her mouth when Myra Tarrant held out an open palm. "I didn't get one."

"They're all gone. This is my last."

"Give us it and I'll let you come to my birthday party on Sunday."

Clarrie hesitated. The bell was ringing—a signal for the girls to form lines and march into school.

Clarrie dropped the biscuit into Myra's palm. "What time's your party?" she asked. When Myra didn't answer, she asked again.

"Three o'clock," Myra said. "You're supposed to bring a present."

"I thought you didn't like that girl," Clarrie's mother said.

"That's because she didn't like me."

"And now she does?"

"She must have changed her mind. She says I have to bring a present."

"It's bad manners to ask for presents. If that's the only reason she invited you, you shouldn't go."

"Everyone in my class is going," Clarrie said.

"Stay with Billy, then, while I do my errands. I'll see what I can find."

Clarrie was surprised to find Myra's house in one of the poorer streets where the houses had no gardens or bay windows and the front doors opened directly onto the pavement. She was surprised again when Myra answered the door dressed in her ordinary school clothes. In her pale green voile frock (her mother had sewed it for her by hand) with a matching green ribbon in her hair, Clarrie had thought she looked fine, but if nobody else was wearing a party frock she'd look silly. She handed Myra the tin of toffees her mother had bought for her to bring to the party.

"Happy birthday."

"Thanks."

Somebody called from inside. "Myra, come and hear what Doris said!"

"What?" Myra darted down the lobby, leaving Clarrie in the doorway. A sharp-faced woman, her drab hair flattened by a hairnet, came down the lobby.

"Was you invited?"

"Yes. Myra said . . ."

"You better come in and shut the door. The rest of 'em's inside."

Clarrie followed the woman through the doorway into a bare kitchen where a small coke fire smoldered in the grate. Three straight-backed chairs were lined against the wall. On the opposite wall, under the back window, an oilcloth-covered table was set with a plate of thin, dry-looking sandwiches, curling at the edges. There was nothing—not so much as a streamer or a balloon—to show that a party was in progress. Clarrie's hopes shriveled.

Myra came in from the back yard, followed by three girls from school. No one but Clarrie had worn party clothes.

"Gather 'round, everyone," Myra said. "I'm going to open my presents." Gasps of admiration went up as Myra unwrapped a string of glass beads, a bottle of purple scent, and a yo-yo. She hung the beads around her neck.

"I hope you like toffees," Clarrie said, as Myra tore the paper from her gift. "They're Quality Street."

"Ooh . . . yes! I love Quality Street." She popped one into her mouth and put the tin on the mantelpiece with the other gifts. "When is my party going to get started?" she asked her mother.

Myra's mother seemed none too sure how one went about getting a party started.

"Well—line up then, if you're all here." She pointed to the sandwiches. "Them butties is potted meat. Just take one apiece 'cause they've got to go 'round."

The girls stood around the table, nibbling politely and darting furtive glances at each other. They saw each other every day at school, but this was a party and they weren't sure what they were supposed to do.

Myra's mother took a cake out of a box and set it in the middle of the table. "My cake!" Myra squealed. Everyone gathered around the table to watch Myra's mother stick eleven tiny candles into the icing and light them. Clarrie recognized the cake as one that had been sitting, unsold, in the bakery window for several days. Myra's mother gave each guest a slice of cake and a cup of orange squash, then shooed them into the street.

"Play quiet," she said. "Mr. Tarrant's a knocker-up. He has to get up in the middle of the night to start his rounds. He gets proper ratty if he's woke up before he's had his sleep out."

Myra said that it was her party, so she would pick the games. They started a game of "Truth or Dare." Everyone took a turn, each girl choosing to answer silly questions about which boy they would like to kiss. Clarrie decided to accept a dare instead, but when her turn came, the girls began quarreling over what the dare should be. Myra's mother stuck her head out of the front door, and told them they were making too much noise and would have to go home. The party was over.

"Back already?" Clarrie's mother said. "How was the party?"

"Myra's mam gave us each a meat-paste butty and a slice of cake and told us to play outside. We were making too much noise, though, so she sent us home. Mr. Tarrant's a knocker-up and he has to get his rest."

"Sounds too bloody hilarious for words," her father said.

On her way to school the next morning, Clarrie caught sight of Myra walking with Hilda Peacock on the other side of the street. Clarrie waved, but Myra and Hilda had their heads together. "Myra, wait for me!" she called. She would avoid mentioning the party in case Hilda felt hurt that she hadn't been there. Clarrie dodged behind a passing horse and cart and darted across the street. Myra didn't look up at Clarrie's greeting.

"You'll never guess what she had the nerve to give me for my birthday," she said in a loud voice to Hilda. "A lousy tin of caramels—it couldn't have cost more than threepence!"

Clarrie stopped, not sure she'd heard right. Hilda kept her eyes focused on the ground. The blood pounded in Clarrie's temples.

"You told me you liked them!"

"Talk about cheap!" Myra said to Hilda. "My mam would only let me invite four; I should have picked you instead of her. I bet you'd have given me a better present than that."

Miss Hughes was droning on and on about Lancashire's role in the industrial revolution, and Clarrie, who'd been fighting tears all morning, was finding it hard to concentrate. She'd overheard Myra telling everyone in the cloakroom how mean and stingy Clarrie Hancock was and what a lousy present she brought to the birthday party. She'd heard them snickering. Nobody had stuck up for her. Had they forgotten how she'd given away all her chocolate biscuits, how they'd crowded around her begging for more? If she had the money she'd buy a whole bag of those chocolate biscuits and hand them out to everyone in the schoolyard. Then they'd see who was stingy.

Passing Timson's on her way to school the next morning, it occurred to her that it would be easy to pop in and order biscuits on tick. Mr. Timson would write it in his book, and at the end of the week her mam would pay the bill. Nobody would be any the wiser. She doubled back to the shop.

As she entered the schoolyard, she opened her bag and began ostentatiously munching a biscuit. Several girls left off playing and ran to her side. Clarrie freely dispensed her bounty. From the corner of her eye she saw Myra Tarrant glowering. Hilda stepped forward, her hand outstretched. Myra pulled her back. "You don't need her old biscuits. Tell her to keep them."

"Let me go!" Hilda said, breaking free.

When the bell sounded, several girls thanked Clarrie as they ran to join their queues. Clarrie smiled. "My pleasure," she said. The Bible was right, it was more blessed to give than to receive.

The next morning when she gave her order, Mr. Timson frowned as he opened the tick book. "What is your mam doing with all these fancy biscuits?"

Clarrie avoided his eyes. "We've had a lot of visitors lately," she muttered as Mr. Timson handed her the bag. It might be wise not to buy any more biscuits for a while, she thought as she walked to school.

On Friday, when she got home, her mother and father were sitting silently by the kitchen fire. Billy was at the kitchen table crayoning something.

"What's everyone being so quiet about?" Clarrie asked.

Her father folded his newspaper. "We want to talk to you, young woman."

Clarrie felt a sick flutter in her stomach. They'd found out.

"Mr. Timson says you've been over there three or four mornings buying fancy chocolate biscuits on tick. Your mam and I want to know what you have to say about it."

"Chocolate biscuits?" The words ended in a squeak. "On tick? No, not that I remember—well—just that once when Mam sent me to get some for Arthur's birthday."

"There, you see." Her mother rose from her chair. "Timson's been padding the bill and when I caught him at it, he blamed it on our Clarrie. If he'd said it was Annie, I might have believed him."

"You're sure it was only one time?" Her father was watching her closely.

"Monday, I think it was." Her glance slid towards the lobby. "Can I hang up my coat?"

"Keep your coat on. You're going over there to settle it."

Clarrie glanced desperately towards the stairs. Perhaps she could faint. "I . . . I'm supposed . . . I have to write a composition."

"This is more important." Her mother's mouth was set in a determined line. Clarrie was trembling. She cautioned herself to stay calm and stick to her story. Whatever happened she must not cry.

Mr. Timson was standing behind the counter in his white coat. At the sound of the bell he looked up quickly and then went back to weighing a slab of cheddar cheese for Mrs. Robertson.

"That'll be one and sevenpence, love. It's a little bit over." Mrs. Robertson handed him the money and put the cheese in her shopping bag. With a smile and a nod all around, she left the shop.

Clarrie's mother stepped up to the counter. Clarrie hung back.

"Come on. You've nothing to be afraid of," her mother said. Clarrie stepped forward.

"Mr. Timson," her mother said, "our Clarrie here says she never ordered biscuits except for one time, last Monday, when I sent her for them. She doesn't tell lies, so I think you've made a mistake. Perhaps you accidentally wrote it in the wrong column."

Mr. Timson arranged a gauze cover over the wheel of cheese, then carefully wiped the knife on a damp cloth. His pink face was expressionless. "It wasn't a mistake." He looked straight into Clarrie's eyes. "Tell your mother the truth, Clarrie."

Mr. Timson's eyes were blue and clear. They seemed to be looking straight into her soul. She held her face rigid, trying not to blink. She must not break down. The silence hung in the air between them.

"Tell her," Mr. Timson said.

With a wail, Clarrie abandoned the struggle. "I'm sorry. I'm sorry, Mr. Timson!" Tears streamed down her cheeks.

Her mother stared at her as though she had suddenly grown horns. "I don't believe it!"

"Don't be too hard on her, Mrs. Hancock," Mr. Timson said. "She's learned her lesson. She won't do it again, will you?"

Her mother gave her a shove towards the door. "Get on home this minute, you little devil," she hissed. "Embarrassing me like this. You've got some explaining to do." She glanced over her shoulder. "I can't tell you how sorry I am, Mr. Timson. It isn't like her to be underhanded. I can't think what got into her. I'll be back as soon as I can to settle up the bill."

"No rush," Mr. Timson said.

When they got home, Clarrie's father put down his newspaper. "Well? What did he have to say for himself ?"

"He didn't say anything. It was this child who was lying. I've never been so mortified."

Her father glared at Clarrie over his glasses. "You may well cry, young woman. Stealing wasn't bad enough, I suppose; you had to lie about it, too. You'd better get upstairs to bed, before I do something I'll be sorry for. I'll deal with you tomorrow."

"She hasn't had her tea yet."

"She can do without. You're too damn lenient with them, that's the trouble."

Clarrie got into bed with her clothes on. Gradually her sobs subsided. Fragrant cooking smells rose from the kitchen. She heard Annie and Arthur come home, and then the sound of laughter and the clatter of dishes. They were enjoying their tea without her. A lot they cared that she was up here starving.

After a while, she heard the front door slam shut. Her father must have left for work. Soon she heard a creaking on the stairs. Her mother pushed open the bedroom door.

"Sit up. I've brought you something to eat."

"Dad said I wasn't to have anything."

"Yes . . . well . . ." Her mother put the tray on the bedside table. "He was angry with you. That was a terrible thing you did. And there was I blaming poor Mr. Timson. I swore up and down you would never do a thing like that—and for a few chocolate biscuits!"

"I didn't eat them myself—well, just one. I gave the rest away."

"Gave them to who?"

"The girls in my class." She started to cry. "I wanted them to like me."

Her mother sat down on the edge of the bed. "Friends who can be bought are not worth having." She plumped Clarrie's pillow. "Sit up and eat your dinner. I can't have you getting poorly again. I'll be back in a little while to get your tray." She stopped at the door. "There's no need to mention this to your dad."

Clarrie, who'd been about to tuck in, put her fork down. It made her feel even more guilty to see her mam going behind Dad's back like this. But the stew looked and smelled delicious—it was one of her favorite dinners, too—lamb, carrots, onions, potatoes, and dumplings, all drenched in delicious gravy. Her mam had gone to the trouble of carrying it upstairs. She would be very upset if Clarrie didn't eat it. Clarrie picked up her fork.

She was jolted awake by a loud, angry voice. Her father had come home from work upset about something. She glanced at the bedside table. The tray was gone. Had he found out about her mother bringing her supper? She got out of bed and tiptoed along the landing to listen. He was talking about something that had happened at the rink. ". . . bloody tables with a loaded tray—boiling hot tea—Eccles cakes, everything—all over the damn place."

"I thought you'd memorized where the tables were."

"Aye, so I did. Some busy bugger shifted 'em around without telling me."

"Was anyone hurt?"

"No, thank God. But I'm finished at the rink. He says he can't take the chance of it happening again; I didn't even see the damned thing—my mind was on summat else."

"Never mind, love. We'll manage somehow. Sit down and have a cup of tea."

Clarrie tiptoed back along the landing with a leaden feeling in her stomach. Had her dad been worrying about the bad things she'd done? Was she the reason he'd crashed into that table and got the sack?

Chapter Twenty-three

Clarrie awoke to the sound of rain pinging into a tin bucket The roof in her bedroom had sprung another leak. As soon as breakfast was over, her father, who had scarcely said a word during the meal, left the house, saying he was going to the machine shop where Arthur had just begun his apprenticeship as an armature winder. He hoped to find a job there for himself.

Her mother left shortly afterwards, taking Billy with her. Mr. Hutchins had asked her to mind the shop while he took care of some business at the abattoir. In the meantime, Clarrie was to do her usual Saturday jobs—except for stoning the steps. Her mother said there was no sense doing that in the pouring rain. She was not to leave the house until Annie got home from the mill at half-past one.

Clarrie had almost finished her tasks when Annie burst in, dripping wet and in an evil temper. Her hair, coat and stockings were plastered with cotton fuzz. In an attempt to placate her, Clarrie asked how everything was at work.

Annie pushed aside a tin of Brasso and a heap of grimy rags. "I hate the damned place and everyone in it," she said. "Get this muck off the table. Where's my dinner?"

"It's warming in the oven."

Annie wolfed down her plate of stew, then plunked herself in her father's chair, lit a cigarette, and clapped her hands for Clarrie's attention.

"Fetch me the bowl, flannel, soap, towel, hairbrush, comb, and the big mirror from the lobby. I'm going out tonight with Jessie. There's a dance at the Sale Lido, and I want to look my best."

The mirror was shield-shaped, framed in dark mahogany and so heavy it was all Clarrie could do to lift it from its hook and carry it into the kitchen. Annie was perched on the table by the window, where she could get the full benefit of the feeble light. She told Clarrie to stand in front of her and hold the mirror high while she plucked her eyebrows and searched for blackheads.

"I need to improve my complexion," Annie said. "Jessie says it looks muddy."

Clarrie studied Annie's face. "It looks all right to me." She was not fond of Jessie. She'd once overheard her compliment Annie on the way she'd trained Clarrie to obey. "I wish I could get our Donald trained like that," Jessie said. "I don't know how you do it."

"You have to be firm," Annie replied. "Let 'em know who's boss."

Clarrie brooded long over that exchange. How dare they talk about her as if she were a dog being trained to fetch! It was her own fault for being such a coward. She must learn to stick up for herself.

Annie's beauty routine was taking longer than usual, and the mirror was growing heavier by the minute. "Hold it higher. I can't see a flaming thing."

"The mirror's too heavy for me. Why can't you use Dad's shaving glass?"

"It's too small. Shut up and hold it higher."

Clarrie raised the mirror an inch or two. The pain in her shoulders was excruciating.

"Higher!" Annie pushed Clarrie's arms up. "Higher, you stupid nit."

"It hurts my arms."

"Stop whining and hold up the damn mirror."

Clarrie's arms were trembling from the effort. She struggled to keep the glass from slipping from her fingers, but she could hold it no longer. The glass tilted, hitting Annie on the head. With a yelp of pain, Annie fell sideways.

"Annie!" Clarrie pushed the mirror aside. "I'm sorry, I'm sorry! Are you all right?"

Annie opened her eyes and stared at Clarrie with a dazed expression. A trickle of blood ran from her nose. "What are you trying to do, kill me?"

"The mirror slipped."

"Slipped?" Annie sat up, dabbing at her nose. "You slammed it on my head, you little liar." She stared at the blood on her handkerchief. "Look what you've done."

"I told you it was too heavy for me. I couldn't hold it. I'm not holding it for you anymore, so don't ask me."

Annie slapped her across the face. "You'll do as I say, you cheeky devil. If I tell Mam and Dad what you just did, they'll pack you off to reform school, or to the lunatic asylum."

"It couldn't be any worse than living with you!" Clarrie shouted. She ran out through the wet yard and took refuge in the lavatory.

It had been raining for days, the slate-colored sky blending into the roofs of the houses, so that one scarcely knew where sky left off and roofs began. Clarrie was late getting home from school. She had stopped at the library to return *The Blue Fairy Book* and select *The Water Babies*. The librarian allowed children only one book at a time so Clarrie found it necessary to pay frequent visits.

Ordinarily, she'd have started her book while she walked home, but since it was still raining she wrapped the book in a black oilcloth bag she'd brought for the purpose. As she walked, she searched the road for lost coins or other treasures, but found only crumpled cigarette packets and sodden fish and chips wrappers bobbing along the streaming gutters. In the middle of the street, where the cobbles were sinking, the rain gathered in oily puddles. Clarrie stirred a puddle with her foot; a dark rainbow swirled, making intricate patterns across the surface. A rainbow in the sky was a sign that God would never again destroy the world. What was a rainbow in an oil puddle a sign of?

At the corner of Thurlow Street, opposite Timson's grocery, water was gushing from a broken roof-spout.

"A crystal cascade!" Clarrie cried. She set her bag down on the garden wall and stepped into the torrent, gasping as the cold water hit her face. "Cascade" a lovely word. She'd come across it first in a poem called "The Highwayman." In it, the landlord's daughter's hair was described as a black cascade of perfume.

Behind closed eyelids, Clarrie watched the highwayman canter along the moonlit road on a black stallion. She was Bess, the landlord's daughter—tied and gagged by the Sheriff 's orders so she couldn't warn her lover. Suddenly Bess heard the clop-clop of hooves on the cobbled courtyard, and knew her lover was approaching. She struggled to free herself from her bonds. She must warn her lover that he was riding into a trap, but her cries were muffled by the gag in her mouth. The ropes chafed her wrists and ankles; the musket barrel they'd placed at her chest was digging into her ribs. Clarrie tightened her finger on an imaginary trigger.

The shot rang out across the courtyard. The highwayman's horse whinnied and reared. The highwayman, unaware that his sweetheart was dead, wheeled around, and spurred his horse to a gallop, leaving the landlord's daughter slumped over the musket barrel with a black cascade of perfume rippling over her bloodstained bosom . . .

"Clarrie Hancock. Get out from under that water, you'll catch your death of cold." Mrs. Barlow eyed her sternly from under a black umbrella. Clarrie stepped away from the gushing spout.

"Just look at you. You'll be lucky if you don't come down with pneumonia. Get on home, before I tell your mother what you've been up to."

Clarrie pushed her dripping hair from her face. "I was already soaked."

"Soaked! So she stands under a spout to get even wetter!" Wagging her head and clucking her tongue, Mrs. Barlow walked away.

Coming down with pneumonia might not be so bad Clarrie thought as she walked home. She could stay in bed all day, reading—and she'd have time to write her own poems and stories. The backyard door was bolted shut. She jumped up, catching the top of the yard door with raw, wet fingers, then scrambled up and over and dropped into the yard. Sliding back the bolt, she picked up the book she'd set down on the step. The scullery door was unlatched. The house smelled of soap and bleach. Wet washing was strung from wall to wall across the kitchen. Clarrie picked a scrap of brown paper from the table—a note written in her mother's firm, round hand.

Mrs. Hutchins has sent for me. Something's wrong at the shop. See to the fire and lay the table for tea. Billy's with Mrs. Phipps. Be back soon as I can. Love, Mam.

Clarrie peeled off her sodden coat and threw it on a chair. The fire was nearly out and the coal bucket in the hearth, empty. She ran down to the cellar to fill it. While she was shoveling, she heard someone step on the lid of the coal-hole overhead. Good! Mam must be home. She lugged the bucket up the steps into the kitchen and was surprised to find her father standing in the lobby doorway, glowering at her. He took off his bowler hat and poured a trickle of water from the brim.

"Where the hell is your mother? Why did you let the fire go out?" He barged into the room heading for the fireplace and became entangled in a line of wet drawers and knickers. He yanked at the rope, pulling the nail from the wall and sending the clothes flying. "Damn washing all over the place!"

He grabbed the bucket out of Clarrie's hand and tossed the coal onto the fire. A cloud of ashes and coal dust flew out in their faces. "Don't stand there gawping. Shut the flaming door." He removed his jacket and draped it over a hook, tugging at the sleeves. "Where's your mother?"

"Hutchins's. They sent for her."

"Bring me a towel, and dry your hair, child, you look like a drowned rat."

"There aren't any dry towels," Clarrie said. The towels were on the floor, with the rest of the wash.

"Find me summat else, then." He pushed the cat out of his chair and sat down. He unlaced one of his boots and eased it off. Beneath a film of rainwater, the boot gleamed with polish. From inside the boot, he removed a wad of black and shredded cardboard and tossed it into the fireplace. "I might as well be a flaming coolie."

Clarrie rummaged in the dresser drawer. These days her father was always angry—especially if her mother was out when he came home. She'd heard her mother complaining about it to Mrs. Phipps. "I don't know what's got into Mr. Hancock. He expects to find me when he walks through the door, standing right where he left me. You'd think I'd nothing better to do."

Mrs. Phipps nodded her head, and said that her old feller was the same. Men were all alike, the gormless buggers.

But Clarrie understood how her father felt. She, too, wanted her mother there when she came home. She handed her father a torn pillowslip from the sideboard cupboard.

"Ta." He peeled off his wet socks and removed his spectacles to examine the chilblains on his toes. His feet were red and narrow, the second toe longer than the first. My feet are just like his, Clarrie thought. Everyone said she took after her mother—and it was true that she had the same round face and rosy cheeks—but lately she'd been noticing the many ways in which she was like her dad. They had the same slender hands, the same grey-green eyes—his good eye, anyway—and the same silky, fawn-colored hair. They were alike in another way, too. It was hard to pin down exactly what it was, but it had to do with not being satisfied—with wanting more out of life than life seemed prepared to offer.

Her father finished drying his feet, and handed her the pillowslip. He stuffed paper through the bars of the grate. Flames flared up and quickly died. Together they stared gloomily at the curling, blackened paper.

"It didn't catch," Clarrie said.

"I can see that." He removed his spectacles and wiped away a film of ash. "Get yourself dry—make yourself useful. Set the table or summat. You're nine years old, aren't you? Old enough to know what to do, without being told."

"I'm only eight," Clarrie said. She rubbed her hair and tried to stop her teeth from chattering.

"Where the devil is your mother, then? She ought to be home by now. Go to the parlor window and see if she's coming down the street."

Clarrie went into the front room and moved aside the half-curtain at the bay window. A woman was rounding the corner into Wynford Street, but it wasn't her mother. She could tell her mam's walk a mile away—she walked quickly, pointing out her toes and swinging her right arm as if she was rowing.

Clarrie went back into the kitchen. "She's not there."

Her father broke into a fit of coughing. "She ought to be home by now," he muttered. "I've got this bloody bronchitis to contend with, on top of everything else."

Clarrie wished her mother would hurry. She loved her dad, but being alone with him was like being lost. At the sound of the big iron key rattling in the front lock, Clarrie and her father turned expectantly towards the lobby. Her mother came in with Billy, slumped over her shoulder asleep.

William dropped the poker in the hearth. "Where the hell have you been?"

Her mother put her finger to her lips, pointed to Billy, and carried him upstairs.

"Where were you?" he repeated when she came down again.

"Hutchins's. Didn't you get my note?"

She twisted several sheets of newspaper and laid them in the grate. "Fetch me a firelighter, Clarrie, they're under the sink."

"I thought today was your day off," William said.

Sally laid the paraffin-soaked bundle of sticks on top of the twisted paper, placed coals on top and struck a match. The fire burst into flames. Her father lit a cigarette with a flaming scrap of newspaper.

"Fill the kettle, Clarrie." Her mother wiped her fingers on the pillowcase and began picking up the clothes strewn about the floor. "I like the way you treat the clean washing. It took me all morning to do these." She piled the clothes in a wicker basket and set them in the corner behind William's chair.

"What's the matter with you?" he asked. "I come home soaked to the skin after trudging the streets all day looking for work, and what do I find? You're out gallivanting—bloody fire's out—washing dripping all over the damn place." He waved a hand towards Clarrie who was kneeling by the fire, drying her hair. "This one skulking about like a drowned rat."

"Albert Hutchins is dead."

Clarrie pushed the hair away from her face and stared at her mother. "Did you say Mr. Hutchins is dead?"

Her father paused, his cigarette halfway to his mouth. "What happened? Was it a heart attack?"

"Suicide."

Suicide. A memory surfaced—a hot summer day in the park—a stinking lavatory—flies buzzing over the muck. One of the stall doors had been nailed shut. Wasn't that the day she'd broken her wrist and collarbone?

"He didn't go home last night," her mother said. "They found him this morning when the missus went over to the shop." Her voice cracked. "It was terrible, Will. He hanged himself from a meat hook. It took three bobbies to cut him down."

A picture of roly-poly Mr. Hutchins, swinging like a side of beef, flashed unbidden into Clarrie's inner eye. She stifled a giggle. Her mother frowned.

"Mr. Hutchins is dead. It's not a laughing matter."

"I know," Clarrie said. "I'm sorry. I couldn't help it." She turned away, struggling to control her unseemly giggles.

"He was one of the nicest people you could wish to meet," her mother said.

"What made him do a thing like that?" her father asked.

"He was bankrupt."

"Bankrupt. Well, I'm not surprised—letting every Tom, Dick, and Harry have meat on tick the way he did."

"And now, I suppose, they'll never settle up. Mrs. Hutchins won't be able to pay me until everything is sorted out. I told her not to worry about it. He'd have given away his last penny if somebody asked him."

"He gave me pennies, sometimes," Clarrie said. "But I never asked for them."

Her mother opened the dresser drawer and tossed Clarrie one of Annie's old frocks—beige wool with sweat stains under the arms. "Take those wet clothes off. Put this on."

"It's too big for me."

"Put it on. You're not going anywhere."

"There'll be an inquest, I suppose," William said.

"I suppose. They'll say it was suicide while the balance of his mind was disturbed. That's what they always say. I suppose it makes them feel better. But there was nothing wrong with his mind. He was just too softhearted, poor fellow."

"It's a coward's way out, all the same."

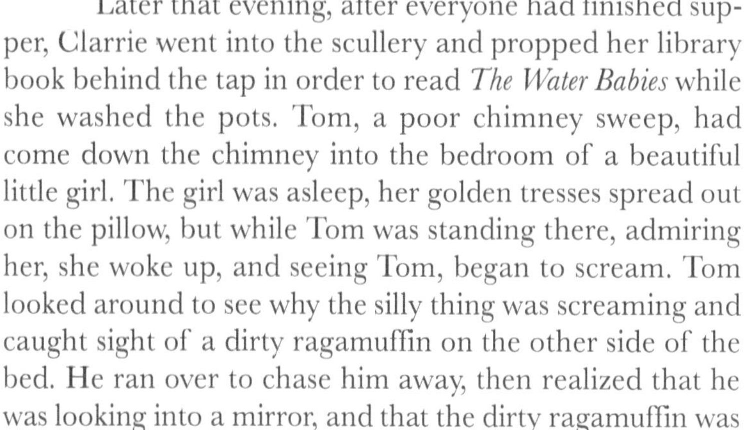

Later that evening, after everyone had finished supper, Clarrie went into the scullery and propped her library book behind the tap in order to read *The Water Babies* while she washed the pots. Tom, a poor chimney sweep, had come down the chimney into the bedroom of a beautiful little girl. The girl was asleep, her golden tresses spread out on the pillow, but while Tom was standing there, admiring her, she woke up, and seeing Tom, began to scream. Tom looked around to see why the silly thing was screaming and caught sight of a dirty ragamuffin on the other side of the bed. He ran over to chase him away, then realized that he was looking into a mirror, and that the dirty ragamuffin was himself!

The tears she'd been unable to shed for Mr. Hutchins rolled freely down Clarrie's cheeks and plopped into the washing-up water. She leaned across to dry her face with the tea towel and caught a glimpse of her reflection in her father's shaving glass. Her round face was smeared with coal dust, her snub nose red and swollen from crying, and a lock of her hair was stuck together in a clump where she had sucked on it. She stuck her tongue out. "What are you sniveling about?" she said. A fresh welling of tears blurred her reflection. She turned the glass to the wall, then lifted the edge of the sooty lace curtain and peered into the dark yard. It was still raining. The wet iron frame of the mangle gleamed. The clothesline hung slack—empty but for a solitary washcloth, dripping and drooping like a discouraged flag.

Chapter Twenty-four

Clarrie and her mother were on their way out of the chapel when Mr. Bassington, the new Methodist minister, bore down on them, his large, good-natured face wreathed in smiles. He asked them to please wait in the vestry as he had something important to discuss.

"I can't imagine what he wants with me," Clarrie's mother said. Mr. Bassington had gone, at her behest, to comfort Mrs. Hutchins after Mr. Hutchins's death. The minister was a kind-hearted, sensible man, Mrs. Hutchins had said afterwards; he'd assured her that since her husband had led an exemplary life, doing all that God required of him, God, in His infinite mercy, would no doubt forgive him his moment of despair. He'd had no qualms about giving Mr. Hutchins a Christian burial.

"Perhaps he's worried about Mrs. Hutchins and wants me to keep an eye on her," she said. "I don't know that I can be of much help. She's got her sister with her now, and she'll be moving to Blackpool soon."

At that moment, Mr. Bassington walked in, motioned Sally to a chair, took his seat behind the desk and clasped his large hands together over the blotter.

"I'll come right to the point, Mrs. Hancock. Our caretakers, as you may have heard, are about to retire. The work has become too much for them, and we need immediate replacements. Mrs. Hutchins happened to mention that, as a result of her—um—recent misfortune, you, Mrs. Hancock, now find yourself without a job. I understand that your husband—I have not yet had the pleasure of meeting him—is also out of work. We need a husband and wife team—a man to handle the heavier work, stoking the furnace, pumping the organ for Sunday services and so on, and a woman for the general cleaning. The salary is modest." Mr. Bassington raised his hands in a regretful shrug. "—but any port in a storm, as they say. In short, I'd like to offer you and your good man the post of joint caretakers here at the chapel. Do you think your husband would be agreeable, Mrs. Hancock?"

Sally nodded as she got to her feet. "I think he'll be only too glad of it, Mr. Bassington, but I'd better ask him first, just to make sure."

"Splendid!" Mr. Bassington spread his fingers on the edge of his desk and rolled away his chair. "Have him come to see me tomorrow, nine o'clock sharp. We'll see if we can't settle the matter."

"So this is how I end up, is it?" William said when he heard the proposal, "a flaming caretaker at everyone's beck and call."

"It'll put food on the table," Sally said, "and I'll still be able to do for Mrs. Perlman. Perhaps now, with Annie and Arthur bringing in a few bob, we'll be able to make ends meet."

"Aye," William said. "If you don't give it away to every blasted tramp and organ grinder who comes knocking at the door. A chap I know told me those chalk marks we found on the gatepost were left by Gypsies to tip off their pals that this house is a good place to stop."

"Surely you don't begrudge anyone a mouthful of bread?"

"The Bible says you should cast your bread upon the waters, Dad," Clarrie said. "And it shall return to you after many days."

"It'd be a bit soggy by then," Arthur said.

The chapel was a solid Victorian building with a balcony, a massive organ, and a great clock tower, all of which had been badly neglected. While their parents worked, Clarrie and Billy explored the chapel, climbing up the narrow staircase into the clock tower, playing hide and seek in the cavernous cellar, among broken cane-bottom chairs, wobbly blackboards, and mildewed leather kneeling cushions.

Clarrie took a proprietary interest in the improvements her parents were making. In addition to the maintenance work, her father pumped the chapel organ for the Sunday services and choir practices. He decorated the rooms with streamers and balloons for the Christmas parties, while her mother helped prepare mountains of sandwiches, shimmering jelly molds, and bowls of creamy custard, and when the parties or meetings were over, both her parents stayed, cleaning up after the volunteers and everyone else had gone home.

Sometimes, on Saturday evenings, after scrubbing her hands thoroughly with carbolic soap, Clarrie was allowed to cut the bread into tiny cubes for the Lord's Supper. She felt honored to have a part in these sacred preparations and thought that her parents were almost as important as the minister.

The money coming in had brought a measure of relief at home. Unfortunately her father's gold watch and her mother's wedding ring had stayed too long in the pawnshop and couldn't be redeemed, but the green bobble-edged cloth was back on the table, and their picture, "A Stag at Bay" returned to its perch above the mantelpiece. Clarrie and her mother spent one Saturday afternoon shopping at the Cross Lane Market, and came home with three striped bath towels and a set of six matching cups, plates, and saucers, decorated with an ivy design. The house was looking cozier, and what was more important, everyone, except Annie, seemed to be in a better mood.

Whenever she and Clarrie were alone, Annie spat forth a running stream of commands—ordering Clarrie to brush the fluff off her coat, fill the coal bucket, run upstairs and fetch her hairbrush. Clarrie obeyed from force of habit, but could never obey quickly enough to suit Annie.

"Are you going to fetch me the damn hairbrush or aren't you?"

"I'm reading. Why don't you get it yourself ?"

"I've been on my feet all day, you cheeky little bitch!"

"Well, I'm not your servant, stop ordering me around."

When Annie slapped her, Clarrie slapped back—an act of defiance that goaded Annie into a fury which invariably ended in an all-out battle. They were struggling in a corner of the kitchen one day, when their father came in from the lavatory.

"Stop that flaming racket," he roared, "before I crack your heads together!"

"I can't understand what's got into them," Sally said, when William complained to her of their behavior. "They used to get along so well."

Clarrie could keep silent no longer. "No, Mam, we never did. Our Annie's bossed me around all my life. You can ask Arthur if you don't believe me. I'm not letting her do it any more."

"Annie's a lot older than you; I've had to depend on her to take care of you and the baby."

"I'm the one who takes care of Billy, not her!"

"It may seem like that to you, love, but . . ."

"Why won't you believe me?" Clarrie shouted. Couldn't her mother see that this was not an ordinary squabble? Couldn't her mother see that she was fighting for her life!

But Annie suddenly stopped making her demands. Clarrie attributed the change to Annie's having left the job at the mill and taken a more agreeable job at the bakery. In a starched white overall, with her red-gold curls peeping out from her starched cap, she bustled happily about among the sparkling glass cases laden with pastries, ringing up sales in the cash register, flashing her toothy smile at the customers. Whatever the reason for Annie's change of heart, Clarrie was profoundly grateful for it.

As Whitsuntide approached, Sally and William worked overtime preparing the chapel for the Whit Sunday celebrations. Sally looped paper flowers around the velvet ropes—designed to keep the smaller children from straying during the Walking of the Scholars. William built a platform with ascending rows of benches covered in white satin for the children's choir. When the congregation filed out after the service, Clarrie heard one of the women comment that it was the first time she'd been able to watch the children's faces as they sang.

"My dad built that platform," Clarrie said.

The lady smiled down at her. "Well, you can tell him from me that he did a splendid job."

Outside, in front of the chapel, the congregation was assembling for the Whit Sunday Walking of the Scholars. The boys were larking about, vying for the privilege of carrying the banner poles. Clarrie was pleased to see Richard Beaumont among the chosen. She'd met him just a few weeks ago when she'd come upon him standing in front of the newly posted honor roll. He'd turned and smiled at her.

"Are you trying to see if your name's on here? What is it?" When she told him her name he'd shaken her hand like a grownup and said, "pleased to meet you." Then he'd pointed to the top of the board. "Yes, here you are, below me, with the Aitches."

After that, whenever they met, in Sunday school or in the street, he'd smiled at her in a way that sent a delicious shiver down her spine. She'd known right away that she loved him. She loved everything about him—the smile that revealed a chipped front tooth, the thick brown lock of hair that kept falling across his forehead. His face lit up whenever he ran into her. She felt sure he would soon declare his love and ask her to be his sweetheart.

Mrs. Jackson, one of the ladies in charge of the scholars walk, had come out of the chapel and was weaving through the crowd, choosing the ribbon girls. Clarrie closed her eyes and crossed her fingers for luck. There were several banners, each with four ribbons to be held. She had never been picked to hold a ribbon, but she looked nice in her new bonnet and being the caretaker's daughter ought to count for something.

When she opened her eyes, Mrs. Jackson had already passed her by and was bearing down on Muriel Monk. Muriel's blue ankle-length taffeta was fastened at the waist with a white sash. Her imitation silver crown sparkled like diamonds in the sunshine.

"Muriel, I want you in front, with the lead banner," Mrs. Jackson said. "Doesn't she look lovely?" she murmured to one of the other teachers.

"Gorgeous," said the other woman. "She's the spit and image of Shirley Temple."

Clarrie suddenly felt plain and dowdy. The green voile frock, and the new straw bonnet she'd been so proud of, could not hope to compete with Muriel's blue taffeta gown and silver-crowned yellow curls.

The parade was starting. In the forefront, behind one of the large banners, came the members of the small chapel band, shaking tambourines and blowing trumpets to the tune of Onward Christian Soldiers. The spectators clustered along Eccles New Road waved at them as they passed by. The day was unusually hot. The sun beat down, melting the pitch between the cobblestones. With every step she took, Clarrie's white shoes accumulated more sticky black tar. The ladies were mopping their faces and complaining of the heat. As they passed the Waverly Hotel, one of them fainted, bringing the parade to a confused halt. After she was revived with smelling salts, the grownups decided it was best to cut the parade route short and return to the chapel for refreshments.

When Clarrie came out of the kitchen where her parents were busy serving sandwiches and lemonade, she spotted Richard Beaumont surrounded by a group of admiring friends—boys mostly. They were passing around Richard's red-leather autograph book. Richard was looking about, searching for someone. He wants me to sign his book, Clarrie thought.

She was racking her brains for something to write—something beautiful that would reveal her love.

A shout of laughter went up from the group. Someone had written something funny in his book, but she was too far away to hear what it was. Suddenly, Richard reclaimed his book and strode towards her. His friends, following close on his heels, jostled for position. Clarrie shrank back, the lemonade glass shaking in her hand.

Richard's eyes were bright with laughter. "Where's my girl? Where's my sweetheart?" he said. "She was here a few minutes ago."

Clarrie's heart hammered so loudly she was sure everyone must hear it. She stepped forward. "Here I am."

Richard turned to one of his friends and shrugged. The friend sniggered.

"Not you," Richard smiled at Clarrie. "I'm looking for Muriel Monk. Have you seen her?"

"It's the caretaker's kid, Clarrie whatsername," someone whispered.

"I was kidding," Clarrie mumbled. She fled down the corridor to the lavatory, and collided with Muriel Monk coming out of the stall.

"Richard Beaumont is looking for you," she said as she brushed past.

Muriel hadn't bothered to flush. Clarrie pulled the chain, lifted the smeared lavatory seat with her foot, and sat down on the cold porcelain rim. She banged her fists against the sides of her head. Stupid . . . stupid! Why had she stepped out like that, saying, "Here I am!" She'd made a complete fool of herself. Nobody had believed for one minute that she'd been joking.

What sort of a boy was Richard Beaumont, anyway, falling for a brainless girl like Muriel? What would he think of his precious sweetheart if he knew about her dirty habits? There ought to be some way to let him know. She could send him an anonymous letter, but he'd be sure to guess who'd sent it, and he'd despise her for it. She'd despise herself.

Clarrie snatched off her new bonnet, threw it against the lavatory door, grabbed a clump of hair and tugged it from her scalp. She stared curiously at the silky strands lying limp across her palm. Why had she done that? The roots reminded her of the roots of a green spring onion.

Chapter Twenty-five

"Clara Hancock!" Miss Hughes flung open her study window and called to Clarrie in the schoolyard below.

"Yes, Miss."

"Wait there for me, please. I wish to speak to you." Miss Hughes withdrew her head.

Clarrie squatted, her back to the wall. What had she done now? Had the headmistress heard about that report on *Tom Sawyer?* She'd described Injun Joe as a half-breed, but Miss Jepson had crossed out the words "half-breed" and written "half-caste." When Clarrie tried to explain that Injun Joe was an American Indian, not the other kind, Miss Jepson had ordered her to stay after school and write "I must not contradict my teacher" one hundred times.

Clarrie couldn't think of anything else serious enough to have come to Miss Hughes's attention—unless she was still upset about that snowball Clarrie had rolled through the streets all the way to school. The ball had grown enormous, picking up ice and grit along the way. Two other girls had helped roll it the last few yards, but when they'd tried to push it through the narrow schoolyard door it became firmly wedged. Miss Hughes, emerging from her car at that moment, had been obliged to wait in the cold while the girls clawed ice and dirt away from the sides in order to force the huge ball into the schoolyard.

"I imagine this is some of your doing, Clara Hancock," she said. Clarrie admitted it was. Miss Hughes made a tutting sound and wagged her head as if in despair. "I thought I recognized your fine Italian hand."

The huge snowball had sat for days in the schoolyard, growing smaller and dirtier, until it finally vanished. But when nothing more was said about the incident, Clarrie thought the headmistress had forgotten it.

The cold wall was freezing Clarrie's back. She got to her feet, shivering as the wind cut through her too-short coat and whipped her bare knees

"Clara!"

Miss Hughes swooped down on her. Her spry little person was bundled from neck to boots in a fur coat, her wispy hair concealed under a matching fur hat. She clutched a leather attaché case, a handbag, and a black book.

"Sorry to have kept you waiting, Clara, my dear. I have good news for you. We have just received the results of the preliminary exam, and you passed with flying colors. You are eligible to sit for the secondary school finals.

The words "flying colors" set Clarrie's heart dancing. For a moment she seemed to be swirling, weightless as a dust mote, through a beam of light.

"Did you hear what I said?"

"Yes, Miss." If she passed the finals, she could go to secondary school, Tootal Road perhaps.

"Well . . . what have you to say?"

"Thank you, Miss."

The pointed tip of Miss Hughes's beak nose was turning pink. She shuddered and drew her fur collar tightly about her neck. "Walk with me to my motor car, and we can talk as we go. My sister is waiting—she will be wondering what has happened to me. Carry my attaché case, please, Clarrie, and take this book. The book is for you."

"Thank you, Miss." Clarrie said again. She wondered if the book was meant as a present—a reward for doing well in the preliminaries?

"I want it back, you understand."

"Yes, Miss."

Clarrie examined the book. Across the black leather spine, in gold lettering, was the word *Algebra.*

"You skipped a standard at some point, did you not?" Miss Hughes said.

"Yes, Miss, twice. But I was out ill for a long time, so I was put back."

"But you are now eleven, am I right?"

"No, Miss. I just turned ten."

"I see. Strictly speaking, you're not supposed to take the examination until you reach eleven."

Clarrie held her breath. Was the gift to be snatched away so soon?

"They occasionally make exceptions. This year, the results of the preliminaries were most disappointing. Only you and Lillian Potter passed, out of the whole school, so it is of the utmost importance that you both do well."

"Yes, Miss."

"Miss Livesey tells me that you are still working with ratios and have not yet started algebra."

"Yes, Miss."

"There may be questions about algebra. I want you to take that book and study at home. You haven't much time, but if you apply yourself . . ."

They crossed the street to Miss Hughes's motorcar. It was the only car on the street, black and shiny, with a lot of steel grillwork in the front. Clarrie was tempted to ask if it was a Rolls Royce or a Daimler. Motorcars in books were always one or the other. Rich people in books had uniformed chauffeurs named Stebbins or Withers, who opened doors and carried parcels from Harrods or Fortnum and Masons. When she grew up, she intended to shop in those places and have lunch at the Ritz afterwards. A posh motorcar like this was wasted parked along the dirty gutters in School Street. It seemed strange that a rich woman like Miss Hughes chose to live in Salford and work at Tatton Memorial School. She was old now—forty at least—and she wasn't married, so the school was probably the most important thing in her life.

Clarrie shuddered. When she grew up she would live in London or Paris or New York. She would be a famous dancer or a film star, or, better still, an authoress. She would marry a handsome gentleman with a country estate and a town house in London. Failing that, she might decide to be an explorer—or a missionary in Africa, like David Livingstone.

"Here is my sister, waiting patiently," Miss Hughes said.

A woman who looked exactly like Miss Hughes but with a different shaped fur hat, was sitting behind the wheel with the motor running. She glanced at them briefly and looked away as though trying to hide her annoyance. Miss Hughes opened the car door. "Just one moment, Freda." She closed the door and turned to Clarrie. "Miss Livesey tells me you are hoping to get into Tootal Road?"

"Yes, Miss."

"It is an excellent school . . . one of the best Salford has to offer, but it is not for everyone. You'll be obliged to buy a uniform and, ah . . . other things."

"Yes, Miss." Clarrie knew all about the uniforms, and the other things, too. Last spring she'd broken her leg jumping off the lavatory roof on a dare. She'd been on the way to the hospital with her mother, to have a plaster cast removed from her leg, when they passed a group of Tootal Road girls on their way to school. Everything about those girls—their ties, their hatbands, the school crests on their blazer pockets, the book-filled satchels strapped to their shoulders—drew Clarrie like a magnet. It was as if the illustrations from all the school stories she had ever read had come to life. She wanted, more than she had ever wanted anything, to be one of them.

"I understand your father is out of work?" Miss Hughes said.

"No!" Clarrie said quickly. "He's the caretaker at the Methodist Chapel—my mother, too. They're both caretakers."

"Caretakers? Well, that's very commendable." Miss Hughes opened the door and got in the back seat. She pulled a purple and green plaid blanket across her knees and leaned toward Clarrie through the half-opened door. "I have some misgivings, Clara. Granted, you made an excellent showing on the preliminary test, but you are not yet eleven, and I believe you are rather weak in arithmetic."

"Yes, Miss."

"These things can be overcome, if you have the will, but I'm afraid you are a dreamer, a procrastinator, and given to acting on impulse. If you are ever to amount to anything, you must first learn to control yourself. Strive—strive for excellence."

"Yes, Miss."

"Please remember to return the book to me as soon as the examination is over."

"Yes, Miss."

Miss Hughes closed the door and the car began to move forward. Clarrie ran after it and knocked on the window. She held up the attaché case. Miss Hughes opened the car door again and stretched out her hand.

"Silly me, I very nearly went off without it." She looked at Clarrie sadly and shook her head. "I wish we had more time, but I suppose it can't be helped. Do your best for the honor of the school." She raised her hand and wagged two fingers at Clarrie as the car pulled away.

Clarrie ran home, her scarf streaming behind her in the wind, her feet barely touching the ground. She scrambled over the backyard door, through the yard and into the scullery.

"Mam!" She pushed open the door to the kitchen. "Anybody home?"

No sound but the dripping of the scullery tap. They must be still at the Chapel. She tossed her coat on a chair and squatted in front of the range. The fire had burned down to a few red embers, filling the hearth with ashes. She shoveled on coal—a small amount so it wouldn't smother the embers—and prodded until a wavering yellow flame appeared. As soon as the fire caught hold, she poured milk into a saucepan and stirred in cocoa and sugar. Gritty lumps of cocoa floated on top. She poured the mixture into a cup and drank it while searching the cupboard for something to eat. Lately she was always ravenous. Nothing but salt, HP sauce, a cup of dripping, four brown eggs nestling in a bowl of sugar to keep them from breaking, and a lone pickled onion in a jar of vinegar. She lifted the wire toasting fork from its hook, speared the pickled onion, and popped it into her mouth. Behind the tea caddy, at the back of the shelf, there was a fresh cottage loaf. She tore the crusty, dimpled knob from the top, impaled it on the toasting fork, and held it to the bars of the grate. When it was nicely browned, she spread it with beef dripping. Lovely. She sprinkled it with salt and took a large bite.

Mister Purrkins, a tabby cat who had strayed one day into the backyard and refused to leave, jumped down from the chair. Mewing, he rubbed against Clarrie's legs. She threw bits of dripping toast onto the enamel hearth plate and watched as he ate them. The milk bottle was almost empty; she poured what there was into a saucer. Purrkins barely gave her time to set it in the hearth before he began to lap. The only time this cat came near her was when he wanted something. She was there to serve him. No wonder the ancient Egyptians thought cats were gods. "Food for the gods," she said, stroking his silky back. Her voice sounded strange in the quiet room. Talking to yourself was supposed to be the first sign of lunacy; she didn't believe it. But then how did an ordinary person become a lunatic? Violet Fawcet's mother was a lunatic. She'd been dragged out of her house and taken to the asylum for pouring a kettle of boiling water over Mr. Fawcet while he slept. Mr. Fawcet had spent weeks in the hospital before coming out with his face all red and lumpy. Violet had stopped coming to school. Clarrie shook her head to send the thoughts away. She didn't want to think about Violet Fawcet.

"The milk's all gone," Clarrie said when Purrkins came back mewing. "If you really were a god, you could say abracadabra and have all the milk you wanted."

The gods of ancient Greece ate and drank nectar and ambrosia. She imagined nectar to be some sort of golden syrupy stuff, like the juice in a tin of peaches. Ambrosia must be like the trifle her mother had made the Christmas Aunt Ruth and Uncle Gerald came to visit.

Her mother bought all the ingredients on tick—cherries, almonds, whipped cream, sherry, and she was still paying for it long after the guests had gone back home to Kent. It had been well worth it, though, her mother said. When treats are hard to come by, you appreciate them more. Clarrie wondered if the gods ever tired of ambrosia. They might have welcomed a change once in a while—some plain old bread and dripping, or fish and chips with a dash of vinegar.

Purrkins gave up weaving around her legs and settled himself by the fire to clean his whiskers. She stroked his narrow head. "This is my lucky day, Purrkie." The cat closed his eyes. She tapped him on the head. "Hey . . . I'm talking to you Mister Purrkins." He turned and fixed her with a cold stare. Green and gold spokes radiated from the narrow black pupils; strange, inhuman eyes. She could gaze into those eyes from now until doomsday and learn nothing. "Are you trying to put a spell on me, you wicked cat?" She was not sure she liked him, after all. The cat blinked and turned away as if he had read her thoughts. She wished her mam and dad would come home so she could tell them the good news. It occurred to her that there was no need to wait—she could walk to the chapel and find them.

Her father was sweeping around the entrance with a large broom. Dust and torn papers blew around him. In spite of the chill wind, he was in his shirt, with the sleeves rolled up above the elbows. He hadn't even bothered to button his waistcoat. She couldn't remember ever before seeing him outdoors without his jacket and bowler hat.

"Hello, Dad," she said. "Where's your jacket?"

He stopped sweeping and straightened his back. Wisps of putty-colored hair waved about his head. He peered at her as though he didn't recognize her, and she saw that he wasn't wearing his spectacles. A milky film covered the pupil of his blind eye; on either side of his nose, where his spectacles had pinched him, the skin was red and sore.

"Where are your specs, Dad?" she said. "You know you can't see without them."

"I dropped the bloody things—cracked the good lens. What are you doing here, anyway?"

"I passed the prelims. I was one of only two girls in the whole school."

"You passed the what?"

"The preliminaries—to go to secondary school. I told you about it, don't you remember?" A little whirlwind, carrying dirt and scraps of paper, blew between them. They turned, quickly, in opposite directions, shielding their eyes.

"You should fasten your waistcoat, Dad, you're going to catch your death of cold," Clarrie said.

"Hold this for me." He handed Clarrie the broom. From his trouser pocket he took a small box of Woodbines, withdrew one and put it between his lips.

"You should smoke Minors, Dad, they're better," Clarrie said. The advertisements for Minors cigarettes showed a beautiful lady standing in a theatre lobby. A handsome man dressed in evening clothes was offering her a cigarette. Underneath the picture it said "Ten minutes to go, so mine's a Minor."

Her father took a box of matches from his trouser pocket. With a hand cupped against the wind, he struck the match. As he bent to light the cigarette, a vein, like a small blue snake, appeared in his temple, throbbing as though it were about to burst out and wriggle free. His hands—long, slender and bony—moved with precision and grace. The inside of the first three fingers of his right hand were stained a deep, yellowish brown. With his thumb and fingernail he flicked away the smoking match. He inhaled deeply on his cigarette and broke immediately into a fit of coughing. Shyly, Clarrie patted him on the back until the coughing subsided.

"Thanks, love." He picked up the broom and began sweeping again. "The flaming wind is blowing it all back at me," he said.

"Where's Mam?"

"Inside somewhere—the kitchen. What do you want her for? Why aren't you at home making yourself useful?"

"I just wanted to tell you and Mam about my test." She hesitated a moment, wondering if he had heard her.

"Well, she's inside," he said.

Squinting, and with the cigarette dangling from his lips, he continued sweeping. Bent over the broom like that, he looked much smaller than he did at home.

She pulled open the heavy oak doors and passed through the narthex into the nave. Before her parents began working here, the whole place had smelled of dust and mildew; now it smelled of Mansion Polish. The red carpet down the center aisle was spotless, the windows sparkled, the pews and choir stalls and mahogany pulpit gleamed. Freed from years of accumulated grime, the massive organ pipes lining the wall above the altar shone. Her dad had spent days up on a ladder, scraping away the dirt. Clarrie took a deep, appreciative breath. She felt better—safer—when things were clean and in order.

Since Mr. Bassington's arrival the chapel bustled with cheerful energy. The sermons were lively—last Sunday he'd thumped the Bible so hard, he'd sent loose pages flying into the congregation, and then he'd made everyone laugh by telling them not to be "wazzers." A "wazzer" was somebody who was about to accomplish something, but never did. Clarrie fervently hoped she wouldn't turn out to be a wazzer.

Clean though the chapel was, there was something missing here—something Clarrie found only in church. She thought it might have to do with the way the light filtered through the church's stained glass windows. Here in the chapel, the windows were plain glass, and now that her father had cleaned them, you could see straight across the yard to a brick wall plastered with peeling advertisements for Beecham's Pills and Keating's Flea powder.

"In my Father's house are many mansions," she whispered. Did that mean that all the churches and chapels in the world were acceptable to God, or that there was room enough for all different kinds of people in heaven? She climbed the three small, curving steps into the pulpit and surveyed an imaginary congregation. An enormous gilt-edged Bible, bound in black leather, lay open at Ecclesiastes. She read aloud, trying to make her voice boom like Mr. Bassington's.

"Vanity of vanities, saith the Preacher; vanity of vanities, all is vanity. What profit hath man of all his labours wherein he laboureth under the sun?" She stopped. What if she got struck by lightning for entering the pulpit and pretending to be a minister? God didn't call girls to preach—except for Joan of Arc, perhaps. He called people like Mr. Bassington and the Reverend Mr. Witherspoon.

Her dad didn't think much of either of them. She'd heard him complaining to her mam that Mr. Bassington was a bloody gasbag. That was because Mr. Bassington always blocked the exit after the service, chatting and joking and not letting anyone pass without a bone-crushing handshake, and her dad had to wait until everyone was out before he could lock up.

Clarrie thought Mr. Bassington was nice. Whenever he noticed her, he patted her on the head and told her to keep up the good work. She imagined God to be a sort of cross between Mr. Bassington and her mother. She wished her dad believed in God, because it would help her to believe in Him, too. She knew lots of hymns and prayers, she'd read many of the stories in the Bible, and in school she'd memorized the ten commandments and the catechism. Why was it then that at home with her family, all her certainty about God vanished like smoke into thin air? According to the Bible, God had spoken to people in the past. Why should He now choose to remain silent and invisible? He could ease her mind in a jiffy if He wanted to.

"Give me one little sign," she whispered. She closed her eyes and waited. Nothing but a clatter of pans from the kitchen. She climbed down from the pulpit and ran along the corridor. Her mother was at the sink scouring a large roasting pan. She looked at Clarrie through a cloud of steam. "What are you doing here?"

Billy, his plump face rosy, his silvery blond hair shining, was on the floor playing with a musical top. Clarrie knelt down by his side and took the top out of his hands to show him how to work it. She pumped the top until it sang and spun out across the floor. Billy started to cry.

"Give it back to him." Her mother said. She began jabbing at the pan with a knife

"I just wanted to show him how to do it."

"He was playing quite well by himself. And that top belongs in the infants' room; we have to put it back before we leave." She rinsed the pan and examined it. "The volunteers were supposed to clean up after the potato pie supper last night, but they left it for me to do. I'll never get this thing clean."

Clarrie hauled herself up onto the draining board.

"Don't perch up there," her mother said. "You look a mess, child. There's cocoa or something all over your face. And when are you going to stop sucking on your hair? It looks like straws on a muck cart."

"I passed the prelims," Clarrie said, swinging her legs. "Now I just have to pass the finals."

Her mother stopped what she was doing. "Well—good for you. That's very nice, love."

"Only me and Lillian Potter passed. Out of our whole school."

"Lillian Potter and I. Your dad will be proud of you when he hears about it."

"I already told him. He's outside sweeping. He didn't say anything."

"Yes—well, I expect he's tired. We've been here all day slaving our guts out, and we're not finished yet."

"Miss Hughes lent me a book on algebra to study."

"I hope you're not getting your heart set on going to Tootal Road. We can't afford those school uniforms."

"But . . . I thought now that you and dad are both working . . ."

"This job doesn't pay well. We don't bring home much more than I did at Hutchins's."

"I can get a job after school, cleaning or running errands or something."

"We'll see. Get down now. Make yourself useful. Take a duster out of that cupboard and dust the vestry."

They stopped at the fish shop to buy codfish for dinner. Clarrie reminded her mother to buy milk.

"Is that milk finished already?"

"I gave the last of it to the cat."

As soon as they got in the house, her mother sat Billy on the three-legged stool and set him to scraping salt from the block with a fork. She told Clarrie to pour milk into a saucepan and stir it, while she peeled the potatoes and chopped the parsley.

"If I go to Tootal Road, I'll have to take a bus."

"Watch that milk. Keep your mind on what you're doing."

The milk bubbled over into the fire. Her mother grabbed the pan out of Clarrie's hand.

"Must I do every blessed thing myself ? Get your head out of the clouds, child. Come down to earth."

While Clarrie was setting the table, her father walked in, wearing his jacket and bowler hat. "Dinner not ready yet?"

"I've only one pair of hands," her mother said.

Annie arrived home from the bakery looking pleased with herself. She handed her mother a white cake box tied with string.

"What's this?"

"Chocolate gateau. Some old biddy squashed it when she put her shopping bag down. She refused to pay for it, so they said I could take it home."

Her mother lifted the lid. "Lovely, that'll be a real treat."

"The boss says I'm doing well. They're teaching me how to ice and decorate."

"Wonderful," her mother said. "Who knows, you might be a manageress one of these days." She set aside a heaped plate of steamed fish, boiled potatoes, parsley sauce, and peas for Arthur, and called the others to the table.

"I passed the preliminaries," Clarrie told Annie. "That means I can take the finals. I might go to Tootal Road."

Annie held a thumb and forefinger to her nose. "Snobs. Stuck up, the lot of them."

"How do you know?" Clarrie said, "have you ever met any of them?"

"I wouldn't go to that school if you paid me."

"You wouldn't get the chance."

"Cheeky bitch." Annie reached over and tugged Clarrie's hair.

"Watch your language, our Annie," Sally said. "You got out of that mill just in time, I'm thinking."

William put down his knife and fork. He had mended the glass in his spectacles with a strip of sticky tape and had to peer over the top in order to see anything. "Can we have a meal in peace for once?"

"She started it," Clarrie said.

Her mother put an extra piece of fish on Annie's plate. "Our Annie's been working hard all day. She has to put up with a lot of things you know nothing about."

"Just wait until she has to do it," Annie said.

"One more word out of either of you, and you can both leave the table," William said.

They ate in silence, until it was time for dessert.

"Look at this lovely cake our Annie brought us," her mother said.

"It's called a gateau," Annie said.

"If it looks like a cake, and tastes like a cake, it's a bloody cake," her father said.

By the time Arthur got home from work, they had finished tea and were clearing the table. Arthur's face and overalls were black with grime. He had cut his hand at work and the injured hand was wrapped in a soiled bandage.

"I've had a rotten day," he said, "I've had to do everything with my left hand."

Sally helped Arthur out of his jacket. "Just look at this poor lad," she said. She sent Clarrie to the scullery for a bowl, some soap, and a clean flannel. Her mother poured hot water from the kettle. "Let me know if that's too hot, love," she said to Arthur.

Arthur's hand was large, with square-tipped fingers, the nails black and broken. The palm, when he turned it over, was covered in cuts and calluses. Sally washed and dried his hands and bandaged the cut. Clarrie took the bowl into the scullery.

"What's up with you, our Clarrie?" Arthur said when she came back. "How is it you're not over here pinching my spuds?"

Clarrie walked over and leaned against his back. "I passed the prelims; I might go to Tootal Road next year."

He turned his head and smiled at her. "Blimey, our kid's going up in the world. We'll need a permit just to talk to you."

Annie let out a snort of disgust. "Most of 'em are common as muck. They may fool themselves, but they don't fool me."

Clarrie reached over Arthur's shoulder and stole a piece of potato. Arthur caught her wrist with his bandaged hand. “Put that spud back,” he said. “You toffs are all alike—taking bread out of the mouths of the workers.”

Clarrie popped the potato into her mouth. “Let ’em eat gateau.”

“I’m the one who provided that cake,” Annie said, “not you, even though you do fancy yourself as Marie Antoinette.” She put on a simpering expression. “I’m going to Tootal Road. I’ve got to have a uniform . . .”

Clarrie looked away as tears sprang to her eyes. She’d be thrilled if anyone else in the family brought home good news. Why couldn’t they be happy for her?

Chapter Twenty-six

Clarrie worked steadily through Saturday morning. By noon she had washed and disinfected the chamber pots, cleaned the lavatory floor, the back steps, and the windowsills with donkey stones, and was free to spend the afternoon studying for the exam. After lunch, while the rest of the family were out, she settled herself at the kitchen table with a pencil, a partly used ledger her father had brought home from the chapel, and Miss Hughes's copy of *Algebra*.

She read the introduction to the black book, and skimmed through the first chapter. The paper was brittle, the print small, and the whole thing incomprehensible. She had no wish to be a mathematician or an engineer, so why did she need to understand it? Because, she told herself, if she didn't, she might not pass. Everything she'd ever hoped for depended on passing this exam. It was her chance of getting into secondary school—her chance to better herself. Failure meant she would have to leave school at fourteen and go to work in the mill, or in some local factory. She'd be stuck there for the rest of her life. That must not happen. She had a very different life in mind.

No matter how long and how intently she stared at them, the symbols in the black book refused to make sense. They might as well be Egyptian hieroglyphics, but she had no Rosetta stone. She rubbed her eyes and looked away. A stain on the wallpaper had taken on the likeness of a gruesome face with glaring eyes and a huge bulbous nose. Ever since she could remember, faces such as this had glared at her from the folds of the curtains, the cracks in the linoleum, the smoldering cinders in the fire. She fancied they were shadowy presences watching from some malevolent spirit world. What did they want of her?

She felt drowsy, as if a heavy hand were pressing on the back of her neck, forcing her head down. She was about to succumb to sleep when she heard a knock at the door. Margie Barlow was standing on the front step, small wads of soiled cotton-wool sprouting from her ears. She jiggled a white paper cone, sending out a tantalizing smell of chocolate-covered toffee. "Banana split," she said. "I'll give you sub if you'll cub out and blay." Margie had a perpetually stuffy nose. The sun came from behind a cloud. Shrill voices echoed from the back street—the kids were playing rounders. It might clear her mind, Clarrie thought, to take a little break . . .

That evening, after the tea things were cleared away, and the washing up done, Clarrie seated herself at the table and with renewed determination opened the black book. "Who knows anything about algebra?" she asked, "How about you, Mam? Can you tell me what they're going on about here?"

Her mother looked over Clarrie's shoulder. "I'm afraid it's all Greek to me, love."

"Give it here," Arthur said. "Let me take a gander at it."

"What does this mean?" Clarrie pointed to the page. "A and B in brackets like that, with those fractions? How am I supposed to add and subtract letters?"

"You're supposed to find the unknown number."

"How do I do that?"

"Keep your shirt on, I'm trying to sort it out for you."

Annie grabbed the book out of his hand. "Let me have a go." She licked her thumb and forefinger and riffled through the pages like the man in the pawnshop counting a wad of pound notes. "It's a lot of gibberish. I don't think they want ordinary people to understand it." Clarrie took the book from Annie and passed it to her father.

"How about you, Dad, do you know what they're asking me to do?" She was surprised he hadn't volunteered to help. He was usually more than willing to explain things. With a sigh, he put down his *Salford City Reporter.*

"Where did you get this book?"

"It belongs to Miss Hughes."

"Suppose summat got spilled on it? What does it tell you in the Bible, eh? 'Neither a borrower or a lender be.'"

"I think that's Shakespeare, Dad. Miss Hughes lent it to me . . . she thinks algebra might be on the test."

"And as usual you've left everything to the last minute."

"Our class hasn't even had algebra, yet."

"I was out earning my own living by the time I was your age. If I wanted to know anything I had to teach myself."

"What do they mean by 'the unknown number'?"

"If you've a barrel of apples but you don't know exactly how many, you've got an unknown number, haven't you?"

A small light dawned and quickly faded. "But what do A and B have to do with it?"

Her father handed the book back to her. "Speak to your teacher; she'll be the best one to explain it."

But on Monday, it was Miss Smallwood, the plump, motherly woman who taught penmanship and needlework and escorted the girls to Halton Bank School for their weekly housewifery classes, who greeted them as they took their seats.

"Good morning, girls. I'm sorry to tell you that Miss Livesey has been taken ill—this dreadful flu. She'll probably be out for several days." Miss Smallwood riffled through a book at her desk. "Where are you up to with your sums?"

Several girls raised their hands to tell her.

"Ratios? Oh, dear! Well, I hope you all understand your ratios well enough to work quietly by yourselves. I have other work to attend to." She began erasing chalk marks from the blackboard. Clarrie raised her hand.

"Yes, Clarrie? Don't tell me you have to leave the room already?"

"No, Miss. Miss Hughes gave me this book last Friday, to learn algebra for my exam, but I can't understand it. She said Miss Livesey would help me."

Pulling in her stomach and buttocks as far as she could, Miss Smallwood moved sideways between the rows of desks. Her ample breasts pressed softly against Clarrie's shoulder as she bent to examine the book. Clarrie felt tempted to lean back and rest her head against the warm bosom. As though sensing her impulse, Miss Smallwood suddenly straightened up.

"I'm afraid I haven't the time to go into it with you, Clarrie. It's not my cup of tea. You must just do your best, try to study at home." She eased herself back along the row, leaving a whiff of Yardley's lavender in her wake.

Chapter Twenty-seven

Clarrie lay in the dark bedroom, listening to Annie's steady breathing. From downstairs came the smell of frying bacon. Her eyes flew open. The test! This was the day of the test! She slipped out of bed, and ran downstairs to dress. Her mother was standing by the bars of the grate, toasting bread.

"What time is it?" Clarrie asked. "Why didn't you wake me up?"

"I was just about to bring you a cup of tea."

"I don't want to be late."

"You've plenty of time. You got everything ready last night, didn't you?"

Clarrie nodded. Before going to bed, she'd had a bath, washed her hair, and replaced a missing button on her white blouse. Her dad had polished her shoes and threaded them with new laces. Her mother had cleaned and pressed her navy serge gymslip and her coat—banging the flatiron down over an ammonia-soaked cloth, filling the kitchen with choking fumes.

"I packed your lunch. It's in there, with your scratch paper and pencils and your carfare." Her mother nodded to the wooden cigar box where they kept tiddlewinks and dice.

"Arthur sharpened your pencils for you. That's all they said you were to bring." Her mother took a plate out of the oven. "There you go, love, tuck in."

Clarrie stared at the heaped plate—two rashers of bacon, an egg, fried tomatoes, two slices of toast. Normally she'd have loved a big breakfast like this, but not this morning.

"I can't eat all this, Mam."

"They said be sure to eat a hearty breakfast."

Her mother put a steaming cup of tea in front of her and slid the sugar bowl across the table.

"Drink your tea while it's hot." Clarrie gulped the milky tea and picked at her egg.

"I don't know what I'm supposed to do—where I have to go or anything." She swallowed the last of her buttered toast. "What if I can't find the right place?"

"Stay close to Lillian—she's older than you. She'll help you. And don't forget to ask the bus conductor to let you off at the right stop."

Clarrie put on her coat. Her mother slipped something in the pocket. "Your apple," she said. "It wouldn't fit in the box." She handed Clarrie the cigar box and tucked a scarf around her neck. "Better get on your way, then."

Clarrie lingered in the open doorway. "What if I don't pass?"

"It won't be the end of the world." Her mother scratched at the corner of Clarrie's mouth with her forefinger. ". . . a bit of egg."

"Well, here I go." Clarrie stepped out into the cold morning air.

The milkman's horse, clip-clopping down the street, had stopped outside the Barlow's house and was waiting while the milkman ladled milk into a small white jug that had been left on the doorstep. He covered the jug with a beaded doily before climbing back on his wagon. The horse, which seemed to know when to move without being told, set off again at the same stately pace, leaving a steaming pyramid of golden balls behind him. Nelly Barlow, the eldest daughter of the numerous Barlow clan, ran out of her house. She had a man's coat thrown over her flannel nightie and was carrying a shovel and a tin bucket.

"Morning, Nelly," Clarrie said.

Nelly grinned, revealing a row of teeth large and strong enough to have belonged to the milkman's horse.

"You've caught me out in my nightie. Don't tell anyone. They'll think I've been down on the docks with the sailors." She broke into a loud guffaw. "I want to get this horse-muck before a motor runs over it. It's a sin to let good manure go to waste."

"Right," Clarrie said, "I collect it myself sometimes." Nelly had shoveled horse manure by the ton for her sooty little garden, but year after year the only things that came up were a few nasturtiums and one straggling sunflower.

In spite of the cold air, Clarrie was sweating. A rancid taste kept coming up in her mouth. At the corner of Eccles New Road, she looked back toward the house. Her mother was standing in the doorway. Clarrie waved, and her mother waved back.

It was still not completely light out and the sky behind the giant chimneys of Howarth's Mill was an ominous red. Red sky at dawning, shepherd's warning—that meant it was supposed to rain before the day was over. She'd pay special attention to the weather on her way back and see if the saying was true. Silhouetted against the red sky, one of the mill chimneys spewed out a cloud of soot that fell like black rain on the houses huddled beneath. Clarrie thought Howarth's must be one of those dark, satanic mills they sang about in school.

She crossed the road where workmen were demolishing what was left of the old workhouse. It was to be replaced by flats for the people from condemned houses in the slums, her father said. A small group of people had gathered to watch the big iron ball swing out, crashing into the side. An old woman cackled with glee. "Bloody good riddance to it, that's what I say."

The bus stop was crowded. Lillian was already there, standing off by herself. She was more than a year older than Clarrie and a whole head taller. Her hair, parted in the middle, hung in glossy, brown plaits over her shoulders. With her navy Burberry coat and her leather book satchel strapped to her back, she already looked the part of a Tootal Road girl. Everyone said Lillian was stuck up and thought she was it. Clarrie was a little in awe of her.

"Is this the right bus stop, Lillian?" she asked. She knew it was but wanted to make conversation.

"It better be," Lillian said.

"Do you think the test will be hard?"

"Hard enough, I suppose."

"Have you had algebra in your class?"

"Yes."

"I haven't. Can you tell me . . ." Clarrie's words fell on air as the bus pulled up and the crowd moved aside to let the people off. Lillian motioned to Clarrie to precede her in the queue.

Clarrie looked back over her shoulder. "I'm afraid I might not pass."

"I'll kill myself if I don't pass," Lillian said grimly.

Lillian, must be joking, of course. Clarrie turned to see if she could read Lillian's expression, but other people had come between them.

The crowd divided, some going downstairs and some upstairs. Clarrie usually begged her mother to let her sit on the upper deck. She went upstairs, chose a seat, and set her box on the seat next to her to save it for Lillian, but Lillian had apparently chosen to sit downstairs. The bus pulled out; Clarrie's stomach lurched. She tried to think if she'd said or done something to make Lillian want to get away from her.

The conductor came upstairs, bracing himself against the seats in order to turn the handle of the ticket machine strapped to his chest. His uniform was greasy. "Where to?" he asked.

"Tootal Road School. Will you tell me when we get there, please?" She handed him her fare, and he gave her a ticket. He hurried away, holding on to the backs of the seats as he swayed down the aisle. She wasn't sure he'd heard her.

The bus stopped outside Weaste Cemetery to pick up and discharge passengers, then pulled away and made a right turn onto another road. She wished now she hadn't come upstairs. What if the conductor forgot to tell her when to get off ? She might go past her stop and ride miles out of her way. Perhaps she should go down and make sure Lillian was still on the bus. As if they'd been waiting for a signal, several people got up and followed her down the steps. Just as the bus drew to the curb, the downstairs section was blocked by a crush of people getting off. The conductor, was trying to prevent others from getting on.

"Let these people off first, please," he said.

Clarrie was swept forward. People were pressing her from behind. She stepped down into the street, intending to wait until everyone was off, to ask the conductor if she had the right stop, but as soon as the last person stepped down, the conductor tugged the cord. The bus pulled away.

"Wait!" Clarrie shouted. The bus gathered speed. She ran after it through a trail of blue fumes, "Wait . . . wait for me!"

When she stopped to catch her breath, the crowd had already dispersed. There was no sign of Lillian, or of any building that looked remotely like a school. Running after the bus had given her a throbbing headache and made her queasy stomach worse. She said a quick prayer, furtively making the sign of the cross the way she had seen Kathleen Rourke do when a funeral passed by. She found the gesture deeply comforting.

An old man was coming towards her, walking a bulldog, and leaning on a cane.

"Excuse me, mister," she said, "can you tell me how to get to the Tootal Road School?"

The man raised an arthritic, freckled hand to his ear. "Tha's a reet bit out of thy way, lass." He jabbed the air with his walking stick. "Keep on down t'road—about a mile—mebbe more. You can't miss it."

Clarrie thanked him and began to run. What a stupid thing for her to do. Lillian was probably sitting at her desk right now, safe and sound, wondering what had happened to her. Her side ached, and her head was pounding. After a few more blocks, she saw a large, grim-looking building on the other side of the road. It had to be a workhouse, a prison, or a school. She crossed the road. To her immense relief, there was a sign above the main entrance, "Tootal Road Secondary School."

She pushed open the gates, crossed the yard, and climbed a flight of wide steps. The doors were closed. She knocked and waited. No response. She turned the knob and stepped into a large, dim hall. The place seemed deserted. There was a strong smell of disinfectant—sheep dip—the same kind they used at Clarrie's school. It was far too quiet down here. The exam room must be upstairs.

She climbed the stairs, trying unsuccessfully to keep her shoes from clattering. At the top of the staircase a corridor stretched left and right. She turned left and passed a row of classrooms with etched glass panels in each door. All the rooms were dark and empty. She turned in the other direction. Where could they be?

At the faint sound of a woman's voice, Clarrie's heart lifted. She followed the sounds to the end of the corridor. The voice was coming from a room with double wooden doors, slightly ajar. She pushed one of the doors. A stout woman wearing a purple crepe frock was addressing the class:

"We will wait for five more minutes, and then . . ." A girl pointed at Clarrie, peeping around the door.

"Clara Hancock?" the woman asked.

"Yes, Miss."

"You're late. Come in and close the door, then take a seat at the back of the room."

The room was long and wide. Clarrie made her way past rows of occupied desks. One girl sat at each desk, and each desk was set apart, unlike the four-seaters Clarrie was used to. Each row was separated by an aisle. The girls she passed were all strangers to her. Clarrie found an empty desk and sat down. She put her cigar box on top of the desk. The others had taken off their coats and draped them over the backs of their seats. Clarrie got to her feet again and removed her coat. The woman in the purple frock came down the aisle and dropped a paper on her desk.

"My name is Miss Urquhart," she said. "I am the proctor. That means this examination will be under my supervision. The exam will be in three parts. This is part one—general knowledge."

Miss Urquhart's hair was black as coal and elaborately curled. She had a red birthmark covering half of one cheek. She sounded southern, Clarrie thought, like her mother's Kentish relations, but more la-di-dah. The expression in her eyes was not friendly.

Clarrie took a pencil from her box and opened the test paper. A plump hand with pink varnished nails shot out to close it.

"Not yet, if you please. I have not finished giving instructions." She walked back to her desk at the front of the room.

"You will begin when I say begin and stop when I say stop. Do not continue writing after I say stop. There will be no talking and no leaving the room for any reason until this part of the exam is finished. Anyone found cheating will be disqualified. Do you understand?" She lifted a watch from her desk and stared at the dial. "Begin."

The first set of questions was easy:

Explain in your own words the meaning of the following expressions:

A bird in the hand is worth two in the bush.
All that glisters is not gold.
Footprints in the sands of time.
To lock the stable door after the horse has bolted.

Quickly, she moved from page to page:

What are parallel lines?
Name the mountain range that forms England's backbone.
Name the present Poet Laureate.

She hesitated once or twice, not sure whether Rio de Janeiro was in Brazil or in Argentina, or whether the Twentieth Century had begun on January 1st, 1900, or January 1st 1901, but she took a guess, and continued on to the end without further difficulty. She put down her pencil. All heads were bent over their papers. The only sounds were the rustle of pages turning and the occasional clearing of a throat. Miss Urquhart sat facing the class—she was reading a book.

Clarrie cleared her throat, noisily. The sick feeling in her stomach was getting worse. Miss Urquhart looked up. Clarrie raised her hand. Miss Urquhart got to her feet and came down the aisle. "What is it?" she whispered.

"I've finished, Miss," Clarrie whispered back.

"Already?"

"Yes. May I start on the next paper?"

"Certainly not. Go over your paper carefully and try to fill in all the questions you haven't answered."

"I've answered them all."

"Then sit quietly and wait until the others are finished." She walked back to her desk, shaking her head.

Sour liquid rose in Clarrie's mouth. She was about to be sick. She clamped her mouth shut. Miss Urquhart had said they must not leave the room until the test was over. Did that mean over for her, or was she supposed to wait until everyone was finished? She raised her hand.

Miss Urquhart's eyes bulged as though she couldn't believe what she was seeing. "What is it now, pray?" This time, she didn't bother to lower her voice, nor did she get up.

"Please, Miss, I have to leave the room."

"For what reason?"

"I don't feel well, I have to go to the lavatory."

"You have managed to make quite a nuisance of yourself this morning, young woman. Since you have finished your paper, you may go, but I will tolerate no further disturbance from you. Be back here in ten minutes."

"Yes, Miss." Clarrie moved quickly down the aisle and out the door. She ran down the corridors searching for the lavatory. Was it perhaps in the schoolyard like it was at Tatton? She was halfway down the stairs when her stomach heaved uncontrollably and a gush of brown vomit hit the steps, splashing over her feet. The stench of vomit filled the hall, overpowering the smell of disinfectant. How was she to clean it up? She must find the lavatory—find a rag, or paper or something. Be back in ten minutes, Miss Urquhart had said. How would she know when the ten minutes were up? She opened a side door and ran down through the passages, searching for a cleaning cupboard . . . a supply cupboard where she might find a sheet of blotting paper . . . anything. There was nothing—and now she had to pee, too. She crossed the hall, pushed open the heavy outer doors and ran around to the back of the building. Several large dustbins concealed the view of a small garden with a birdbath. There was no lavatory. She darted behind the dustbins and pulled down her knickers, squatting to relieve herself. Her new knickers ought to be thick and fleecy enough to soak up most of the vomit. She stepped out of them and rolled them into a ball, shivering as the cold air touched her bottom. Thank God there was nobody around. She ran back inside, scooped up the vomit with her knickers as best she could, carried the dripping mess outside and threw it, knickers and all, into one of the dustbins. There was an inch or so of gritty water in the birdbath. She swished her fingers about in it, wiped them on her skirt, then made her way back to the classroom. The girls were still bent over their desks.

Miss Urquhart glanced at her watch. "You have been gone for more than fifteen minutes."

"I'm sorry, Miss, I . . . I didn't know where the lavatory was."

Miss Urquhart handed Clarrie a test paper.

"Begin," she said.

Clarrie opened the paper. Her heart sank. Algebra.

Perform the necessary operations and combine like terms: 4(d-7) + (d+2) (d-3).

"Perform the necessary operations?" What did that mean? She looked at the next question and the next. She glanced desperately around the room. Most of the girls were busy writing. Everything—her whole future, the honor of the school—depended on her passing this test, and she had no clue how to begin.

If she could get just a hint of the correct procedure, she might be able to work out the answers. On an impulse, she swept the pencil off her desk with the back of her hand. Miss Urquhart glanced up and frowned, then turned back to her book. The pencil rolled slowly across the aisle, coming to rest near the foot of the girl opposite her. The girl glanced down at the pencil, stared at Clarrie with pale, lashless eyes, and, without any change of expression, turned back to her paper.

Clarrie's palms were wet, and she was sweating profusely. If she were to bend down, she'd risk exposing her bare backside. She gathered the hem of her gymslip tightly about her legs, sank to her knees, and crawled across the aisle. Her fingers closed around the pencil. A blob of grayish-pink chewing gum was squashed against the underside of the girl's desk, and in the far corner, a spider waited in a dusty cobweb. Clarrie got to her feet. Her heart was hammering so loudly it seemed the whole room could hear it. Her eyes slid to the girl's desk.

Miss Urquhart swooped down the aisle and grasped Clarrie's shoulder. "What are you doing?"

"Please, Miss, I dropped my pencil."

"I believe you were trying to copy from this girl's paper."

Clarrie opened her mouth to speak, but no words would come. Everyone was looking at her. She began to shake. Somewhere in the room, Lillian must be watching and listening.

Miss Urquhart picked up Clarrie's paper. "I'll take this. You may sit down and be quiet. I'll deal with you later."

Clarrie sat, her face burning with shame. She hadn't wanted to cheat—cheating meant you'd copied the answers—it was the most shameful thing anybody could do. She'd only tried to get a hint about how to proceed. Miss Urquhart would never believe her, nor would she give her a chance to explain. She'd be disqualified, and everyone at home and at school would know about it.

A voice, compelling and urgent, spoke from deep inside her. "Run . . . run for your life! Get away from this room . . . do it now . . . run!"

She stood up, pushed her arms into her coat sleeves, and picked up her pencils. Miss Urquhart gasped, jumped to her feet, and started down the aisle towards her. Clarrie flung the pencils at Miss Urquhart as she darted past. Strong fingers closed around Clarrie's arm, sharp nails dug through the sleeves of her coat.

"Let me go! Get out of my way!" Tearing loose, she fled from the room, along the corridor, down the stairs and out into the street.

Her eyes were burning, her nose dripping, her whole body heaving with the violence of her sobs. The street, which earlier had been deserted, was now bustling with people shopping, gossiping, riding bicycles. Where was she? Which way should she go?

A young lad covered in coal dust, with a burlap bag draped over the back of his head, called to her from his perch atop a coal lorry. "What's up, chuck, have yer lost yer best friend?"

Clarrie stopped to catch her breath. Perhaps she should ask somebody? Three women were standing on the corner, their shawled heads close together, their shopping baskets over their arms. "The bloody nerve of her," one of them was saying loudly. "An old maid teacher telling me I don't know how to bring up my own children!"

A fresh wave of misery washed over Clarrie. She had left the cigar box with her lunch and her return bus fare on the desk. What should she do? Where could she go? She couldn't face her parents—or Miss Hughes either. But she could hardly wander the streets forever with no knickers on.

By the time she reached the end of the road she was shivering violently and there was a rumbling sound like a steamroller in her head. She wanted desperately to lie down and sleep. How far was she from the Hancock House? If she could find her way there, she could perhaps break in through the window and hide out until she decided what to do. She crossed at the corner, turned left and saw to her relief that she was back on Eccles New Road, near the familiar wrought-iron gates of Weaste Cemetery. Pushing open the gates, she made her way down the wide driveway into the heart of the cemetery.

The noise of the traffic fell away. The sky had darkened. Masses of black clouds were moving slowly across the horizon. It was going to pour. Red sky at dawning, shepherd's warning. The saying must be true. In the few hours since she'd noted the red sky, the bright hope of the morning had abandoned her.

Blinded by tears, she walked past the ornamental flower gardens that ran down the center of the lane, past the black marble mausoleum, past the statue of the bride who'd collapsed and died on the church steps in her wedding dress. The story had always struck Clarrie as unbearably sad, but now she almost envied that bride . . . Stumbling down the stony path, she reached the grassy mound near the ash tree—Janet's grave.

Clarrie knelt down, dug her fingers into the damp earth, and pulled out a clump of weeds. The earth around the roots was black and wet. A fat red earthworm wriggled out then dropped to the ground. She picked it up and flung it away in disgust. No wonder her parents did not like to visit the cemetery—it must have been unbearable to leave their little girl in the dark, cold ground and walk away. It mightn't be so bad to do as Janet had done, leave the world. Even if there was no heaven, it might be a relief just to fall asleep forever. Clarrie stretched out face down on the grave and closed her eyes.

Chapter Twenty-eight

She awoke to the patter of raindrops on her back. Where was she? Bits of grass and dirt had found their way into her mouth. She raised her head to spit them out, wincing as a throbbing pain struck behind her eyeballs. The events of the morning surged back. "Oh, God," she groaned. "What have I done?"

She sat up, shivering, and picked at the dirt and gravel embedded in her knees. Her neck was stiff, her whole body chilled. It was clear to her now that the idea of hiding out at the Hancock house was plain daft. Even if she managed to break in, the place would be freezing cold; there'd be nothing to eat, and her mam and dad would certainly have the police out looking for her.

She pulled the apple from her pocket and laid it on the grave. In this rich black earth, perhaps the seeds would take root. When she died they might bury her here, under an apple tree, close to Janet. But not yet. She wasn't ready to leave this world just yet. There was nothing for it, now, but to go home and face whatever was to happen.

The rain came pelting down as she made her way out of the cemetery. Her shoes squelched on the gravel, and she was soon soaked to the skin. The chapel clock struck three, adding its reverberating boom to the rumble in her ears. She'd thought it later than that—her parents would still be at work. On reaching the house, she hauled herself over the backyard door and dropped to the ground, landing with a jolt that sent a blinding pain through her head. The scullery door was locked. She dragged the ladder under the kitchen window and pushed it up with her fingertips, raising it enough to squeeze through into the kitchen.

The black algebra book was still on the kitchen table where she'd left it that morning. The fire was banked, barely glowing. She poked at the coals until a flame broke through, then curled herself into a ball on the rug. Steam rose from her clothes. She ought to take off her wet things, but she couldn't bring herself to move.

The steamroller was rumbling towards her. When she tried to run, her feet seemed to be stuck in black tar that covered her white shoes. High in the driver's seat of the steamroller, a man in a top hat operated a sort of lever. The great roller moved forward, looming over her, blotting out the light. Had he not seen her? The roller was about to flatten her into the tar and gravel.

"Mam!" she screamed.

"Shh, my love! I'm here." Her mother's face swam into view. She slipped a hand around the back of Clarrie's neck and raised her head, offering her a cup of water. Clarrie whimpered. Her mother lowered her head gently back onto the pillow. "Lie still. The doctor will be here soon." From out in the streets, a child's voice came clearly through the open window. "You rat. I'll get you for that . . . just you wait . . ."

Drifting in and out of consciousness, she was aware of being turned and washed with cool water, of being lifted, so that the damp sheets might be pulled from under her, of sputtering as water trickled down her parched throat. And one morning while her mother was bathing her, the rumbling in her head subsided, and the world came back into focus.

"Mam?"

"Yes, love?" Her mother dried her hands and touched Clarrie's forehead. "You seem cooler this morning. Are you feeling better, then?" She set the bowl of water aside. "Can you sit up? I'd like to brush your hair." Clarrie raised her head while her mother arranged a pillow behind her back.

"I'm hungry," Clarrie said.

"That's good. It's a good sign. You haven't eaten anything solid for weeks. Would you like some tea and toast?"

"Yes, please—with marmalade."

Her mother picked up the towel and washbasin and carried it downstairs, returning with the breakfast tray. "I put golden syrup on the toast. I'll get marmalade later, when I go out to do my errands." She set the tray in front of Clarrie and sat on the edge of the bed.

"Clarrie, your dad and I were wondering what happened to you that day of the test? What happened to your knickers?"

Clarrie began to cry.

"Never mind. I can see you don't feel up to talking right now."

"I threw up all over the stairs. I had to take my knickers off to clean up the mess."

"I thought it might be something like that." Her mother wiped a smear of syrup from Clarrie's chin. "Never mind, eh? It's all over now. We got a letter, you know, from those test people."

"A letter?" Clarrie's hands shook as she sipped her tea.

"They said you made a perfect score on the first part of the test." Her mother smiled. Her grey eyes were clear, free of condemnation. "Since you were only ten when you took the exam, perhaps they'll let you have another go at it next year."

Clarrie shook her head. "I can't go through that again."

Her mother took the cup and set it back on the tray. "No need to get upset. You can manage all right without any fancy schools." She got to her feet. "The important thing now is for you to get better. You've been very poorly, love. You had us scared to death. All your skin peeled off, don't you remember?"

Clarrie shook her head.

"You were rambling about being stuck in pitch—something about a steamroller. You had scarlet fever, love, we didn't realize it. And just when you were getting over it, you came down with yellow jaundice—red and yellow! Our Arthur said you must be doing your bit for the Labor party."

"Labor?" Clarrie said. "I thought dad was conservative."

Her mother held up a small mirror. "See how funny you look."

Clarrie looked. A yellow, thin-faced stranger gazed back at her.

"You'll look better once we get some nourishment into you. We'll have you back to school in no time."

Clarrie sank back on the pillow and closed her eyes.

The prospect of facing Miss Hughes had made her break out in a cold sweat.

Fighting an impulse to turn and run, Clarrie climbed the stairs to the headmistress's study and knocked on the glass-paneled door.

"Come in," trilled the headmistress. Clarrie opened the door. Miss Hughes looked up from her desk. She frowned.

"It's me, Miss, Clarrie Hancock."

"Speak up child. Why are you whispering? I can hardly hear you."

"Clarrie Hancock, Miss. I came to return your book."

Miss Hughes's expression cleared. "Clara, but of course! You've changed. I didn't recognize you for a moment. Come in, come in. Sit down." She took the book from Clarrie's hand. "Are you quite recovered, then, from the . . . er . . . scarlet fever, was it?"

"Yes, Miss. Jaundice, too. But I'm better now."

"Your mother stopped by some time ago, to tell me about it. It was most unfortunate, that you were taken ill in the midst of such an important examination. Lillian fared somewhat better. She was the only girl from our school to qualify this year."

Clarrie nodded. She remembered that Lillian had sworn to kill herself if she failed.

"—now that you are back with us, after such a long absence" Miss Hughes was saying, "you must put your shoulder to the wheel, and work hard to make up for lost time."

"Yes, Miss." Why was the headmistress being so nice to her? Could it be that she hadn't heard about the terrible thing she'd done?

Miss Hughes drew a sheaf of papers towards her and picked up a pen. "Well, Clara, if there's nothing more . . ."

Clarrie didn't move. What did she mean by "If there's nothing more?" Was she prompting her to make a confession?

Miss Hughes glanced up from her paperwork as if surprised to see her still there. "Run along, then, child," she said, "return to your class. Be sure to shut the door on your way out." She tapped her pen against a paperweight—a blue iridescent butterfly trapped in a ball of dusty glass.

Chapter Twenty-nine

Now that all chance of going on to secondary school was lost, Clarrie scarcely knew what to hope for. She had made a mess of everything. She had let down her school and her family. If anyone in the family were to succeed in moving up in the world, it would have to be Billy.

Billy was now five years old, and it had fallen to Clarrie to take him to school each morning and bring him home in the afternoon. Remembering Annie's harsh treatment of her when she was Billy's age, she resolved to be always gentle and patient with Billy, and to use her influence to steer him in the right direction.

"Don't forget to say your prayers every night," she told him as they walked home. "And whenever you walk by a church, remember to go in and pray."

"What if I'm in a hurry?"

"Just bow your head, or make the sign of the cross like the Catholics do."

"We're not Catholics."

"We're not *Roman* Catholics. Catholic means universal—and that means everybody, including us. Anyway, you don't need anyone's permission to make the sign of the cross."

To pass the time until her parents got home from work, she invented exciting games for Billy and herself to play. Sloshball was her favorite—it involved rolling the dustbin and the corrugated wash barrel, one to each end of the back yard, to serve as goals, and smacking a ball around the back yard with wet mops. Billy respected the rules she laid down, always remembering to take off his glasses before a game. Near-sighted though he was, he played well, moving quickly to slam the ball back to her and never whining when he got slapped with a dirty mop.

On days when it rained too heavily to play outside, she read him fairy tales, and stories from *King Arthur and the Knights of the Round Table,* just as Arthur had done for her. After extracting a promise from Billy to fight for truth and justice and never to back down when he was in the right, she had him kneel in front of her, on the three-legged stool, while she touched him on each shoulder with the fireside tongs, saying, "I dub thee, my royal knight, Sir William Hancock."

Sometimes her mother gave her fourpence to take Sir William to the matinee at the King's Cinema on Trafford Road.

Returning from one of these outings, and finding the rest of the family out, she and Billy discovered a bag of day-old custard tarts that Annie had brought home from the bakery. After they'd eaten their fill, Clarrie tried to persuade Billy to join her in a pie-throwing fight.

Billy shook his head. "We shouln't waste food."

"We'll throw just one each. These tarts are already a bit battered. Remember how funny it was when Laurel and Hardy did it? You laughed so hard you almost fell off your seat."

"You'll get in trouble, our Clarrie."

"I'll clean it up afterwards. You stand here," she pointed to the inside of the front door. I'll stand at the other end of the lobby. You go first, because you're younger." She held out a custard tart. "This may be the only chance we ever get to have a pie fight."

"You first, then," Billy said, reluctantly.

Clarrie walked to the other end of the lobby. She raised her arm.

Billy folded his arms across his chest and clamped his mouth shut, his eyes on the tart, waiting like a small, bespectacled Saint Stephen to be stoned.

"Here goes," she said.

Billy ducked; the tart sailed over his head, splattering against the inside of the front door.

"Your turn!" Clarrie said

"No. " Billy took off his glasses and polished them on his shirt. It was clear that nothing she could say would make him change his mind. With a sigh, Clarrie went into the scullery to fetch the washing up bowl and a rag. Billy was a bit too sensible at times, but still, she was proud of him. She couldn't help thinking that some of the credit for his strong character was due to her influence.

"There's never anything to do around here," Clarrie said.

Her mother was up on a ladder, cleaning the kitchen windows. "Why don't you find someone to play with?"

"There isn't anyone." Since Gladys died, there'd been nobody she could call a close friend, and Clarrie was pretty sure that even if Gladys had lived, they would eventually have drifted apart.

Her father looked up from the cobbler's last, where he was mending Arthur's work boots. "Help your mother, if you want something to do."

"I've done all my jobs."

"Why don't you play with Billy?"

"He's playing with Noel."

"What about Maisie Barlow?" her mother said. "She's always knocking at the door, looking for you."

"She's too young for me."

"Read your book, then."

"It's boring. I think I've outgrown school stories."

"Go to the library, then, and find something else," her mother said. "You can use my card if you can't find anything in the children's department." She came down from the ladder and fished in her apron pocket for her purse. "Take the shopping bag, and stop at the greengrocer's on your way back for a nice cabbage."

Clarrie sighed as she put on her coat. "I can see I'm not wanted around here."

She made her way to the library in a cloud of self-pity. Perhaps as a punishment for something she'd done—she wasn't sure what—an evil fairy had cast a spell over her, isolating her in some kind of invisible tower, where she was condemned, like the Lady of Shallott, to remain alone, weaving her web of words, and watching the world reflected in her invisible looking glass. The Lady of Shallott had turned to look upon a handsome knight riding by on his horse. That forbidden glimpse of reality had brought about her death. Words and images from Tennyson's poem flashed through her mind:

She left the web, she left the loom,
She took three paces cross the room,
Out flew the web and floated wide
I am half sick of shadows, cried
The Lady of Shallott.

Two girls, emerging from the fish and chip shop on the corner, broke into giggles as they passed her. Clarrie realized she'd been speaking out loud. She'd also walked a block past the library, and was obliged to cover her embarrassment by slapping her forehead, and abruptly changing direction, as though she'd suddenly remembered something.

Sidestepping a patch of ice on the pavement, Clarrie flipped a page of *The Scarlet Pimpernel.* Relentlessly the tumbrels rolled through the streets of Paris. The aristocrats, contemptuous of the jeering rabble, held their noble heads high. This time it looked as though Madame Guillotine was not to be thwarted, but . . . thank heaven! A wagon had made it through the barrier and out of the city. The driver, a toothless old hag, would, Clarrie felt sure, turn out to be none other than the Scarlet Pimpernel, cleverly disguised.

"Clarrie!"

Maisie Barlow, scarf flapping and arms flailing, dashed across the street. "Someone in your house has died. There's a man come. He's in there now." Her eyes were excited, full of importance at being the bearer of bad news.

Clarrie closed her book. "What are you talking about?"

"I don't know who, but someone in your family must have died. There's a strange man in your house. He went in about half an hour ago and hasn't come out, and someone's closed all the curtains."

Sure enough, the curtains were drawn at the bay window and the front bedroom. Nobody closed their curtains during the daytime unless there was a death in the family. With Maisie close at her heels, Clarrie ran to the back of the house. The kitchen shutters were closed. On summer evenings, while they were at the table having tea, her dad sometimes closed the shutters to keep the sun from dazzling his good eye. But this was February—the sky was as grey as an old dishrag. "Come out and tell us who died," Maisie said. "My mam will draw our curtains, too."

Clarrie's mother intercepted her at the back door.

"Cousin Clifford's here," she whispered. "Your Aunt Dora's had an accident. She slipped on the icy steps and hit her head."

"Is she dead?"

"Yes, love, I'm afraid so." Her mother handed her a tray laden with the cups and saucers they'd bought at the Cross Lane Market. "Take these in. Be careful with them. I'll bring in the sandwiches as soon as I finish making them. Don't forget to tell Clifford you're sorry about Aunt Dora."

Clifford was sitting by the fire talking to her father in a low voice. From the corner of her eye she saw the plush cloth move on the side of the table. Billy was hiding under there, listening to the grownup conversation just as she used to do. Clifford twisted around and smiled at her. She smiled back. She liked Cousin Clifford—he wasn't a tease like his brother, Norman. He'd grown a moustache since she'd last seen him. It made him look much older.

"I'm sorry to hear about Aunt Dora's accident," she blurted.

"Yes, love. Thank you."

The truth was she barely remembered Aunt Dora—they hadn't been to Oldham for years, and Uncle Jack and Aunt Dora never came to Salford. Clifford put down a half-eaten sandwich and said he must be getting back; his father was taking things hard and was relying on him to handle all the funeral arrangements. William shook Clifford's hand and asked the time of the funeral. Clarrie followed her father and Clifford down the lobby, trying to think of something comforting to say, but everything she thought of seemed false and unnatural. Her father stood in the doorway, a cigarette dangling from his fingers, watching until Clifford turned the corner onto Eccles New Road.

When Annie and Arthur came home from work that evening and heard the news, Annie burst into tears. Clarrie stared at her, puzzled. How could Annie feel so sad about Aunt Dora? It was years since they'd been to Oldham. Christmas Day, wasn't it? There'd been a terrible row over something Cousin Beryl had done. Uncle Jack had slapped Beryl, then Aunt Dora had started screaming at him to leave her daughter alone. Aunt Dora had tripped over the fender and fallen into the hearth . . . and . . . Clarrie closed her eyes, trying to conjure up Aunt Dora's face.

"Why are you scrunching up your face like that?" Arthur asked. "Are you trying to make yourself cry?"

"I'm trying to remember what Aunt Dora looked like."

William began collecting everyone's shoes to be polished. "We leave first thing in the morning," he said, "and I want you all on your best behavior. There'll be a lot of Dora's people there, so don't show us up."

"I have to work," Arthur said.

"We're the only family Jack's got. The rest of 'em are all from Dora's side. You can tell your boss there was a death in the family."

"What can I wear?" Clarrie asked.

"Wear your gymslip, it's dark enough." Her mother tore the black sateen lining from an old coat, cut several diamond-shaped patches and handed them to her. "Here. Sew one of these patches on the left sleeve of everybody's coat. I have to bake a cake."

Clarrie spread the patches out on the table and gathered the coats from the hall stand. "Why the left side?" she asked. Gladys had worn such a patch on the left sleeve of her Teddy bear coat when her granddad died.

"That's where your heart is."

"Miss Hughes says it's not good form to wear your heart on your sleeve."

"Well, those are not hearts, they're diamonds. Just sew the patches on." Her mother set out sugar, butter, flour, and caraway seeds, and began greasing a cake pan. "This cake was supposed to be for your birthday," she said. "but we'd better not mention that when we get to Oldham."

Clarrie was about to remind her mother that she didn't like caraway seeds, but she stopped herself in time. She had long understood that her birthday could never be an occasion for celebration. It only served to remind her mother of Janet's death.

Arthur went to the window. "It looks as though it's going to snow."

William finished polishing the shoes and set them by the hearth. "We leave at nine o'clock sharp," he said, "snow or no bloody snow." He tapped Clarrie on the head with his newspaper. "Finish your sewing and go to bed."

"I feel dizzy," she said, "peculiar."

"They don't come any more peculiar than you," Annie said.

Chapter Thirty

Clarrie awoke feeling achy, with a muffled ringing in her ears. The room was cold as ice. She ran down to the kitchen in her petticoat and sat shivering by the fire. Through the back window, the sky hung heavy over the rooftops.

"Hurry and eat your breakfast," her mother said. "Everyone else has finished."

Clarrie bit into a slice of marmalade toast. "My throat hurts."

"Oh, for heaven's sake, not again!" Her mother put down the teapot and felt Clarrie's forehead. "She's very warm, Will." She pressed Clarrie's tongue down with a spoon handle and looked in her mouth. "We'd better stay home."

"We're not staying home."

"Well, our Clarrie can't go out with a fever in this weather," her mother said. "She's barely over the last lot."

Her father lit a cigarette with the end of the poker. "She can stay home by herself for an hour or two, can't she? She's almost twelve years old."

"I am twelve already. Today's my birthday, but nobody has even wished me many happy returns."

"Many happy returns of the day," they said in unison. Her mother went to the cupboard and produced three tissue-wrapped parcels.

"We almost forgot your presents with all this going on. I hope you like them, love."

Clarrie opened the parcels, carefully folding the paper for future use—three white handkerchiefs, each with colored embroidery in one corner, a pink celluloid brush, mirror, and comb set, and a book, *Girl of the Limberlost.*

"I know you've been wanting your own brush and comb set," her mother said, "and that book looked like something you might enjoy."

Clarrie forced a smile. "Thanks, Mam." She had already read, *Girl of the Limberlost,* and when she'd mentioned a brush and comb set, she'd imagined an embossed and monogrammed silver-backed affair on a fancy tray.

Her mother patted her hand. "I knew you'd be pleased." She touched Clarrie's forehead again. "I don't like leaving you alone, especially on your birthday."

"I'll be all right."

Her mother went upstairs and came back with some old coats, and a threadbare flannel nightgown. "Stand up a minute." She slipped the nightgown over Clarrie's head. "I'll make up a bed up for you on the sofa."

"The horsehair is too scratchy," Clarrie said.

"I'll put one of these coats under you. Just keep your feet tucked in the nightie."

"What if I have to go to the lav?"

"Annie can fetch the pot from under your bed. It's clean."

Annie ran upstairs and came back with the chamber pot. "Here, you can piddle to your heart's content."

Her mother took a bottle from the cupboard and poured clear liquid into a teaspoon. "I'll give you a drop of

Doctor Fenning's Fever cure," she said, "it'll make you feel better."

"Hasn't that stuff got laudanum in it?" William asked.

"I'm only giving her a teaspoon. It'll help her sleep and it's the best thing for fever." She put the bottle on the mantelpiece. "Don't take any more," she said to Clarrie. "I'll pop over to Mrs. Phipps and ask her to look in on you. I'll give her my key, so you won't need to answer the door to anyone."

"For the love of God!" William emptied the last fragments of coal onto the fire. "We'll only be gone a few hours." He handed the bucket to Arthur and told him to run down to the cellar and fetch more coal.

"If a burglar breaks in, she can just grab the poker and hit him on the head. Like this." Billy, his hair slicked back with brilliantine, his wire-rimmed glasses slipping down his nose, hit an invisible burglar with an imaginary poker.

"Shut up, you," Annie said. "You're giving her the willies."

"Our Clarrie's not afraid, are you love?" Her mother said.

"No." She was anxious, now, for them to leave. There was something she had wanted to do for a long time, and this was the perfect opportunity.

As soon as the house was quiet, Clarrie read the final chapter of *The Scarlet Pimpernel,* gave the book a kiss meant for Sir Percy Blakeney, then threw back the covers and got unsteadily to her feet. She took a swig of Doctor Fenning's Fever Cure, straight from the bottle, before making her way upstairs. Her legs seemed to be made of rubber, and there was a strange buzzing noise in her head. The alcove at the end of the landing was icy cold. Shivering, Clarrie lifted the lid of her father's wicker trunk.

A smell of mothballs rose from the brittle, discolored tissue paper as, one by one, she lifted out her father's costumes: the gold mandarin suit with wide sleeves done in embroidery, the Pierrot costume—black and white satin diamonds—the Cossack suit with its baggy black trousers and crimson satin tunic. From the bottom of the trunk she brought out a large leather make-up case. She fiddled with the clasp until the lid sprang open. Underneath the top tray, hidden by a jumble of false hairpieces, was a bundle of letters tied with a blue ribbon and a mottled exercise book. This was what she was looking for.

Without stopping to put the costumes back, she carried the letters and the exercise book down to the kitchen and climbed back on the sofa between the covers. She'd stumbled on these things years ago, but this was the first time she'd been alone in the house long enough to study them without fear of discovery. The exercise book was filled with practice loops and capital letters—light upstrokes, heavy downstrokes. Her dad must have been practicing his penmanship. At the back of the book were three folded letters written in her father's narrow Spenserian hand:

Dear Sir: In reply to yours of the first inst., I have known Mr. William Hancock for more than ten years and can attest to his intelligence and character. I know him to be a man of good personal habits—honest, sober, industrious, punctual and reliable—and I have no hesitation in recommending him to the position of clerk in your establishment.

The letter was signed, Thomas F. Black, Esquire. Except for different dates and signatures, the other two letters were identical. Poor Dad—he'd written these letters of recommendation himself. Clarrie slipped them back into the exercise book and set the book on the floor.

The thicker bundle must be love letters—why else would they be tied with blue ribbon? The envelopes had a sad, yellowed look; the ink had turned rust color. She untied the ribbon, reminding herself to be careful to tie it back exactly the same way.

The letters were addressed to her father in a sprawling, almost illegible hand that slanted far to the right. This wasn't her mam's handwriting—her writing was clear, round, firm, and upright. She selected a letter. She knew it wasn't nice to read other people's letters, but how else was she to find out anything?

"My Darling," the letter began. "Darling" was a word used only in books and films; she'd never heard it used in real life. The handwriting was impossible—a tangle of oversized loops and flourishes that dwindled to a wavy line at the end of each word. She managed to make out a phrase here and there: ". . . can't be too careful . . . he keeps threatening me with . . ." The last words were heavily underlined. The letter was signed, "Your own Dolly."

Dolly. That was the name of her father's old partner in his skating act—Dainty Dolly Davis. She'd heard her mother speak of Dainty Dolly, always with an edge to her voice. "Yes, I scorched your shirt. I'm very sorry. Perhaps you should have married Dainty Dolly Davis."

Clarrie set aside the letters and went to the sideboard for the photograph album. Was it possible that her dad was still in love with Dainty Dolly and had married her mother only because he couldn't have the one he really wanted?

Most of the photographs were ancient, taken before her parents had met—several of her father in various skating outfits, one of him whirling around, one of him soaring over a row of barrels. And here she was—Dainty Dolly Davis—perched on her roller skates, simpering for the camera and holding out her short ruffled skirt to reveal the bloomers peeping out underneath. Her body curved out and in and out again, like an egg timer. Her frizzy hair was piled up like a bunch of cauliflower on top of her head. At the lower right corner of the picture, she had written, "With love, Dolly," in that same sprawling hand. The card was dated 1910.

1910. That was when her dad was with the Bostock tour—four years before he joined the army in the Great War. Her mam would have been about twelve then—the same age as I am now, Clarrie thought. In any case, it was her mother he'd married, and she was younger—and far prettier—than Dainty Dolly Davis.

Satisfied that her mother had nothing to fear from Dainty Dolly, Clarrie returned the photograph album to the sideboard, then carried the letters upstairs and put everything back in the trunk.

Returning to the kitchen, she took another gulp of Doctor Fenning's Fever Cure and set the bottle on the floor near the sofa, in case she wanted more later. She picked up her book, slid down in the covers, and put her head back on the pillow. She was almost asleep when the door banged.

"It's only me, love." Mrs. Phipps's iron clogs rang on the stone floor of the scullery. She pushed open the kitchen door, shook the snow from her shawl and hung it on the doorknob. "It's fit for neither man nor beast out there," she said. She gave Clarrie a snaggle-toothed smile. "Are you comfy enough, then, love?"

"Yes, thank you, I'm fine."

The voluminous black skirt Mrs. Phipps wore couldn't quite hide her bowed legs. Clarrie's mother said that bandy legs were caused by rickets during childhood, and it seemed that half the people of Salford had suffered from it. Mrs. Phipps picked up the bucket and threw some coal on the fire. She cracked open the larger lumps with the poker. Sparks flew up the chimney, and a blue-green flame licked at the pitch bubbles.

"I'll warm you this drop of soup," she said, "then I'll be on my way." Bent over the fire, stirring the saucepan, she looked like a witch in a fairy tale.

"It were a sad thing, your poor auntie passing away so sudden like." She handed Clarrie a bowl of steaming soup and a thick wedge of bread. "Your dad's Auntie Nellie—the one as used to live in this house—died the same way. She fell indoors, though, down them very stairs. When we're called, ready or not, we have to drop everything and go. I won't be sorry when my time comes—I've seen enough of this world."

Clarrie broke the bread in the soup. "You don't mean that, Mrs. Phipps," she said. The day she'd run out of the exam she, too, thought she wanted to die. She didn't like to think about that. She told Mrs. Phipps she couldn't imagine anyone feeling that they'd seen enough of this world.

"It's true, all the same," Mrs. Phipps said. "I've spent fifty years in t'mill, and I've been married for thirty-seven of 'em—that's enough misery for anybody." She pulled her shawl over her head. "Leave the basin on the floor, love, when you've finished. There's not much coal left in the bucket, but your dad or your mam'll take care of it when they come home." She set the soup pan on the hearth. "She's the salt of the earth is your mam—not like some of the rubbish you get these days." She touched Clarrie's forehead, "You don't seem too bad, so I'll get on home. My old fella has a fit if he calls and I'm not there."

Clarrie drank most of the soup, then got up, walked over to the window and pressed her head against the cold glass. Thick flakes of snow flew past the window. Already there was more than two inches of snow on the ground. She imagined pallbearers carrying Aunt Dora's coffin through a snowstorm. Inside the closed box, Aunt Dora lay as though sleeping. Her face was indistinct except for her plucked eyebrows, raised, just as Clarrie remembered, in perpetual surprise.

Clarrie dropped the curtain and knelt to stroke the cat. She no longer felt sleepy. She padded in her bare feet over to the bookcase. Most of the books were her father's and had been on the shelves for as long as she could remember. She'd read, or attempted to read, them all: *The Vicar of Wakefield, A Tale of Two Cities, Ivanhoe, Trilby, The Constant Nymph, J'Accuse, Collected Poems of Ella Wheeler Wilcox.* Tucked away at the back of the top shelf was the book her father had recently acquired through some sort of newspaper offer—*The Fifty Most Amazing Crimes of the Past Five Hundred Years.* The book was thick as a Bible, bound in green imitation leather and embossed with a black skull and crossbones. She lifted it down and glanced at the lurid illustrations—a man with a hatchet raised to strike—a bare female leg hanging over the side of a bathtub—a body sprawled in a pool of blood. She carried the book back to the sofa.

It was dark out now, and the light of the fire was not enough to read by. She dragged a chair into position under the gas bracket, lit the mantle with a flaming scrap of newspaper, adjusted the brightness, and settled down to read.

Except for the distant mooing of a foghorn from the ship canal, the world outside was silent—muffled in snow. Inside the only sounds were the ticking of the clock on the mantelpiece and the occasional fall of a cinder into the hearth. Clarrie devoured story after story; Jack the Ripper, Doctor Crippen, Lizzie Borden. The spirits of murderers, long since hanged, rose like wraiths from the pages of the book and swarmed her couch.

Clarrie shuddered. Hadn't these murderers once been children, more or less like herself ? What could have turned them into such monsters? Could it happen to anyone? She suddenly remembered the evil dream she'd once had—she'd been forcing a dead baby down the sink drain! The dream had convinced her that a demon had tried to possess her while she slept. With God's help, she believed she'd defeated him. If there really were such things as demons, then murderers might also be victims—people who'd failed in their struggle with evil. What if she hadn't really vanquished the demon? What if he was hidden deep inside her—waiting?

She could not put the book down. She wanted to explore the murderers' twisted minds, to probe their grisly hearts, to understand why they had failed in their struggle with evil—for surely they must have struggled.

A faint clanging reached her ears, as though the iron lid had been lifted from the coalhole. After listening intently for several minutes, she decided she'd imagined it.

She was immersed in a story of a prim little Victorian girl who drowned her infant brother in a well, when the gaslight flickered and went out. The firelight was too dim. If she wanted to finish the story, she'd have to venture into the cellar and put money in the meter.

In the tin on the mantelpiece, where her mother kept the gas money, she found a shilling. The prospect of going down into the dark cellar set her heart racing, but she had long ago made up her mind never to give in to fear. She reminded herself that there was nothing down there in the dark that wasn't there in the light. But where were her shoes? And she'd need a candle.

She found the stub of a candle on the shelf over the sink, and went back into the kitchen to light it, before beginning her barefoot descent into the cellar. Near the bottom of the stairs she stepped on something sharp. With a yelp of pain, she dropped the candle and staggered down the last few steps. The candle extinguished itself on the cellar floor.

Sick with fear, but still clutching the shilling, she groped her way along the damp, flaking walls. She turned through the arched doorway into the inner cellar, pulling her hand quickly away from the wall when it came in contact with something soft and squishy—must be one of the frilly brown fungus things that grew between the bricks. The cellar smelled of cats and creosote. And something else—a faint pungent odor of human sweat; probably my own, she thought.

The meter was in the far left corner, a few inches below the ceiling. She was reaching for the coin slot, when she felt something touch her hand. With a scream she dropped the coin and ran, slamming her head against the arch as she raced through the doorway, and back up the stairs. With shaking hands, she bolted the cellar door behind her.

Arming herself with the poker, she sat huddled by the fire, whimpering, and calling upon her guardian angel for protection, until she heard the blessed sound of a key in the lock and the music of familiar voices.

Chapter Thirty-one

"You spend far too much time with your head in a book," Clarrie's father said. "Do something useful—help your mother around the house."

"She does plenty," her mother said. "But you do need to get out more, our Clarrie. Why don't you try making friends with Reenie Perlman? Mrs. Perlman is worried about her; she says Reenie feels like an outsider at Tatton. I told her you felt the same way."

Clarrie groaned. "I wish you wouldn't talk about me to Mrs. Perlman, Mam. It's not easy to be friends with Reenie—she's like an old lady. All she ever does is sit on the schoolyard steps, knitting."

"You'd be doing her a good turn, and you might get along better than you think."

"I doubt it," Clarrie said.

But on her way home from school the next day, she called out to Reenie to wait.

Reenie stopped. "What do you want?"

Clarrie ran to join her. "I'm on my way to the library, and I thought, since it's in the same direction, I might as well walk part of the way home with you."

"Suit yourself." Reenie's coat was carefully buttoned, her dark hair a bit too tidy. Her face revealed nothing.

After walking in silence for a while, Clarrie tried to break the ice. "Have you tried out for the netball team?" she asked.

"No."

"Miss Riding might put me on. She says I'm fast enough on my feet, but I don't get in there and grab the ball."

Reenie selected a piece of Turkish delight from a white paper bag and offered the open bag to Clarrie.

"Thanks." Clarrie popped a piece into her mouth. Turkish delight sounded a lot better than it tasted.

"I never bother to try out for anything," Reenie said. "She doesn't like me."

"Why do you say that?"

"You know why."

Clarrie didn't know. "Is it because you're not a fast runner—because you're a bit plump?"

"Plump? You think I'm plump?" Reenie's pale face reddened. "Is that what they're saying about me, that I'm plump?"

"Nobody's said anything. I just thought . . ."

"Anyway, that's not why. It's because I'm Jewish. She doesn't like Jews."

"Why?"

"How should I know? You saw that magic lantern slide she brought back from Germany."

Miss Riding had gone to Berlin for the Olympic games and had come back bubbling over with enthusiasm. The lantern slide was a disappointment—nothing much of the games, just a boring gymnastics display—row upon row of German schoolgirls wearing baggy gym suits and arm-bands with bent crosses.

"Look at those splendid girls!" Miss Riding said. "See how healthy and wholesome they are—not a slacker to be found! We have much to learn from the Germans, much to learn."

Her father had snorted when Clarrie told him what Miss Riding had said. "Much to learn from the Germans? Well, they bear watching, all right."

"My dad thinks the Germans are getting ready for another war," Clarrie said. "But what does the lantern slide have to do with you being a Jew?"

"Herr Hitler's the German prime minister or something. He hates the Jews."

"I don't know anything about Herr Hitler, but I think you're wrong about Miss Riding. She just likes gymnastics and sports." Clarrie cast about for another topic. "I've got to go to the library to take this book back—*Judith Paris*—have you read it?"

"No."

"It's part of a series, *The Herries Chronicles* by Hugh Walpole. You should read *Rogue Herries* first, though, because . . ."

"Is it made up? I don't like made-up stories."

"Oh. What do you like to read, then?"

Reenie shrugged. "I read my mother's magazines. They have some nice knitting and crochet patterns. I've almost finished a cardigan for myself—cable stitch."

"I'm not very good at that stuff," Clarrie said.

"Yes," Reenie said. "I saw what you did in sewing class."

"What else do you like to do?"

"I play cards."

Clarrie smiled. "I know how to play 'Snap,' and 'Fish'. We could have a game sometime, if you like." She and Gladys had often played cards together.

"I don't play those baby games. I'm talking about 'whist'."

"You'd have to show me how."

"It would take too long. I've been playing since I was little. I compete in whist drives with my mother and my Aunt Sophie. Last week I won a bottle of scent—*Evening in Paris,* it's called."

"You must be pretty good," Clarrie said.

"I'm not bad."

Neither of them seemed to be able to think of anything more to say. They walked in silence until they reached the library.

"Why don't you come in the library with me?" Clarrie asked. "It's not all made up. They have biographies—some of them are great—*Stanley and Livingstone* is as good as a novel."

Reenie shook her head and went on walking

"I'll say ta-ra then." Clarrie ran up the library steps feeling as though a lead weight had been lifted from her shoulders.

Each Wednesday morning from Shrove Tuesday to Easter, the combined Tatton schools assembled in church for Lenten services. For Clarrie, the soot-blackened church with its soaring spire and its murky stained-glass windows was a place of mystery and beauty; and it comforted her—so long as she was obliged to be there—to cast doubt aside and immerse herself in God's purported presence.

Miss Riding gathered up her coat, hat, and prayer book and announced that it was time for church. "Roman Catholic girls have permission to leave for the service at St Cyprian's."

Kathleen Quinn raised her hand. "We don't call it a service, Miss, we call it mass, but it's only religious instruction on Wednesdays."

"I know, I know." Miss Riding waved her away. "Get your coats from the cloakroom and wait in the yard—quietly—if you please."

Reenie raised her hand. "What about me, Miss?"

Miss Riding frowned. "Oh, dear! What did we do with you last year? We can't have you running wild."

An image of Reenie, sitting on the schoolyard steps, munching on toffees and knitting while everyone else was shrieking and dashing about, flashed through Clarrie's mind. Anyone less likely to run wild would be hard to imagine.

"I went home early, Miss."

"Can't your parents arrange for you to have some sort of religious instruction—in a synagogue perhaps?"

"My father's an atheist," Reenie said.

Miss Riding raised her eyebrows. "An atheist? And yet he sees fit to send you to a church school?"

"Yes, Miss. There's nowhere else to go."

"That's unfortunate," Miss Riding said. "But I suppose beggars can't be choosers."

"We're not beggars, Miss." This time Reenie didn't even bother to raise her hand. A girl in the back row giggled. Reenie turned her sleek, shingled head, and the girl fell silent.

Miss Riding's face was splotched with pink. "That's merely a figure of speech, as well you know."

There was an uncomfortable tension in the room. Clarrie, mindful of what her mother had told her, felt she should come to Reenie's defense. She raised her hand.

"Yes, Clarrie?"

"My father is an agnostic, Miss. That means . . ."

"I know what that means," Miss Riding said. "And if this is your way of trying to wriggle out of going to church, Clarrie Hancock, it's not going to succeed."

Clarrie's face grew hot. She was not trying to get out of going to church. She didn't want Miss Riding to think that. She raised her hand again.

"For heaven's sake put your hand down, child. I don't want to hear any more about it. Reenie is Jewish. She is not required to attend church. You will come to church with the rest of us. I don't care if your father is a Hottentot."

A ripple of laughter ran through the class. Miss Riding twinkled at them to show that she too could enjoy a joke.

The other classes had already formed a crocodile and were waiting in the street. Miss Riding's group took the lead, walking the half-mile through the wet streets to the church. At the church entrance Miss Riding closed her umbrella, put a cautionary finger to her lips, and motioned to them to enter. Tattered banners hung limply from the rafters, their emblems and mottoes effaced by years of soot. A hundred pairs of shoes and clogs set up a clatter that ricocheted throughout the church. A trail of muddy footprints marred the black and white tiles.

Miss Riding stood aside to let her class file into the pews. Her face took on a pious expression. She pulled down the wooden kneeling bench and motioned them all to kneel. The benches groaned and shifted. Somebody giggled and Miss Riding swung around, her eyes alert for mischief makers.

Clarrie tried to shut out the noises around her so she could think about God. Reenie's father just plain didn't believe in Him. How could he be a Jew and an atheist at the same time?

A disturbance from the doorway signaled the arrival of the boys. Miss Riding got up off her knees and sat back in the pew. The girls followed suit, craning their necks to watch the boys file down the aisle.

During Lent, everything—the altar, the lectern, the pulpit, even the Reverend Nigel Witherspoon himself—was draped in purple. There was little ceremony—an opening hymn, and a prayer, then, stoop-shouldered and melancholy, the rector climbed into the pulpit and began his sermon. His high-pitched voice rippled out, bouncing from wall to wall, from floor to ceiling. The echoes made it impossible to understand a word he said. What happened to sermons that didn't reach their target, Clarrie wondered. Perhaps they rattled around forever, like ghosts among the rafters.

The Reverend's nose was very thin and red. Maud next door said it was because he tippled, and that the rectory dustbin was always full of empty brandy bottles. Clarrie didn't believe it. He was a minister, after all—a man chosen by God—one of those "pastors, masters, elders and betters," who, according to the catechism, she must promise to honor and obey.

She'd been ill when the rest of the girls in her class were confirmed, and her parents had told her she must decide for herself whether or not she wanted to do it. She had studied the catechism backwards and forwards, but she still wasn't sure. The bit about "dwelling content in that state to which it has pleased God to call you" was a stumbling block. She might be able to do it if she was certain it was God's will, but she found it hard to believe that God didn't want her to better herself. Wasn't that what the parable of the talents was all about?

From the corner of her eye she saw a scrap of paper fly across the aisle. A girl in the pew behind her tapped Clarrie's shoulder and pressed the paper into her hand. Clarrie glanced down at the paper, about to pass it on, and saw that it was addressed to her. Had Richard Beaumont decided he liked her, after all? She slid the note between the pages of her hymnbook and opened it.

"Dear Clarrie," she read. "Will U B my sweetheart? If your answer is yes, nod your head at me on the way out." It was signed "H. Wardle."

Herbert. She might have known.

Clarrie crumpled the note into a ball and slipped it in her pocket. At least someone liked her, but why did that someone have to be Herbert? Fat, baby-faced, good-natured Herbert. Decked out in his blue and red uniform, a pillbox hat perched on his head, and a leopard skin across his chubby belly, he played the big bass drum in the Boys' Brigade. After practice, he always marched home alone, straight down the middle of the street, banging on his drum and singing "Onward Christian Soldiers" at the top of his lungs. He was so comical, it was impossible to picture him as a sweetheart.

The sermon ricocheted to a close. The rector stepped down from the pulpit. The children riffled through their hymnbooks to find "O God Our Help in Ages Past," a hymn Clarrie loved. By the time they got to "Time like an ever-rolling stream bears all its sons away" her voice was faltering. She buried her face in the hymnal to hide her tears. With a hollow clatter, the kneeling benches were lowered for a final prayer, and the Rector strode down the aisle to deliver the benediction. From that end of the church his voice rang out clearly; "—and the blessing of God the Father, God the Son, and God the Holy Ghost, be with us all now and evermore."

A final Amen. Miss Riding knelt briefly, then stepped into the aisle, standing aside to allow the girls to file out of the pew.

Conscious that Herbert would be trying to catch her eye, Clarrie kept her gaze fixed on the wall as she went by. The sun had broken through, and for a fleeting moment, the saints, apostles, and shepherds trapped in the stained glass windows burst into shimmering life.

Chapter Thirty-two

A girl with frizzy blonde hair approached Clarrie in the schoolyard. Clarrie had noticed the addition of this new, interesting, face, but had not yet spoken to her. The girl stood with thrust-out out chin, her arms folded across her chest like a teacher about to scold. She fixed Clarrie with bold brown eyes.

"My name's Celia Scott," she said. "I'm new here. I'd like to talk to you if you have a minute."

Clarrie started to introduce herself. The girl raised a hand to stop her. "I know who you are. I've been making inquiries about you."

Inquiries? What sort of person was this?

"I've been on the lookout for a friend—someone intelligent I can talk to. So far, you seem to be the only possibility."

Clarrie stared at the girl with admiration. What audacity! Most of the girls she knew, including herself, would rather die than come right out and admit they needed a friend.

Celia held out her hand. "Show me what you're reading?"

"It's just a library book."

Celia leafed through it. "*She*, by Rider Haggard. Is it any good?"

"I'm only halfway through—it's exciting so far."

"I'll read it when you're finished." Celia handed the book back. "What do you say to my idea—about us being friends?"

"I don't mind giving it a try," Clarrie said, aware that she was blushing. The bell was ringing. It was time to take their places in line to file into school.

"Wait for me after school, then." Celia said. "I live nearby. You can walk me home."

While they were walking to Celia's house, Celia peppered her with questions—where did she live? How many sisters and brothers did she have? What sort of work did her father do? What were her favorite subjects? Who were her favorite authors? When her answers to the last two questions received an approving nod, Clarrie glowed with pleasure.

"We're going to get on like a house on fire," Celia said.

Warmed by Celia's approval, Clarrie brushed away a momentary misgiving.

"Speaking of houses," Celia said. "Here's mine."

Clarrie had expected Celia's house to be a pleasant, homey place, filled with books and flowering plants. She was disillusioned, even before stepping inside, by the stale smell and grimy windows. The kitchen chairs were heaped with dog-eared magazines and unwashed clothes, but there were no books to be seen. A woman, bent over the fire, stirring something in an iron stewpot, looked up as they came in, then without a word went back to stirring.

"Is that your granny?" Clarrie whispered.

"No, that's my ma. I was a change-of-life baby." Celia threw her coat on a chair and led Clarrie into the front room to play records. "Here's where my Uncle Paddy stays," she said, "he was blinded by mustard gas in the war."

In the parlor, sitting in a rocking chair by a small fire, was a shriveled looking man with a stubbly chin. He took a white clay pipe from his mouth. "Who's there?"

"It's only me," Celia said. "I brought a friend of mine from school."

"You woke me up, so you did."

"Well, you shouldn't fall asleep with your pipe lit. You'll burn the house down. Is it all right if we play some records?"

"Don't scratch 'em."

Celia took a stack of gramophone records off the table. "They're already scratched." To Clarrie she said, "He's had 'em for donkey's years."

Watching her new friend wind the gramophone, Clarrie was reminded of the day she and Gladys were locked in Gladys's parlor. She started to tell Celia the story, but Celia put her finger to her lips for silence. A scratchy male voice was singing "Phil the Fluter's Ball."

"Sure they don't write songs like that any more," Uncle Paddy said. "Put on "Finnegan's Wake" will you now, tha's another grand song."

When "Finnegan's Wake" ended, Clarrie said she'd better be getting home. "I'll walk part of the way with you," Celia said.

While they walked, Clarrie asked Celia if her father was at work. Celia hesitated, "He doesn't live with us anymore."

"Why not?"

"He's taken up with another woman. Good riddance to him, I say. He never gives my ma so much as a penny. My sister's a dressmaker. She helps support us."

Suspecting that Celia would later regret blurting out such a shameful family secret, Clarrie offered one of her own. "My granddad threw my granny and their two boys out in the street with nothing but the clothes on their backs," she said, "but it wasn't over a woman. It was over some dead birds. They lived in this big house off Eccles Old Road. The house is still there. The name Hancock's written in wrought iron on a big gate, and there's a fountain on the front lawn."

"An old family mansion, eh? You've been reading too many books."

"It's true."

"I'll believe it when I see it," Celia said.

"I'll take you there next Sunday."

The garden at Hancock House was knee-deep in buttercups, otherwise everything was much as Clarrie remembered. Celia's reaction was gratifying. "It's smashing. I wouldn't call it a mansion though."

"I never said it was."

"I bet your dad could hire a solicitor, then you could claim the house and move in. I could come and spend the night with you. I bet this place is swarming with ghosts."

"Bird ghosts," Clarrie said. "We could have a ghost hunt, like that one in *The Mystery of St. Winifred's Tower.*"

They walked home with their arms around each other's waists, making plans for furnishing the house and giving a party. "A masquerade ball," Clarrie said. "With Chinese lanterns strung along the drive."

"And servants to open the door and announce the guests," Celia said.

They chose their costumes and planned the menu. Celia thought they should serve cocktails, like they did in American films, but Clarrie, mindful of the stories her mother had told her about life among the upper classes, thought cocktails might stamp them as *nouveau riche.*

"The gentry don't drink cocktails," she told Celia, "they serve a different wine with each course and after dinner the men retire to the library or the drawing room with cigars and brandy."

"What do the women do?"

"I'm not sure—they probably sit around and talk about the servants."

"While the servants are in the kitchen talking about them," Celia said.

Clarrie laughed. "And eating the leftovers," she said. "Which reminds me, my mam says you're welcome to come to tea if you like."

Celia drooped her wrist. "Delighted, I'm sure!"

Celia and Clarrie would soon be turning thirteen; their birthdays were just three days apart. Celia told Clarrie that her older sister, Noreen, was making her a frock for her birthday. "She'll make one for you, too, if you like."

"Let me know what she charges. I'll be glad to talk to her about it," Clarrie's mother told Clarrie.

"Too late, they're almost finished," Celia said when Clarrie told her. "Mine's green and yours is brown. My sister is embroidering the letter C on the breast pockets.

When the dresses were finished, Celia brought Clarrie's frock over to her house, with a bill for fifteen shillings.

"I thought your sister was going to discuss it with me first," Sally said. "She's lucky I have the money. As it happens, Mister Hancock and I have just been paid."

After Celia left, Clarrie's mother grumbled about being billed without first being consulted, but when she saw Clarrie in her new frock, she said no more about it.

Celia and Clarrie arranged to wear their frocks to school on the same day. They strolled about the schoolyard, basking in the envious glances they drew from the other girls.

"You and I are the cream of the crop in this place," Celia said. "We're head and shoulders above this riffraff."

Riffraff ? Clarrie shifted uncomfortably. Most of the girls were not as clever as Celia, it was true, but they were not riffraff. What if she, herself, were to do something to disappoint Celia? Would she be cast into outer darkness with the rest of the riffraff?

"I've got to take my uncle for his walk after school today," Celia said. "He can't be trusted out by himself." She told Clarrie that, left to himself, Uncle Paddy would end up in the gutter. "He doesn't know when he's had enough. I want you to come with me. Between the two of us, we ought to be able to handle him."

Celia told Clarrie to walk on the other side of Uncle Paddy, and on no account to let him go in the pub. Uncle Paddy had other ideas. He seemed to know exactly where each pub was, and as they went by he made every effort to steer the girls in that direction. Celia shoved him roughly past the pub doorways and told him he was being a pest. She dropped her uncle's arm.

"Watch him for me. I have to run to the lav." She darted away before Clarrie could voice an objection.

"Good riddance to her," Uncle Paddy grasped Clarrie's arm. "You seem like a nice little girl." He tapped her on the shoulder with the handle of his cane. "Drop me at The Ship, or The Waverly. I'll make me own way home."

"Celia wants us to wait here."

"She's never coming back. She's pulled this one before, so she has—palming me off on any Tom, Dick, and Harry."

"I can't leave you, Uncle Paddy. You might hurt yourself."

"I know how to take care of meself. Just do as I tell yous!" He tore himself away and struck out with his cane. Clarrie grabbed the rubber tip and tried to wrest it from him. Out of the corner of her eye, she saw her father approaching from across the street.

"Dad!" she cried. "Help me!"

Her father hurried to her. "Easy there, Paddy old chum!" He grabbed the cane. "What's going on?" he asked Clarrie.

Clarrie tried to explain.

"Jesus," Uncle Paddy shouted. "Can't a man wet his whistle with his own pension money? I thought this was a free country. Give us back me stick."

Her father took a firm grip of Paddy's arm. "I'll take you in for a quick one, Paddy me lad, and then I'm taking you home, so you might as well save your breath."

"Those people had no business expecting a child to take care of that old devil," Clarrie's mother said when she heard the story. "Blind, or not, he had no business trying to bash your head in with his cane. I don't want you going over there anymore."

"But Celia's my best friend."

"What sort of a friend runs off and leaves you like that? You shouldn't let her boss you around so much."

"She doesn't boss me," Clarrie said, but she knew that her mother was right. When she was with Celia, she went where Celia wanted to go, and spoke only to the people Celia approved of. And Celia had started choosing her books for her. "Not that one," she'd say, taking the book out of Clarrie's hand, "I like this one better."

"Friendship is a matter of give and take, love," her mother said. "You must learn to speak up for yourself."

"She won't like me anymore, if I do that," Clarrie said.

"If she's a true friend, she'll respect you for it. If she doesn't, you're better off without her."

Clarrie fell silent. She'd gone from being bossed about by Annie to being bossed about by Celia. With Annie, she'd been afraid of getting hit, but what reason had she to be afraid of Celia?

On their next Sunday walk to the park, Clarrie suggested taking the shortcut across the railway bridge and down Hodge Lane.

"No," Celia said. "let's go the way we always go, down Langworthy Road. It's nicer."

"If we go over the bridge we can watch the trains go by and wave at the people," Clarrie said. She felt herself blushing.

"Why do you want to do that. It's so childish."

Clarrie tried to explain. "We are all in this world together—the people on the train and us—sharing this earth, and this moment in time. We catch sight of each other for a fleeting moment, as the train goes by. Our paths will never cross again, so we greet each other, wishing each other well as we go our separate ways. We make a small connection."

"You're never going to see them again, so what's the point? We'll go the way I said."

Clarrie was trembling. "Why can't you do what I want for a change?"

Celia examined her fingernails. "Why are you making an issue of it? Hodge Lane stinks. It's better down Langworthy Road."

"Today I just feel like going over the bridge."

They walked on in chilly silence. Clarrie felt like crying. She wanted to tell Celia she was sorry—that she didn't really care one way or the other—but as they reached the bridge she stopped and took a deep breath, then placed her foot on the first step. "I'm going this way," she said. Celia stared at her in disbelief. Clarrie stuffed her clenched fists in her pockets and looked down at her shoes.

There was a momentary silence, then Celia turned away. "Suit yourself," she said.

Clarrie ran up the steps. A train was chugging along the tracks, but she didn't have the heart to wave. She looked down at the street, watching the rhythmic bounce of Celia's curly yellow hair as she walked away. Clarrie closed her eyes, silently willing Celia to turn around and come back, but when she opened them again, Celia had already vanished in the distance.

Chapter Thirty-three

The headmistress breezed into Clarrie's classroom and pinned a sheet of paper to the bulletin board. Here, she said, was an opportunity for the class to join a newly formed international pen-pal organization. Any girl interested should leave her name and address on the sheet when the class was over. Thinking it might be easier to maintain a friendship at a safe distance, Clarrie added her name and address to the list.

Several weeks passed, and she'd almost given up hope when she received a letter from an American girl living in Washington, D.C. In a large, free-flowing hand, the girl introduced herself as Saundra Jette. She told Clarrie that her school had gone to see King George and Queen Elizabeth when they visited the White House. She peppered Clarrie with questions; had she ever been invited to Buckingham Palace? Which programs did she listen to on the radio? Who did she like best, Count Basie or Duke Ellington? Her own favorite song, she told Clarrie, was "Deep Purple." What was Clarrie's favorite? She ended her letter with, "Yours 'til the ocean wears rubber pants to keep its buttom dry."

Clarrie admired Saundra's handwriting, and gave her the benefit of the doubt about her spelling. Perhaps that was the way Americans spelled "bottom." Making an effort to control her own untidy scrawl, she wrote back, telling Saundra about the royal visit to Salford on the occasion of King George the Fifth's jubilee.

Armed with small union jacks, the local schoolchildren had traipsed crocodile fashion down to Eccles New Road where they'd waited for hours under a hot sun for a glimpse of the royal procession. To mark the occasion, each child had received a jubilee beaker decorated with pictures of King George and Queen Mary. Clarrie's beaker got broken in the sink a couple of days later.

Clarrie confessed to Saundra that she'd never heard of Count Basie or Duke Ellington. She liked most of the songs she learned in school—"Where ere You Walk" and "On Linden Lea" and many others too numerous to list. She closed her letter with, "I think this darn thing is long enough, as the sword-swallower said . . ."

In her next letter, Saundra told Clarrie that she'd spent her thirteenth birthday having a picnic in the park with her boyfriend and his family. She'd taken her radio, and they'd eaten fried chicken and danced on the grass. Her boyfriend, Tyrone, had kissed her right in front of his mother.

America must be a strange place indeed, Clarrie thought, if a thirteen-year-old girl felt free to kiss a boy in full view of his mother. And how could they take a big thing like a wireless on a picnic? And how could anyone fry a chicken? The few chickens she'd eaten had been stuffed with breadcrumbs, thyme, and parsley, and roasted in the oven.

She'd shared Saundra's first letter with the family, but, embarrassed to have them read about the kissing, she hid the second. If anyone should ask to see it, she'd pretend she'd lost it.

Saundra had asked Clarrie for a photograph, so in her next letter, Clarrie enclosed a small photograph cut from a class picture. She studied it critically. Her fringe came straight down from the crown of her head, cutting across her broad forehead, emphasizing the width of her face, but it was the only photograph she had. She asked Saundra to send her a snapshot in return, and waited eagerly for the next letter.

Days turned into weeks, but no letter came from America. Thinking her letter had gone astray, Clarrie wrote again. Again there was no reply.

"Must be that photograph," Clarrie said to her mother. "I look too childish for her."

"You are a child," her mother said. "That's how you're supposed to look."

"Well, she didn't like me."

"Perhaps the shoe is on the other foot. Perhaps she's afraid *you* won't like *her*."

"I doubt it," Clarrie said. She made no further attempt to write to Saundra. Instead, she wrote a letter to herself:

Dear Clarrie,

When you read this letter, many years hence, please do not laugh at me. Remember, I am you as you were at twelve. I am not sure what will become of me. You know the answer to this, I don't. I am wondering what has happened to you, and where you are. Did you ever travel abroad? Are you married? Are you famous? Whatever has happened to you, whoever you may have become, you must never forget that you were once this twelve-year-old child. Please think kindly of me and do not scorn me.

I remain, your former self,
Clara Maud Hancock.

She folded and sealed the letter, addressed it to herself, wrote "Not to be opened until I am twenty-one" on the envelope, and hid it behind a loose brick in the backyard wall.

One evening after dinner, while the rest of the family moved their chairs closer to the fireplace, Clarrie settled herself at the kitchen table while she waited for the washing-up water to boil. She'd recently read Tennyson's "Maud"—drawn to it, because Maud was her own middle name. The poem had moved her to tears and stirred in her a desire to write a poem of her own. She read over what she had written so far.

Tonight love, when the drifting moon,
Dapples the tangled trees,
And dreaming bats hang all aswoon,
Fanned by the shivering breeze,
Tonight will I dare,
Though death may follow,
To meet thee there,
In that little hollow . . .

Behind closed eyelids she saw a woman running down a moonlit path, deep into the woods—her raven tresses, her silken gown, her hooded cloak swirled about her in the breeze. Bare branches caught at her clothing, twigs snapped beneath her slippered feet. The odors of leaf mould and violets mingled with vapors from the damp earth . . .

Clarrie chewed her pencil. At the beginning of "Maud" Tennyson mentioned a "dreadful hollow." She didn't want people to think she'd stolen his words—perhaps it would be better to change "little hollow" to "secret hut." But then, she'd have to take out "though death may follow," and find something that rhymed with hut. She considered the possibilities—cut, strut, rut, nut . . .? How about shut?

Tonight will I dare,
To meet thee there,

In our secret hut,
And we'll make quite sure
That the wooden door, is firmly shut. . .

Annie poked her in the ribs. "Wake up, gormless, your water's boiling over."

Clarrie sighed. Alfred Lord Tennyson would never have finished anything if he'd had to put up with this. She got up and removed the kettle from the fire. " 'Gormless' is not even a proper word," she muttered. "It's working-class slang."

Putting on her haughtiest expression, Clarrie rumpled Billy's hair as she went by with the steaming kettle.

"Your hair is untonsured, Billy."

"It's what?"

"Untonsured. It means your hair needs cutting."

Clarrie came back with a fresh kettleful of cold water, saying the kettle had almost boiled dry.

"You got that word out of that last book you brought me, *Ulysses*," her mother said.

Her father looked up from his paper. "Wasn't that book banned?"

"It wouldn't be in the library, Dad, if it was," Clarrie said.

"They needn't have bothered banning it," Sally said. "I doubt anyone's going to finish it. I couldn't make heads or tails of it, myself. I expected it to be about the ancient Greeks, but it's all about Dublin. You can take it back tomorrow."

"I want to read it myself, first," Clarrie said. She had read the first few pages of *Ulysses* in the library and been intrigued by the unfamiliar words and the strange bantering conversation with a man who appeared to be shaving himself at the top of a tower. "If I'm going to be an authoress I need to know what's being written—what's going on in the world."

Her father rattled his newspaper under her nose. "Read the paper. We're heading for another bloody war, that's what's going on."

"You won't have time to read anything when you're working in the mill," Annie said.

"I'm not going to work in the mill. My class went on a tour of Howarth's the other day. The noise was deafening. I don't know how you could stand it."

"That 's why the mill girls screech so," her mother said. "I'm glad our Annie got out when she did. You'll be far better off in service."

"I'm not going into service either."

"Oh? You seem to enjoy hearing about it."

"That's different." Clarrie said. It was true, she never tired of hearing about the stables full of horses, the hunt balls, the variety and abundance of foods served at hunt breakfasts, but she'd never cast herself in the role of a servant.

"It's hard work," her mother said, "but you're not afraid of work."

"I want to be an authoress."

"You can always do your writing on your afternoons off. I quite enjoyed being in service myself. I would have stayed there if it hadn't been for the war, but it seemed more important to do my bit and join the WAACS."

"What if you hadn't been born working class, Mam?" Clarrie asked. "What if you could have been anything in the world you wanted?"

"No sense wanting what you can't have. As long as we're healthy, and we have a roof over our heads and food on the table, I'm satisfied."

"Well, I'm not."

"She'd be a damn sight better off in the mill," her father said, "than bowing and scraping to the bloody gentry."

"Bowing and scraping? I never bowed or scraped to anyone in my life. At The Homestead as long as you did your work and knew your place, they treated you with respect. The mistress herself came into the kitchen every morning to plan the menu, and she never failed to ask after my family. Many's the time she gave me clothes to send home—some of them hardly worn. And the master loved to stop by and dance with us at the servants' ball. I believe he had more fun in the kitchen with us than he did at their own affairs.

"Aye, we've heard it all before," William said. "Next you'll be telling us you were like one, big, happy family."

"So we were. On Christmas Eve they invited us into the main hall to get our presents from under the tree. It wasn't much—a few bath cubes, a scarf, or a box of hankies, but nobody was forgotten. Even the stable boy got something." She resumed sprinkling the clothes. "You can always spot the real gentry," she said. "They practice what they call *noblesse oblige.*"

"Aye, and well they may." William released a trail of cigarette smoke. "Seeing as how the buggers have everything their own way."

Clarrie looked out the window at the grey Sunday morning sky. September always made her feel sad, this year more than ever. Time was slipping away too fast. In a few months she'd be turning fourteen—she'd be too old to skip rope, to run down to the croft with her whip and top, to race through the twilit streets crying "run sheep, run!" She'd have to leave school and find a job. Her childhood would be over forever.

She rose quickly, grabbed her skipping rope off the windowsill. "I'm going out to play," she said.

Her mother looked up from her book. "Don't go far, dinner's almost ready."

Grateful to find the back street empty, Clarrie sang as she skipped.

Up the street and down the street,
Windows made of glass,
Little Clarrie Hancock
Is a fine young lass.
She can dance, she can sing,
She can wear a wedding . . .

She tripped on the rope, breaking off in mid-song. Mrs. Sidebotham, known locally as "the duchess," was bearing down on her. She came to a stop an inch from Clarrie's nose. It seemed a bit early in the day for the duchess to be drunk. Clarrie had once seen her walk, head held high, past a group of gossiping women, and had overheard one of the women say, "It's a bloody marvel the way she sails over the curb without looking, you'd never guess t'owd girl was three sheets in the wind."

"She must think she's Queen Mary with that piss-pot on her head," another woman said, and they'd all laughed.

The duchess leaned closer to Clarrie. "Aren't you too old to be playing in the street?"

"I'm only thirteen," Clarrie said.

"Have you heard the news?"

Clarrie shook her head and stepped back, recoiling from the reek of beer and mothballs. The lapel of the old woman's coat bulged out revealing the chipped rim of an earthenware jug. She shoved it back beneath her coat.

"I'm on my way to get some herb beer," she said. "My old fella fancies a drop with his Sunday dinner."

Clarrie suppressed a smile. The duchess's herb beer was a neighborhood joke.

"You ought to go in and listen to the news on the wireless."

"We haven't got a wireless," Clarrie said. She was surprised to learn that the Sidebotham's had one. She always felt a twinge of envy when she saw people carrying their "accumulators" down the road to be charged. What exactly an accumulator's function was and why it needed to be charged, were mysteries only the lucky wireless owners seemed able to fathom.

"We're at war," Mrs. Sidebotham wiped a tear away with the back of her hand. "Those flaming Germans are at it again."

Clarrie patted Mrs. Sidebotham's arm. "Don't get upset, love. It might not be so bad."

"You're too young to remember the last one, or you wouldn't say that. It'll be terrible." She blew her nose on a soiled handkerchief. "All the young lads will have to go. They'll get theirselves killed in the trenches. It's mustard gas I'm worried about."

"People are more civilized nowadays," Clarrie said. "They won't use gas any more."

"Aye, that's what folks thought the last time." Mrs. Sidebotham stuffed her handkerchief back in her pocket. "You better go in and tell your mam and dad we're at war."

War! The word seemed to reverberate in the quiet street. Not long ago, the Prime Minister had gone to Germany to reason with Herr Hitler. He had stepped off a plane in London waving a sheet of paper and saying there would be peace in our time. Clarrie had seen it on the news at the Empire cinema.

Her father had been skeptical. "Peace in our time? I wouldn't trust that Hitler fella as far as I could throw him. They ought to listen to Winston Churchill."

"I thought you had no use for the man," her mother said.

"Aye; well, he made a bugger of it at Gallipoli, but this time he's right."

Her mother said she thought Mr. Chamberlain was a nice old gentleman doing his best to keep us out of war.

"He's a chinless wonder," her father said. "He doesn't know his arse from his umbrella."

Clarrie had no idea which of her parents was right, but she wished her father would show more respect for the Prime Minister—after all, he'd been educated at Oxford or Cambridge—somewhere like that—so it stood to reason he must know what he was talking about.

She ran into the back yard, threw her skipping rope behind the dustbin and stopped to use the lavatory before going in the house. When she pulled her knickers down, she was astonished to find them stained with blood. She'd heard rumors about this mysterious blood business—girls in school whispering about being excused from gym class because they had "the curse."

"What sort of curse?" she'd asked

"Haven't you got yours yet?"

"I don't even know what it is"

"You get blood in your knickers," one of the girls told her. "It means you've become a woman. When it happens you can't go to gym or wash your hair or play with boys, and you have to tell your mam right away, or you'll bleed to death. My mam knew a girl who was afraid to tell her mother. She bled to death in the lavatory."

Clarrie's mother was sitting by the fire absorbed in a book. She looked up. "Good, you're back. It's time to set the table."

Clarrie cleared her throat. She walked around to the back of her mother's chair. When she tried to speak she succeeding only in emitting a strangled whimper.

"What is it?" her mother said. "Why are you pacing about?"

"I . . . I . . ."

"What is it for heaven's sake?"

"There's blood all over my knickers," Clarrie blurted. She could feel her face burning.

Her mother got up and closed her book. Her normally rosy color deepened. "Well, now, that's nothing to get upset about. It happens to all girls sooner or later." She spoke in a quick, high voice. "It's perfectly natural. You've probably heard about it in school." She seemed to be addressing someone in the corner of the room over Clarrie's left shoulder. "Come upstairs with me and I'll give you something to put on."

Clarrie followed her mother into the big bedroom. Her mother rummaged through a drawer at the bottom of the wardrobe and brought out several thick white pads. She thrust them into Clarrie's hands.

"Pin one of these inside your knickers. Tomorrow when the shops open I'll buy you a proper belt. From now on, every month, you can just take what you need out of this drawer."

"Every month?" Clarrie's voice squeaked.

Her mother flashed her a startled glance. "Yes, love—every month. It's called a period. It comes every month, it lasts for a few days then goes away until the next month."

Every month! Why had nobody told her that? It would take some getting used to. But she felt better for having summoned up the courage to tell her mam, and relieved that her mam hadn't gone into a lot of embarrassing stuff about staying away from boys. She'd said nothing, thank God, about becoming a woman.

"I'll leave you to it, then," her mother said. "Change your knickers and run those stained ones through some cold water right away.

"Oh, by the way," Clarrie called as her mother walked away. "I almost forgot, Mrs. Sidebotham says the King has just been on the wireless. We're at war with Germany."

Chapter Thirty-four

The war seemed to be taking its time getting started, but there were changes taking place, nevertheless. The lamplighter, that familiar, mysterious being, no longer walked the streets at dusk, leaving pools of yellow light to mark his passage. On moonless nights, the streets were plunged into inky blackness. Men in tin helmets and ARP armbands patrolled the streets, looking for chinks of light in blackout curtains. People who ventured out at night were allowed to carry electric torches, provided the glass was covered with paint or paper, with only a small hole left for a needle of light to escape.

Maud Halliwell followed Clarrie down the lobby and into the Hancock's kitchen where Sally was pouring boiling water into the teapot.

"Hello, Sally," Maud said. "It looks like I've come at the right time."

"Have a seat," Sally said.

"Don't mind if I do. It's black as the hobs of hell out there. I just slammed into a flaming pillar box and said 'sorry' before I realized what it was."

William rose and pulled out a chair. "It's a bloody nuisance all right."

"The blackout doesn't bother me," Sally said. "I got used to the dark growing up in Kent. There were no street-lights in those country lanes."

"I wouldn't live in the country for all the rice in China," Maud said. "There's nothing to do. You can't even pop out to the pictures. But speaking of the blackout . . ." Maud paused to accept the cup of tea Sally held out to her. "Thanks, love. Did you hear about that daft fella who went on the prowl down Trafford Road the other night, to pick up a you-know-what . . ."

Sally shot a warning glance to Maud.

"She's not a baby any more," Maud said. Clarrie watched uneasily as Maud dropped a second cube of sugar into her teacup. She hoped Maud wasn't going to say anything embarrassing in front of her parents.

"Anyway," Maud went on, "the silly sod got the shock of his life when he got her into the light and found he'd picked up his own missus!"

"I imagine his wife was a bit surprised, too," Sally said.

Billy burst in, his hair in disarray, his cheeks glowing from the chilly air.

"You're late, young man," William said, "where've you been?"

"There's a whopping pile of sandbags around the Waverly Hotel. Noel and me—Noel and I—are using it for a fort."

"Stay away from it. Those sandbags are there to shore up the walls in case of bomb blast."

Sally made a wry mouth "Ah, yes," she said. "Let us protect the booze by all means."

Maud searched her handbag and produced a packet of Woodbines. She tapped a cigarette against the back of her hand. "I think they're making a to-do over nothing with all these precautions. The Jerries would be daft to fly all the way to Salford to bomb a few pubs and chimney pots."

William struck a match and lit Maud's cigarette. "We're right next to the Manchester Ship Canal and the docks—not to mention Trafford Park. Metro-Vicks is where they're making the Lancaster bombers."

"Anyway, what I came in to tell you was, the police found old Granny Witchy dead on her scullery flags, in a pile of rubbish. She'd been dead for a couple of days. They say the stench was terrible."

Sally paused in the act of buttering a slice of bread. "Oh, that poor soul! I was afraid of something like that. Yesterday, Mr. Timson told me she hadn't been by to pick up her basket, so I offered to take it over. I banged on the doors, front and back, but got no answer. I took the stuff back to Timson's. He said he'd call the police."

Maud flicked her cigarette ash into the hearth. "It was Timson who told me. Nellie Barlow came in while I was in the shop, and right away she starts collecting for a wreath. I gave her a threepenny bit. I think that's plenty, don't you? I never even spoke to the woman. You could smell her a mile away. And I have my own family to think of."

"I don't think she had any family, poor thing. We should have done something . . ."

Maud rose from her chair. "Anyway, Timson asked me to let you know. I better go in and get Johnny his tea."

Clarrie tried to imagine Granny Witchy lying dead in a pile of rubbish. She'd been old, ill, half-daft, and shunned like one of the lepers in the Bible—forbidden even to set foot in the corner shop to collect her groceries. The words from her prayer book flashed in her mind, "We have done those things we ought not to have done, and have left undone those things we ought to have done, and there is no health in us . . ."

"I carried her groceries home for her once or twice," Clarrie blurted, "and I always said hello when she went shuffling past our house with those rags trailing under her skirts."

"Yes, love," her mother said. "I know you did."

When Annie came home from work there was more talk about the old woman's death. "I'd have cleaned the place up for her, if she'd asked me to," Annie said.

"Well, it's too late now, " Sally said. "We all let her down. Wash your hands and have your tea. I wonder where our Arthur is? I don't like him riding that bike of his in the dark."

"I forgot to tell you," Annie said. "He told me he might spend the night with one of his pals. He said you're not to worry."

The following evening, William came down the lobby tearing open a telegram. "A lad just handed me this on my way in," he said. "It's from our Arthur. The damn fool's ridden his bike all the way to Kent. He's gone to stay with Ruth. He says he'll write and explain."

"Kent?" Sally said. "He rode all the way to Kent in one day? Why didn't he tell us he was going?"

"I think he's planning on joining up," Annie said.

"He could go to the barracks at Cross Lane to do that," William said. "The Lancashire Fusiliers is a good outfit."

"He's got his heart set on the Royal Marines," Annie said. "He was afraid you and Mam might try to stop him."

On Monday morning a man in a Home Guard uniform arrived at Clarrie's school, bringing with him several boxes filled with gasmasks. The masks were made of grey rubber with adjustable straps and a round filter in the front. The man showed the children how to put the masks on and told them they were theirs to keep for the duration of the war. Every man, woman, and child in England was to get one, free.

The children beamed at the prospect of getting something for nothing. Clarrie wondered how the government could afford to give away gasmasks to so many people.

The masks had a rubbery smell, and when you breathed out they made trumping noises that set the girls giggling. Miss Livesey grew red in the face, and told them they must try to breathe out quietly. Gasmasks, she told them, were not a laughing matter.

The Home Guard man held up several small wooden boards. These boards were being set up throughout the city, he said, to warn people of exposure to poison gases. If they saw one of the boards change color, they must put on their gas masks immediately. He set the boards aside and looked over the assembled classes.

"Which of you is willing to fight for King and country?" Every hand shot up. "Well done, young ladies," he said. "That's the ticket."

The children listened in rapt silence while he explained that in the event of a German invasion—which might happen at any moment—they were to resist the Germans to their last breath. All the able-bodied men were being called up into the armed forces. Only those too old or infirm to fight were being left behind to defend dear old England. It would be up to the children to fend off an invasion. The bundles of barbed wire at the street corners were to be stretched across the street the minute they spotted a German tank. And if they saw German soldiers marching down the street, they were to attack them with bricks, bottles, or anything else that came to hand.

Miss Livesey stepped forward and told the children to please stand and give the gentleman a round of applause. When the applause died down, she walked over to the piano and struck the opening chords of "I Vow to thee my Country." Her heart overflowing with emotion, Clarrie joined the singing:

I vow to thee my country, all earthly things above,
Entire and whole and perfect, the service of my love.
A love that will not falter, A love that pays the price.
That lays upon the altar, the eternal sacrifice . . .

Two days later, Arthur's promised letter arrived. William scanned it quickly and handed it to Sally. "He's joined the Marines. Why couldn't he wait until they called him up?"

"I seem to remember that you volunteered yourself in the last lot, Will."

"I was twenty-eight—old enough to know what I was doing."

"You can join the Home Guards this time Dad," Clarrie said. "England expects that every man shall do his duty."

Annie poked her in the ribs. "Eat your breakfast and don't talk so flaming daft. In case you haven't noticed, your old man's nearly blind."

"I was quoting Lord Nelson," Clarrie said. "Nelson only had one eye, didn't he, Dad?"

"Aye, he did. And I'll join the Home Guards when Nelson gets his eye back."

Chapter Thirty-five

Shortly before Christmas, Miss Hughes came into Clarrie's classroom. Her sharp, bird-like face was flushed. Wisps of greying hair had escaped from her topknot. She leaned over and whispered something to Miss Livesey behind her hand. Miss Livesey nodded and rose from her chair.

"May we have your attention, please? Miss Hughes has an announcement to make."

Miss Hughes cleared her throat. "As you are all no doubt aware, many of your schoolmates have already been evacuated. Several teachers, too, have left to help with the war effort, and half our classrooms are empty. Because of these things, and because of the severe fuel shortages, we find that we can no longer . . ." She broke off and then resumed. "The girls who expect to turn fourteen within the first six months of the coming year—and I believe that takes in all of you—are free to go." She fumbled in the pocket of her smock, produced a handkerchief, then turned abruptly and left the classroom.

The girls looked at one another. Clarrie raised her hand. She had done exceptionally well in all her subjects this year, even arithmetic, and Miss Livesey had told her in confidence that there was little doubt she would be top girl. Being top girl meant she'd get a prize—a book or something—and the privilege of choosing the closing hymn on leaving day. To honor Arthur and the other Marines, she'd picked "Eternal Father Strong to Save"; the heartfelt refrain, "O hear us when we cry to Thee, For those in peril on the sea," always moved her to tears.

"Yes, Clarrie, what is it?"

"Please Miss, what about Leaving Day?"

"Leaving Day . . . yes, you've been looking forward to it, I know. I . . . er . . . I'm sorry to say there will be no Leaving Day ceremony this year. The customary certificates and prizes have been dispensed with for the duration."

"But . . ."

"I'm afraid there's nothing to be done about it."

Miss Livesey picked up a chalk eraser and began rubbing at the clean blackboard. "Miss Hughes has said you are free to go. Please tell your parents there is no need for you to come to school any more." Nobody moved. The girls looked at each other, dazed.

"Class dismissed," Miss Livesey said firmly.

Clarrie stumbled to her feet, close to tears. Her school days were over. She wouldn't get to pick the closing hymn after all, nor would she have the thrill of going up to receive her prize. "There's a war on, love," her family would say when she told them. They'd think she was making a fuss about nothing.

Barrage balloons floated above the rooftops, basking like silvery whales in the gray sky; sandbags and rolls of barbed wire marked every corner. At the corner of Cross Lane, forty or fifty children, all about Billy's age, were huddled together in the care of a large, matronly woman. The girls wore their Sunday best, their knitted wool scarves sewn, according to the latest fad, into pixie hats. The boys looked unnaturally spic and span—their hair combed, their knee socks smartly pulled up, their boots polished to a high gloss. They each had a gas mask slung across their shoulders and carried a pillowcase stuffed with belongings. Pinned to each child's coat was a buff-colored luggage tag bearing a name and a destination. Behind a barrier, a crowd of mothers waved handkerchiefs, dabbed at their eyes, called out last-minute instructions to their children. Clarrie walked over to the woman in charge and asked her where the children were going.

"They're being evacuated, love," the woman said. "That's all I can tell you."

Evacuated. It was one of those new words, like, *Axis*, *salvage*, and *austerity*, appearing every day in the newspapers. Many of the new words were German—words like *fuehrer*, *swastika*, and *ersatz*. All of them were being quickly absorbed into the public vocabulary.

At the corner of Thurlow Street, several small boys were climbing over the sandbag barriers around the Waverly Hotel, shooting cap pistols and rubber-tipped arrows in their game of cowboys and Indians. The sandbags had proved irresistible. Already several bags had burst open, spilling sand onto the pavement. Clarrie spotted Billy crouching behind the sandbags.

"Dad told you not to climb on these sandbags," she said.

"I'm not climbing on them, I'm hiding behind them. I'm lying in ambush. You're giving the game away."

"Better not let Dad catch you," Clarrie said. A lorry, piled high with scrap iron, was parked outside her house. Two men were busy removing the spiked railings and the wrought-iron gate.

"May I ask why you're taking away our gate and railings?" she asked.

"They're to be smelted down to make torpedoes," one of the men said. "There's a war on, chuck, haven't you heard?"

"I'm aware that there's a war on," Clarrie said haughtily. "My brother happens to be a Royal Marine."

Over tea that evening, she recounted the events of the day. "I won't even get a leaving certificate, and I was supposed to get a prize, but they've suspended prize-giving for the duration." Her description of the evacuees set off a discussion about the advisability of sending her and Billy away, too.

"I wouldn't mind going to America," Clarrie told them.

Her mother dished out mashed potatoes from a saucepan. "You're finished with school now, so you're not eligible to be evacuated."

"I want to go to one of those ranches in Texas," Billy said. "I can sleep in a bunkhouse and ride the range on a horse, like Tim McCoy."

Sally patted his arm. "I don't think they let you choose where you go, love."

"I bet it's only rich kids who get sent to America, anyway," Annie said.

"A bloody daft idea it is, too," William said. "The Atlantic is crawling with U-Boats."

Sally placed the pan back on the hob with a bang. "Well, we're not sending him to live with strangers. What if he got in with rum'n's? I'll write and ask my sister, Ruth, if she can take him."

Somebody was knocking at the front door. Billy ran down the lobby to open it.

"What makes you think the lad will be any safer there?" William said. "Kent is right on the channel, in the flaming line of fire."

"We'll keep him home, then, and take our chances together."

Billy ran back into the kitchen shouting: "The Marines have landed!"

Arthur, looking handsome as a film star in his uniform, came in hauling a duffle bag. Everyone at the table rose to greet him.

"How long are you in for, then?" his father asked when they were seated again.

"Thirteen years."

"Thirteen years! You're out of your mind, lad. Whatever possessed you to do a thing like that?"

"Don't shout at him," Sally heaped Arthur's plate with potatoes and onion gravy, and gave him the sausage off her own plate. "Your dad's proud of you, love. He just wants what's best for you."

"It was the only way I could get in. The Royal Marines are a crack outfit, Dad. They're very particular "

"You've signed your blasted life away," William said.

"I'll be okay."

"When will you be finished with your training, then?"

"I'm pretty much finished. Everything's speeded up in wartime. I expect I'll be getting a berth on a ship when I go back. I don't know where they're sending us. We're not supposed to talk about that, anyway."

As soon as the meal was over, William got to his feet. "Come on, Arthur, m'lad. I'm taking you to a game of snooker."

Sally smiled. "Your dad wants to show him off to his pals," she said after they'd gone.

For the next few days, Billy and Clarrie followed Arthur about the house, asking him questions, watching with interest as he polished his boots and whitened his belt with

Blanco. He told them bits of Marine lore, explained how the Marines got the nickname "leathernecks."

"I want to join the RAF," Billy said, "but it will be just my luck to have the war over by the time I'm old enough."

Two days before Arthur was due back at camp, William came in, staggering under the weight of a large metal box. He set the box on the table.

"What's that you've got, Dad?" Clarrie asked.

"A wireless."

Arthur grinned. "Finally broke down and decided to join the modern world, eh, Dad?"

William fiddled with the knobs. Crackling voices and tinny music came and went.

Sally came in from the scullery. "What on earth's that?"

"What does it look like?"

"You swore you'd never have a wireless in the house."

"Aye, well . . . I changed my mind. This is a short wave. Chap sold it to me dirt cheap. We can bring in Germany . . . find out what's going on over there."

"All we have to do is learn German," Annie said.

Sally had her hands over her ears. "I don't wonder he got rid of it."

"It needs a bit of adjusting, that's all."

The room was suddenly filled with a raucous voice speaking German. "Shh! That's him," William said. "That's Hitler!"

"Listen to him rant," Sally said. "You don't need to understand German to know the man's stark raving mad. Those Nazis must be deaf, dumb, and blind to fall for a man like that."

"Turn the silly bugger off," Annie said. "Let's have summat with a bit of life to it—Arthur Askey, or Tommy Handley, or Gert and Daisy."

William turned the knobs again. A Cockney voice was singing "The Lambeth Walk."

"That's more like it," Annie said. "I think that's Lupino Lane."

"Your dad was on stage with one of the Lupinos," Sally said. "They're related to Ida Lupino, the film star, you know."

On New Year's Eve, William took the family on an unprecedented outing to the Koh-i-noor restaurant in Manchester to celebrate Arthur's last day at home.

"This place is named for the Koh-i-noor diamond," Sally said. "I remember reading about it in *The Passing Parade*. It was Queen Alexandra, I believe, who . . ."

Her story was interrupted by a waiter who showed them to a long table in the center of the room. The air smelled deliciously of curry. Clarrie, conscious that they were causing a small stir, took her place at the table. Two young women at a nearby table cast warm glances at Arthur.

"What are those two gawping at?" Annie asked.

"They're admiring your handsome brother," her mother said.

"Or perhaps they're admiring your younger brother," Billy said.

Everybody laughed. Clarrie looked around the room. Candles winking in little red glass bowls on the tables cast a rosy light over all the faces. She was proud to be in this fancy restaurant in the company of her family, and fiercely proud of Arthur, so strong and manly in his Royal Marine uniform. She knew she would never forget this moment.

When the waiter came to take their order, Clarrie was suddenly overcome with shyness. Her hands felt bigger and heavier than normal. She didn't know where to put them. She tried resting her wrists on the edge of the table, but that felt awkward, so she slid them into her lap.

"I don't know what to ask for," she whispered to her mother.

"Leave that to your dad," her mother said. She turned to William. "You can order for us all, Will."

Her father took control of everything—scanning the menu, quietly consulting with the waiter, ordering for everyone as though it were something he did every day. Her mother seemed shy but happy. Annie laughed softly at something Arthur had said, and her pretty white teeth flashed. Billy was peering at the menu through his new glasses, like a miniature professor examining a student's paper. Clarrie had a sudden vision of Billy, grown up, wearing a mortarboard and academic robes. Billy would become a teacher—a university professor—she was sure of it.

The waiter brought a platter of curry—the same thing for everyone.

"This isn't at all bad," her mother conceded, "although I myself would never serve curry with potatoes."

As soon as they got home, William told Billy to get off to bed. He was too young to stay up to see in the New Year.

"Let him stay up a little longer, Will," Sally said. "It's Arthur's last night."

"You'll have to get up early, tomorrow," Clarrie said to Billy. "It's New Year's day." On New Year's day, Gladys and she had always waited on Timson's step while he opened the shop. It seemed so long ago . . . she could hardly remember what Gladys had looked like.

"I doubt they'll have much to give away this year," Sally said.

They gathered by the fire to await the stroke of midnight and the arrival of Mr. Perlman who had promised to bring in the New Year. Tradition demanded that the first person to enter a house at New Year be a dark-haired man—anyone else would bring bad luck. They had just finished singing Auld Lang Syne, when they heard a rat-a-tat-tat on the front door.

"That's destiny knocking on the door," Clarrie said, "like in Beethoven's fifth thing-a-mebob." But it was only Mr. Perlman. He stepped into the kitchen, removed his trilby, and placed a small parcel on the table.

"Coal and salt—I believe they're supposed to bring good luck," he said. His face was blue from the cold. He stepped over to the fire to warm his hands.

William rose from his chair. "Let me take your coat; have a glass of wine with us."

Mr. Perlman said he'd keep his coat on, but he wouldn't say no to a drop of port.

"Thanks for bringing in the New Year for us." William said. He poured wine for Mr. Perlman, for Annie and Arthur, and a smaller glass for Clarrie.

"Will!" Sally said.

"A drop of port won't do her any harm."

"Well . . . since it's a special occasion." Sally gave Billy a glass of ginger beer and poured one for herself.

William raised his glass. "Here's wishing you a happy new year . . . and let's hope 1940 will bring a quick end to this bloody war."

Chapter Thirty-six

According to the "Help Wanted" column in the Manchester Evening News, girls, fourteen years or over, were needed for factory work and should apply by letter to Mr. Arnold P. Grimsby, owner and general manager of A. Grimsby & Son, Packers and Makers-Up. The advertisement made no mention of experience. Clarrie circled the item with a pencil. She hadn't yet reached her fourteenth birthday, but perhaps a week or two made no difference. She asked the family if anyone knew what a "Packers and Makers-up" did.

Billy, who was sprawled on the mat by the fire, looked up from his *Beano* comic. "I imagine they pack stuff and make it up."

Clarrie swatted him with the paper.

Her father took the paper from her hand and brought the page close to his face. "Judging by this address, it's got to do with the cotton trade."

"Not a mill, I hope."

He handed the paper back to her. "It's in Manchester. There are no mills on that street."

"There's no need to go into Manchester," her mother said. "Mrs. Perlman says she could use some help in the shop."

"Why can't Renee do it?"

"She's not interested."

"Neither am I." Clarrie said. Perlman's shop window displayed faded pink corsets, bust bodices, and open boxes of lisle stockings. Working there, she'd see nobody but the Perlmans and a few old women customers—and she'd have to work the till. What if she were to give somebody the wrong change?

"Why don't you want to work at Perlman's?" her mother asked.

"I'd rather find my own job."

She wasted several sheets of paper composing a letter of application, trying to strike the right balance between modesty and self-confidence. She borrowed a phrase or two from the letters of recommendation her father had written on his own behalf. When she was finally satisfied, she showed the letter to her father. He read it and handed it back to her, saying, "Aye, it'll do."

On her way up the stairs to bed, Clarrie overheard him saying to her mother, "She writes a damn good letter, does our Clarrie."

"Why didn't you tell her so, then?"

"No sense giving her a swelled head."

Clarrie tiptoed upstairs, smiling.

After several days of anxious waiting she got a reply. She was to present herself at Grimsby's on Friday morning for an interview. The time had come to step out into the larger world.

"Should I wear my best?" She asked her mother.

"Yes, love. You want to look nice for the interview. If you get the job, you probably won't start until Monday."

"What about my hair?"

"You can go to the hairdresser's. We really can't afford it, but it's not every day."

On Friday morning, Clarrie rose before it was light and ran down to the scullery. Her mother had started the fire in the kitchen, but the water in the kettle was not yet warm, so she washed in cold water by candlelight. The day before, after visiting the hairdresser's for the first time in her life; she'd gone to bed in one of Annie's hairnets, but the hairnet had come off in the night, and the fringe across her forehead was sticking out like a bookie's eyeshade. She ran tap water over her fingers and tried to press the fringe back in place.

Annie shouted for her to hurry up. "You're not the only one who needs to use the sink."

Clarrie gave her fringe a final tug and went into the kitchen. "Do I look all right?"

"What happened to your curls?" Annie asked.

Her mother set a plate of toast in front of Clarrie. "You look fine."

"I don't look like a working girl, though. Should I put lipstick on?"

"You're not even fourteen," Annie said. "I was sixteen before I was allowed to use lipstick."

Billy, his arms folded, looked Clarrie over critically. "Noel's cousin, Doris, uses an eyebrow pencil," he said, "and she's only twelve."

"That's because she has no eyebrows," Annie said.

Billy said he thought Clarrie would look nice with lipstick.

William handed Clarrie her freshly polished shoes. "You don't need any of that muck. That's only for the stage. Your mam doesn't paint her face, and where could you find anyone better looking?"

"Mam's a natural beauty, I'm not."

"Eat your breakfast, love," her mother said. "You're good enough as you are."

Clarrie swallowed a mouthful of toast and gulped her tea. "What if they want to see my leaving certificate?"

"Tell them the truth. They didn't hand them out this year."

"What if they ask me to do something I don't know how to do?"

"You haven't landed the job yet," her father said.

Her mother took a few pennies out of her purse. "Here's your carfare. You'll probably be home in time for lunch."

"I wish you were coming with me, Mam."

"Bringing your mother with you on a job interview? What a mard arse!" Annie blew a breath of contempt. "You won't last five minutes in a factory. They'll make mincemeat out of you."

Her mother tucked a scarf around Clarrie's neck. "If you don't like the look of the place, don't bother with them; you can work for Mrs. Perlman."

Fine needles of rain stung Clarrie's face as she walked to the bus stop, but by the time the bus pulled to a stop at Deansgate, the sun had broken through. She asked the conductor for directions.

"Go down Princess Street and cross over the canal," he said. "You can't miss it."

Princess Street was lined with office buildings, four and five stories high, with gleaming windows and massive window ledges. Charwomen were cleaning steps and polishing the shiny brass nameplates outside the buildings. In spite of the walls of sandbags and the barrage balloons overhead, there was energy and a sense of purpose in the air that made Clarrie lift her chin and walk more briskly.

The street narrowed forming a bridge across the canal. Clarrie peered over the low wall. Below was a barge, with a slatternly woman sitting on a pile of sacks, breastfeeding a baby. A horde of scruffy, flaxen-haired children were chasing one another about the deck. What a strange life the barge people must lead. Didn't the children have to go to school? Didn't they mind strangers gaping at them as though they were animals in a zoo? As if in answer to her unspoken question, one of the ragamuffins looked up and thumbed his nose at her. Embarrassed, Clarrie moved away.

She turned onto a side street lined with ancient factories and ramshackle warehouses. Halfway down the block she found the address. A painted sign, barely legible across the two halves of a splintered double door, confirmed that these were the premises of A. Grimsby and Sons, Packers and Makers-Up.

Clarrie's heart sank. This building was even shabbier than its neighbors. The double doors opened into a cobbled yard full of oily puddles. Two men and a boy of fifteen or sixteen were loading paper-covered bales onto a lorry. The yard reeked of petrol and urine. The boy, struggling with a bale that was bigger than he, stopped what he was doing to stare boldly at Clarrie as she approached. His right eye was almost closed by a sty.

"Yer looking for someone, love?" he said.

"Yes. Mr. Grimsby." Both of the men on the lorry were scrawny, wizened, and dressed in greasy trousers and leather waistcoats. One had a withered arm that hung, apparently useless, by his side. He held a grappling hook in his good hand.

"Ted, this 'ere lass is lookin' for t'gaffer," the boy yelled.

"I have an appointment," Clarrie said. One of the men whispered something to the other, and they both laughed. Clarrie flushed. Perhaps "I have an appointment" was an expression only used in books and films. She couldn't recall hearing anyone she knew say it.

The men were grinning at her like idiots. Was there something peculiar about her? Was it her hair?

The man with the withered arm gestured with his grappling hook towards a side door. "He's in t'office."

Clarrie thanked him and knocked timidly at the door. There was no response. She knocked again. Nothing. She pushed open the door a crack.

"There's nobody here," she called to the man.

"Wait inside, lass, I reckon 'e won't be long."

She stepped into a cramped, dusty room, with barely enough space for a desk and chair. Shelves, crammed haphazardly with cardboard boxes, bolts of cloth, reels of twine, and bottles of ink, lined the walls. The desk was heaped with yellowing invoices and receipts, some of them impaled on steel spikes. A man's dark blue jacket and a bowler hat hung from a brass hat-rack in one corner. Her letter lay open on the desk. Someone had marked it with a large red checkmark.

A voice sounded outside and a sharp-faced, middle-aged man burst into the room. His white shirtsleeves were rolled up above the elbows; his dark waistcoat was open and covered in cotton fuzz. He shot Clarrie a surprised look, but before he could speak, he was followed by another, older man, wearing a long canvas apron. The older man was explaining something. When he saw Clarrie he stopped.

"Yes, yes . . ." the man in the waistcoat said over his shoulder. He turned back to Clarrie. "And who are you, young lady?"

"Clara Hancock. I'm looking for Mr. Grimsby."

"Well, you've found him." He turned to the older man. "You'd better take care of that right away. We can't hold up that order any longer."

"What do you expect me to do about it, then?" The older man said. The expression on his cadaverous face said he wasn't about to hurry for Mr. Grimsby or anyone else.

"It's got to come off the rollers. It's got to be put right, the quicker the better."

The older man gave a perfunctory nod and walked out.

"Bit of an emergency," Mr. Grimsby said. "I'll have to make this brief." He sat at his desk and picked up Clarrie's letter. "Did you write this yourself, or did someone write it for you?"

"I wrote it."

His eyes seemed to be accusing her of something. Clarrie looked back at him and tried not to feel guilty.

"It's a good letter," he said finally. "Better than most. I can see you know how to spell, but do you know how to work?"

"I'm not afraid of work. I do plenty at home."

"I don't stand for any nonsense. You work for me, you have to earn your wages."

"I understand."

"Right. It's twelve and six a week. The hours are half past eight to half past five, with an hour for lunch and half a day on Saturday. You can start right away. I've a nice little job for you."

Mr. Grimsby got up. "Come with me."

She followed him out the door and up a rickety outside staircase. The two men and the boy stopped loading the lorry, to watch. Mr. Grimsby pushed open the door to a large loft. There was a buzz of machinery. Girls in wraparound aprons were operating machines that whirled cloth around boards. Four or five other girls stood at a long shiny wooden bench doing something with bolts of cloth. The older man she'd seen in the office came forward to meet them.

"This here is Mr. Blackwell, the foreman," Mr. Grimsby said. "He's in charge of all the girls up here." He pushed Clarrie forward. "This is the new girl, Clara Hawkins," he said.

"Hancock," Clarrie said.

"Hancock, right. You can start her on that rush job. Have you decided how you're going to do it?"

"I thought we'd just let her throw it back like, and pull it down." Mr. Blackwell scratched himself under the arm. "I've already got Joan working on it." The two men walked over to the bench where a plump blonde girl was tossing blue silk to the back of the bench and pulling it down off its wooden roller. She was breathing heavily from the effort, and her pink face was beaded with sweat. Layer upon layer of slippery silk lay in folds at her feet.

"Too slow . . . too slow. It'll take forever that way," Mr. Grimsby said. "And she's taking up all the bench space. Remember what we did last time? A few years ago, it was—one of the Bloom jobs was lapped wrong?"

Mr. Blackwell said no, he didn't remember.

"Well, I do," Mr. Grimsby said. "You get those lads in the yard to bring up a couple of the big weights. I still have the pole and the handle somewhere."

Mr. Blackwell nodded. "You can show the new girl where to put her coat—show her the ropes and so on," he said to Joan.

The blonde girl smiled at Clarrie. "Come with me." Clarrie followed her to a coat-rack at the end of the room. "We knock off for lunch at twelve," she said. "We get a whole hour—which is a lot more than you get at some jobs. You'll have to go for the lunches. I've been filling in, but the new girls are supposed to do it. All the girls, and the blokes in packing, too, will give you their money and their orders. You can get most of the stuff at Vernon's chip shop, next street down. You'll need a cardboard box to carry it all."

Mr. Grimsby beckoned to Clarrie, who followed him to a makeshift contraption set up on wooden blocks a few inches from the floor. A pole that held the silk was secured at either end by two enormous iron weights, with an iron handle attached to one end of the pole.

"Kneel down here on the floor," he said, "and keep turning this handle until all the silk is off the roller. When that's done, there're forty more to unwind. This job's supposed to be finished and on boards by half-past five."

Clarrie knelt obediently on the rough wooden floor and began to turn the handle. A thick layer of rust rubbed against her palms as she worked. Soon her knees were hurting so much that she had to keep changing positions to get more comfortable. The girls at the benches nudged each other and giggled. Mr. Blackwell glared at them. "The next one who thinks it's funny can take her place," he said.

Mr. Grimsby stopped by to see how she was getting along. She had unwound only four or five rolls of silk, but she felt as though she had been turning the handle forever. Her back ached and the palms of her hands were blistered and covered with rust.

"Faster, faster!" Mr. Grimsby said. From the bottom of the stairs, a man shouted that the boss was wanted on the telephone. Mr. Grimsby hurried away.

Clarrie wiped her hands on her skirt. Her new yellow blouse and her brown dirndl skirt were covered in dust. The blisters on her palms and on the insides of her fingers had broken open and were oozing.

Mr. Blackwell came by with a wad of coarse cretonne for her to use as a kneeling mat. It was better than kneeling on the wood, but rough on her knees, even so. She wished she could go home and sit by the fire and have a cup of tea. There was nothing to stop her from walking out right now, but that was exactly what Annie had predicted. She wanted to prove Annie wrong. She would stick this job out if it killed her.

By the time twelve o'clock rolled around and the machines were turned off, she was so stiff she could barely rise to her feet. "You all right, lass?" Mr. Blackwell asked gruffly.

"I'm fine." She kept her hands hidden behind her back." Joan says I'm supposed to fetch the lunches."

"You better get a move on, then."

The reek of frying fish and hot grease rushed at her as she opened the door and stepped inside the shop. Girls and boys in work overalls shoved and jostled, calling out orders to a little woman who was flitting about doing several things at once. A large man with a drooping moustache and a greasy apron was pushing peeled potatoes through a cutter.

Pressed on all sides, Clarrie inched her way to the counter. A sharp elbow jabbed her in the ribs and Clarrie stepped back, waiting for a path to clear. A cockroach scuttled along the steamy wall and disappeared behind the stove, loosening a flake of curling green paint that broke from the wall and dropped into a vat of boiling grease. At last she succeeded in getting the woman's attention. The woman slapped fish and chips and peas and beans into squares of greaseproof paper and bundled them up in newspaper. As she worked, she wiped her hands on an apron already black from grease and newsprint.

When Clarrie returned with the lunches, the girls were sitting on the workbench, waiting. A girl with furtive eyes and a hairline so low it almost met her eyebrows thrust her face close to Clarrie's. "You took your sweet time, kiddo. Lunch hour is almost over. We were beginning to think you'd run off with the money."

"They were very busy."

"You've got to shove your way through—use your elbows," the girl said. "What did you say your name was?"

"Clarrie."

The girl with low forehead laughed. "Where did you get your hair set, Clarrie?"

Clarrie smiled. "Riley's. It's in Salford."

The girl with the low forehead winked at the others. "Thanks for warning us. We'll know enough to stay away from Riley's." She looked around for approval from her cronies, who giggled on cue. "By the way, Mr. Blackwell wants you to whitewash the lavatory tomorrow. He'll supply the whitewash but you have to bring your own pail and brushes."

Clarrie handed out the rest of the lunches and then ran to the lavatory. In the dirty stall, she sat on the porcelain rim, wiping her tears with the back of her hand. When would she learn? No matter how many times she ran into this kind of spite, she was never prepared for it.

There was a knock at the door and somebody asked her to hurry up. She pulled the chain and left the stall, brushing past the girl who was waiting. She splashed her face with cold water, and spun the dirty roller towel; failing to find a clean spot, she wiped her face on her sleeve and ran back upstairs. The machinery had started up. She searched a waste barrel for something to protect her hands. Nothing but more scraps of the coarse cretonne. She wrapped them around her hands and went back to work. No matter how fast she turned the roller, she would never be able to finish it all by half-past five.

At last the buzzer sounded, signaling the end of the workday, and the machinery ground to a stop. Clarrie stared in dismay at the stack of bolts still waiting to be unwound. The girls around her had dropped what they were doing and were grabbing their coats. Within seconds, the room had emptied.

Mr. Blackwell came over. "Time to go home, young lady," he said.

"But I haven't finished, and tomorrow they said I'm supposed to . . ."

"Go home. You're not being paid to work overtime." He walked away.

Clarrie struggled to her feet. Blood had soaked through the cretonne around her hands; her knees were excruciatingly sore, her whole body ached. She lifted her coat from the peg but found that her arm wouldn't go through the armhole; someone had sewn together the linings of the sleeves—probably that girl with the low forehead and her cronies—they must have done it while she was out getting their lunches. She took a pair of small scissors from the workbench, and holding them gingerly to avoid the blisters on her fingers, snipped away the stitches.

She walked to Deansgate in swirling fog, reaching the bus stop just as the bus was pulling away. She'd have to walk back to Salford, but it was only a couple of miles. As she walked, she mulled over the events of the day. Joan was nice, but as for the rest of them . . . what was it about her that made some people want to hurt her? Perhaps they sensed how easy it would be. She needed to grow a thicker skin, to find a place inside herself where they couldn't reach her—an interior fortress where, safe in her own secret center, she would remain unmoved, indifferent.

The fog had thickened. As she cut down Blackfriars, a dim bobbing light loomed out of the darkness. She laughed. It was the same bus she would have caught had she not been delayed, but it was crawling along through the fog, guided by the conductor swinging a lantern. At the rate it was moving, she would be home before it reached Eccles New Road.

The door flew open at her knock. Her mother stepped aside to let her pass. "Hurry, love, before the fog gets in. We've been worried sick about you. We thought you'd got lost. Did you get the job?"

"Yes. I had to start right away, and then I missed the bus." She winced as she tried to remove her coat.

Her mother grasped Clarrie's hands and turned them palm up. "Good God, what have they done to you?" Clarrie explained what she'd had to do.

"That settles it," her mother said. She helped Clarrie out of her coat and steered her into the kitchen. "Look what they've done to her hands," she said to William. "She's not going back there. Miserable devils!"

"Why didn't you say something to them?" her father asked. "When are you going to learn to speak up for yourself?"

"You can find a better job," her mother said. "If you don't want Perlmans, perhaps our Annie can put in a word for you at the bakery."

"No!" Clarrie said quickly. "I'm all right, Mam, honest. I'm just not used to it."

"Look at your hands. If they're expecting you to work tomorrow, you'll have to tell them you can't."

"I have to bring a bucket and a whitewash brush when I go in tomorrow," Clarrie said. "New girls are supposed to whitewash the lavatory."

Her mother tore a strip of the bandage in half with her teeth and tied it around Clarrie's hand. "I'll have to get you some ointment."

Her father laughed. "Whitewash the lavatory? You're being had, you silly bugger."

"No—everyone said so. I don't mind. It really needs doing, and I'd rather whitewash the lavatory than have to turn that handle again."

"They're making a jackass out of you," her father said. "You'll look a right numbskull showing up for work carrying a bucket and a whitewash brush."

Her mother set a cup of steaming tea in front of Clarrie. "Listen to your dad, love. If you must go in, go in without them. If anyone mentions whitewash, tell them you thought they were joking."

Chapter Thirty-seven

The next morning the silks and the contraption with weights had vanished. Nothing was said about whitewashing the lavatory. With a glance at her bandaged hands, Mr. Blackwell set her to stamping "Made in England" along the selvedges of a stack of folded calico. Clarrie worked diligently, finishing one bolt and picking up another. Joan, who was working next to her, pointed to where Clarrie was briskly stamping "Made in England" down the center crease of the fabric.

Clarrie looked up, aghast. "What should I do?"

Joan pushed Clarrie aside, grabbed the shears and quickly slit the damaged material away from the bolt. In less than a second, she had thrust the spoiled material to the bottom of the scrap barrel. When Clarrie, conscious that she ought to pay for the damage, started to protest, Joan whispered "You'll get us both in trouble." Clarrie nodded, switched the material around, and resumed stamping along the selvedge.

Several days had passed but Clarrie still hadn't mastered the art of getting served at the fish and chip shop. Rita, the girl with the low brow, was complaining to anyone within earshot about having to wait too long for her lunch.

"I'm sorry," Clarrie said, "but you're supposed to wait your turn, and that's what I do."

Joan told Clarrie she'd be happy to go for the lunches if Clarrie would make the tea and clean up the kitchen afterwards. Clarrie followed her down to the kitchen to see how it was done. The kitchen was nothing more than a ramshackle lean-to under the stairs, sparsely equipped with an ancient sink, a splintery shelf for cups and teapots, and two gas rings on a small oilcloth-covered table. In spite of being open to the elements along one side, the place smelled strongly of stewed tea and leaking gas.

"I'll leave you to it, then," Joan said. "I'll fetch those lunches before you-know-who starts on me."

Shortly before twelve on Clarrie's second Saturday, Mr. Blackwell came by with a cardboard box filled with small buff-colored envelopes. He dropped one on the bench in front of her. Clarrie tore open the envelope and shook out several half-crowns and a sixpence. The coins fell with a satisfying jingle into her palm. Her first wages! This was not just money; it was tangible evidence of her worth—proof of her ability to earn her bread as other people did. Her mother had said she could spend her first wages in any way she chose, but she knew without being told that starting with the next pay envelope, she'd be expected to hand everything over to her mother. She'd get a shilling for spending money, as Arthur and Annie had done when they first started work.

She took a deep breath as she stepped out into the air. Sometime during the morning, a lively March wind had sprung up, chasing the scudding clouds across the sky and blowing away the last vestiges of fog. Instead of going straight home, she'd walk to Market Street and do some shopping.

Market Street quivered with vibrant energy. The plate-glass windows sparkled. Shoppers bustled past, laden with parcels. A policeman, with immaculate white-gloved hands, was directing traffic. Red double-decker buses rollicked down the street. Even the barrage balloons shimmering overhead, and the sandbags stacked against the buildings failed to detract from the general air of prosperity and well-being.

She stopped first at Boots chemists. The mingled smells of talcum powder, coal-tar soap, rubber hot-water bottles, and loofahs seemed more than ordinarily potent. After some indecision, she chose a packet of Yardley's lavender bath cubes for Annie. In Woolworth's, she bought a kite for Billy and a writing pad for herself. From there she went to the tobacconists and bought a packet of De Reske cork-tipped cigarettes for her father. At the corner of the street, a flower seller, sitting on an upturned crate, solved the problem of what to get for her mother by thrusting a bunch of daffodils under Clarrie's nose. "Buy some lovely daffs, first of the season," she wheedled.

Clarrie bent close, breathing in the moist, raw, scent. "I'll take two bunches," she said, "for my mother."

The woman lifted the dripping flowers from the tub beside her and wrapped them in green tissue paper. "Is your mam in hospital, love?"

"Oh, no—she's fine. It's just that she grew up in the country, and she loves flowers."

She stopped again at the fishmongers and bought a bag of fresh herrings—something the whole family would enjoy. Clarrie counted her change. She had intended to buy wool to knit a pair of warm gloves for Arthur, but that would have to wait for next payday. She'd better get on home while she still had money for bus fare.

A brisk breeze lifted scraps of paper from the gutters and whipped at her hair as she walked to the bus stop. The windows along Deansgate sparkled in the pale sunlight. Out of the corner of her eye, she saw a slender girl striding towards her. The girl's fair, silky hair fluttered about her face, the flaps of her open coat billowed back, revealing a slender body, and long, shapely legs. Clarrie smiled at the girl. The girl smiled back. She, too, was laden with parcels and had her arms full of daffodils. They were about to pass one another, when the girl suddenly vanished. Clarrie stopped in confusion. She took a step backwards. The girl reappeared. She stepped forward. Again the girl vanished. Clarrie burst out laughing. She had been admiring her own reflection. The pretty, windblown girl in the plate glass window was herself. When had such a transformation taken place and why hadn't she noticed it?

In the early months of summer, air-raid sirens began disturbing the nights with their eerie wailing. There were one or two bombs dropped, but it was not until August that the air-raids began in earnest. The Methodist chapel, rendered unsafe by a bomb blast, was permanently closed, leaving William and Sally once more out of work. William lost no time applying at the docks again. This time he was hired on the spot as a checker. He came home looking pleased with himself.

"Now that the buggers need me," he said, "it seems my blind eye is no longer a handicap."

He went off to work each morning dressed in a blue serge suit, a bowler hat, and white celluloid collar, his breast pocket bristling with a fountain pen and several freshly sharpened pencils. He returned each evening, tired and grimy, with barely enough time to bolt a hurried meal before returning to Trafford Park, where he had volunteered as a roof-spotter.

"A blind roof-spotter!" Annie rolled her eyes. "Why should England tremble?"

"Blind or not," Sally said, "your dad will do a better job than most."

Sitting on the damp cellar steps in the middle of the night, aided by the light of a solitary candle, Clarrie began to read *Gone With the Wind,* the latest novel from America. With the opening sentences, the cold, gritty steps of the cellar were transformed into the steps of Tara. The smells of coal dust, tomcats, and creosote vanished, dispelled by the magnolias and honeysuckle of antebellum Georgia. Stopped by an unfamiliar word, Clarrie looked up from her book, uncertain for the moment where she was.

"What's a 'barbecue'?"

"Some sort of roast beef, I believe," her mother said.

"That can't be right. The girl in this book is getting dressed for a ball. She's supposed to rest at the barbecue."

There was a rumbling overhead, followed by an explosion that shook the house. The lid of the coalhole jumped out of its groove and rolled down the front path. Icy air whipped through the open hole into the cellar.

Her mother jumped up. "I'd better put that back before we freeze to death."

The breeze fluttered the pages of *Gone With the Wind.* Clarrie riffled through the book, searching for her place. She heard the sound of the coalhole cover being put back, then a rapid pounding from the mobile antiaircraft gun out in the street.

Her mother hurried down the cellar steps, squeezed next to Billy, and tucked a blanket around him. "All hell's breaking loose out there," she said, "and there's your poor dad, out on that rooftop like a sitting duck."

Clarrie, swept by a rush of anxious love, imagined him on his rooftop, sitting on an upturned crate, coughing and shivering, peering into the night sky through scratched binoculars.

"God only knows where our Arthur is," her mother said.

"He can't be much worse off than we are, wherever he is," Annie said.

Billy sat up. "I bet he's out on the Atlantic, sinking U-Boats."

The noise from an antiaircraft gun shook the house. Clarrie said a silent prayer for Arthur, and for her father.

"What a life!" Annie said. "Whatever have we done to deserve this?"

Clarrie closed her book. She couldn't concentrate. The cold of the stone step had eaten through the cushion into her backside, and she could feel blood running down her leg. Her sanitary pad must be saturated. She hoped nobody could smell it. She tucked the blanket tightly around her legs.

Here she was, sitting in a dirty coal cellar in the middle of the night with menstrual blood trickling down her legs, not knowing if she and her family would live to see the dawn, while strangers, men who didn't even know her, had flown across the channel in the dead of night to blow her, her family, friends, and neighbors, off the face of the earth. She hadn't the vaguest idea why.

The bombers were directly overhead. Everyone looked up to the source of the sound, as though it were possible to see through the roof. There was a rattling overhead, then the sound of someone thumping on the wall that divided them from the Halliwell's house. "Sally . . . Sally!" Maud Halliwell shrieked. "Can you hear me?"

"I hear you. Are you all right?" Sally's words were half obliterated by the pounding of the guns.

"What did you say?" Maud shouted.

Billy was imitating the throb of a Messerschmidt, the hum of a Spitfire, the whistle of falling bombs.

"Get down." Sally said. A long whining sound that seemed to come straight towards them ended in an explosion. The coalhole lid went flying again.

"I think they got us," Maud called. "They're dropping 'em like bloody peas."

"Peas?" Annie raised her eyebrows and rolled her eyes. "Did she say peas?" Clarrie giggled.

There was another explosion, followed by a prolonged rattling sound.

"Sally . . . Sally," Maud screamed. "We're on fire . . . I've just been upstairs—the mattress is spitting pinwheels—one of them intenduerry bombs. I can't put it out. We've got no water."

"I'll be right over, don't panic," Sally called.

"Intenduerries?" Annie rolled her eyes again. They burst into gales of laughter.

"I'd better run upstairs and make sure we're not on fire too," Sally said.

Annie got up. "I'll do it." In a few moments she was back. "Everything's okay up there."

"I'll pop next door, then," Sally said.

"I tried the tap," Annie said. "Our water's off too, but there's a bowl of washing-up water in the sink. I'll take that over. Every little helps."

When Annie and her mother left, Clarrie ran to the lavatory to change her sanitary napkin. She threw the soiled one in the fire, jabbing at it with the poker until it burned.

"Where did you go?" Billy asked.

"To the lav," Clarrie said. The ack-ack gun outside the house kept up a steady pounding, drowning out the rattle of incendiaries and the throb of the engines overhead.

"Can't we go out for a minute?" Billy asked. "I want to see what's happening." Clarrie hesitated. She too wanted to see what was happening.

"I suppose there's no harm just standing by the door."

"Oh, look!" Billy cried, stepping out onto the front path. Bright searchlights crisscrossed the sky. Green flares fell, illuminating clouds and barrage balloons with flashes of emerald light. Just above the chimney pots, a plane, clearly marked with the British bull's-eye insignia, swooped low, rolling over and over. "That's a spitfire," Billy said, adjusting his glasses. "He's doing the victory roll. He must have shot down a German plane." Clarrie followed Billy off the step and down the path. They waved wildly at the Spitfire, shouting "Hurray for the RAF! Hurray for England!" As if in response, the plane rolled over again before flying off.

Sally stuck her head out the Halliwell's bedroom window. "Get back, you two . . . out of the way!"

Clarrie and Billy jumped back as a smoldering mattress hurtled past them, landing in the garden patch. Through the open doorway of the Halliwell's house, they could see smoke swirling down the lobby. Mr. Robertson, the local shoemaker, stood at the foot of the stairs looking dazed, his air raid warden's helmet covered with tea leaves. Soapy water dripped down his face and chest.

"What happened to you, Mr. Robertson?" Clarrie said, stifling a giggle.

He wiped his face with his sleeve. "Some daft bugger's just sloshed me with a bowl of washing-up water."

"That was our Annie!" Clarrie and Billy stumbled, helpless with laughter, through the doorway of the Halliwell's kitchen, where Maud's mother was on her knees in front of "The Old Rugged Cross." Her grey hair hung in two long plaits over her nightgown.

"Help me up, Clarrie love," she said. "I'm not as young as I used to be."

Clarrie bent to help her. Through the open neck of the nightgown, she caught a glimpse of the old woman's shriveled, elongated breasts, and quickly looked away.

Sally led the old woman to a chair. "I thought I told you to stay in the house," she said to Clarrie. "Get on home out of this smoke, and take Billy with you. See if there's enough water left in the kettle to make us all a cup of tea."

"None for me, love," the warden said. "I've got work to do out there."

"I think you've had enough tea for one night, Mr. Robertson," Annie said. Everyone laughed, even the warden. Maud handed him a rag to wipe his face, and the rest of the party went next door to the Hancock's house. They were sitting around the table, drinking tea, when the all-clear signal sounded.

"My side hurts," Annie said. "I've never laughed so much in my life."

Clarrie thought of the newsreels she'd seen at the King's Cinema—Chinese peasants scuttling for cover from Japanese bombers; Spanish women in black dresses running through the streets of Barcelona. It had all seemed so frightening and horrible, but this air raid had been more like a Laurel and Hardy comedy. What would the Luftwaffe bombardiers think, she wondered, if they could look down and see these English people laughing their heads off?

Sirens sounded in the daytime, too. At Grimsby's, as soon as the wailing started the machinery ground to a halt. Clarrie and the others grabbed their knitting, their cigarettes, their magazines, and filed down into the ancient cellars that lined the canal bank. Clarrie always carried a book and a knitting bag. She was trying to knit a pair of warm socks for Arthur, but she wasn't making much progress. She found it hard to read and knit at the same time.

In an attempt to give the enemy a fair hearing, she had checked *Mein Kampf* out of the library and struggled conscientiously through the first few chapters. She searched in vain for a shred of evidence to support Hitler's rambling attacks on the Jews, before finally abandoning the effort. Reading *Mein Kampf* was like wading through sludge. She returned the book to the library unfinished, and went to the poetry shelves to cleanse her mind.

She chose a volume by Walt Whitman—a poet she'd never heard of—opened it at random to read, "Whoever you are holding me now in hand . . ." The small hairs on the back of her neck stood up. She read on, savoring the strange new cadences, and felt the ice that had been crystallizing around her heart begin to melt.

She was sitting in Grimsby's cellar, absorbed in *Leaves of Grass*, when someone snatched the book out of her hands. Rita jumped onto an empty skid, waving the open book.

"Goody two-shoes is reading a dirty book!" she crowed. "Listen to this—'All is missing if the moisture of the right man is missing . . .' "

"It's not a dirty book," Clarrie said "It's poetry. Give it back."

Rita flipped the pages. "You call these poems? They don't even rhyme. He's just a dirty old man if you ask me."

"What would you know about poetry? I'm surprised you can even read."

Rita threw the book at Clarrie, hitting the side of her face, just as Mr. Blackwell came down the stairs, shouting "What's going on here!"

"She called me ignorant!" Rita shouted. Clarrie picked up her book, trying to piece together a torn page.

"There's the all-clear," Mr. Blackwell said. "Get back to work."

The following Monday, Mr. Blackwell met Clarrie with the news that one of the girls who ran a lapping machine had left to join the ATS. Two new girls had been hired, and would take over the lunch errands and the kitchen clean-up duties. Starting immediately, Clarrie was to begin training on the lapping machines.

She had mixed feelings about her promotion. She'd be free to spend her lunch hour as she pleased—she could find a quiet place to sit and read by the canal—but she was afraid of being in charge of a lapping machine. Doris, a quiet girl who ran the next machine, showed her how to adjust the slats for various widths of material, and how to thread and remove the bolts of cloth from the metal grips

Mr. Blackwell stopped by to see how she was getting along. "That's right. Keep it up, you're doing fine."

Rita came over, her eyes blazing. "Why does she get a machine? I've been here longer than her."

"Go back to your bench," Mr. Blackwell said. "I don't have to explain my reasons to you."

"Arse kisser," Rita said, casting a malevolent glare at Clarrie as she went by.

Clarrie fought back welling tears. She hadn't asked for the job. Mr. Blackwell had chosen her. She would do her best not to let him down.

The job called for a delicate coordination of hand and foot: too much pressure on the foot pedal set the machine whizzing, the cloth flying out of control; too tight a grip on the cloth made the bolt bend in the middle. As she pressed her foot on the pedal, and guided the cloth through her fingers, she felt a thrill of mastery. Was this how her dad felt, she wondered, when he was skating?

She had been working at the machine for several days, when a shipment of thick, khaki material was brought into the department.

"This lot has to be out of here tonight," Mr. Blackwell said. "It's for army uniforms."

Clarrie and Doris set to work, stacking up bolts so fast that the bench girls, whose job it was to stamp, tie, and label them, were unable to keep up. Soon, the skids were stacked to the ceiling.

Rita left her bench, walked over and thrust her face into Clarrie's. "Slow down, arse kisser," she hissed. "Are you trying to show us up?"

Clarrie stopped her machine, and without a glance at Rita, took a place at the bench.

"Now she's going to teach us how to do our job," Rita said.

"Why don't you shut up," Joan said. "Can't you see she's trying to help us?"

Clarrie worked deftly, at a furious speed, scarcely glancing at the other girls. By the time the day was over, the benches were cleared, the skids were empty and the job had been handed over to the packers for shipment.

Mr. Blackwell stopped by to congratulate them. "Damn good job," he said. "See what you can do when everyone pulls together?"

Chapter Thirty-eight

"Wake up, Clarrie, we have to get to the shelter." Clarrie kept her eyes shut, trying to hold on to her dream.

"Come on, child, there's going to be a raid."

"I didn't hear any sirens."

"Trixie's waiting by the door with one of her kittens in her mouth. She must have heard something."

Trixie, a stray tabby cat who'd adopted the family shortly after Mr. Purrkins disappeared, had recently produced four kittens of which she was fiercely protective. Earlier in the week she'd astonished the family by waiting at the closed scullery door with a mewling kitten dangling from her mouth, and following them out to the newly opened brick shelter in the back street.

"There go the sirens, now," her mother said.

"I don't care," Clarrie moaned, "I want to go back to sleep."

Her mother hauled her to her feet, threw a coat over her shoulders, and hustled her along the landing and down the stairs.

"My book!" Clarrie pulled away from her mother. She darted back up the stairs and down again. "I got it," she said.

As they stepped from the back yard into the street, the throb of the bombers, already loud overhead, was followed by a burst of antiaircraft fire.

"You'll get us all killed one of these days, you silly girl," Sally pushed Clarrie ahead of her into the shelter.

Built above ground, the street shelters had no windows, no heat, no lights, and no door to cover the entrance, but they were reputed to be safer than any other type of shelter. Maud next door was not convinced, and announced that she and Jack would stay with the cellar steps. It had been left to Mrs. Barlow, Mrs. Sidebotham, and Sally to furnish the shelter with candles and a blanket to cover the entrance.

Mrs. Barlow and two of her grown daughters were already in the shelter. "We beat you to it tonight, Sally."

"We'd have been here sooner, but this child insisted she must run back and get her book."

"One of them bookworms, is she?" Mrs. Barlow squinted at Clarrie over her knitting. "I like a good read myself, but you shouldn't let her do it in this light, Sally."

"Try stopping her."

Mrs. Sidebotham moved aside the curtain and stepped into the shelter. She had struck a compromise between haste and propriety by lacing a soiled pink corset over the top of her flannel nightgown. Her husband, Fred, came in after her. He was busy trying to buckle his belt. "The buggers didn't even give us time to get dressed," he muttered.

Mrs. Sidebotham nodded in agreement. "You'd think they'd leave us in peace, seeing it's only two days 'til Christmas."

The whine of a falling bomb was followed by a deafening explosion.

"Ha-ha, you missed us," Billy crowed

"They say you never hear the one that gets you," Mr. Sidebotham said.

Annie stroked the gold kitten on her lap. "Trixie hasn't come back with her other kittens."

Clarrie jumped up. "I'll go and see if they're all right." Her mother caught her by the wrist. "Stay where you are. Read your book."

When the pounding of the antiaircraft guns stopped for a moment, Mrs. Sidebotham proposed a sing-song, and without waiting for encouragement, took her stance in the middle of the small shelter. The throb of bombers and the renewed pounding of guns briefly drowned her quavering contralto. Mrs. Sidebotham increased her volume and sailed unruffled through all twelve verses of "Speak, Speak, Speak to me, Thora." The audience applauded, politely, and Mrs. Sidebotham took her bows with the aplomb of a veteran performer on stage at the Hippodrome.

"I hope you could hear me all right over that bloody racket," she said.

The cover they'd hung in the shelter doorway moved aside. A man stepped in, his face streaked with soot. He grinned.

"Is this what they mean by keeping the home fires burning?"

"Arthur!" Sally rushed to greet him. "Oh, thank God, thank God you're home! Your dad was sure you'd be home for Christmas."

"Where is he?"

"Fire-spotting."

Arthur brought a tiny black and white kitten out of the top of his duffle bag.

"I found this little fellow crawling around outside. "The mother's dead—she's got a chunk of shrapnel through her skull."

Clarrie ran to the doorway and pulled aside the curtain. Outside, brilliant green flares were falling, and a barrage balloon, suddenly bursting into flames, curled and shriveled as it descended. Arthur pulled her back.

"It's too dangerous out there, love." He glanced down at his blackened uniform. "All England's on fire," he said. "It's taken me three days to get here from Portsmouth; every time the train stopped, all men in uniform were called off to help fight fires and rescue people. Right now, Salford is getting the worst of it." He told them that on his way down the street, he had seen two small children standing in an open doorway. "Poor kids were scared to death . . . crying. I asked them where their mam and dad were, and they didn't know. I wasn't sure what to do."

"Must be the Watkins children," Sally said.

"Watkins?" Mrs. Sidebotham said. "Wasn't that the fellow who went to Borstal for breaking into houses and stealing money from the gas-meters?"

"I believe so," Sally said.

"I bet he was the one who touched my hand in the cellar that time," Clarrie said.

"He married that scruffy Maisie what's her name," Mrs. Barlow said, "not a minute too soon, neither."

"Bowker," Annie said. "Maisie Bowker. She was in my class at Tatton. Her hair was full of nits."

"It's no wonder the poor girl doesn't know how to take care of her children." Sally got up. "It's quieted down a bit. I think I'll go over to get them."

"I'll come with you," Arthur said.

Annie got to her feet. "I'm going too."

"You stay here," her mother said. "If need be, Arthur will help me carry them."

In a little while, she was back with two children—a boy of three or four and a girl of two. Even in the dim light, it was plain to see that the children were filthy, their dun-colored hair matted.

"The coal-yard's on fire," Sally said. "Arthur and another chap are trying to save the horses. You can hear the poor things screaming."

Annie went to pick up the girl, but her mother stopped her, pointing to the open sores on the girl's face. "I think that's impetigo."

Mrs. Barlow shook her head, clucking sadly. "Breaks your heart."

The little boy whimpered and rubbed his sleeve across his runny nose. Sally held out her handkerchief. "Blow your nose, like a good boy. Don't cry. Your mam will be back soon."

"She's out on the game, that one," Mrs. Barlow said. "They ought to take these kids away from her."

"It's better not to talk like that in front of the children," Sally said.

"They're too young to understand."

"They may understand more than you think."

The all-clear sounded at last. An ARP warden stuck his head through the shelter doorway.

"You folks all right?" he asked cheerfully. "Eleven bloody hours they've been at it, but we're still here. Gas mains got it, and the water's contaminated—you've got to boil it for at least ten minutes."

"How are we supposed to boil it, love?" Sally asked. "We've no coal and no gas."

"There's plenty of fires out here," he said.

"If anyone comes looking for the Watkins youngsters, tell 'em they're with us," Sally said.

The Watkins boy tugged at Sally's coat. "Can you give us summat to eat, Missus?" His sister had fallen asleep.

"Of course, love." She lifted the girl up in her arms, and told Annie to take the boy into the house and find him something to eat.

Trixie was lying in the gutter outside the back door with a piece of twisted grey metal in her head. Clarrie squatted and stroked her narrow back. "Poor old Trix, going back for your kittens. I'll bury her in the garden when I come home."

"Billy can do it," her mother said. "You see if the shops are open. We'll need a bottle to feed the other kittens."

"I have to go to work."

"I doubt there'll be any buses running. You might as well stay home today."

"Mr. Grimsby says air-raids or no air-raids, we get in on time, or get the sack"

"Your dad's not home yet. I hope to God he's all right."

"I'll walk down to the docks and look for him," Annie said.

"No. Wait a while. He won't want you wandering about down there. He's probably helping put out fires."

Clarrie followed her mother into the kitchen where they began assembling things to burn—a mop handle and some stray bits of wood Billy had found near the sawmill. Her mother unscrewed the legs from the three-legged stool.

"You're not going to burn that, are you, Mam?" The stool had been part of the kitchen furniture ever since she could remember. As a little girl she had loved to sit on it by the fire and read her fairy tales; she still sat there when she toasted bread or crumpets.

Sally laid the legs of the stool across the grate and put a match to the paper. "It's only furniture. I'm just hoping it'll burn long enough to boil the water for our tea."

Arthur came back, his face and hands covered in soot. He looked weary.

"What happened to the horses?" Clarrie asked.

"We bashed the door down. Three of the horses ran out, but two of them panicked and ran back into the flames before we could stop them. The other bolted; last we saw of him, he was galloping like mad down Wynford Street. The coal-yard's demolished."

Clarrie washed in icy water, wondering if it was polluted enough to poison her through her pores. She made herself a cold baked-bean sandwich and stuffed it into her gas mask case. "I'll be off then," she said.

The sulphur smell—familiar aftermath of the air raids—was worse than she had ever known it. Flying sparks, fragments of burning paper, stung her face as she walked. Billowing black smoke rolled towards her across the rooftops. When she turned the corner onto Eccles New Road, she stopped. Rubble and broken glass completely covered the road, gutted buildings smoldered, dazed-looking people crunched through the rubble, trying, from force of habit, to walk along some invisible pavement. Women pushed prams laden with whatever they had been able to salvage, followed by children carrying pillows and grimy blankets.

"I don't know where the hell I'm going," a young woman said as she passed Clarrie. A boy, no bigger than Billy, traipsed behind her dragging a wagon loaded with blankets, a washboard, and various household goods—the whole thing topped by a cast-iron teakettle. He stumbled as he passed Clarrie, and the teakettle wobbled and fell off. The woman didn't pause or look around. Clarrie picked the kettle up and returned it to the wagon.

"Is it broke?" the boy asked.

"Just the tip of the spout."

"Me mam'll kill me for that," he said. "We haven't got much left. Jerry got us dead on. We're takin' this stuff to me Gran's to see if she'll have us."

"Your mam has enough to worry about without that old spout," Clarrie said.

He shook his head. "You don't know her like I do."

Clarrie crossed the road, glass crunching under her feet. Rows of enormous icicles, glowing pink, hung like teeth of prehistoric monsters from every gutted building. Stretchers were lined up among the rubble, their lumpy burdens covered by khaki blankets. Clarrie had never seen a dead body. She had a powerful impulse to raise the blankets to see if there was anyone she knew, and would perhaps have done so had it not been for the presence of two firemen struggling with a hose trained on the burning flats.

The flats had been built on the site of the old workhouse to accommodate people uprooted by slum clearance. The outer wall facing the road had been blown away in the night, exposing rooms strewn with fallen plaster.

Clarrie joined a small knot of people gaping up at a double-decker bus that was hanging half in and half out of a second-story flat.

"That's what I call service," a man said. "The bloody bus stopped right at my bedside." The crowd laughed.

Clarrie gazed, fascinated, into the exposed bedroom. The walls were painted a garish magenta. A painting of a Spanish lady, dancing with castanets, hung tipsily above a brass bed covered in rubble. The dresser had fallen face down, and a pair of dusty trousers dangled by their braces from a hook on the bedroom door. She turned and walked on, ashamed to be stealing a forbidden glimpse into someone's private life.

And last night, while she'd been grumbling about not getting enough sleep, her neighbors had been dying, and while she was mourning the death of a cat and the loss of her wooden stool, others had been—still were—fighting fires, dismantling bombs at risk of their lives. The bus-stop sign lay twisted amongst the rubble. There'd be no traffic into Manchester today. She would have to walk.

At the corner of Cross Lane, a young woman pushing a pram stopped in front of her.

"Clarrie? Clarrie Hancock? Oh, thank God! I was hoping to see somebody I know."

Clarrie tried to place her. The low-bridged nose, the coarse mouth . . .

She nudged Clarrie with her elbow. "It's Vi'let—Vi'let Fawcet—don't you remember me?"

"Violet Fawcet, of course!" Clarrie said. Violet was the girl whose mother was in the lunatic asylum for trying to scald her husband to death. Violet had been absent from school a lot after her mother was put away, and last year she'd stopped coming altogether. She'd had a baby—by her own father, it was said. Mr. Fawcet had gone to prison, was still there probably.

"We've been bombed out. I've been pushing this pram all over Christendom. Everywhere we go they send us somewhere else."

Clarrie was casting about wildly for some way to make her escape without having to mention the baby. A cry came from inside the pram. Violet rocked the pram, and the crying stopped.

"I've nowhere to turn," she said. "I haven't even got a clean nappie for the baby."

Clarrie glanced into the pram. Violet pulled aside the blankets. The baby's outfit looked familiar—a white knitted hat and a matching cardigan with the red letter "B" embroidered on it. The baby was remarkably ugly, its flat face covered in an angry rash.

"Lovely." Clarrie could feel herself blushing. "What's his name?"

"It's a girl. Lily. We was in the shelter last night when the bomb hit. When we come out, the house, and everything in it, was blown to smithereens."

Clarrie dug in her pocket and handed Violet a shilling. "This is all I've got, but you're welcome. I'm in a hurry. I'm on my way to work."

"Thanks, love. I'll pay you back when I can." Violet put the coin in her pocket. "But I don't know where to go."

"What about the police station?"

"You can't get near it. I've tried. I went over to Tatton, thinking they might be letting folks in there, but there's nowt left of it."

"The church?"

"No, the school."

"What do you mean, 'nowt left'?"

"Demolished—girls' school, boys', infants'—the lot."

Tatton gone? Surely Violet must be exaggerating. Aeons might pass and empires crumble, but Tatton School would be there forever.

"Are you sure?"

"I saw it with my own eyes. The street's gone too—houses, everything."

"What happened to the people on School Street?" School Street was where Celia and her family lived.

Violet shrugged. "Don't know." She blew on her fingers. "God, I'm freezing, and this poor baby's not had a thing to eat."

Clarrie hesitated. She had no wish to get mixed up with the likes of Violet Fawcet. The expression, "common as muck" flashed through her mind.

Violet delved down into the carriage and lifted up the baby. She kissed the inflamed cheeks, and murmured: "Hush, love, you're all right, your mam's here."

"Why don't you go over to our house?" Clarrie said quickly. "It'll get you and the baby out of the cold at least.

My mother's taking care of the Watkins kids at the moment, but if she can keep the fire going, she'll boil some water and give you a cup of tea."

Violet brightened. "She won't mind?"

"No. She won't mind."

"Your mam's a lovely woman, isn't she? She's the only one that came over when I . . . when our Lily was born. She give me a box of baby clothes, lovely and clean they were, all ironed and folded. Baby's wearing some of 'em right now."

"I'd best be on my way," Clarrie said. So! Her mother had given Billy's baby clothes to Violet Fawcet. She'd said nothing about that to the family, and no wonder. What had happened to Violet did not bear thinking about. Except for the rash, the baby seemed normal enough—much like any other baby—but still . . . Clarrie shuddered. Thank God for her own parents, her own life.

A crayoned sign on the bakery door offered free tea and barm cakes to bombed-out people. Too bad she hadn't known about that to tell Violet. Several strangers smiled at her and made cheerful comments or "thumbs up" gestures as they passed. An old woman rummaging through the smoldering ruins of a house gave her a toothless grin.

"I'm looking for me teeth," she said. "I left them in the glass. I knew I should have took 'em to the shelter with me. I can't chew butter without 'em."

"I wish I could help you search," Clarrie said, "but I'm on my way to work."

"Never mind, eh?" the woman said. "Keep smiling, even if you've got no teeth. I've nowt to eat, any road."

St Peter's Square was roped off, with a warning: "Danger. Unexploded Bomb." Clarrie leaned across the rope, trying to see into the huge crater. A young man in a raincoat walked over and stood beside her.

"This is bloody inconvenient, isn't it," he said. "Where are you trying to get to?"

"Canal Street. I usually get off the bus here and walk down Princess Street."

"I go that way, too," he said. "I'm already half an hour late for work. I've backtracked along Deansgate in both directions, but it's blocked off. We'll have to go miles out of our way."

"I think I'll take a chance and dodge under the rope," Clarrie said.

The man opened his eyes in exaggerated astonishment.

"If you're game, so am I." He raised the rope and they slipped underneath. Clarrie moved towards the crater to get a better look at the bomb. The man grabbed her arm and steered her away. "That thing could blow us to kingdom come at any minute," he said. He walked swiftly, with a strange jerking rhythm, pulling her along. Within seconds they were safely under the ropes on the other side. The man pretended to wipe the sweat from his brow.

"I knew it wouldn't explode," Clarrie said. Together they walked down Princess Street. No sign of bomb damage here. At the curb, the man paused and swung his leg stiffly up onto the pavement. A wooden leg. That would explain why he wasn't in the army. He stopped at the entrance of a bank. "This is where I get off." He raised his hat to her. "You've got a lot of guts, for a girl, but you mustn't make a habit of dodging unexploded bombs."

"I won't," Clarrie said.

Up ahead, the sky was a brilliant orange. As she approached the bridge over the canal, she saw a row of burning factories. Flames roared, leaping and licking about the buildings. No firemen were in sight, but a dozen or so people stood on the bridge watching the fire engulf an ancient factory, five or six stories high. Next to it, the frame of a gutted three-story building glowed red hot.

A familiar voice at her side said, "Looks as if we're all out of a job."

"Mr. Blackwell?"

"Aye!" She caught sight of Mr. Grimsby and several of his employees standing nearby. "That's Grimsby and Sons, over there," Mr. Blackwell said, "what's left of it."

"Oh, God . . . I didn't realize . . ." As she spoke, the girders buckled, bulging outwards. The whole structure swayed and hurtled with a mighty hissing noise into the canal. Everyone stepped closer to the wall to watch the fiery fragments floating on the murky water. Reflected, they appeared to open out like full-blown poppies before they sank at last into darkness.

Mr. Grimsby stared into the canal. "That's that then," he said. "My whole life—my father's before me—my son's future, gone up in smoke."

The girls from Grimsby's had gathered in a group, talking in low voices. Doris broke away from them and approached the two men. "What shall we do now then, Mr. Grimsby?"

"You'd best get on home," Mr. Grimsby said. "I've got your names and addresses on file at the house. I'll see you all get what's owing to you." He blew his nose. "You've been good workers. You'll soon find something else. There's nowt to be done for Grimsby and Sons. We're finished."

Chapter Thirty-nine

Clarrie made her way down Blackfriars Lane to Regent Road. Turning at Trafford, she threaded her way through smoking ruins to where Tatton Memorial Schools ought to be. A scene of utter devastation confronted her. Of the three school buildings, the walled schoolyards, the streets and houses that had surrounded them, not one brick was left standing.

How was this possible? Tatton School was the soil in which her own mind, heart, and soul were rooted; it was, here that she'd discovered poetry and music, here she'd been introduced to an endless parade of heroes—explorers, inventors, scientists, writers, artists, reformers, saints, and martyrs, who had walked the English earth before she was born.

Out of the eerie silence and desolation, their illustrious ghosts rose to comfort her: Thomas a Becket, Shakespeare, Milton, Shelley, Keats, Latimer and Ridley, Florence Nightingale, William Wilberforce, Charles Dickens, Elizabeth Fry . . .

Something was shining in the rubble. Stepping across the still-hot ashes, she bent to retrieve it. A faint pinging sound confirmed her suspicions—the brass bell from Miss Hughes's desk! It was dented and blackened and dusty, but when she tapped the button at the top, the tone rang out as clear and peremptory as ever. She slipped the bell into her pocket and headed home.

At the gutted remains of the coal-shed she came across Nelly Barlow searching through the rubble.

"Are you looking for coal?" Nelly asked. "I'm not having any luck—it's burnt to cinders."

"I'm on my way home. The place where I worked is at the bottom of the canal. Tatton's gone, too—the whole lot—streets and all."

"I know. My Auntie's house got it. She's all right, though. She was in the shelter."

"Have you heard anything about the Scott family?"

Nelly shook her head. "That blind uncle of theirs came through okay. He sneaked out for a drink and passed out in the men's bog behind the pub. The warden found him this morning, safe and sound." She picked up a cob of coal and threw it in her wagon. "The cemetery got hit."

"Weaste?" Nelly's brother, Jimmy, was a gardener there.

Nelly nodded. "They came to fetch our Jimmy first thing this morning. They said there're bodies strewn all over the place, and no way to tell who belongs where. They're shoveling 'em back, any way they can."

"That's where our Janet and my grandmother Hancock are buried," Clarrie said. "So much for resting in peace."

The house smelled of burning coke and laundry soap. Violet Fawcet was huddled over a small fire in the kitchen, the baby asleep on her lap. Steam rose from a few wet nappies and baby clothes strung across the fireplace. Violet looked up, surprised.

"You're home early."

"The place where I worked burned down. Where is everybody—where's my mother?"

"She's out trying to find somewhere for me and Lily to stay. Lily's got a fever and your mam thinks it's measles. Annie took the Watkins kids to the police station and then went to work."

"What about our Arthur and my father?"

"Don't know where they are." Violet lifted the lid of the teapot. "There's a drop of tea left if you want some."

"No. I didn't get much sleep last night." She was already heading for the stairs. "I just want to lie down."

She slipped off her coat and shoes and crawled between the cold sheets. Lovely bed. After she'd rested, she'd go to the police station to find out if Celia and her family were all right. And she'd walk to the cemetery . . . see if the Hancock grave had been disturbed.

She woke up shivering with no idea how long she'd slept. The bedroom was freezing, but someone had thrown an extra coat over her. She drew the coat around her shoulders and went downstairs. Her mother was sitting by the fire. Violet and the baby were gone.

"Where is everyone?"

"Your dad's resting. He's burned his hands, badly—I had to tear up one of Annie's bakery aprons to bandage them. Arthur's gone looking for coke and firewood with Billy."

"What about Violet?"

"The baby has the measles. They've taken her to Salford Royal. Violet's staying in the hospital with her."

"Grimsby's burned down."

"So Violet told me. I hope nobody was hurt."

"No, but Mr. Grimsby says he's finished. Tatton schools are gone, too, and all the streets around. It's a wasteland."

"Thank God no children were there."

Clarrie took the bell from her pocket. "I found this. I think it belongs to Miss Hughes, but I don't know where she lives."

"We can find out. Right now I'm going to lie down for a minute or two. Then I'll see what I can rustle up for tea."

Clarrie tied a scarf around her head and buttoned her coat. "I'm going out. I want to know what's happened to Celia and her family."

The tired-looking woman at the ARP station could tell her nothing. "We haven't traced everyone yet, love," she said. Clarrie thanked her and set off to the cemetery.

The wrought-iron gates were twisted off their hinges. Part of the railings were down, their spearheads jutting across the pavement. A man wearing an ARP helmet sat in a makeshift shelter, blowing on his mittened hands. He pointed to a chalked sign. "Cemetery closed."

"When will it be open?" Clarrie asked.

"As soon as everything's back to normal."

Clarrie turned down a side street, where the railings had sunk. Easing herself over the spikes, she dropped onto a pile of leaves, stiff and silvered with frost, and made her way between the gravestones to the ornamental flower beds, filled now with the brown and shriveled remains of chrysanthemums. The statue of the bride was still standing, but the path leading to Janet's grave had been obliterated, and the graves themselves had vanished into a sea of frozen mud. On a jagged slab of black marble she read the letters ARDSL. That must be from the Bardsley monument. The Hancock grave had been very near, but the tree she had always used as a landmark was gone.

At the edge of a crater, a silver handle attached to a slab of wood caught her eye. She hooked the toe of her shoe under the handle to raise the wood. A skeletal hand was sticking out of the dirt as though fending off an attack. She lost her footing and slid down the side of the crater, setting off a small avalanche of pebbles. Near her face, half buried in the dirt was a skull, with long grey hair attached. Gasping, spitting out dirt, Clarrie clawed her way up and over the edge of the crater and ran. A man in a cap, pushing a wheelbarrow, appeared from behind a mound of frozen mud as though rising up out of the ground.

"Hey!" he shouted, "What're you doing here?"

Clarrie kept running until she reached the railings. Breathless, she scrambled up the heap of frozen leaves and dropped over the spikes into the street.

She walked home wondering what to tell her parents about what had happened in the cemetery. Her mother was frying something over a small coke fire. Annie and Billy were already eating.

"Where on earth have you been, love?" Her mother removed a sliver of wood from Clarrie's hair. "Just look at the sight of you. You'd better wash your hands before you eat."

"I was looking for firewood, but I had no luck" Clarrie removed her coat and went into the scullery.

"Where's our Arthur?" she took her place at the table.

Her mother put a plate of fried potatoes in front of her. "He went out. He's got a date."

"With one of those Rourke girls," Annie said. "Sheila. She's skinny as a toothpick, and Irish as Paddy's pig. I don't know what our Arthur sees in her. Remember when the Rourkes used to go round singing in the streets? She was the one with the long black curls." Annie crossed her hands on her bosom and broke into the opening bars of "O Take Me Home Again, Kathleen."

"You leave our Arthur alone," Sally said. "He's entitled to a little relaxation. He's spent his entire leave, so far, digging through rubble and pulling people and animals out of burning buildings."

"She might be trying to worm information out of him for the Germans," Annie said. "The Irish claim they're neutral, don't they?"

"Now you're being silly," her mother said. "It's only the southern part—Eire—that's neutral. And two of the Rourke lads are in the navy if I'm not mistaken."

"She does have a lovely singing voice," Annie conceded. "I'll grant her that."

"I hope he brings her home so she can sing for us," Clarrie said. "I love those Irish songs." She told them about her unsuccessful search for Celia's family.

The cold dark days of January and February, which seemed to last an eternity, were spent searching for food, fuel, and warm clothing to make it through the winter.

The air-raids had tapered off after the Christmas blitz, but the sirens still sounded, and more often than not the nights were spent in the freezing cold shelter. Clarrie kept herself busy helping with laundry and housework. She borrowed a rusty old pram from Mrs. Phipps—the same pram she and her mother had used to take the wet sheets to the washhouse—and brought it home filled with sacks of coke to share with Mrs. Phipps.

"God bless you, lass," Mrs. Phipps said. "I'm getting too old to be lugging loads of coke home, and my old fella's not fit for anything these days. I don't know how I can pay you back."

"You've done plenty for us already," Clarrie said. "My mother said that when our Janet died, you were a godsend. She feels beholden to you."

"Aye. It was a bad time for your poor mam, but she came through it. She'll come through this lot, too, I'll warrant."

Clarrie searched the "Help Wanted" columns of the newspaper every evening in hope of finding an interesting job.

"What exactly are you hoping to find?" her mother asked.

"I don't know. Perhaps I ought to join the WRENS."

"You'd stand a better chance with the ATS," Annie said. "The WRENS don't take working-class girls."

"That's not so," her mother said. "But you're too young to join anything. Starting next week, I'll be working full-time for the Perlmans, helping them salvage what they can from the old shop. There'll be plenty for you to do right here at home."

Shortly after her fifteenth birthday, when Clarrie had almost given up hope of finding anything, an item in the Manchester Evening News caught her eye:

Strong young girl needed to work in Kitchen of a small college in the Lake District. Wages, plus room and board. Apply in writing to Miss McBride, Rook How, Bramblebeck, Westmorland.

She read it again. A college in the Lake District! She was already half in love with the Lake District from reading *The Herries Chronicles*. Of course, she'd be working as a kitchen maid—it was the same as being in service, something she'd sworn never to do—but this was different, this was a college. In a way, it would be almost like going to boarding school.

Chapter Forty

The train slowed, and a grizzled porter poked his head into the compartment to announce "Bowness." Clarrie thrust Miss McBride's letter into her coat pocket, hauled down her cardboard suitcase from the luggage rack, and tucking the newspaper-wrapped lighthouse picture under one arm, stepped into the corridor. On her way down the steps she missed her footing and dropped the suitcase. It burst open, spilling underwear, socks, and ribbons onto the platform. She snatched up her belongings and shoved them back in the suitcase, but the latch would no longer hold. A schoolboy in a green blazer and cap produced a length of string from his pocket and handed it to her. It was the sort of kind thing Billy would have done, she thought, as she tied her suitcase back together.

The train whistle blew. A young corporal threw his cigarette stub down and ground it under his boot. He winked at Clarrie and made a clicking noise out of the corner of his mouth as he jumped aboard the train. She assumed a haughty expression. The cheeky lads who leaned against the walls outside the Salford pubs made those sorts of noises whenever a pretty girl walked by, but sometimes, if a girl wasn't to their liking, they did it anyway, in mockery.

Clarrie looked down at her plain black, low-heeled, lace-ups. Her lisle stockings were already twisted like corkscrews around her thin calves, and the hat she was wearing—a shiny black straw that perched like a saucer over one eye—probably looked ridiculous. Rosalind Russell had worn a hat like it in her last picture. Clarrie had bought hers hoping it would make her look older, more sophisticated. She pulled the hat off, accidentally dragging her burgundy rayon snood with it. Her hair, released from the net, fell limp and straight across her shoulders. So much for spending the night in pipe-cleaner curlers.

There was a deal of door slamming, and then, with a piercing shriek and a great belching of steam, the train took off again. A porter, so ancient he was barely able to walk, shuffled by trundling an almost empty luggage cart.

Clarrie intercepted him. "Excuse me. Can you tell me where I get the bus to . . . ?" The porter pointed to an exit and said something in an unfamiliar dialect.

"Thank you," she said to his receding back.

Clutching the picture and the string-tied case, she made her way up a flight of steps to a wide road and settled herself on a bench near the bus-stop sign. According to Miss McBride's letter, the last bus for Bramblebeck left Bowness at four-thirty. She had no watch. Perhaps she should go back to the station and ask the porter the time, but then she might miss the bus. What if it had already gone? A twenty-minute bus ride, Miss McBride's letter said. That would be a long walk. She'd arrive late and nobody would want to hire a girl who couldn't be on time her first day on the job. What would she do if they sent her away? She didn't have enough money to go back home.

Her father had warned her not to let her suitcase out of her sight, but it was a nuisance juggling the hat, the picture, and the case. She left everything on the bench and walked to the crest of the hill to see if the bus was coming. A glossy, blue-black crow, eating something bloody in the road, flew off at her approach. Other than that, all was quiet. There were no barrage balloons in the sky, and not a living soul in sight. She could perish here and be picked clean by the crows before anyone found her.

A bus was approaching. She ran back, grabbed her belongings, and dashed out into the road, waving frantically. The bus squealed to a stop.

"Does this bus go to Bramblebeck?"

"Bramblebeck. Aye." The driver reached out to haul her up the steps. "Tha' shouldna run out in front of t'bus, lass. Tha'll get thysel' killed."

Clarrie settled into a window seat, luxurious as the ones in any posh Manchester cinema. She ran her hand over the fern pattern in the blue plush upholstery and took a deep breath. Even inside the bus, the air was sweeter than in Salford.

They were riding past a clear blue lake, bordered by masses of yellow daffodils. A fierce joy swept through her. Wordsworth's daffodils, just as he had described them! On the other side of the lake, mountains loomed gold and green, their crevasses lost in purple shadows. A faint bleating came from a field, where black-faced sheep were grazing, and new-born white lambs were frisking about. She began to sing, under her breath, "Little Lamb, Who Made Thee?"

She stopped in mid-verse. One of the little lambs was unmistakably trying to mount another little lamb. She looked away. Surely they were too young for that? Across the aisle two women in tweed suits and sensible hats were chatting amiably, their placid pink faces showing none of the weariness and irritability of Salford and Manchester folk. They looked well-fed, well-groomed, contented—as if nothing unpleasant had ever happened to them, nor ever could. Seeing them, she thought, you'd never guess there was a war on.

The bus ran down into a narrow valley. Treeless mountains rose steeply on either side. Clear water bubbled and splashed, dripping over outcroppings of slate and stone. The mountains were crisscrossed, haphazardly, with low stone walls. What was the purpose of the walls? Why should anyone go to the trouble of building little walls over the mountains?

A wide street lined with gift shops and a few small hotels rose steeply uphill. At the top of the hill, the street opened into a square. In the center of the square, among a bed of bright flowers, stood a granite soldier with a rifle on his shoulder, a memorial to soldiers of the first world war perhaps? Judging by the uniform, it might be even older—the Boer war, or even the Crimean. The bus pulled into the station under a green glass roof.

"Bramblebeck!" the driver called. Two old men sitting together on a bench jumped up as Clarrie stepped down. One of them pulled the suitcase from her hand.

"The college is it, Miss?"

"Yes." She wondered if he was a chauffeur sent to collect her. In the books she'd read, chauffeurs were always picking servants up at the station. "Rook How," she said to make sure there was no mistake. But the old man was already halfway across the square. She hurried after him, thinking that if he was a thief making off with her suitcase, he'd be in for a big disappointment. She was relieved to see him stop in front of a large, white brick building, where a painted sign, Rook How, swung above the lintel. A flight of stone steps, worn hollow in the middle, led up to double glass doors. On either side, ornamental pots were filled with colorful spring flowers. The man pushed open the door and dropped her suitcase on the black and white tiled floor.

"Right you are then, Miss."

They were in a large hall, empty except for a table along one wall and an enormous brass gong. An imposing staircase with a thick banister led to the upper floors. A warm aroma of stew or meat pie filled the air. From somewhere in the back, she heard voices and the clatter of dishes. The man removed his cap; he seemed to be waiting for something. Clarrie smiled. "Thank you," she said. "I can manage now."

The man put his cap back and stalked away, slamming the door behind him. Clarrie stared after him. Had she done something to offend him?

To the right of the entrance was a small office with a half-open window. She knocked and called "Hello!" When nobody answered, she followed the sounds at the back of the hall. There was a shriek of laughter. She turned down a passage and bumped into a middle-aged woman coming around the corner. The woman reached out a manicured hand and grasped Clarrie's arm.

"Whoa! Hold on." She glanced down at Clarrie's suitcase. "You must be Clara, the new scullery maid." Without waiting for confirmation, the woman smiled and held out her hand. Large, white, prominent teeth glistened. "Flora McBride. You received my letter, then? Did I hear you talking to somebody a minute ago?"

"A man from the bus-station carried my case over."

Miss McBride raised strongly marked eyebrows. "That flimsy little thing? Rather extravagant, my dear, in your position—wasting your money on tips."

A tip! The man had been waiting for a tip. Clarrie's face grew hot. "He grabbed my case before I could stop him." She'd never had to tip anyone before. She didn't know what you were supposed to give. She hoped she wouldn't run into him again.

"No doubt he mistook you for a student." Miss McBride had a voice that boomed and squeaked at the same time, and a la-di-dah accent that would make the people in Salford die laughing. Her salt and pepper hair was pressed close to her horsy face in an out-of-date Marcel wave. Her pearl earrings and pearl necklace glistened like her teeth. Her firmly bound and corseted person swelled under a crocheted beige cardigan and a nubby tweed skirt. Her feet were clad in expensive-looking brogans with little serrated flaps covering the laces.

"You mustn't stare so child," Miss McBride said. "I imagine you would like to wash your hands after your journey. Let me show you to the bathroom, and then we can have a little chat before I introduce you to the kitchen staff."

She followed Miss McBride down a long hallway to the bathroom. A real bathroom. Pink. A film of steam covered the mirror over the washbasin, and droplets of water trickled down pink-painted walls. The pink paint of the bathtub was blistered, with scabby patches of rust underneath. Long black hairs and soap scum coated the sides and bottom. She'd have to give the tub a good scrubbing before she took a bath. In the lavatory cubicle a sign said PLEASE DO NOT STUFF THE BOWL WITH LAVATORY PAPER. Underneath, someone had drawn a cartoon of a girl jamming rolls of flying paper into the bowl with maniacal glee. Clarrie smiled. This was the sort of thing she was hoping for.

Miss McBride was waiting for her in the hall. "The working day for kitchen staff is from six in the morning until eight in the evening," she told Clarrie, "with time out for meals, of course, and two hours free in the afternoon. Each member of the kitchen staff gets one full day off a week. The only day open at the moment is Monday."

Clarrie said that would be fine.

"Splendid! You can start tomorrow. I'm afraid you must work this coming Monday and wait for your free day until after you've been here a full week. Come, let me introduce you to the others."

The kitchen was in turmoil. Two women in white caps were straining an outsize cauldron into the sink, steam billowing across their faces. A small plump woman with a cigarette in the corner of her mouth stared into a toasting oven, jiggling a shelf that seemed to have jammed. Suddenly she gave a yelp and jumped back. The shelf fell with a clatter, and slices of toasted bread flew across the floor. Clarrie picked one up and handed it to the woman.

"Use an oven pad, Winnie!" Miss McBride said as she went by. "That's Winnie, one of the chambermaids," she told Clarrie. "She prepares the trays for those teachers who prefer to dine in their rooms." One of the women who had been straining the cauldron ran to a long black range and stirred a bubbling pan. "Ah! Here's our cook," Miss McBride said. "Mrs. Marten, I'd like you to meet Clara, our new scullery maid. She answers to 'Clarrie,' so she tells me."

Mrs. Marten scowled, her features bunched up like a Pekingese dog about to bite. She raked Clarrie with sharp eyes. "'Bout time," she said. She elbowed Miss McBride out of the way as she carried the gravy pan over to the table. "I'm too busy to be bothered with her right now."

Miss McBride smiled graciously as though she had not noticed the rudeness, and steered Clarrie across the room to where an enormously fat woman was mashing potatoes. This was Mrs. Battle, she told Clarrie, the assistant cook. Mrs. Battle wiped her hands on her apron, and held out her hand. She had a pronounced squint and coarse black hair—very much like the hair in the pink bathtub, Clarrie thought. Before she could shake the proffered hand, Mrs. Marten pushed between them with a steaming cauldron. "They're queuing up out there, Mrs. B.," she said, "no time for gabbing."

On the long stove, another iron pan was boiling over. Mrs. Battle withdrew her hand. "I got me spuds to finish, and me suet puddings 'as to come out." Breathing noisily through her mouth, she waddled to the stove and removed the lid from the boiling pot.

Miss McBride led Clarrie over to a counter where a girl was slicing bread and tossing it into baskets. "Nora here is our other kitchen maid. She's been working very hard since Betty left. I know she'll be glad to meet you."

The girl looked up with green slanted eyes set wide apart in a wide face. Her mouth curved up at the corners so that it was difficult to tell if she was actually smiling. Clarrie held out her hand.

"How do you do."

Nora wiped her hand on her apron and touched Clarrie's outstretched hand with her fingertips. "How do."

"A nice girl, Nora," Miss McBride said as she led Clarrie away. "I'm afraid she, too, will soon be leaving us. She'll be getting married to her handsome Tommy."

For some time, Clarrie had been aware of a murmur of voices coming from behind a glass-paneled door. The murmur had swelled to a high-pitched babble interspersed with laughter and the shuffling of feet.

"We'll come back after dinner," Miss McBride said. "It sounds as though the natives are getting restless." She motioned to another door at the back. "We'll avoid the crush."

Clarrie looked in the direction of the noise. She'd been hoping to catch a glimpse of the pupils, or scholars, or whatever they were called.

"Did you remember to bring your ration book?"

"Yes, miss, it's in my suitcase."

"Splendid. Give it to Cook at the first opportunity. Your room here is not quite ready; for the moment you'll be housed at the Royal Hotel across the street. It's where the men sleep, but it will only be for a few days." She led Clarrie to the doorway and pointed down the street. "The Royal is on the right. You may have noticed it on your way up the hill. If you go up the stairs and along the passage to the last door, and introduce yourself to Miss Charteris, she will take care of you. Be back before seven or you'll miss dinner. Cook won't wait. She doesn't tolerate tardiness."

The Royal Hotel was more up-to-date than Rook How, but smaller. Clarrie was mounting the carpeted stairs when a bearded young man ran down. He stopped as they came abreast.

"Helloo! What have we here?"

His voice was thick and rich. Deep creases ran down his cheeks. His hair, a mass of chestnut curls, blended with a full red-brown beard. He wore corduroy trousers splotched with green and blue paint, his bare toes protruding from scuffed leather sandals.

A bohemian! Clarrie had read about bohemians in *Trilby* and *The Constant Nymph.*

"Are you looking for the women's quarters?" he asked. He had an air of experience that made it difficult to judge his age; he might be anywhere from eighteen to thirty.

"I'm looking for Miss Charteris," she said.

"She's in her lair. Second floor, last door on the left."

His mischievous brown eyes were teasing her. She felt herself blushing. Was he waiting for her to say something? Should she introduce herself and offer her hand? It was the woman's prerogative to do so, her mother had told her, but not if the other person was older, or clearly one's social superior. The palms of her hands were moist; she wiped them surreptitiously against her coat. Better not to risk it.

"Thank you," she said.

"My pleasure." He blew her a kiss as he ran down the last few steps.

Chapter Forty-one

Clarrie was on her knees in front of the range, her face close to the fire-pit. The clock on the wall read six a.m. She'd been here since five, raking out yesterday's cinders and ashes, carrying wood and coal up from the cellar, but she hadn't yet been able to get the fire going. The fire bed was enclosed at the top and sides, making it necessary to work blindly, thrusting her arms through the narrow front opening deep into the dark cavern. She'd managed well enough setting the paper, wood, and coal, but when she struck the match and carried it into the cavern, the draft blew it out.

She was about to strike yet another match, when a grey-haired gentleman came in. "You must be the new kitchen maid," he said. "How are you getting along with this monster?"

"I've used half a box of matches trying to get it started."

"Let me give you a hand." He slipped off his jacket, rolled up his sleeves, lit the tip of a twisted scrap of newspaper and jammed the brand into the stove. Flames flickered in the dark pit, the fire crackled.

Clarrie looked away in embarrassment. Why on earth hadn't she thought of that?

"These old ranges can be tricky," he said, rolling down his sleeve. "I'm Mr. Warren, supervisor of buildings and grounds, and you are?"

"Clara Hancock." She put out her hand, saw that it was black with soot and quickly withdrew it. "My dad was a caretaker too," she said, "for a Methodist chapel, but it got damaged in the blitz so he doesn't work there any more."

An odd smile quivered for a moment on Mr. Warren's face. "Perhaps you ought to run along now, Clara," he said. "You'll need to wash and put on a clean apron before Cook arrives."

Clarrie followed his glance. Her hands and arms were filthy, her starched green overall smeared with soot. The cook had told her to use one fresh overall each day, but she took another from the storage cupboard and ran up the back stairs. When she returned, Mrs. Marten and Mrs. Battle were already at work.

"I see you got the fire going," Mrs. Marten said.

"Mr. Warren did. He showed me how . . ."

"It's Nora's day off," she said. "And Winnie's gone to Newcastle—to a funeral, so she says. I have my doubts. Mrs. Battle will be doing her trays and I'll take care of the teachers, so you'll have to serve the students by yourself. Give 'em each two slices of bread, one pat of butter, two scoops of porridge, one spoon of sugar—no seconds until everyone has been served. If they want more tell 'em there's a war on." She pointed to a glass-paneled door. "That's where they come in, and when they've been served, they file through the other door with their trays out to the common room."

"The common room?" Clarrie smiled. Common rooms were a familiar feature in her old boarding school stories. She'd assumed they were places for studying, not for eating in.

"Time to start slicing the bread," the cook said.

Clarrie found a bread knife and took her place at the table where Mrs. Battle was setting up trays for the teaching staff.

"You're cutting 'em too thin, ducks." Mrs. Battle elbowed Clarrie aside and began sawing thick slices of bread and throwing them into the basket. "Mr. Warren must have took a fancy to you," Mrs. Battle said. "He ain't much for getting his hands dirty, that one."

"He seems a bit posh for a caretaker," Clarrie said.

"Oh, he ain't just a caretaker. He's what they calls a 'poverish gentleman.' He's only working 'ere to pay his daughter's way."

"His daughter?" Clarrie paused, knife in hand. "Is she one of the pupils?"

"Students. We calls 'em students."

"Can anyone go to this college, then? I mean—if my dad worked here, could I be a student, too?"

Mrs. Battle sniffed. "It don't work that way, do it? You ain't one o' them."

"One of them?"

"The nobs, ducks. Where did you grow up? They don't mix with the likes of us." From the hall came the sound of laughter and shuffling footsteps. "Give me an 'and with this 'ere porridge," Mrs. Battle said, "then get a holt o' that ladle and stand by that hot plate while I opens the door."

Clarrie took one end of the huge iron pot and Mrs. Battle the other. "Will you point out Mr. Warren's daughter to me when she comes through?" Clarrie said.

Mrs. Battle didn't answer. She waddled over to the door and stepped aside as the students surged through, chattering, laughing, and helping themselves to tea from the large urn.

Clarrie stared in astonishment. This was not at all what she'd been expecting. They were grownups, almost—older than she at any rate—and strikingly different from anyone she'd seen in Salford or Manchester. The women wore no lipstick, and they'd made no attempt to fashion themselves after Rita Hayworth or Betty Grable. There were no bleached blondes, no permanent waves, but there was hair in abundance, worn long and free—even when it was as straight as her own. The women favored loose-fitting blouses and flaring cotton skirts in oddly mixed colors—blue and orange, green and purple. The men also wore their hair unfashionably long, and they sported beards of all varieties—wild and bushy, sparse and wispy, neatly trimmed. One young man had a Svengali affair, split in half and twisted into oily corkscrews. The men favored corduroy trousers and paint-stained shirts, such as she'd seen on the man she met on the stairs. Men and women alike seemed partial to leather sandals. They were all bohemians—wild and colorful as tropical birds. She was prepared to love every one of them.

A slender girl was filling her cup at the tea urn, her head bent in concentration. Her hair, the color of daffodils, divided at the nape of her neck and fell smoothly over her small breasts. She set her cup on a tray, picked out what she needed from the cutlery drawer, and moved along the line.

"Oy!" Mrs. Battle called to Clarrie. She nodded toward the girl. "That's her," she mouthed, "Jane Warren."

Clarrie handed the girl a bowl of porridge. "Miss Warren?"

"Yes?" The girl fixed her with slightly prominent blue eyes. Her face was pale, delicate, pretty but for her receding chin. She looked, Clarrie thought, a bit like a goldfish.

"I just met your father this morning. He was so nice—he . . ."

"Really?" The girl put the bowl on her tray and walked away.

Clarrie felt the blood rush to her face. Obviously, she had made a blunder. Jane Warren had no wish to talk about her father. She must be sensitive about his position.

Mrs. Battle walked over to whisper in Clarrie's ear. "Keeps to herself, that one. She don't talk to nobody."

A young man with a flowing cravat shook his head as she handed him his plate. "Porridge again? Oh, dear. I wonder what culinary delights are being plotted for dinner. If it's toad-in-the-hole and Ma Battle's shoe-leather tart, I believe I'll go back to bed and catch up on my sleep."

A pleasant clatter of plates came from the common room. As the students filed past, she searched each face, hoping to see the bearded man who had spoken to her on the stairs. Cryptic scraps of conversation drifted towards her; ". . . attributed to Holbein, I believe . . . Mummy was quite distraught . . . an iridescent green, like those lovely ducks in St James's Park . . . too damned invigorating . . . only in London . . ."

Clarrie strained to hear. The accents were distinctly upper class. This was a different world entirely from the one she'd left behind. Perhaps, in this place, she'd be free to be . . . whatever it was she was.

After the students had finished breakfast, and the staff had eaten theirs, Clarrie gathered up the dirty dishes.

"Soon as you've finished the washing up and put everything away," the cook said, "I want you to help Mrs. Battle with the pies." She turned to Mrs. Battle. "I'll be in the office with Miss McBride if anyone needs me. We've got to sort out that muddle with the ration books."

Mrs. Battle dumped flour and salt and lard into a white enamel bowl. She told Clarrie to grease the pastry trays.

"It's a lot of work isn't it—feeding all these students," Clarrie said, trying to be sociable.

Mrs. Battle plunged her fat hands into the bowl. "This ain't nothing to what it used to be, when we was in London.

We had plenty of staff, then, and there wasn't no rations in them days." Breathing heavily, she walked over to the stove and jiggled the damper. "It needs to be hot for pastry," she said. "What was I saying?"

"You were telling me about London."

"London. Gawd, we used to do some lovely grub there—chicken, fresh salmon, steak and kidney pud'n'. You oughter seen what we served when we catered the Chelsea Arts Ball—saveloys, veal an 'am pies, jellied eels . . ."

"My mother was in service when she was young," Clarrie said. "She told me . . ."

"Oyster patties."

"Oyster patties?"

"Ain't you never had oyster patties?"

Clarrie admitted she had not.

"I didn't think so. Gorge theirsels sick, the students did, on oyster patties. I was like you in them days, ducks—a scullery maid. There was a Mrs. Pearson was assistant cook. When war broke out, and they was packing up to leave London, Mrs. Pearson wouldn't budge. 'I'm London born and bred,' sez she, 'and I'm staying where the good Lord put me, right here in dear old London.'" Mrs. Battle threw down a handful of flour that rose in a cloud. She scratched at her armpit with a floury hand. "Pass me that rolling pin, ducks. Ta." She slapped a lump of grey dough onto the table, and attacked it with the rolling pin. Clarrie began to understand how Mrs. Battle's pastry had achieved its shoe-leather reputation.

"I was nobody then, just like you—never been nowhere, didn't know nothing. I never thought in a million years I'd get a chance to better m'self. But they needed someone as was willing to come down here you see . . . up . . . it's up when you go North, ain't it, and down for the South. Except for London. It's always up to London, ain't it? Well, it don't matter. I saw my chance and I took it." Mrs. Battle paused. Her face was streaked with flour; a strand of stiff black hair had come loose from its tortoise shell slide and was hanging over one eye. She wiped her face with a tea towel. "You'll get your chance, some day. You ain't common like Nora and that other one before you. If you minds your P's and Q's and works hard and watches how things is done, you'll get on like a house afire. Someday you could be like me—standing right here doing the pies."

Clarrie tried to imagine a day when she might be like Mrs. Battle. Mrs. Battle's belly and hips could scarcely be contained by her wraparound apron. With every movement she made, her great loose breasts jostled wildly about as though struggling to escape. She had dug into a large pot of jam and was spreading it on the pastry with the back of a spoon. Clarrie pointed to the jam dripping down the side of the jar. Mrs. Battle scooped it up with her finger and licked it off, then licked the handle of the spoon. A glob of jam attached itself to the fugitive strand of hair. She carried the tray to the stove and slid it in the oven.

"You oughter seen the toffs as used to come to them balls," she went on. "Dolled up to the nines—masks—wigs. The Prince of Wales—him as abdicated—he wouldn't miss the Chelsea Arts Ball for the world. They coulda locked him in the palace at night, but he'd of got a ladder and climbed over the walls. Him and his pals kept going all night, dancin' and swiggin' down champagne. I'd be stuck at that sink 'til all hours, washing up. In they'd come barging right through the kitchens—kissing the maids, swinging the cook round. His nibs would grab a spoon and a pan lid, and go banging through the halls, raising Cain—shivaree they calls it, and the rest of 'em followin'. He wore a mask, but we allus knew who it was."

"Did he kiss you?"

Mrs. Battle winked. "That would be telling. He was a great one for hanky-panky, though. Took after the old King

Eddie, I shouldn't wonder. Anyway, when war broke out they said if I was willing to leave London for the duration, they'd make me assistant cook. I didn't like leaving Battle, and my boy, Norman, but my old china says, 'You go me old cock sparrer—it's a chance to better yourself. I'll take care of the boy.'" She stopped with the jam spoon in midair. Her eyes filled with tears.

"What is it? What's the matter?" Clarrie asked.

Mrs. Battle put down the spoon and fumbled in her apron for a handkerchief. Tears spilled down her cheeks, making rivulets in the flour.

"Do you miss London?"

Mrs. Battle blew her nose with a loud trumpeting. "It ain't that, ducks. Me and Battle lost our only child in them air-raids." She looked up with tear-filled eyes. "Just turned seventeen, he was. I wasn't there to wake 'em up, see. I was allus the one to do that. They could sleep like the dead. They never heard nothing."

Clarrie walked around the table and patted Mrs. Battle's shoulder.

"Battle was throwed clear, but they got our boy, Norman . . ." Mrs. Battle's bosom heaved. She blew her nose again. "I was going to pack it in and go back to London, but they said if I'd stick it out for the duration, they'd take Battle on as handyman. So here we are, the two of us, like fish out of water."

Clarrie felt deeply ashamed. She'd been thinking of Mrs. Battle as a comic servant in a novel—a caricature—and had been mentally composing a comic description of her for a letter home. The smell of burning pastry drifted from the stove

"I think the pies are done, Mrs. Battle," Clarrie said. "Shall I take them out of the oven?"

It was after eight and Clarrie's first day was almost over. The rest of the staff had gone for the night, leaving her to finish the pots and pans. She was scrubbing the wooden drain boards and singing, "Do ye ken John Peel?" when she heard gentle clapping. She turned. The man with the chestnut beard stood in the doorway.

"You sing very well," he said. He was wearing the same paint-splotched shirt, brown corduroy trousers, and scuffed sandals he had worn the day before.

Blushing, Clarrie picked up a tea towel and clutched it to her stomach to conceal the large wet patch on her pinafore. "Did you want something?" The words came out with a brusqueness she had not intended. Should she call him "Sir?"

He stepped into the kitchen. "Did I want something? Yes, I believe I did—or rather do."

Clarrie frowned. Was the fellow correcting her grammar?

"I'd like a glass of water," he said. "If that is permissible." He strode with a quick bouncing walk over to the sink and stood looking down into her face with bright, fox-colored eyes. He was standing uncomfortably close. She lowered her eyes, and found herself staring into a clump of curling reddish-brown chest hair. She took a step backwards.

"You're the girl I met on the stairs," he said. "What's your name?"

"Clara." Her voice came out in a cracked whisper.

"Clara? Clara what—what is your surname?"

"Hancock."

"Hancock." He raised his eyebrows as though there was something surprising about her name. She twisted the tea towel, trying to think of something to say. His manner was subtly different, now, from when they had met on the stairs. Perhaps he, like the man who'd carried in her suitcase, had mistaken her for a student.

"And you are from where?"

"Manchester." She thought it unlikely that he'd heard of Salford.

"Ah, Manchester." He nodded wisely. Did he think her being from Manchester explained something?

Clarrie waited. She felt unnaturally alert, as though she might be in some sort of danger. She ran the water tap and rinsed an already clean tumbler. He reached over, took the glass from her and filled it with cold water. She caught a whiff of sweat. It was not unpleasant. As he brought the glass of water to his mouth, his elbow brushed against her breast. Clarrie jumped back, dropping the dishcloth. She bent to retrieve it, aware as she did so that he was gazing at her, speculatively.

"How old are you, Clara Hancock from Manchester?"

Clarrie hesitated.

"You can't be more than sixteen. Sweet sixteen and never been . . . ?" His eyes were teasing her, enjoying her discomfort. A right ninny he must think her . . . a gormless skivvy.

"I'm fifteen," she said crisply. She might be just a skivvy, but she wasn't about to be taken for a fool. Her cheeks blazed, but she plunged in. "Is there anything else you'd like to know?"

His smile vanished and something like shock flickered in the depth of his eyes. He put the glass on the draining board. "Yes," he said, softly. "Do tell me—when is your afternoon off?"

Clarrie caught her breath. Was he about to ask her for a date? She kept her eyes cast down.

"Monday. I get the whole day. Why do you ask?" There was a soft rasp of corduroy, and when she looked up again he had gone. She caught a glimpse of his frayed trouser cuff as it disappeared around the doorway. Bewildered, she stared after it, half expecting him to return. Her face burned as though it had been slapped. He'd asked her when her day off was, and then walked away without waiting for an answer! Had her show of spirit struck him as impertinence, obliging him to put her in her place?

She picked up his glass to rinse it, and then slammed it so hard on the draining board it shattered.

Chapter Forty-two

"These floors need a good scrubbing," the cook said. "Betty, the girl who had the job before you, thought herself too high and mighty to get down on her knees. She said the red stuff off the tiles stained her hands." The cook snorted contemptuously. "Bone idle that one; all she knew how to do was slosh a mop around." She nodded towards the pantry. "You'd best start in there—wash and straighten the shelves then do the floors."

Clarrie, anxious to acquit herself well, filled a bucket with hot soapy water and attacked the long-accumulated grime. Hidden away at the back of the top shelf, she found a dozen identical white vases covered in dust. She washed and dried them. With a few wild flowers, they'd make nice centerpieces for the common room tables.

Although it was large and airy, with a huge stone fireplace and a row of long windows opening onto the gardens, the common room was spoiled by walls the color of pea soup, and cracked brown oilcloth on the tables. The teachers took their meals in a cozy paneled room where the tables were set each day with freshly starched white linen cloths, and vases of fresh flowers. Clarrie thought the students deserved the same consideration—they were artists, after all, and probably sensitive to their surroundings.

Once the shelves were finished, she refilled the bucket, and got down on her knees to scrub the floors, singing as she worked, drawing pleasure, as she invariably did, from banishing dirt, making things shine. There was a clatter outside and the door burst open. Two yellow-haired, pink-cheeked farm lads came in. Twins, obviously. They carried between them a large, double-handled milk churn. Clarrie stopped singing. The lads nudged each other, put down the milk churn and began talking to her in a broad Westmorland dialect. She smiled politely.

"Sorry. I don't understand what you're saying—I'm not familiar with the accent." This brought slaps and guffaws from the twins. The cook stuck her little Pekingese face around the door.

"You boys are late," she snapped. "Bring in that milk and let my girl do her work." Still laughing, they carried the milk churn into the kitchen.

Clarrie went back to her task and her singing. She was in the middle of a heartfelt rendering of "The Raggle-Taggle Gypsies" when she felt a rough hand slide up under her skirt and grasp her buttock. She swung around and slapped the owner of the hand with her scrubbing brush. Two identical ruddy faces laughed down at her. The twins pointed fingers at each other.

"'Tweren't me, 'twere 'im!" they cried in unison.

"Idiots!" Clarrie picked up the bucket, threatening to throw the soapy water at them. The twins ran out, laughing and clanging the milk pail against the door as they ran.

Later that afternoon, as she walked with Nora to the beck to see where the tealeaf bucket should be emptied, she told Nora what had happened.

Nora's green eyes glinted with amusement. "That's the Dobbs twins. They try it on with all the girls."

"They'd better not try it with me again."

"They're having a bit of fun with you. Their father's a right old devil. Got 'em exempted from the army because he needs them on the farm. Milking cows and mucking out stalls is all they know. They daresn't even go to the lav without his permission—they've never seen the inside of a bus or a train. They sneaked out to a dance one night with Betty and me—I really miss Betty—she was the scullery maid before you. We used to laugh ourselves sick. But she got herself in the family way and had to leave. Anyway, the old man come after the twins with his belt flying—chased them right off the dance floor. Johnny—he's the one with the big mole on his cheek—told me he was in love with Betty, but his old man put the kibosh on it."

"Is he the father of Betty's baby?"

Nora hesitated. "She won't say. All I know is the old man slipped her twenty quid and told her to stay away from his lads."

"Why don't the twins stand up to him?"

"That's easier said than done. I stood up to my stepmother, and look what it got me." Nora lifted a clump of brown hair from her scalp and bent to show Clarrie a bald white patch the size of a florin. "Tipped boiling fat from the chip pan over me, she did. She claimed it was an accident. My dad believed her, but I know better." She pushed up the sleeve of her cardigan to reveal a twisted rope-like scar on her upper arm. "Got me here, too, the old witch."

"A wicked stepmother!"

"She poisoned my dad's mind against me, that's why I ran away from home. I was only twelve, but I was well-developed for my age. I took the bus to Kendal and got a job as a maid at a boy's school. I haven't been home since."

"Didn't your dad try to find you?"

"I wrote to him a couple of times, but he never answered. I think he was glad to get rid of me so the old witch would leave him in peace."

"Perhaps he didn't get your letter," she said. "Your stepmother might have kept it from him."

Nora shrugged. "They can both go to hell for all I care."

Clarrie had an impulse to put her arm around Nora's shoulder, to comfort her, but proud as Nora seemed to be, she would no doubt resent any show of sympathy.

They had reached a rocky bank looking down on a gurgling beck. "Here's where we empty the bucket," Nora said. "Just turn it upside down and give it a shake . . . try not to hit the rocks . . . let everything get carried away by the water."

During their afternoon break, Nora offered to show Clarrie around the village. They stopped first at Boots chemists for Nora's shampoo, and then strolled down the hill. When they reached the bookshop, Clarrie stopped. Shielding her eyes from the reflected glare of the spring sunlight, she brought her face close to the window. The chestnut-haired man was sitting on the floor between the stacks, poring over what looked to be an oversized art book.

Nora tugged at her sleeve. "What are you gawping at?"

"That man. Isn't he one of the students?"

"Aye. Griff Williams." Nora shot her an amused glance. "What's so interesting about him?"

"He came in for a drink of water while I was finishing up last night."

"So?"

"Oh . . . nothing." Last night's insult still rankled, but it occurred to her that perhaps she'd hurt him a little first. "He's nice looking, don't you think?"

"He might be all right if he got rid of that beard."

"I rather like the beard."

"You're not the only one," Nora said. "He's not my type, but lots of girls are after him. There's this girl Margot, she's always right behind him when they come through for meals, but she looks down her long nose at everyone else. And last year, before you came, there was one of 'em—Greta somebody—traipsed after him like a dog—proper moon-struck. He wouldn't give her a tumble. She was deformed, poor thing, all twisted and funny looking. One day she disappeared, and they found a note in her room saying if she couldn't have the man she loved, she didn't want to live."

"I wouldn't chase after any man," Clarrie said.

"You've never been in love, then."

"I thought I was, once."

"What happened?"

Clarrie fell silent, remembering the awful day in Sunday school when she'd stepped out, smiling, so sure that Richard Beaumont was looking for her. She'd never leave herself unguarded again, if she could help it.

"Did some fellow jilt you?"

"We were just children."

"Puppy love?" Nora made a wry mouth. "That's not the real thing."

"So they tell me." Clarrie turned from the bookshop window. "So what happened to that girl, Greta?"

"They sent a search party up on the fells, looking for her. Griff Williams was leader of the rescue squad. He found her half dead from starvation and exposure on Langdale Pike. They had to carry her down on a stretcher."

"Did she die?"

"All I know is her parents came to take her home and she never came back." They had crested the hill. In the distance, a ribbon of bright water shimmered.

"There's the lake!" Clarrie cried. "It's so lovely. Let's walk down."

"You're just like the students." Nora sounded scornful. "They're forever raving about the scenery. You'd think they'd never seen grass or water before." They walked on in silence until they came to a row of small stone cottages. Nora stopped. "My feet are killing me," she said. "And I've seen the lake a million times. I want to pop in here and cheer up my friend, Betty. They're all giving her the cold shoulder now because of the baby—rotten lot of hypocrites."

Nora knocked at the cottage door. Clarrie caught a glimpse of a dark-haired young woman holding a baby. The door closed behind Nora. Clarrie hesitated for a moment. The lake would still be there tomorrow. She turned back up the hill and went into the bookshop. Griff Williams had gone.

Chapter Forty-three

The domestic staff were eating dinner around the long, well-scrubbed kitchen table, when a slender, well-dressed woman entered and went straight to the refrigerator.

Mrs. Marten gave an exasperated sigh. "Can I get you anything, Mrs. Howland?"

"Oh, Cook!" Mrs. Howland feigned surprise, as though she hadn't noticed Mrs. Marten and the eight other people sitting around the table. "I didn't wish to disturb you while you were eating." She spoke with a flat drawl that Clarrie recognized as American. "My cats are awfully hungry. I thought I might take a few scraps."

Mrs. Marten stood up, pushing her chair back. "Here, let me . . ."

"Don't trouble yourself. I see a small piece of fish here, under some wax paper. I'll make do with that."

"That's not scraps," the cook said. "That's a nice bit of codfish. I put it aside for Nobby Clark." She poured a saucer of milk from a jug on the table and handed it to Mrs. Howland.

"What are my cats to eat?"

"If you didn't pamper them so much, they might get rid of some of the rats for us."

"I shall speak to Miss McBride about this," Mrs. Howland said.

"A fat lot of good may it do you," the cook muttered as Mrs. Howland walked out with the saucer of milk. An awkward silence followed.

Clarrie ended it by asking what, if anything, there was to do in the village on a Monday. Her day off was coming up, and she didn't intend to spend it indoors.

"There's a little tea room near the Royal," the cook told her. "They make a very nice scone."

Mr. Battle winked. "And if that's too much excitement for you, ducks, you can sit by the lake and watch the grass grow."

Clarrie laughed. "Does anyone know the quickest way to get up into the mountains?"

"You can take the road past the beck, cut through Dobbs Farm, and over the stile," Nora said. "You'll be right there on the fells."

"Is that where you and your Tommy go to do your spooning?" Mrs. Battle asked. She looked at Clarrie. "Nora's engaged to a soldier, but we ain't seen no ring yet."

Nora reddened. "He's bringing it next time he comes on leave, and what me and my fiancé do is nobody else's business." She turned to Clarrie. "It's quite a climb," she said. "You'll need a walking stick—there's an old one in the hall cupboard that doesn't belong to anyone; it's got a handle carved like a fox's-head."

Next Monday morning, Clarrie left the hotel right after breakfast. Stuffing a sandwich into one coat pocket, a paperback book of poetry into the other, and carrying the walking stick with its fox-head handle, she set off to explore the fells.

Fluffy clouds dotted the sky, forming haloes around the mountain peaks before breaking and scudding away. Along the lanes, the hedges had burst into sticky bud. The air reverberated with bird cries and the bleating of lambs. Waterfalls splashed down between massive outcroppings of rock. As she climbed, the breeze became brisker, changing at last into a blustery wind that slapped at her face, whipped her hair back, and filled her ears with a powerful rushing sound. Rough plants, gorse or bracken, scratched her legs. A sheep scrambled over a wall and ran off.

These low stone walls, straggling over the mountains, bore silent witness to the wildness, the loneliness, of the fells. They didn't prevent the sheep from straying, so what on earth was their purpose?

She had been climbing for a couple of hours and was very near the top. From the valley, the mountains looked much higher than they actually were. As she clambered over the last rocky rise, the roar of the wind subsided, and she found herself in a scooped-out bowl, at the center of which lay a dark tarn, the water smooth as glass. Right here, protected from the wind, would be the ideal place to stop and eat her sandwich.

She took off her coat, shoes, and socks and walked around the grassy bowl, looking into every crevice. Down in the valley, the lakes ringed with daffodils sparkled. She was above the clouds, at the very crest of the world. The sun beat down on her head and back. She sat on the grassy bank, gazing into the depths of the tarn. Since passing Dobbs's Farm, except for the odd sheep, she hadn't seen a living soul. She had the world to herself. She could take off her clothes and step naked into the water. Nobody would see her.

Quickly she undressed, folded her clothes into a neat pile, and stood for a moment looking down at her own naked body, exposed to fresh air and sunlight for the first time in her life. Her skin was pale as a mushroom.

She walked to the edge of the tarn and put one foot into the dark, still water. There was a sucking noise, and a cloud of black sludge swirled up around her ankle. She moved along the rim to where the water was undisturbed and rinsed her foot, taking care not to stir the mud at the bottom.

She rolled her coat into a pillow, and lay on her back, naked to the sky. Shivers of pleasure rippled through her. "What wondrous life is this I lead?" she whispered. A funny green insect was making his way up her thigh as laboriously as she had made her way up the mountain. Normally she would have swatted him, but today, killing anything was out of the question. She brushed the insect off. Overhead, the clouds were changing shape, drifting, melting. She too, was drifting, melting, becoming one with the earth and sky . . .

She heard a munching noise and turned her head. An old grey sheep, its matted wool marked with a streak of blue paint, was staring at her, a bunch of grass hanging from its mouth. "Shame on you," she said. "Go away." The sheep obediently trotted away. She closed her eyes. The long climb had tired her.

She wasn't sure how long she'd slept, or what had woken her. Half-opening her eyes, she saw, no more than three feet away, a man in khaki shorts, bent by a haversack on his back, tiptoeing past with a broad grin on his face. It was too late to cover herself—he had already seen everything there was to see. She shut her eyes again, pretending to be asleep.

When she was sure he had gone, she got to her feet, dressed quickly and started the long trek back. Twilight descended, veiling the crags. She skirted the emerald green patches she suspected were treacherous bogs, and made her way down the mountain to the stile that led across the fells to the Dobbs farmyard. A dog ran out yapping at her heels, but a rough male voice from the direction of the barn called the dog to heel and the animal turned and loped away. It was almost dark by the time she reached the road, but the blackout curtains were not yet drawn, and she was relieved to see the welcoming lights from the college winking in the distance. She was hungry. She hoped the cook had saved her something to eat.

Later that night, sitting up in bed after a hot bath, she wrote a letter home:

Dear Mam, Dad, and all,

Well, my first full week is over. I love it here. There are daffodils growing wild all over the place. You wouldn't believe your eyes if you could see the students, they're real bohemians. The boys all have beards and wear corduroy trousers. The girls dress like Gypsies—long hair, skirts round their ankles, no stockings. Men and women alike go about with bare toes sticking out of sandals (but what you really need here is stout walking shoes). You can tell they're upper class, though, because they all sound like Lord Haw-Haw.

There seems to be plenty of food. Eggs and milk come fresh from the farm every day, but the cooks could do with a few lessons. You could sole your shoes with Mrs. Battle's pastry and they boil the life out of the vegetables.

The kitchen has ancient wooden sinks that we have to scrub to get the grease out; the wood is all soft and splintery. And the kitchen is plagued with cockroaches. When you switch on the light at night, they run like mad up the walls, over the counters and the silverware trays—one even crawled up my leg while I was scrubbing the floor. Nora, the other kitchen maid, says there are rats, too, but so far I haven't seen any.

There are only a few Northerners working here. Nora's from Cheshire, and Doris—one of the chambermaids—is a Geordie from Newcastle (she calls the ash on her cigarette a dottle). Then there's old Nobby, who takes care of the furnaces—he has a dewdrop forever dangling on the end of his nose, and he talks to me in a thick, Westmorland dialect. I have no idea what he's saying.

The locals have some lovely words for things. A hill is a fell, a stream, a beck, and a deep mountain pool, a tarn. I think a ghyll means a waterfall, but I'm not sure.

Most of the domestic staff are Cockneys who came with the college from London. One of them, Mr. Battle, greets me in the mornings with "Watcher me ole cock sparrer!" If I say "Good morning, Mr. Battle," he thinks I'm putting on airs. He whistles and says "Coo! 'Ark at her!"

Today was my first day off. I climbed to the top of a mountain and got back late for supper. The cook hadn't left me anything to eat, so right now I'm in my room, starving . . .

She broke off and read the letter over. She was pretty sure that nobody—except perhaps Billy—would be interested in all that stuff about the local words. And her mother would get upset if she knew her daughter was going to bed hungry.

Bone-tired though she was, she tore the letter up and began again.

Dear Mam, Dad, and all,

I hope you got my telegram. Sorry not to have written sooner. There really isn't much to tell. They keep me busy here, scrubbing floors and peeling spuds, etc., but the work isn't too hard, and so far, everyone seems very nice . . ."

Chapter Forty-four

Miss McBride poked her head into the kitchen to tell Clarrie her new room was ready. "Miss Charteris needs your old room right away, Clarrie, so run across to the Royal and fetch your belongings."

The few days Clarrie was supposed to spend at the Royal had turned into more than two weeks. She was curious to see her permanent quarters, but living at the Royal had one important advantage—it was where Griff lived. After that incident in the kitchen, there'd been no opportunity for anything more than a brief greeting in the hall or on the stairs, still . . .

"Is it all right if I go with Clarrie to help bring her things over?" Nora asked Miss McBride.

"Yes, by all means."

Mrs. Battle, who seldom missed an opportunity to hint that Nora was too free and easy with the men, winked at Clarrie. "I ain't sure we oughter let Nora loose with all them fellas over there, Miss McBride."

Clarrie had been about to say she didn't need any help, but seeing ominous red patches staining Nora's cheeks, she thought better of it.

"Did you hear that old cow?" Nora said, as they walked over to the Royal.

"Mrs. Battle? She was just teasing. She doesn't mean any harm."

"She's had it in for me ever since Christmas. Her husband gave me a little kiss under the mistletoe, and she's never forgiven me for it."

"You're young and pretty and you've got your whole life ahead of you. Her only child was killed in the air raids."

"I know." Nora thrust out her chin defiantly. "It's her husband I feel sorry for—fancy being married to that back-street Cockney bitch. She only takes a bath once a fortnight, and she doesn't even clean the tub when she's done. I hate going in there after she's used it."

"Why don't you take your baths in one of the upstairs bathrooms? That's what I'm going to do."

"Better not let Cook catch you. She'll tell you that you don't know your place."

"She's a fine one to talk about knowing your place—the way she treats Mrs. Howland."

"Howland's a Yank," Nora said as they went into the Royal. "Nobody knows what her place is."

"What exactly does she do?" Clarrie asked. Mrs. Howland seemed to spend an inordinate amount of time looking for Roly and Poly, her overfed cats. Her position at Rook How was not clear to Clarrie, nor, it seemed, to anyone else.

"She's supposed to be in charge of the girls' rooms, but I've never seen her do a lick of work," Nora said. "Her husband was a famous artist. When he died, they let her stay on. If that was us, we'd have been sent packing before the body was cold."

"Perhaps she had nowhere else to go."

"She's like her cats. They've got a comfy place to stay and servants to take care of 'em. Nice work if you can get it."

"Doesn't she pay for her keep?"

"No. They pay her."

"She's so elegant and well-turned out, don't you think?"

"We'd be, too, if we had nothing to do all day but groom ourselves."

Clarrie said no more. It would take more than grooming, she thought, to turn either of them into someone like Mrs. Howland.

"Splendid!" Miss McBride said when Clarrie and Nora returned with her suitcase. "Nora, you may go back to work. Clarrie, come with me." She led the way up the main staircase. "We'll go this way, rather than traipse through the kitchen. But from now on, you must use the servants' . . ." the rest of her words were obliterated by the drone of a vacuum cleaner. Winnie, one of the chambermaids, was cleaning the corridor. Pulling the Hoover after her, she backed into an open doorway to allow them to pass.

Clarrie caught tantalizing glimpses into rooms crammed with books, canvases, paintbrushes, gramophone records, and ice skates. One room had a heap of silky underclothes and a blue satin dressing gown strewn on the floor.

"Such dreadful disorder . . ." Miss McBride clucked her tongue. "It doesn't seem to trouble them . . . the artistic temperament, I suppose."

Mrs. Howland appeared in a doorway, immaculately dressed in a dark woolen frock and a matching, beige-trimmed jacket. She was holding one of her cats. "Is there anything I can do to help?"

"I believe we have everything under control, thank you Mrs. Howland," Miss McBride said briskly. "I'm just showing Clarrie to her new room." They had reached a landing at the end of the corridor. She pointed to a crooked flight of stairs that disappeared into a dark hole. "The servants' staircase. Be careful when using it—there's no banister. If you follow it down, it will take you straight to the scullery."

She pushed open a door and motioned for Clarrie to enter. The room reeked of fresh paint. Miss McBride swept back the shiny black chintz curtains, and flung open the casement window. "That's better—a little fresh air."

Clarrie put her suitcase on the floor. This part of the building looked very old. A layer of shiny cream-colored paint had done little to disguise the lumps and ridges in the woodwork or the patched plaster on the walls. The room was sparsely furnished with a straight-backed chair, a white-painted dresser, a washbasin with a small wooden shelf over it, and a narrow bed, its caved-in mattress covered by a threadbare chenille spread. One corner of the room had been curtained off to serve as a wardrobe.

"You'll be comfortable enough in here," Miss McBride said. "Clarrie," she lowered her voice. "Cook told me about that unfortunate incident with the Dobbs twins. I intend to pay Mr. Dobbs a visit, and tell him, in no uncertain terms, that I will not have my staff subjected to . . ."

"Oh, please no! I don't want to get them in trouble with their father. I suppose it was their idea of a joke."

"As you wish. But if they do anything like that again, you must let me know immediately. Your mother wrote me a nice letter asking me to take good care of you."

Clarrie shot a startled glance at Miss McBride.

"She's understandably concerned about your welfare. I promised to keep an eye on you."

"Thank you. I don't think they'll bother me again."

"You'll be responsible for making your own bed, of course, and for keeping your room dusted and in order. Winnie will come by on Fridays to vacuum and leave you fresh sheets and towels. Remember to strip your bed and put the soiled linens by the door."

Clarrie nodded.

"I'll leave you to it, then. Don't be late getting back to work." Miss McBride left, closing the door behind her.

Clarrie walked over to the window and took a deep breath of the sweet air. The window overlooked the cobbled courtyard at the back of the hotel, and to the left, a coppice, broken by the narrow path which led to the beck. The air was filled with the sound of rushing water.

She unpacked her frock, skirt, and coat, and put them on wire hangers behind the wardrobe curtain. Her underclothes, socks, and nightgown went into the dresser, where they took up one corner of one of the drawers. On her pillow, she arranged the nightdress case her mother had brought home for her from the chapel jumble sale. She suspected that the frilly pink satin wasn't in the best of taste, but it didn't much matter. Nobody but Winnie would be coming in her room, and Winnie would think it was lovely.

The top of the dresser was marred by cigarette burns. She must find some sort of runner to cover them, but for the moment, she could hide them under her celluloid brush and comb set. She removed the newspaper wrappings from her picture—a diamond-shaped plaque depicting a lighthouse overlooking a stormy sea. It was made of some sort of hard, dark lacquer work, with the moon, the lighthouse window, and the beam of light touching the waves picked out in mother-of-pearl. A strip of curling paper on the back read "For those in Peril." Mr. Bassington had removed it from the wall of the vestry and given it to her mother. Since the picture did not have a biblical subject, he said, it was not really suitable for the vestry. He had replaced it with a framed photograph taken of himself and some friends at a ministers' conference. Tomorrow she'd ask Miss McBride if it would be all right to knock a nail in the wall.

That evening, she was coming out of the bathroom with her towel over her arm, when she bumped into another girl going in.

"Whoa!" the girl cried, dodging the door.

"Sorry!" Clarrie said.

"No harm done." The girl put out her hand. "Jennie Alwin. I don't believe we've met. Is this your first term?"

"I'm not a student. I work in the kitchen. My name's Clarrie."

"Ah! A fellow Northerner, if I'm not mistaken?"

"Yes," Clarrie said, "Manchester."

"I live not too far from there—well, far enough, I suppose—Morecambe. I was supposed to be here at the beginning of the term, but I had a spell of pneumonia." She pulled together her fuzzy white dressing gown. "It's late. I'd better get my bath before someone beats me to it."

"I'm sorry if I kept you waiting," Clarrie said. "I'm supposed to use the bath downstairs, but . . ."

Jennie flashed her a warm smile. "Your secret's safe with me. We Northerners must stick together."

Clarrie thought Jennie quite the most beautiful girl she had ever seen. It was the way she imagined her sister, Janet, might have looked, had she lived.

Although she and Nora got along well during working hours, it had soon become clear that they had little in common. After work, as if by mutual consent, they went their separate ways.

On her free Mondays, Clarrie tramped the fells alone, exhilarated by the pure air, the clear water bubbling over stones, the bleating of sheep, the rushing winds that whipped her hair, reshaped the scudding clouds, and whistled through the bracken.

The daffodils were gone now from the lakeside, but the woods around Rydal Water were knee-deep in bluebells. The delicate flowers would look lovely, she thought, in the white vases she'd discovered in the pantry when she first arrived—the perfect things to brighten the tables in the common room. She gathered as many flowers as she could hold and carried them back to the hotel.

She was in the common room, arranging the bluebells in the vases, when she heard someone rather deliberately clearing his throat. Stephen Wentworth was standing in the doorway, watching her with his sad dark eyes. Those eyes, and his marble-pale slab of a forehead, gave him an ethereal quality that reminded her of the picture of Lord Byron in her poetry book. Under other circumstances—if she hadn't met Griff first, for instance—she might easily have fallen in love with Stephen Wentworth.

"I saw the light," he said. "I wondered who . . ."

"It's only me. I thought a few flowers might dress up the tables."

"You'll be disappointed, I'm afraid. Bluebells are notoriously fragile, by morning they'll be dead."

Clarrie shrugged. "I've already picked them . . ."

The next morning, before the students began filing in for breakfast, she ran to the common room to check on the bluebells. As Stephen had predicted, they now drooped lifeless over the rims of the vases. She scooped them up and dropped them in the rubbish bin.

Throughout April, lilacs burst into bloom, drenching the village lanes with heady perfume; these were followed by roses—creamy yellow, dusty pink, crimson, and white, they flung themselves in riotous profusion over walls and fences. As Clarrie strolled along a narrow lane, entranced by the scents and sights around her, her skirt caught on a thorny stem and a creamy, scarlet-tipped bud brushed her cheek. She stroked the petals, filled with wonder that such a fragrant, delicate, and lovely thing had thrust its way through layers of dank earth to dance for a moment in the bright air.

In spite of, or perhaps because of, the heartbreaking beauty around her, Clarrie was lonely. In the evenings, the rest of the staff went off, leaving her to her own devices. When she'd read the few books she could get her hands on, and used up her writing paper, there was little to do but lie on her bed, listening to the bursts of laughter, the clamor of voices, and the jangling of the out-of-tune piano, drifting up from the common room.

At times the solitude weighed so heavily, she took to stealing down the main staircase to secrete herself in a dark nook in the passage that led from the main hall to the kitchens. From there, perched on an upturned barrel, she watched the comings and goings of the students unobserved. From time to time, she caught a glimpse of Griff Williams. Although longing to talk to him, she resisted the impulse to make her presence known. She'd be hard-pressed to explain why she was sitting on a barrel in the dark hallway.

Chapter Forty-five

Summer brought an exodus of students, teachers, and most of the domestic and office staffs. Nora had arranged to spend the holidays with her prospective in-laws at their home in Liverpool, leaving Clarrie, along with Mr. and Mrs. Battle, to cater to the few students and staff members who, for one reason or another, had chosen to remain.

The handful of students who'd remained behind were not inclined to be sociable. One day, on her afternoon break, Clarrie came upon two of them—a dark-haired girl named Leah, and her constant companion, a handsome, silent, young man, known to Clarrie only as Tanner—locked in each others arms in the deep grass. Mumbling an apology, she made a hasty retreat.

Mrs. Howland and two elderly male teachers took their meals together in the small dining room. The remaining domestic staff—Charlie, the gardener, Old Nobby, the handyman, and two chambermaids from the Royal—ate their meals in the kitchen and went their separate ways immediately after. Clarrie served the handful of students and cleaned the common room after meals.

The holidays were only a couple of weeks underway when Mr. and Mrs. Battle were called unexpectedly to London, where Mrs. Battle's aged mother was dangerously ill. Clarrie was unable to reach Miss McBride, and found herself with no choice but to handle the kitchen alone.

She kept the cooking simple—confining her efforts to things she remembered her mother making—shepherd's pie, Lancashire hotpot, sausage and mash. The compliments she got were gratifying, but she was glad the cook and Mrs. Battle were not there to hear them. On her days off, she left porridge for breakfast, sandwiches for lunch, and instructions for warming dinner.

The extra work did not trouble her, but the lonely evenings were hard to bear. Driven more by the urge to get out of her room than by hunger, she took to venturing down the servants' staircase in her nightgown, and braving the army of cockroaches that scuttled for cover when she switched on the light, in order to forage in the refrigerator for a sandwich, a slice of pie, or a glass of cold milk to carry back to her room.

One evening, catching a glimpse of herself in the bedroom mirror, her cheeks bulging with pie, her mouth stained with blackberry juice, she was overcome by shame. Arthur and his fellow Marines were out on the ocean risking their lives for their country; the rest of her family were dealing with all manner of hardship and deprivation, and here was she, feeling sorry for herself, stuffing her face with sweets, not doing one blessed thing to help the war effort. She leaned close to the mirror. "What is wrong with you?" she asked her reflection.

"Is it always this quiet in the summertime?" she asked the man who ran the bookshop.

He took his pipe from his mouth. “Nay. Summer was our busiest season before war broke out—we did a great business with the tourists—but now . . . If it weren’t for you young people from the college, I’d have to close up shop.”

“I’m not a student,” Clarrie said, hastily. “I just work there.” She had gone in the shop intending only to browse, but in view of his remarks, she felt obliged to buy something. She chose a suede-bound copy of *Leaves of Grass*.

She was on her way back to the hotel, reading, when she ran into Mrs. Howland. With her waxy smooth skin, well-tailored clothes, and carefully manicured hands, Mrs. Howland seemed out of place in a country lane. She’d be more at home, Clarrie thought, behind the plate glass of a fashionable shop window.

“Ah, Clarrie. Have you by any chance seen my cats along the road?”

“I’m sorry, Mrs. Howland, I was reading. I wasn’t paying attention.”

“And what is so interesting, may I ask, that you must read while you walk?” Mrs. Howland took the book from Clarrie’s hand and riffled through the pages. “Whitman? My dear child, you never cease to amaze me. You are truly a chameleon.”

“A chameleon?”

“You don’t have them in this country, I suppose. A chameleon is a lizard that changes color in order to blend in with its background.”

Clarrie didn’t much care for being likened to a lizard, but she was flattered that Mrs. Howland should take an interest in the doings of a kitchen-maid.

“I caught a glimpse of you from my window when you first arrived. You were wearing a rather dashing hat, I remember—the very image of a sophisticated young woman about town. A few days later I saw you striding along the road wearing knee socks and carrying a walking stick, like any hardy Lakeland hiker. And just before the vacation started, I was in the corridor near the kitchen, looking for Roly and Poly, when I heard you singing. I peeked in and there you were—you and Nora—engaged in a sprightly rustic dance."

Clarrie blushed. She'd been teaching Nora some of the country dances she'd learned in school. She and Nora had grown a bit rowdy, kicking up their heels, singing "Roll me Over in the Clover," and "Knees up, Mother Brown." She hoped Mrs. Howland hadn't witnessed that.

"Was that a square dance you were doing?" Mrs. Howland asked.

"It's just country dancing. The dances have different names—Black Nag, The Barley Mow, Picking up Sticks . . ."

"Charming. And now I see you are a bookworm and a lover of poetry." Mrs. Howland handed the book back. "You are much too young, my dear, for Whitman. If you're interested in American poetry, I shall find you something more suitable. Are you familiar with *The Spoon River Anthology*?"

Clarrie shook her head.

"You'll like it better than Whitman," Mrs. Howland said firmly. She fluttered a pale hand in dismissal. "I must be off to look for those naughty cats of mine."

That evening, Clarrie found *The Spoon River Anthology* on her bedside chair. She read the poems that night, but the voices from the graveyard, their stories of betrayal and regret, brought with them a whiff of corruption that left her depressed. She waited a decent couple of days before returning the book, and was grateful when Mrs. Howland simply invited her to look over her bookshelves and borrow whatever she wished. She selected Dorothy Wordsworth's *Journal*, and inspired by the journal, went on her next Monday to visit Dove Cottage.

The cottage was quaint, the interior low-ceilinged and sparsely furnished. Clarrie imagined William Wordsworth lying on his couch, thinking about the daffodils. The cottage must have looked different in those days, she thought. There were probably lots of books and cushions strewn about, and a cheery fire burning, and William's sister, Dorothy, trotting to the kitchen to fetch him tea and buttered scones. The only other visitors at the cottage were an elderly man and woman who communicated with each other in sign language, and the tour was over sooner than she had expected.

Having the rest of the day on her hands, she strolled through the nearby woods, gathering wild flowers, which she carried to the Grasmere churchyard. Offering up a brief prayer, she dropped them over the railings onto Dorothy Wordsworth's grave.

Cutting across a meadow on her way back , she came upon a crowd of people watching some sort of ceremony. Women, crowned with blossoms, paraded in a stately circle around a trench filled with rushes. Clarrie joined the spectators. Some of them—a group of a dozen or so young men and women—appeared to be members of some sort of cycling club.

"What's going on?" Clarrie asked a pretty blonde girl standing near her.

"It's the rush-gathering ceremony," the girl whispered. "It's as old as the hills . . ."

The women had stopped circling. A clergyman stepped forward and began speaking. Clarrie strained to hear, but the wind carried his words away. When he'd finished, he stepped back, and four men, their trousers tied below the knees with strings of bells, picked up a sort of stretcher laden with rushes. With the clergyman leading the way and the bells tinkling, the rush-bearers carried their burden across the fields to the square-towered church. Most of the spectators—all except the cyclists—followed the procession to the church. Clarrie was tempted to join them, but she'd put her prayer book aside when she'd left school, along with her whip and top, her skipping rope, and her ball. She hadn't set foot in a church since. These people were obviously stalwart churchgoers. They would spot her immediately as an outsider—an intruder.

Turning away, she saw the cyclists pushing their bicycles over the grassy hillocks. Snatches of conversation, bursts of laughter blew across the field towards her. They were arranging to stop for tea at the Boar's Head Inn. Clarrie felt a pang of envy. In spite of the war, life was going on all around her—people were joining clubs, going to church, taking part in ancient ceremonies. She, on the other hand, was always on the outside, always alone.

She quickened her pace, hoping to catch up with the cyclists and perhaps make an acquaintance, but on rounding the hill, she saw that they had reached the road and were already mounting their bicycles. The blonde girl's laughter rang out across the valley; her hair fluttered like a golden banner as she sped away.

Tired of her usual haunts, on the following Monday Clarrie set out with her walking stick to hike the Kirkstone Pass to wherever it led. The sky was overcast and rain appeared imminent. She chose to disregard it. She hoped to make it all the way to the end of the pass and back before dark. She'd been climbing about half an hour when the rain began. A car drove up, slowing to a crawl as it came alongside. A balding, middle-aged man leaned out of the window.

"Where are you bound, lass?"

She hesitated. He'd think her mad, trudging about in the rain without a destination.

"Are you lost, then?"

"I'm trying to get to Keswick," she said. She remembered reading somewhere that the Lake Poets had from time to time gathered at Keswick, and that Keswick lay some miles to the north of Bramblebeck.

"Taking the scenic route, eh?" He raised his bushy black eyebrows. "I'm on my way to Keswick myself. It's much too far to walk. Hop in, I'll give you a lift."

"I'll be all right, thank you," she said primly.

"Nay, don't be daft—you're getting drenched. Hop in. I'll be glad of the company." The man spoke with a broad Lancashire accent, much like her Oldham relations. He had pushed open the door and his arm was getting wet. Unable to think of a plausible reason to refuse, she climbed in.

"Braithwaite's the name, Albert Braithwaite, owner of Braithwaite Woolens. You've heard of Braithwaite Woolens?"

"The name sounds familiar," she said politely.

"I should hope so. It's costing me enough to advertise."

The rain was pelting down now, sliding in sheets across the windshield, the wipers making frantic arcs across the streaming glass. Mr. Braithwaite slowed the car to a crawl.

"Don't worry, I know every twist and turn of this road. If it gets any worse there's a spot where we can pull over and wait it out." Clarrie shifted in her seat, her eye on the door handle.

"I've been thinking—perhaps I shouldn't go to Keswick after all. I didn't realize it was so far."

"Don't you worry—I'll see you back safe. You're lucky it was me as picked you up. As a general rule, you shouldn't go getting into cars with strangers. When you've lived as long as me, you'll find there's a lot of rum 'uns in this world."

"That's what my father says, too."

"Where are you from? Are you one of them artist lassies from the college, then?"

"I'm from Manchester. I just work at the college."

"Doing what?" he asked. Clarrie told him.

"A kitchen maid. A bright young lass like you? It's honest work, I'll grant you that, but you can do better. What is it you want to do?"

"I'm not sure. I haven't much education." Her fantasy of becoming a novelist seemed too absurd to mention.

"You can't let that stop you. Operation bootstrap, that's what I recommend. You know what that means? It means you've got to pull yourself up by your own bootlaces."

Bootlaces. The word triggered an image of her father, squinting through his cracked spectacles as he struggled to tie together scraps of broken bootlace. Sometimes your own bootlaces weren't even strong enough to do the job they'd been designed for.

". . . shorthand and typewriting," Mr. Braithwaite was saying. He fumbled in his pockets and produced a business card. "Take my advice. Go back to Manchester. Get someone to teach you shorthand and typing, then look me up. There's always an opening for a good shorthand typist."

"Thank you," Clarrie said. "It's very kind of you." The prospect of going back to Manchester and becoming a shorthand typist left her cold. She loved the Lake District, and her job at the college, lowly though it may be, had many advantages; she had a room of her own, plenty to eat, and money enough to buy a book or two and an occasional train ticket home. And, what was more important, she was in daily contact with the students—with Griff.

"You can do it as well as the next one," Mr. Braithwaite said. "I know what I'm talking about. I've no more education than you. I am a self-made man and proud of it—started wi' nowt, I did. I was barely ten years old when my dad told me to clear off and earn my living—give me a clout across the ear'ole, he did, for good measure. Now I've my own business and my own car, and I've only m'self to thank for it."

His working-class background was obvious, Clarrie thought, and all the money in the world wouldn't rid him of that drawback. But he was right to feel proud. "That's wonderful," she said.

"Nay, lass, there's nowt wonderful about it. Perseverance is what it takes, and guts. Guts and perseverance."

The rain had slowed to a drizzle. "We're almost there," he said. "What are you planning to do with yourself in Keswick?"

"I thought it might be interesting to see where Wordsworth and Coleridge and all the Lake poets and writers used to meet."

"Wordsworth, is it? Well, you've found the right chap. The place where I eat my lunch is the selfsame one where those chaps used to get together. You can have lunch with me there. The rain's letting up a bit, so after lunch you can walk around while I take care of business. I'll drive you back later this afternoon."

"I brought my lunch. It's in my pocket."

"It'll keep. Lunch is on me if it's money you're worried about. You'll be doing me a favor, lass. I can't abide eating by myself."

They passed under a stone archway and pulled up in front of an old, prosperous-looking hotel. It was certainly old enough to have been known to Wordsworth and Coleridge. Mr. Braithwaite got out and came around to open the door for her. She followed him through the polished doors, shaped like a church entrance, and into a red-carpeted lobby. The place was spotlessly clean and well-kept, with a pleasant smell of good food cooking. A waiter in a red jacket recognized Mr. Braithwaite and came over to show them to a table by the window. On their way, they passed a bronze bust on a pedestal. Wordsworth. The tablecloths and serviettes were snowy white, stiff, the glasses sparkling.

The man in the red jacket pulled out a chair. Clarrie, painfully conscious of her wet, straggly hair and red chapped hands, sat down. Mr. Braithwaite took the starched serviette from his plate, opened it and placed it across his knees. Clarrie followed suit. This was her first meal in a restaurant since the New Year's Eve visit to the Koh-i-noor in Manchester almost two years ago. She looked at the intimidating array of silverware spread out by her plate. Were you supposed to work your way from the outside in, or was it the other way around? She wished she'd paid attention when her mother had told her. She should let the waiter know when she was finished by placing her knife and fork close together in the middle of her plate. She remembered that.

Mr. Braithwaite passed her the bill of fare. "What shall it be, then?"

Clarrie had made up her mind to choose the cheapest thing no matter what it was. She was surprised to find no prices listed.

"Shall I do the ordering, then?" Mr. Braithwaite asked. "I'm partial to a bit of fish myself."

"Yes, please."

"My young friend here is interested in Wordsworth and those poetry chaps," Mr. Braithwaite said to the waiter. "I've been telling her this is the place where they used to meet."

"Yes, indeed, Miss. In fact, you're sitting at the very table." The waiter reached past Clarrie and lifted a corner of the tablecloth. "Those are Mr. De Quincey's initials. He's the fellow that wrote *Confessions of an English Opium Eater*. Not very nice of him, carving his name in the wood like that, but it's the sort of thing that brings in the tourists—used to, that is, before war broke out."

Clarrie plucked up the nerve to ask where the restroom was. When she got back to the table, lunch had arrived. She was relieved to find it simple—fish, chips, peas, bread and butter, and a dish of mixed pickles.

"Tuck in, then, lass." Mr. Braithwaite sprinkled his chips with vinegar. "You can keep your caviar and all that fancy French stuff," he said. "Give me a nice bit of cod or hake any day."

He questioned her about the art students and cautioned her not to take up with bohemians. "I've run into a few of them in my time. I've no use for them—all that free love claptrap. They think they can have their cake and eat it too, but when all's said and done, it's the poor lass who's left holding the baby."

Clarrie nodded. Her father might have said the same thing, but the truth was that right now, the art students were the only people in the world who interested her.

The waiter put an apple dumpling and a jug of custard in front of her. Mr. Braithwaite picked up the bill, glanced at his watch.

"Eat up, lass. It's quarter past two—time I was on my way. There's a small museum down the road if you're looking for something to do. Be out in front here at four sharp if you want me to drive you back."

Clarrie walked along the main street to the museum. It was small indeed. In less than half an hour, she had seen all the exhibits and read the story of the musical rocks of Keswick. She made her way down to the lake and sat on a flat stone that jutted out over the water. Low clouds obscured the fells. Rain needles pierced the glassy surface of the lake. She fed her soggy sandwich to a family of ducks, then, anxious about the time, walked back into town.

She was relieved to find Mr. Braithwaite waiting at the front entrance of the hotel. On the journey back, he urged her again to improve herself. "If anyone tries to keep you down, don't you listen to 'em. My guess is you've got what it takes." As she walked up the path in front of Rook House, he called to her. "Don't forget what I told you—operation boot strap!"

Chapter Forty-six

It was after nine, and Clarrie was still working. She wanted everything in order before Cook and the others returned. She had her head in the refrigerator searching for things to be consigned to the pig-bin, when she heard a rich, familiar voice.

"Hello Clarrie."

"Griff?" She withdrew her head and turned to face him.

He grinned. "You sound surprised."

"I wasn't expecting anyone back until Monday. "You're early."

"Where's Cook, Mrs. Battle and the rest?"

"Cook is supposed to be back late Sunday. I'm not sure about the Battles."

"You're alone, then?"

"For the moment."

"Is there any chance of getting something to eat?"

"There's salad and the remains of a cheese and onion pie. It's cold but I can warm it if you like."

"Cold sounds fine. We're ravenous."

"Is somebody with you, then?"

"Alan. I caught a ride from London with his parents. They're en route to Scotland—the parents that is, not Alan."

"Will they be eating, too?"

"No. They're anxious to be on their way. Alan's outside, saying goodbye."

The dishes rattled on the tray as Clarrie carried pie, milk, and salad from the refrigerator. Griff watched her as she sliced the pie.

"Looks wonderful," he said, "and so do you. I've missed you, you know."

His words sent the blood rushing to her face. Had he really missed her, or was he just practicing his charm on the naive skivvy? Compliments, in her experience, were best handled warily.

"There's plenty to eat if that's what you're worried about," she said crisply. "No need to butter up the cook."

Griff's smile faded. "I'll wait in the common room, then. When Alan comes in, perhaps you'll be good enough to give him the tray and let him know where to find me."

Clarrie watched him leave. She had offended him again. Why, with Griff, did she invariably say the wrong thing? And why was he always so quick to take offence?

Ten minutes went by with no sign of Alan. She picked up the tray to carry it into the common room, and ran into Griff on his way back to the kitchen.

"Alan's too tired to eat; he's going to bed. It's just me for dinner I'm afraid." He took the tray from her hands. "Come and sit with me awhile."

Clarrie followed him to his favorite table near the fireplace. He set down the tray and motioned to the seat opposite.

"Did you really think I was just trying to butter you up when I said I'd missed you?" He was looking at her intently.

Clarrie looked away. "Sometimes I say things I don't mean."

"I never say things I don't mean."

A long silence followed. Clarrie fought an impulse to blurt out the truth—that she'd spent every waking moment longing for his return. "I'm glad you're back," she said, blushing again. "It's been too quiet with everyone away."

Alan appeared in the doorway. "I changed my mind. I decided I'd sleep better if I had something to eat."

"You're just in time," Griff said. "I was about to demolish the last piece of pie. It's delicious."

Clarrie got to her feet and began piling plates on the tray. "The tea has gone cold. I'll fetch a fresh pot." Alan took the vacated chair. "Please don't leave on my account."

Clarrie forced a smile. "I'll bring the tea, and then I must get back to work." She liked Alan, but at the moment she could have cheerfully strangled him.

By the end of the next week, most of the students and staff were back. Among the returning students, Clarrie noticed several newcomers. An effete young man named Vivian Braswell, wearing white flannels, a silk cravat, and an embossed blazer, stood by the tea urn, mocking Arnold Piper's squeaky voice for the amusement of his companions. There were spoilers everywhere, she thought, even here, among the enlightened.

Miss McBride, who wasn't usually given to imparting personal information about the students, cautioned the kitchen staff to be particularly considerate of the new student, Erna Jasinska, a Polish refugee. Miss McBride explained that she had been a dispatch rider for the Polish guerillas, and had been thrown from her motorcycle while on a mission and left unconscious for two days in a snowy ditch. Her compatriots had found her and managed to smuggle her out of the country to England, where her toes were amputated due to frostbite, which caused her to walk with a strange clumsy gait, coming down heavily on her heels. Erna made no attempt to mingle with the other students.

Clarrie was incensed when she overheard Vivian Braswell mocking Erna in the common room.

"Ah, the importance of being Erna!" he said as Erna passed by his chair. He spoke loudly enough for her and everyone in the room to hear.

Clarrie, who had been wiping off a table, stopped what she was doing. "It's a good thing there are people like Erna in the world," she said to Vivian, "or Hitler would be having everything his own way."

Vivian Braswell raised his eyebrows and looked about in exaggerated astonishment. "Tsk, tsk! I do believe I've been put in my place!"

Dinner hour was almost over. Clarrie was scraping the burned scraps off the hot plate, when Arnold Piper walked through the door reeking of the chemicals he used for his etchings. He helped himself to tea and came over to the hotplate, watching her as she served him. He shifted from one foot to the other and cleared his throat. Clarrie slipped an extra rissole on his plate.

"Um . . ." He cleared his throat again.

"Can I get you anything else?"

"I—well—to tell the truth, I'm rather at loose ends this evening." His voice was even squeakier than usual. "I thought, if you're free later, you might like to join me at the pub for a drink."

He pronounced the letter r, as if it were a w—fwee, dwink. Clarrie felt a stab of pity. He was lonely. Why not have a drink with the poor fellow? She, too, did not look forward to spending yet another evening alone in her room.

"Clarrie!" Nora called from the inner kitchen. "Cook says you're to stop serving and come to supper. We're waiting."

"Be right there," she called. To Arnold, she said: "I don't finish here until eight, and I have to be back by eleven, before Mr. Battle locks up for the night."

"I'll see you at eight thirty, then, The Rose and Thistle."

After dinner, while she and Nora walked to the beck with the tea bucket, Clarrie told her about Arnold's invitation. Arnold was said to have been discharged from the Navy for reasons unknown. With his bushy side-whiskers, his puffy shirtsleeves, and his baggy corduroy breeches tucked into rubber Wellington boots, he looked as if he'd stepped out of a bygone era. Clarrie was reminded of the illustrations in her father's copy of *Silas Marner.*

"Are you going, then?" Nora asked.

"I guess. Don't say anything to the others. They'll never let me live it down."

"Who do you take me for," Nora said, "Mrs. Battle?"

"He wants me to meet him at the pub."

"Wonders never cease. I could of swore he was one of them morphodites. I thought that's why they kicked him out of the Navy."

"Morphodites?"

"You know—those queer fella's that don't like women."

Clarrie resolved to look up morphodite as soon as she could get her hands on a dictionary.

Arnold was certainly strange, she thought as she washed and dressed, but she'd probably be safe with him. This wasn't exactly a date, anyway—she was keeping him company for the evening—it would give her a chance to wear the pretty frock her mother had made for her fifteenth birthday.

She examined herself in the misted glass; the delicately flowered fabric clung to her slender body, revealing the outlines of her small, but nicely shaped breasts. She didn't like the way the nipples showed. Next payday she'd buy herself one of those brassiere things. Her hair, still damp, hung straight on her shoulders, but there wasn't time now to do anything but tie it back with a blue grosgrain ribbon. She powdered her nose and dabbed her lips with a newly acquired pink lipstick. That would have to do. A shiver of anticipation swept through her. The Rose and Thistle was a popular gathering place for the students. Griff might be there.

The cobbled lane that led to the pub was drenched in moonlight. Clarrie hesitated outside the door. How old were you supposed to be before you entered a public house? If someone asked her age, she'd have to say she was sixteen. But what if they wanted proof ?

An old farmer came trudging up the hill and passed her with a curious glance, then opened the door. Loud male voices, laughter, came from inside. The farmer stood to one side and held the door for her.

"Make up tha mind lass, is tha going in, or isn' tha?"

Clarrie thanked him and stepped inside. The room was ancient—whitewashed walls, low-beamed ceiling, and flagstone floor. Several men, ancient too, sat around a fire smoking clay pipes; the air above their heads was blue and hazy, the smell of ale and pipe smoke richly blended, as though it too had been there so long it had soaked into the oak rafters. A man in a canvas apron was bent over a trestle table wiping up spills.

"Excuse me," Clarrie said, "I was supposed to meet someone here, a Mr. Piper?"

"Piper? That'll be one o' them college lads?"

Clarrie nodded.

"You'll most likely find him in t'back parlor, then."

He waved the cloth towards a low archway.

Clarrie ducked under the arch and walked down a whitewashed passage. The shriller cadences of upper class voices drifted from a half-open door at the end. She pushed open the door to a room crowded with students at small tables. Vivian Braswell, sitting with some of the newer students around the fire, leered at her. Arnold was alone in an alcove by the window. Clarrie threaded her way among the tables towards him, and the buzz of conversation subsided. Arnold half-rose, pulling out a chair for her. He had taken off the leather apron but otherwise was dressed as usual. He gestured to a glass on the table in front of him, half-filled with amber liquid.

"What will you have?" he asked.

Clarrie's palms were wet. She could feel people watching her. "I'll have the same as you."

"It's a double whisky. Will that be all right?"

"Fine. Yes. That'll be fine."

He crossed the room to a small hatchway to give the order.

Clarrie remembered an American film in which Mickey Rooney or someone had choked and sputtered and made a fool of himself over his first sip of alcohol. She resolved not to give any hint that this was her first encounter with the stuff.

"Sorry to be so long!" Arnold set the drink in front of her. Clarrie thanked him, lifted the glass to her lips and swallowed. The whiskey burned, but it was no worse than some cough medicines. She took another drink, surprised by the warm sensation coursing through her body.

Arnold raised his eyebrows.

"I was thirsty," she muttered, lamely. She set her glass down, wondering how long she should wait before finishing the drink. There was an awkward silence. Arnold stared morosely into his empty glass.

"Drink up," he said. Clarrie did as he said. Arnold pushed back his chair. "Same again?" She nodded. He picked up the glasses and crossed to the bar. As he passed the group around the fire, Vivian Braswell took hold of his sleeve and spoke to him. Arnold brushed him away.

Clarrie kept changing the position of her hands. They felt enormous. She didn't know where to put them. She ought to take up smoking—it would give her something to do with them. She glanced around the room. Vivian and two of his friends raised their glasses to her, then turned away, laughing. Her face grew hot. Had they seen the outline of her nipples through the flimsy frock? Was that why they were laughing? She studied the ashtray in front of her—a black glass octagon inscribed in gold lettering with the words "Players Please." She saw with relief that Arnold was weaving his way back with the drinks.

The buzz of voices around her had grown muffled. Blue cigarette smoke drifted up from the tables, leaving gossamer veils over the paneled walls and pewter mugs. The laughing faces of the students struck her as extraordinarily beautiful.

"You remind me of Silas Marner," she said, as Arnold set the glass down in front of her.

"He was an old miser, if I remember correctly," Arnold said coldly.

"That's not what I meant." Clarrie giggled. "It's your clothes—that little waistcoat over the full sleeves, and the leather apron you wear."

"I spend a lot of time etching—I work with acids," he said coldly. "The apron protects me from burns."

"Etching," she said. "I'm not sure how that's done."

"I doubt if it would interest you."

She swallowed a large mouthful of whisky. Her shyness had miraculously evaporated. "On the contrary," she said, "I find it fascinating. I'd like to watch you work sometime. It must be wonderful to be an artist—to be able to capture this room, for instance—the firelight, the faces, everything—it's so lovely."

Arnold's lip curled. "'Lovely' is not a word I use."

"What word would you use, then?"

"I find more to interest me in things grotesque."

"But things grotesque have a kind of beauty of their own, don't they? Like—like those gargoyles on . . ." She stopped. Margot had come into the room, followed by Griff and Alan. Griff was in his shirtsleeves. His face, his curling auburn hair, and his beard, burnished by firelight, seemed to hold all the mystery and wonder of the universe.

Griff pulled up a chair for Margot by the fireside, then spotted Clarrie and waved. Margot glanced over in her direction and quickly looked away. It occurred to Clarrie that Margot might be jealous of her.

Arnold was rambling on about something.

"I'm sorry," she said. "I didn't catch what you said."

"I said, it's awfully noisy in here. I think it's time we left."

"Already?"

"If you don't mind."

Clarrie rose unsteadily. Her head was reeling. As if on cue, Vivian Braswell and his friends got up and filed out of the room. Clarrie lost her balance and staggered against one of the tables, knocking over a glass and spilling its contents.

"Steady!" Arnold gripped her elbow and steered her to the exit. The floor rolled with every step she took. As they emerged from the passage into the back alley, she tripped and almost fell. She giggled. "The ground is closer than it looks."

Arnold propelled her along the alley, down the cobbled lane to the bottom of the hill, towards the lake. A full moon sailed from behind the clouds.

"O moon of my delight that knowsht—" Clarrie tried again. "That knowest no wane." She giggled. "I don't know no Wayne, neither, do you?"

Silvery ripples swished around the rocks at the edge of the lake. In the woods an owl hooted. Clarrie held up her hand for silence. "What owl poems do we know?" The owl hooted again. She began reciting "The Owl and the Pussycat." From the other side of the bushes came a crackling sound, like footsteps treading bracken. "We're being followed," she whispered.

"Probably a rabbit." He took her by the arm, steering her to where the softly lapping water ended in rocks and boulders. They veered away from the lake and followed the road along a stone wall. In spite of the fog in her brain, some part of her mind remained lucid. If she wanted to, she could make herself sober again by an act of will, but thoughts and new sensations were rising and tumbling about like the bits of colored glass in a kaleidoscope. She had stepped into another world and didn't choose to be sober just yet. "What smells so sweet?" she asked.

"It's the hay." He pointed to a haystack in the middle of a field.

She broke away from Arnold's grip, climbed the stile, and stumbled across the new-mown field to the haystack. The moon flooded the field with pearly light. She threw herself onto a heap of soft and fragrant hay. Arnold lowered himself stiffly beside her. He pulled her up into a sitting position.

"Sit facing the road," he said. He slipped an arm around her shoulder.

"Why?"

Arnold did not answer. Clarrie looked at him. His profile, outlined in the moonlight, was that of a sharp-beaked bird. Why was she here with this fellow? He wasn't the one she should be with. This balmy evening, the moonlight, the hay—all were going to waste because of this tiresome old maid of a man. Why wasn't it Griff sitting here beside her? It ought to be Griff.

"It's getting late," she said, "I'd better get back before Mr. Battle locks the doors."

Arnold took his arm from around her shoulder and raised his hand high, wiggling his fingers as though he were waving to somebody. ". . . arm's numb," he said, "slide over onto my lap for a minute."

Feeling foolish, Clarrie did as he asked. He brought his mouth down on hers. His lips felt wet, sticky, and unpleasant. She pushed him away and scrambled to her feet.

The sound of muffled laughter came from the other side of the wall. Several shadowy figures rose and flitted away.

"There was someone there," she whispered. "Someone was spying on us."

Arnold stood up. "Some of the local yokels, I imagine," he said.

They walked in silence back to the hotel. Clarrie felt sick; her head was throbbing. Arnold wished her a brief goodnight and left her at the door without making any further attempt to kiss her.

She was heading to the lavatory to wash her mouth, when she noticed Griff's corduroy jacket hanging from a peg in the cloakroom. She lifted the jacket and buried her face in the lining, breathing deeply. There was a crinkly sound of paper. Something was in the pocket. She drew out a crumpled letter, addressed to Griff at a Chelsea, London address. Margot's name and an address in Hampshire were on the back flap. Clarrie pulled the letter from the envelope. "Darling,"

she read, "I can hardly wait until we can be together again. The thought of you and London . . ."

Voices sounded outside the entrance. She slipped the letter back into the envelope, shoved it in the pocket of the jacket, and darted into the lavatory.

"You're drunk," she muttered to her image in the mirror. She removed some wisps of hay from her hair, splashed water into her mouth, spat it out, and rubbed her mouth with the back of her hand. Her first kiss, wasted. She'd wanted to save it for Griff. "Griff darling," Margot had called him. Had they ever been together in London? Were they lovers? The word "darling" might not mean anything; people like Margot called everyone darling.

The outer door opened, and a female voice said, "I think they're despicable." Clarrie slipped into one of the two stalls. "What merry pranksters they must think themselves." The voice sounded like Jennie's roommate, Kay Gresham.

"Plying a poor little skivvy with whisky."

Skivvy? Whisky? Clarrie froze. They were talking about her.

"Vivian Braswell's a juvenile specimen." That was Jennie's voice. "Someone should have warned her."

The tile floor rocked and shifted. Clarrie pushed open the door of the stall. "I'm sorry, but I couldn't help overhearing. What poor little skivvy were you talking about?"

Jennie was combing her hair at the mirror. Kay was leaning with her back to the sink, smoking a cigarette. They exchanged stricken glances. "Oh, God!" Jennie said.

"Were you talking about me?"

"About you?" Kay's voice rose to a squeak. "Why, whatever makes you . . ."

"Stop it, Kay," Jennie said quietly. She turned an unhappy, scarlet face to Clarrie. "I'm so sorry, Clarrie. We only just found out about it."

"Found out about what?"

"That idiot, Braswell, and some of his cronies," Jennie said, "They were teasing Arnold about his aversion to women. It was a stupid bet."

"The joke was supposed to be on Arnold," Kay said. "He was to get you tipsy—take you for a walk—and, well, you know . . ."

"Arnold knew about this?" Clarrie felt cold sober now, but the hammering in her head was deafening. "Who else was in on this so-called joke? Was Griff Williams in on it?"

Kay and Jennie exchanged glances. "I very much doubt it," Jennie said. "It's not his style."

Kay put out a tentative hand and touched Clarrie's arm. "You mustn't take it personally."

Clarrie shook Kay's hand away and brushed past them. Her head was pounding, her whole body shaking. Upper class indeed! They were contemptible. To hell with the lot of them. She would keep to herself from now on.

Chapter Forty-seven

Neither Arnold Piper nor Vivian Braswell came in for breakfast, and if Griff and his friends had heard about the Piper incident, they did not show it. Several of the students cast curious looks at her as they passed down the line; Clarrie held her head high.

Stopping by the staff mailbox on her afternoon break, she found two letters from home—one in Annie's spiky scrawl, the other in her mother's firm round hand—and promptly burst into tears.

Annie had left the bakery, her mother wrote, and was working in a munitions factory in Trafford Park. She was courting a soldier named Walter, but didn't see much of him because he was overseas. They wrote to each other almost every day, and intended to be married when he came home. Billy had sprouted up like a weed and was begging for his first pair of long trousers, but Dad thought he was still too young. Nobody had heard from Arthur for a while, so perhaps he was not able to go ashore to post anything.

They had been issued an indoor shelter that took up most of the room in the kitchen; it was as ugly as sin, but the steel top served as a dinner table, and underneath there was enough room for three or four people to sleep. Dad was still roof-spotting, so most of the time it was just Annie, Billy, and herself. At night, when the sirens sounded, they no longer went out into the cold, but stayed right where they were.

Annie's letter was harder to read because she wrote with little punctuation:

Hello love Mams probably told you about me and Walter. I met him first through his wife Jessie that friend of mine who moved to Stockport. I ran into him a few months ago while he was home on leave and he told me Jessie died in the blitz. Any road, we hit it off and we've been writing to each other. Wasn't it lucky Celia Scott went to Liverpool to visit her father and didn't get killed with the rest of her family you never know do you, her old man was good for something after all. Did Mam tell you about the scandal next door? Remember Maisie Watkins her that left her poor kids alone during the blitz well she was found dead in Halliwells back bedroom. It turns out Maud was doing abortions for years and everyone knew but us. I always thought there was something fishy going on and now shes gone and got herself arrested for manslaughter what a scandal eh?

Gladys's mother—her own godmother—an abortionist! Suddenly, she was back in the Halliwells' dark house, with its gloomy oil painting of the woman clinging to the cross in the middle of the ocean. Abortion. Was that what was taking place the afternoon she and Gladys were locked in the Halliwell's parlor? It explained the mysterious cries from upstairs, the trail of blood along the lobby and the unhappy woman by the front door . . .

Clarrie slipped the letters into her apron pocket. She was overcome by a sudden yearning to go home.

Shortly before Christmas, Miss McBride hired a girl from the village to work part-time in the kitchen and gave Clarrie leave to take a few days off to visit her family.

Arriving at the railway station in Salford, she found the grey sky, the smoky air, and the familiar, grimy streets oddly comforting. Much of the bomb damage and rubble had been cleared away, leaving gaping holes, reminiscent of missing teeth, between what had once been solid rows of shops and houses. A queue of shabby, exhausted women armed with shopping bags waited patiently outside the butcher's shop. The sandbags had gone from around the Waverly Hotel, but the bay window of the Halliwell's house was still boarded up.

Annie came to the door in answer to Clarrie's knock, her face smeared with calamine lotion.

"I'm just getting over the scabies," she explained. "We've all had a dose of it—the whole city has been plagued with it. You needn't worry about catching it, though, it's not contagious at this stage."

"The house looks different," Clarrie said. "It's smaller than I remember." She cast a critical eye on the ugly steel structure that filled up the tiny kitchen, leaving no room for fireside chairs. "This thing doesn't help, does it?"

"It's a flaming eyesore," Annie said.

Billy came in from the backyard lavatory. "You can have my room while you're home," he said, "so you won't have to share with Annie. I don't mind sleeping under the table."

Clarrie opened her suitcase and handed her mother six brown eggs wrapped in newspaper. "Miss McBride sent them."

"Lovely. I must write and thank her. Your dad misses his fresh eggs. We've been eating those powdered ones from America—glad to get them, too—but they don't taste the same, and of course, you can't eat them soft-boiled. I'm thinking of buying a few chicks and raising them in the backyard. They tell me it's against the law to keep chickens in the city, but I doubt anyone will try to stop me. A law like that makes no sense with all these shortages."

When her father returned from the docks, Clarrie kissed him shyly. He looked exhausted. "I wish you and Mam could get away to the Lake District for a few days," she said. "The country air would do you good."

"Seems to agree with you, right enough," he said. "You look the picture of health." Clarrie glanced at her mother and raised her eyebrows in mock surprise. It was the closest thing to a compliment her father had ever uttered.

Over a meal of baked beans and soft-boiled eggs, the family filled Clarrie in on the doings of some rowdy new neighbors.

"But where's Mr. Halliwell?"

Annie shrugged. "Who knows? He packed up and left after Maud was arrested."

"Everyone disappears," Clarrie said.

"Violet Fawcet's still around," Annie said. "She's always asking about you. She's married now, you know, to the window cleaner—that skinny fellow with the rotten teeth. He's old enough to be her father."

The teacup shook in Clarrie's hand, spilling tea onto the worn-out counterpane that was serving as a tablecloth.

"What's the matter?" Annie said. "You look as though you've seen a ghost."

"That man was so awful."

"The poor fellow can't help his bad teeth," her mother said. "He must have a good heart; he adopted that little girl of hers, Lily. They're living in a caravan down on the tip."

Clarrie set her cup down in the saucer. She should have told somebody about that man, years ago, but even now, she still couldn't bring herself to mention such a thing to her parents. It was too late anyway, she had no proof. Perhaps he'd mended his ways. Whatever the case, she could hardly walk down to the tip, knock on that caravan door, and accuse Violet's husband of being a child molester.

Chapter Forty-eight

On her return to the Lake District, Clarrie found the lakes frozen over and the village digging out from a heavy snowfall. She breathed deeply, filling her lungs with clean, cold air. She could hardly wait to be up on the fells again.

Late one afternoon, as she was walking along the snowy banks of Rydal Water, she heard the whoosh of blades on the ice. A figure in a red knitted cap was skating alone in the middle of the lake. She moved aside a bare tree branch. The skater raised a gloved hand, waved, then with his scarf flying out behind him, skated over to the bank and made his way through the snow towards her. It was Griff. He brushed the frost crystals off his beard.

"Clarrie, what are you doing here—why aren't you skating?"

"I have no skates."

"You can borrow mine if you like. I was thinking of packing it in, anyway."

He took off his gloves, stuffed them into his pockets, and leaning against a tree to balance himself, removed a skate.

"I can't skate," Clarrie said. "I don't know how."

"There's nothing to it. You should learn. It's exhilarating." He put on a boot, and removed the other skate.

"My father was a professional skater."

"Professional? And he didn't teach you?"

"He was a trick roller skater. His skates were too fast for a learner."

"I've been on the ice as long as I can remember—there was a pond near our house in Llanduddno, where I grew up."

"I thought I detected a Welsh lilt."

"Ah, yes." He assumed a Welsh accent. "So there you are then—a Welshman isn't it, look you." He lapsed into his normal speech. "I'll be going back to Chelsea, though, when I finish here."

Clarrie cast about in her mind for something to say to keep him with her. "I've been to Wales," she said. "I spent a week there at a children's holiday camp in Prestatyn."

"My grandmother lives in Prestatyn," he said. "I know the place well. I remember seeing children from that camp playing on the beach. I thought they were orphans."

"No. Just poor kids from places like Salford. The school sent home a notice with every child in my class. They gave us a list as long as your arm—things we were supposed to bring."

She smiled at the memory. Her mother had thrown the list down in disgust, saying that if people could afford all that clobber, they wouldn't need a poor children's holiday camp.

"My mother rustled a few things together—a borrowed suitcase, a green bathing costume that had belonged to someone she worked for. It was a sorry object, miles too big for me, but better than nothing. I was terrified that someone would inspect my suitcase and turn me away for not complying with instructions."

"How was the camp?"

"I loved it." She remembered the salty tang of the air, the endless whoosh of the waves, the feel of pebbles under her feet. "Although I didn't much care for the earwigs and the moldy bread."

"Moldy bread?" Griff shook his head in disbelief. "Was that the best they could do?"

"I was happy just to be at the seaside. The day before we were to return home, I took a small butter knife with me to the beach. I wanted to start a pearl in an oyster, but there were no oysters to be found. I'd seen mother-of-pearl lining mussel shells, so I forced open a mussel and inserted a few grains of sand."

He grinned. "You're an optimist."

"I left the mussel in a shallow pool and marked the spot with a mound of pebbles. I hoped I might get the chance someday to go back and find my pearl."

"I'll be sure to look for it the next time I visit Granny."

He slung his skates over his shoulders and pulled his gloves on. They were standing so close she could feel his breath on her face.

"I'd better be on my way, then," he said.

She nodded. She wanted to leave too, but what if he didn't want her company? He might rather not be seen walking out with a kitchen maid. While she hesitated he reached out a gloved finger and stroked her face, then bent and kissed her lightly on the mouth.

"Don't hang about too long," he said softly. "You'll freeze to death out here."

She watched him walk away, waiting until his red knitted cap disappeared through the trees before starting her own long walk back to the village.

That night she dreamed that Griff came up behind her in the snowy lane and cupped her breasts in his hands. She woke up filled with longing, and lay there, shivering, savoring again the sweet, snow-cold touch of his mouth, the rough scrape of his beard. In the days that followed, she returned to the frozen lake again and again, hoping to catch a glimpse of Griff's red cap, to hear the whoosh of his skates across the ice. In the end, the paralyzing cold always forced her to abandon her vigil and trudge back to the hotel alone.

The long, dark days of winter dragged on and on, but just when Clarrie had begun to think that spring would never come, the melting snow started trickling downward from the mountain peaks, dripping over rocks, gathering force as the rivulets ran together, cascading from crag to crag, sending up clouds of spume as they crashed into the swollen becks. Soon, the snowdrops and crocuses would blindly poke through the melting snow, and the lakes would once again be ringed with daffodils.

Chapter Forty-nine

The term was nearly over and the excitement racing through the college was almost palpable. Nora had left to marry her soldier and would not be coming back, making it more than likely that Clarrie would be expected to put her holidays on hold again. She had mixed feelings about it. She didn't mind the work but, as she confided to Jennie, she dreaded the long, empty evenings in her room with nobody to talk to and no bustle of students coming and going through the halls.

"Alan and Griff are working on a fantastic mural for the end-of-term dance," Jennie said. "It's a masquerade kind of thing. Why don't you throw together a costume and join us?"

"I wouldn't know what to wear."

"Use your imagination. The theme is 'Nature Red in Tooth and Claw.' I'm going as a wood sprite. It should be lots of fun. This is a last fling for those of us who are leaving."

"Leaving? Why are you leaving?"

"Didn't you know? Those of us who've been here two years and have earned their associate's degree will be leaving. Alan and I are going. We hope to be married soon, but we want to make sure we have jobs first. Kay's lucky—she's already found a good job in a gallery."

Clarrie was speechless. She hadn't known. She'd assumed that they would all be coming back. How could Jennie and the others she'd grown fond of just go away? Did this mean Griff would be leaving too—that she'd never see him again?

"We're going to miss you, Clarrie," Jennie said. "Do come to the dance."

While Clarrie was serving dinner, Margot came in alone. She lingered by the tea urn until the rest of the queue had gone. She approached Clarrie, her haughty face a little flushed.

"Clarrie, if you can spare me a moment I'd like to ask you something."

"Of course." What on earth could Margot want? Did it have something to do with Griff ?

"Have you made plans yet for the spring holidays?"

"No, not really." Why was Margot feigning an interest in her?

Margot leaned across the counter. Her voice dropped to a whisper. "The thing is, I'm hoping you'll agree to come home with me. We have a place in Hampshire—scads of room—you'd love it there."

Other latecomers had arrived and were helping themselves to tea. Margot straightened herself and picked up her tray. "There's no need to decide right now," she said. "Think about it, and let me know."

Clarrie watched Margot stride off with her tray. If Jennie had invited her, or even Kay, it would not seem so very strange. But Margot? Margot had hardly exchanged two words with her. Could Griff have had something to do with it? Was he on the guest list, too?

After her work was over for the night, she went up to her room and examined her wardrobe—one coat, one hat, one pair of flat-heeled shoes, one cardigan, one summer frock, one brown dirndl skirt, one yellow blouse, three pairs of knickers, three pairs of socks, one underskirt, two nightgowns.

She had a vision of herself arriving at Margot's large country house clutching a cardboard suitcase held together with string. In novels she'd read and in her mother's accounts of her days in service, there were hunt balls and weekend house parties. They'd hardly be carrying on like that in wartime, but perhaps they'd still dress for dinner. She'd be totally out of place in her little rayon frock—a laughing stock—but that might be exactly what Margot intended.

There was a knock at her door and Margot stepped into the room.

"Clarrie, have you given any thought to . . . what I spoke about earlier today?"

"Actually I . . . it was awfully nice of you to think of me, but . . ."

"I do hope you'll say yes. I've already written to Mummy about you. She's anxious to meet you."

"I think Miss McBride is expecting me to . . ."

"Of course she is." Margot sat on the edge of the bed and laid a narrow hand on Clarrie's arm. "It's wicked of me, I know, to try to steal you away from her. I wouldn't dream of doing so if Mummy weren't so desperate."

Desperate? Clarrie gazed blankly into Margot's protruding brown eyes. What on earth was she talking about?

"She's at her wit's end. Most of our people have joined the army or gone into some sort of war work. We've had to close up half the rooms. You have no idea how gloom-making it is with everything under dust covers."

Clarrie's confusion vanished. She took a deep breath. Thank God she hadn't given herself away.

"I'm awfully sorry," she said firmly. "But Miss McBride is counting on me, and I've more or less given my word."

"Mummy will make it worth your while," Margot said. "I can't quote an exact sum at the moment, but I'm sure it will be more than you're getting here."

"I'm sorry."

"Ah, well, so am I," Margot said. "So be it. I think you're rather foolish to pass up such an opportunity. Let me know if you change your mind."

It had been a mistake to ask the cook for permission to leave early.

"You have no business at those dances," Mrs. Marten snapped. They're meant for students, not kitchen staff."

"But I was invited. Jennie invited me."

Mrs. Marten released an exasperated sigh, and walked away without saying anything more, but before she'd left for the night, she'd given Clarrie several extra jobs to do. She was to pull out all the trays and the pots and pans from under the counters, wash the shelves, and scrub the floor thoroughly before putting everything back. From where she knelt, Clarrie craned her neck to see the clock. Eight-thirty. The dance would be half over before she got there.

Her costume wouldn't take long to throw together—she planned to go as a witch. It probably didn't have much to do with the theme of the dance, but all she'd have to do was pin the blackout curtains around her like a strapless gown. Jennie had promised to help her with it and to lend her a blue-green cape to cover her shoulders. The witch hat was the only problem. She'd rolled up a sheet of black construction paper, but the glue refused to hold, and she couldn't think of any good way to attach the brim.

She began pulling out the trays from under the counter, and was startled to see two beady eyes fixed on hers. A fat brown rat darted towards her. Clarrie screamed and scrambled to her feet, knocking over the bucket. The rat scurried through the spreading puddle and vanished behind the pudding steamers. Footsteps sounded along the corridor. Stephen Wentworth came through the open door, his eyes wide with alarm.

"Did somebody scream?"

"I saw a rat. It ran back there behind the steamers."

He tiptoed across the wet floor, peered into the narrow crevice behind the steamers. "I can't see a thing. Not enough light."

"It was horrible."

"Yes. Rats are not pleasant. I'll stay a while, if you like, in case it comes back."

"Thanks." She got down on her knees again to sop up the water.

"Do you like this sort of work . . . scrubbing floors and so on?"

"I'm used to it."

He watched her as she soaked up the water. "I had a strange dream about you last night."

"About me?" Clarrie stopped what she was doing. So far as she knew, nobody had ever dreamed about her before.

Stephen hesitated. "I was in the desert, dying of thirst. You appeared out of nowhere. You were wearing that same green apron."

She glanced down at her overall.

"You offered me a glass of water, but when I went to drink it, the glass cracked in my mouth. Blood and water dripped onto the sand."

She shuddered. "What happened then?"

"I don't remember anything after that. It was the end of the dream."

"I wonder what it means. It reminds me of that film, *The Four Feathers.*"

"I don't believe I've seen it."

"A man gets some white feathers in the post. He sets out to prove to himself and everyone else that he's not a coward. I've forgotten the details, but somebody ends up wandering in the desert with his tongue cut out."

"White feathers? I don't understand."

"In the first world war they used to send them to the men who . . ." She stopped; Stephen—all the male students in fact—had for one reason or another managed to avoid the call-up.

"Who what?"

"I think I may have it confused with another picture—*Beau Geste* or something."

"If you like films, there's a new one playing in the village; *Blossoms in the Dust.* Greer Garson's in it I believe. If Greer Garson is not your cup of tea, we could go for a walk."

Stephen's pale, lofty forehead was faintly clammy, his dark eyes full of pain. He seemed to be waiting for her answer as though something important hung on her decision. At any other time she'd have been tempted to accept his invitation, but she'd thought of nothing but this dance all week. Griff might be there.

"I'm sorry," she said. "I . . . I've made other plans."

Stephen nodded. "Some other time, perhaps. I'll say good night, then." He walked out of the kitchen without another word.

Clarrie was suddenly moved by a strong impulse to run after him and call him back. She dropped the rag she was holding and ran into the passage. Stephen was nowhere in sight.

On the way to her room, she ran into Jennie dressed as a wood sprite in a costume of semitransparent leaves and gauzy wings.

"Is the dance over already?" Clarrie asked.

"It's still in full swing, but I had to get out of there. Alan and I had a tiff—nothing important—it's all this excitement. How is your witch costume coming along?"

"I haven't been able to finish the hat."

"Bring it to my room, I'll see what I can do."

It took only a few minutes for Jennie to solve the problem of the hat with a staple gun. "Now you need some witchy make-up," she said. She darkened Clarrie's lashes, and smoothed green shadow over her eyelids. "Better. But I'm afraid it's impossible to make you look sinister. You're altogether too wholesome." She held up a mirror.

Clarrie stared in dismay at her reflection. "Like a bowl of porridge."

"Like a pretty milkmaid." Jennie handed her a blue-green bundle. "Here's the cape, but if my back and shoulders were as spectacular as yours, I wouldn't hide them."

Clarrie twisted around to see her back. Against the black drapery, her skin gleamed. She thanked Jennie, threw the cape over her shoulders, and ran down the stairs.

The cool air cut through her costume as she flitted across the moonlit square. Three old men, sitting in the shelter of the bus station, stopped talking to stare at her. One of them looked like the man who had carried her suitcase for her when she'd first arrived. She waved her broom at them.

Snatches of "Amapola" rose and fell as the door to the pavilion opened and closed. A cluster of fantastically garbed students blocked the entrance. Easing her way through the crowd, Clarrie removed her cape and dropped it on a chair. The room had been transformed into a jungle. Ferns banked the walls, filling every corner. Green fronds hung snake-like from the ceiling, brushing the heads of the dancers moving around the floor. Tropical birds, flowers, and butterflies blazed across the long wall facing the door. Against a dark background, a yellow-eyed tiger lurked, half obscured by spiky undergrowth.

Griff was not here, or if he was, he was so disguised she couldn't recognize him. Crossing the room to examine the jungle scene, she stumbled over a pair of sandaled feet sticking out from behind a wall of ferns. "Sorry!" she said. Vivian Braswell stepped out, dressed as the Hunchback of Notre Dame. He leered at Clarrie. "Want to ring my bells? He looked at the broom she was carrying. "Or would you prefer to sweep me off my feet?"

Nancy Barraclough stepped forward, dressed for a safari in a khaki shirt, riding breeches and solar topee. "And into the gutter, where you belong?" she said.

Clarrie smiled. As she walked away, she felt a hand lightly stroke her back; she swung around annoyed, prepared to find Vivian Braswell leering at her, but it was Nancy Barraclough standing close behind her. Nancy rubbed together her thumb and forefinger. "You had talcum powder . . ."

"Oh, thanks."

"Would you care to dance?" she asked Clarrie.

Surprised by the invitation, but not wanting to offend Nancy by refusing. Clarrie set her broomstick aside and allowed herself to be led onto the dance floor. Nancy gripped her so tightly she could hardly breathe. She seemed reluctant to let Clarrie go when the waltz was over.

Alan approached. He was painted from head to toe in an intricate paisley pattern. His hair, shaved Mohawk fashion, was streaked with orange, green and purple dye; his only clothing, a loincloth. He raised his hand to Clarrie in an Indian salute.

"How."

"How," Clarrie said. "Have you seen Griff by any chance?"

"Griff . . . Griff . . . Why do they all ask about Griff?" Alan said. "Am I my brother's keeper?"

"Apparently not," Clarrie said. Who else, she wondered, had been asking after Griff. Was it Margot?

"Sorry," Alan said. "I'm in a foul mood. Jennie and I have had a bit of a row."

"What about?"

"You'd better ask her."

The music stopped. The dancers broke apart and headed for the refreshment table. Hilary came from behind the refreshment stand bearing an empty glass pitcher. "I say!" She flashed a warm smile at Clarrie. "Would you mind most awfully popping over to the kitchen and fetching more of that ghastly ersatz ginger beer? We seem to have gobbled it all up."

Clarrie took the pitcher and went across the square to the hotel kitchen. On her way back with the pitcher of ginger beer, she saw Griff, dressed as usual in his baggy corduroys, heading in the same direction. She slowed down so that they would reach the door at the same time.

"One of the Lancashire witches, I presume?" He held the door for her.

Hilary swooped down to claim the pitcher. "Thanks, most awfully," she said. "It was jolly decent of you. You're an absolute brick."

Griff waited until Hilary was out of earshot. "Brick? She sounds as if she's just walked off the hockey field at St. Agatha's school for girls."

"Where's Margot tonight?" Clarrie asked.

"Summoned home for reasons I can only guess at. I was curious to see how this room would look with the ferns in place."

"I think it's lovely, particularly the wall painting."

"Mural. It's called a mural. Thank you."

"Did you paint it?"

"Yes. I had some help. It's rough, I'm afraid, but it isn't meant to last. It will all have to be painted over before we leave."

Clarrie felt she should say more. She remembered something she'd overheard in the Manchester art gallery. "It's quite effective when viewed from this angle," she said, blushing.

"Ah! Yes, well . . ." The music stopped, then started again. A tango: "Jealousy." Griff raised his eyebrows. "Shall we?"

"I'm afraid I don't tango very well."

"Just follow me."

Clarrie suppressed a smile. She had seen Griff dancing with Margot at one of the Saturday hops. He had loped around the room dragging Margot with him without any feeling for the music. Wiping her damp palms against her skirt, she allowed herself to be steered to the dance floor. Griff pulled her close to him and held her tight. Her nose was a fraction of an inch from the cluster of curling red brown hair sprouting through the open neck of his shirt. She was tempted to bury her face in it. Griff's hand stroked her bare back. She stumbled, and he gripped her more tightly.

"You're trembling," he said. "Are you cold?"

Nancy Barraclough was watching them from the sidelines, an elaborately sardonic smile on her face. "Seducing virgins out of season, Griff?" she said.

"Better me than thee," Griff said as he steered Clarrie away.

"Pig," Nancy said.

"What was all that about?" Clarrie asked.

"I gather that Nancy doesn't like my dancing with you."

"Is it because she's a friend of Margot's?"

"She's not a friend of Margot's. She's a lesbian. I suspect she has her eye on you."

"Why, is she putting on a play or something?"

"A play? Not that I know of. Why do you ask?"

"I thought . . . isn't a lesbian something to do with the theatre? An actor?"

He laughed, and pressed her closer. "You're thinking of a thespian. A lesbian is a woman who prefers to make love to other women—the word is derived from the Isle of Lesbos . . . home of Sappho."

Clarrie darted a backward glance at Nancy. She was still watching them. Sensing Nancy's isolation, Clarrie felt a stab of pity. She was glad she'd agreed to dance with her.

"Sappho," she said, "he was a Greek poet, wasn't he?"

"She. Sappho was a woman."

Clarrie lapsed into silence. She was making an utter fool of herself.

"Your hair smells like lemons," he said.

"It's verbena shampoo."

"Sweet little Clarrie." He bent as though to put his cheek against hers, but the brim of her witch hat got in his way. "Can't you take that thing off ? It's hard to dance with a barrier between us."

"I'm supposed to be a witch."

"And so you are," His voice grew husky. "You've got me under your spell. If I hold you like this much longer, I'm afraid I shall have to kiss you."

Clarrie's feet became entangled with his. They stopped dancing.

"Let's sit the rest of it out." He found her a chair. "I'll fetch us something to drink."

"When will you be leaving?" she asked when he returned with the drinks.

"In a couple of days—when the term is officially over."

"You won't be coming back?"

"True. I've passed the final exams. My roommate was not so fortunate."

"Who is your roommate?"

"Stephen Wentworth."

"Stephen?" She hadn't known he was Griff's roommate. She wondered if she ought to mention the invitation to the pictures.

"He was the only one who didn't pass. I'm not sure why. I thought he was rather good at what he did. It was strange and different—startlingly original work."

"The only one who didn't pass?" Clarrie said. She was suddenly ten years old again, running in panic out of the algebra test. "Poor Stephen, he must feel awful."

"Yes. To tell the truth, I'm rather worried about him. He told me to take whatever I wanted of his art supplies—his paints and brushes. I really didn't like the sound of that."

"He came into the kitchen tonight and asked me to go to the pictures with him, but . . . well, I had my costume all ready for this dance."

"He asked you out?" Griff stared at her surprised. "He told me he wasn't going to dinner tonight."

"He didn't come through for dinner. This was later, after everyone had gone. I saw a rat while I was cleaning up, and I screamed. He came running down the hall to see what was the matter. We talked for a while and then he asked me to the cinema. He must have changed his mind about being alone tonight."

Griff was frowning. "How did he seem? Perhaps I should go back . . . make sure he's all right."

Should she tell Griff about Stephen's dream? She didn't want him to leave her. "Yes," she said quickly, "I think you should make sure."

"Come with me," Griff said. "Together, perhaps we can coax him out."

Clarrie took her cloak from the chair where she had dropped it. Griff put his hand on her back and steered her to the door.

Clarrie was shivering violently. "What if Miss Charteris sees me?" Women were not permitted to visit the men in their rooms.

"Her room is way down at the other end of the hall, remember? She never comes out after nine."

The Royal was unusually quiet. Everyone must be at the dance. They passed nobody on their way through the hall or on the stairs. Griff turned the knob of his door and rattled it. "That's strange," he said. "We never bother to lock it." He banged on the door. "Stephen . . . Stephen are you there? Open up!"

"Perhaps he went to the cinema by himself," Clarrie said.

Griff was fishing in his pocket for the key. He turned the lock and pushed open the door.

"Oh, my God!" he said.

"What's the matter . . . what is it?"

He put out an arm to bar her entrance.

Clarrie craned her neck and saw a figure slumped on the floor, a dark puddle on the carpet.

"Wait here, Clarrie," Griff stepped inside and pulled the door closed behind him. In a few moments he stepped out again.

He looked at her, his face ashen. "You'd better go back to Rook How. I'll talk to you later."

"What is it—what's happened?"

"It's Stephen. He's . . ." Griff's voice broke. "Oh, God, Clarrie, he's blown the top of his head off."

Chapter Fifty

Miss McBride came into the kitchen with her empty breakfast tray to tell them that Stephen Wentworth's parents had arrived and were resting in one of the rooms upstairs. The doctor had already been. Mrs. Wentworth was under sedation.

"Why did he have to do that?" Mr. Battle said, his mouth full of toast. "A young bloke like that—his whole life ahead of him."

Clarrie, who had been crying all night, tried to stem her tears. "He'd failed his exams," she said, wiping her face.

"That's no reason to kill yourself. He could have gone into some other line of work." He waved his fork at Clarrie. "Some folks don't know when they're well off."

Clarrie nodded. Apparently it wasn't enough to be an artist and a member of the upper classes. They too felt despair in the face of failure.

"My boy was happy every minute of the day," Mr. Battle went on. "Always singing, full of life. He was took before his time and he didn't have nothing to say about it." Mr.

Battle shook his head. "It's his poor old mum and dad I feel sorry for—he wasn't thinking about them, now, was he?"

Clarrie cried herself to sleep for the second night in a row, and dreamed she was in a railway station looking for a clean lavatory, but all the stalls were smeared with blood and feces and feathers. She found one that seemed clean and was about to sit when she heard a voice say, "She ought to be reported." Clarrie realized there was no door to the stall and that she was in plain view of every passer-by. She woke up with her eyes swollen, her nose raw.

She picked up her towel and sponge bag and went down the hall to the bathroom. The room next to Jennie's had a sign on the door, "Do not disturb." That must be the room where Stephen's parents were staying. Her tears welled up again. In the bathroom she remembered that this was Monday—her day off. Thank God, she need not go down for breakfast.

In the afternoon, Jennie tapped on Clarrie's door. She too had been crying. "May I come in?" She sat on the edge of Clarrie's bed. "Griff told me you were with him when he found Stephen," she said. "He thinks you might be in shock."

Clarrie sat up, wiped her wet cheeks with her hand. "I'll be all right."

"Some of us are going up to the Kirkstone Inn for tea." Jennie patted Clarrie's arm. "We all need to get away for a while. Why don't you come along?"

Clarrie shook her head. "I look terrible."

"Splash a little cold water on your face. I'll be back for you in a few minutes."

When Jennie came back, she said. "It looks like rain, but we're going anyway."

Clarrie put on her coat, wrapped a blue and white kerchief around her head and followed Jennie down the main staircase to join the rest of the party. Clarrie was the only one who wasn't wearing a rain slicker or carrying a walking stick.

Griff and several of his friends led the way, walking a few paces ahead of Clarrie, Jennie, and Kay. The fells, their crevices filled with snow, looked bleak and barren; the sky, overcast. As they climbed, rain blew in gusts across their faces. Clarrie's kerchief was whipped off by the wind and blown away before she could catch it.

"Perhaps this wasn't a good idea, after all," Kay said.

"It suits the mood," Jennie said.

Strong winds buffeted them as they climbed, snatching the words from their mouths. They stopped trying to talk. The only living thing, beside themselves, was a lone sheep huddled near a wall. Despite the exertion of the climb, Clarrie was shivering. She could not keep her teeth from chattering.

When Clarrie, Jennie, and Kay reached the inn, Griff and his friends were already being served tea and cakes. Conscious of her red, swollen nose and puffy eyes, Clarrie chose a seat behind a wooden beam, where Griff could not see her.

They were drinking tea, talking in desultory tones about Stephen, when an agitated young man in a yellow sou'wester and rain cape burst in. A gust of cold air blew the menu off Clarrie's table. When she rose to retrieve it, she saw the man in the sou'wester whisper something to Griff. Griff got up and spoke to the waitress, who ran back to the kitchen. Griff, Alan, and the other men hurried outside.

"Now what's happened?" Kay said.

Jennie was about to go outside to see, when the innkeeper came out of the kitchen. Clearing his throat to get their attention, he announced that there had been an unfortunate accident. A party of cyclists had been blown over by the wind as they topped the rim of the pass. He had called for help. The ambulance was on its way. They had asked him to clear the room to make way for the injured.

Clarrie took her coat from the hook and trooped out with the others. The rain was heavier now. A few yards down the road, they came across Griff and Alan on their knees, rigging up a makeshift stretcher out of broom handles and a raincoat. Dazed-looking cyclists sat on the low wall. Buckled bicycles lay strewn about. Along the side of the road lay two still forms covered with rain capes. A pretty girl, sitting apart on the wet grass, caught Clarrie's attention. There was something familiar about her, about the long blonde hair that hung, dripping wet, almost to the ground. It was the girl she'd spoken to at the rush-gathering ceremony, that first summer.

Jennie put her hand on Griff's shoulder. "Are they . . . is there anything we can do to help?"

"We've done everything we can. The ambulance should be here soon. It might be best if you all just go."

"I'll never forget this," Kay said as they trooped back down the Kirkstone pass. "The rain . . . the sense of doom . . . everything . . ."

And how we are all wallowing in the drama, Clarrie thought bitterly. Even the weather seemed to know its part.

She was in bed, still weeping, unable to stop, unable to sleep, when she heard someone knock lightly, then rattle the handle of her door. Miss McBride poked her head in the room. "Are you decent? The doctor's with me. I called him to give a sedative to Mrs. Wentworth, but I'd like him to take a look at you."

Clarrie sat up and blew her nose. The doctor came into the room and put his black bag on the chair next to her bed. He tapped on her back with his fingertips then put his stethoscope into his ears and told her to take a deep breath.

"Why all this weeping, young lady?" he asked. "Was the young man who died a special friend of yours?"

Miss McBride walked over to the window and looked out. Clarrie shook her head.

"And you two hadn't been up to mischief ?"

Clarrie closed her eyes. "I hardly knew him."

The doctor took the stethoscope out of his ears. "What did you say?"

"I said I hardly knew him."

"And yet they tell me you've been crying nonstop for three days. Now why is that? It's not natural to carry on like that for someone you hardly knew." He turned to Miss McBride. "It's her nerves. She's having some sort of nervous breakdown. It's not uncommon in girls of this age." To Clarrie, he said: "Do you have a home to go to, young woman?"

Clarrie nodded.

The doctor put the stethoscope back in his bag. "I recommend that you go home for a while, and try to pull yourself together."

"I'll take her myself, tomorrow," Miss McBride said. "If we leave early I can be back in time for the last bus."

Clarrie looked at her in alarm. She couldn't imagine Miss McBride in that cramped and shabby kitchen at home. Miss McBride was not the sort of person her mother would wish to have drop in unexpectedly. "I'll be all right by myself," she said.

"I'll feel better if I go with you, and while I'm in Manchester perhaps I can do some much needed shopping."

"We live in Salford, actually," Clarrie said. "Its another bus ride to Manchester."

"Perhaps your mother would like to go with me."

There seemed to be no polite way to put Miss McBride off. As soon as she and the doctor left the room, Clarrie slipped on her coat and dashed out to the telegraph office to warn her mother.

Chapter Fifty-one

A chill wind gusted across the railway platform as they came down the steps. Miss McBride shuddered and pulled up the collar of her coat. Clarrie held onto the brim of her hat—the black straw she had worn when she first arrived. She hoped the veil would hide her puffy eyes.

Near the station house, a green canvas sheet covering a stack of wedge-shaped boxes had torn loose on one corner and was flapping in the wind. "Coffins." Miss McBride said. "For our poor soldiers, no doubt."

Clarrie stared at the boxes, the flapping canvas. She'd almost forgotten about the war.

The train was crowded. Clarrie followed Miss McBride down the corridor, stumbling over soldiers and sailors perched on duffle bags. Miss McBride glanced into the compartments.

"Oh, dear, no seats," she said. A young sailor rose and offered her his place. Miss McBride thanked him as she sat down and opened a copy of *Britannia and Eve.* Clarrie left her suitcase at Miss McBride's feet and went into the passageway. The sailor followed her out. He lit a cigarette and offered one to Clarrie. She shook her head.

"Was that your mother?" he asked.

"Yes," Clarrie said. She leaned against the compartment wall, pulled a paperback book of poetry from her coat pocket and pretended to read.

"You're holding your book upside down, darlin'," the sailor said. Clarrie thrust the book into her pocket and went back in the compartment. "It's too crowded out there," she said.

At Cross Lane Station, they stepped down from the train into a blur of khaki jackets, blue trousers trimmed with red, young men on crutches, men with slings, bandages.

"Perhaps you'd better lead the way," Miss McBride said.

Some of the wounded men whistled as Clarrie picked her way through stretchers and wheelchairs to the exit. She held the door open for Miss McBride and followed her into the street.

"Oh, dear!" Miss McBride opened her handbag and brought a dainty handkerchief to her nose. "What is that smell?"

Clarrie smothered a flicker of resentment. Growing up here she'd hardly noticed the smell, but now, after living in the Lake District, she was acutely conscious of it, and of how it must seem to Miss McBride.

"City air," she said. It was the mixture of the dank effluvia of canal and river waters, the reek of outdoor lavatories, the beery vapors from the pubs, the greasy fumes from the fish and chip shops, the smoke of a million chimneys, the daily deposits of spit and coal dust, of horse dung and vinegar-soaked newspapers. It was the smell of her childhood, the unmistakable, unforgettable, smell of Salford.

"This way," Clarrie said, turning onto Eccles New Road. The place where Perlman's old shop had stood was now a weed-grown patch. Most of the shops still had boarded-up windows, one bearing a chalked message, "Blasted, but not buggered."

The bay window of the house next door was still boarded up. Clarrie was relieved to see no sign of the scruffy new neighbors. "Here we are," she said, leading the way up the path to the house. "We used to have a wrought-iron gate and railings separating the houses, but they took them away when the war started."

Her mother opened the door, looking flustered. "Come in, love, if you can get in," she said, bobbing her head and smiling as she ushered Miss McBride into the kitchen. "Let me take your coat. I'm afraid you've caught us in a bit of a mess . . ."

Clarrie groaned inwardly. Her mother was going to spend the rest of Miss McBride's visit apologizing—a sure sign that she was feeling intimidated.

"The old table and chairs are in the parlor. You can take Miss McBride in there, Clarrie."

The table was in the bay window, set for tea, with a green checked cloth and the ivy-patterned tea set she had helped her mother pick out at the market. A small fire burned in the fireplace.

"Make yourself at home, Miss McBride," her mother said. "I'll fetch some tea."

"I'll help you," Clarrie said, following her mother into the scullery. "You needn't be so humble, Mam," she snapped as soon as they were out of earshot. "It's not a visit from the queen."

"I was just being polite."

"You were practically curtseying to her."

"We haven't much to offer her, I'm afraid. A bit of salmon paste, a loaf of Hovis, some digestive biscuits . . ."

"It's good enough."

"What happened? You didn't say much in your telegram. It looks as though you've been crying. Why did she come home with you?"

Clarrie explained briefly about Stephen and told her mother what the doctor had said. "And Miss McBride wants to do some shopping in Manchester. She's hoping you'll go with her."

Over tea, Miss McBride broached the matter of the shopping trip. "And afterwards, if you'll point me to the station, I can catch the train straight from Manchester."

Clarrie's mother said it would be her pleasure.

"We'll leave you then, Clarrie, to get some rest," Miss McBride said when the tea was finished. She told Clarrie to take her time recuperating and be sure to keep in touch.

Clarrie washed the cups and saucers then went upstairs to lie down. Her eyes were dry and burning. She was all cried out.

She'd been home for about two weeks, when Annie asked her, over Sunday breakfast, when she intended returning to the college. Clarrie didn't answer. "You ought to get yourself a job at Metro-Vicks, like me. Do your bit for the war effort instead of moping around the house with a face like a wet week."

"Annie's right, love," her mother said. "I think you'll feel better if you keep busy."

"I wish everyone would just leave me alone."

"You mustn't go blaming yourself for that boy's death, love," her mother said.

"I'm not." Clarrie's eyes filled with the ever-impending tears. "It isn't that."

"What the devil ails you, then?" her father said.

"No need to shout at her, Will."

"Well . . . anyone would think she'd got the troubles of the world on her shoulders." He glared at Clarrie. "For God's sake, why won't you tell us what's the matter?"

Clarrie said, quite truthfully, that she didn't know what was the matter.

"Perhaps you'll feel better if you get dressed," her mother said. "Go for a nice walk."

"I have nowhere to go."

"What about the park? You used to love the park. You can go to Chimney Pot if you don't want to walk all the way to Buille Hill. Take a book with you—it might warm up a bit later."

Clarrie got up from her chair and put on her cardigan and coat.

"That's my girl," her mother said.

Clarrie put on the knee socks and stout shoes she had taken to wearing in the Lake District. She tied a kerchief around her head.

"Here." Her mother pushed a sandwich wrapped in greaseproof paper into Clarrie's coat pocket. "In case you get hungry."

Except for a few old men circling in slow motion around the bowling green, Chimney Pot Park was deserted. Clarrie sat on a bench to watch them play. They looked like the same old men who had played bowls here when she was a little girl. How could that be? How could they go on, day after day, year after year, with nothing better than this to occupy their time?

It was too cold to sit here. She stood up, stamped her feet, blew on her hands . . . best to keep moving. She'd walk to Buille Hill . . . see if the museum was open, or the greenhouses.

Two girls, heavily made-up, were leaning against the gateposts at the park entrance. They looked at her boldly as she approached. One of the girls nudged the other and whispered something. They stared pointedly at her legs. "Now I've seen everything," one of the girls said. They burst into derisive laughter.

Clarrie turned and, instead of entering the park, crossed to the other side of the road. The blood pounded in her temples. Stupid girls! What were they sniggering about? "Now I've seen everything," the one with the leg paint had said. She should have confronted her. She should have told her that, far from having seen everything, it was clear she'd seen nothing outside of her own back street. It would have been better to ignore them completely—to walk through the gates and into the park as she'd originally intended.

Perhaps she ought to go home. But her parents had made it clear they didn't want her moping about. They were probably sick of the sight of her, and she didn't blame them. She was sick of herself. She decided to keep walking until she reached the Hancock house.

Evidently the salvage people had been here, too; the iron railings and the gate with the *Hancock* scroll were gone. An overgrown hedge laden with blood-red berries blocked her view. She walked partway up the drive and stopped to look through a gap in the hedge. The house appeared to be intact, but where was the fountain? She squeezed through the hedge, scratching her cheeks and hands on the sharp holly leaves, and plodded through a tangle of weeds and overgrown grass. The fountain lay on its side, its bowl cracked. She tried to raise it and set it back on the pedestal, but it was too heavy. She abandoned the effort and went to sit on the front steps.

It was no use. She couldn't stay in Salford. There was nothing here for her. And if she went back to the college, Griff and Jennie and most of the students she knew would be gone.

It had fallen apart so suddenly, just as she and Griff were . . . just as something wonderful was about to happen. "Sweet little Clarrie," he'd called her. He'd almost kissed her, right there on the dance floor, and he would have, too, if it hadn't been for . . . A knot of misery had lodged like a stone in her chest. Griff. She wanted Griff. There was something unfinished between them. It was impossible that she would never see him again. She felt in her pockets for a handkerchief and found, instead, the sandwich her mother had made for her. She unwrapped it and took a bite, but couldn't swallow. She broke the bread into bits and flung it out for the birds.

"I'll be staying in my flat in Chelsea," Griff had said. The letter she'd taken from his pocket the night she got drunk had been addressed to him somewhere in Chelsea. She wished she'd had the presence of mind to write down the name of the street.

That evening, Clarrie told her mother she wanted to go to London.

"You can't go to London by yourself—you're only sixteen."

"I'll go mad, Mam, if I have to stay in Salford."

Her mother stared at her, bleakly. "I'm sorry you're not happy here, Clarrie, love. If you don't want to go back to the college, I'll write to Aunt Ruth, and see if they'll have you for a while. Will that satisfy you?"

Clarrie said it would. Arthur had stayed with Aunt Ruth and Uncle Gerald before going into the Marines, and he'd got along well with them—but then Arthur got along well with almost everybody. Still, they were probably fairly decent—and, what was more important, from Aunt Ruth's house she could take a train and be in London in less than an hour.

Chapter Fifty-two

It had been six years or more since Uncle Gerald and Aunt Ruth had paid their one and only Christmas visit to Salford. Driving along the Great North Road, Uncle Gerald had skidded, overturning his car in a snow bank and, although nobody was hurt, Uncle Gerald had spent a great deal of time complaining of the difficulties of driving along the Great North Road, the impudence of Lancashire garage mechanics, the nastiness of Lancashire weather, and the general inferiority of the north. After the visitors had gone back to Kent, her father observed that Gerald acted as though the blizzard was a plot hatched by northerners to inconvenience him.

Uncle Gerald might look very different after six years, Clarrie thought, but when the train pulled into the Orpington station, she saw the bullet head crowned by tight yellow curls and the fleshy raw ham face, and knew they could belong to nobody else.

"Uncle Gerald?"

"Clarrie? Well! You've certainly grown up since I last saw you." He relieved her of her suitcase with fingers so thick they could scarcely fit around the handle. "It's a good thing the train was on time. I've got the van parked in a loading zone. We have to pick up your Aunt Ruth at the café—she should be just about finished work."

"Café?" Clarrie said. Uncle Gerald ran his own coal delivery business, and he and Aunt Ruth owned their own house and an adjoining apple orchard, so why would Aunt Ruth take a job at a café?

"I bought the place a couple of months ago." Uncle Gerald went on. The owner was killed in action, and his widow didn't want the bother of running it, so I got a good deal." He opened the door of a black van and threw Clarrie's suitcase in the back. "For now, you'll stay in the spare room. It's where Arthur slept. My mother will be coming from Bournemouth after she sells her house. When she gets here, you'll have to make do with the settee in the drawing room."

"That'll be fine," Clarrie said as she climbed in. "How are Aunt Ruth and the boys?" Trevor would be about fourteen by now, and Nicholas eight.

"They're fine. The boys are home right now, loading bags for tomorrow's coal delivery. I keep 'em busy so they've no time for getting into mischief."

Uncle Gerald lit a cigarette. "What do you hear from Arthur?" he asked, as they drove through the High Street. "How's he doing in the marines?"

"He seems to like it."

"He's a good bloke, Arthur. When I strained my back, he took over all the coal deliveries for me. He helped put up the Anderson shelter, too. He wanted to dig deep and pour a proper concrete foundation. I told him not to bother. The Jerries were concentrating on London at the time, so I thought there was no need of it, but now they've got these damn buzz bombs, and you never know where they're going to land. Ruth is scared to death of them. I hope you're not like that."

"I'm used to it. We were pretty well pounded in the blitz."

"That's what I thought. 'If your niece is anything like her brother,' I said, 'she won't give us any trouble.'" He patted Clarrie's hand with his fleshy fingers. "Of course we'll expect you to get a job and pay your own way."

"Naturally."

Uncle Gerald said he would help her find a job—there were one or two people who owed him favors. In the meantime, she could make herself useful at the café.

"I'll be glad to help in any way I can," Clarrie said.

A sign on the door of the café read "Under New Management." Aunt Ruth was waiting for them in the doorway. She greeted Clarrie warmly. "I hope you had a pleasant journey."

"Yes, but tiring. I'm glad it's over."

"I'm tired, too," Aunt Ruth said. "I've been on the go since six o'clock this morning."

She was younger than Clarrie's mother by two or three years, but she seemed older. There were streaks of grey in her hair; her face was pretty, but more lined and weather-beaten, and she didn't smile as readily.

They drove along a wide road lined with detached brick houses. Clarrie thought the names on the gates rather uninspired—Honeysuckle Cottage, The Larches, Sunnyside . . . This was nothing more than suburbia. It was not the Kent her mother had described.

Uncle Gerald's house, Narrowfield, stood by itself at the corner of a gravel lane.

"Why Narrowfield?" Clarrie asked.

"It was named when we bought it," Aunt Ruth said. "I expect it's because of the long back garden."

"I rather like the name," Clarrie said.

"The trades people can't seem to get it right. We get letters addressed to Marrowfield, Harrowfield, Barrowfield. Still, the name is better than some. If it had been Bide a Wee or Dun Rovin or something of that sort, we'd have changed it."

Clarrie stepped down from the van and shrank back as a red setter ran up barking.

"She won't hurt you." Uncle Gerald slapped the dog on the muzzle. "Stop that, Molly, down girl!" He led the way around to the back of the house, past the garage and the Anderson shelter. Further back were chicken coops and rows of beanpoles.

"Where's the orchard?" Clarrie asked.

"It's half a mile down on the other side of the lane," Uncle Gerald said. "I keep a dog tied up out there to scare apple scrumpers away."

"What's his name?"

"It's just a mutt. It doesn't need a name."

The boys came forward to greet her shyly, refusing her offered hand because their own were black with coal dust. Trevor was thin and gangly; he had a nervous habit of blinking his eyes rapidly every few seconds. Nicholas was sturdier. His yellow curls were damp with sweat, and there was coal dust on his neck and around his ears.

While the boys went upstairs to wash, Clarrie set the table in the dining room, and Aunt Ruth peeled potatoes. Over dinner, Aunt Ruth complained of the difficulty she was having making the meat rations go round.

"Gerald works hard and needs a lot of food," she said. "And with two growing boys to feed . . .The dogs need meat, too. I feel sorry for that skinny mutt in the orchard."

Clarrie said she didn't care for meat and that someone else could have her ration.

That night, luxuriating in a feather bed, Clarrie fell straight off to sleep. The next morning, while it was still dark, she was awakened by a thumping sound coming from the room overhead and by Uncle Gerald's voice exhorting the boys to rise and shine. A few moments later he hammered on her door. "Rise and shine! We leave for the café in half an hour."

After a hasty and sparse breakfast of lumpy porridge, they piled into the van, and Uncle Gerald dropped them off at the café.

"We put all our tips in that jar over there," he said as he was leaving to drive the boys to school. "While we're getting on our feet, we need every penny put back into the café."

There were half a dozen square tables on the ground floor, each covered with red and white checked oilcloth, and several more upstairs. Aunt Ruth bustled about preparing sausages, cabbages, and boiled potatoes; she told Clarrie to fill the salt and pepper shakers, and put out water jugs and cutlery. When that was done, Clarrie cleaned out a small storage room.

Workmen in overalls began arriving for the midday meal, clumping upstairs in muddy boots.

"There's plenty of room down here, but for some reason the men prefer the upstairs," Aunt Ruth said. "I wish they didn't; it's exhausting, running up and down with these heavy trays."

"I'll take the trays upstairs," Clarrie said. "It won't bother me at all."

Most of the workmen looked to be over fifty. Aunt Ruth said they'd been hired to replace the younger laborers who'd been called up for military service. She found them amiable and easy to please—happy to be working and satisfied with anything they got.

Aunt Ruth, herself, was clearly not happy working in the café. She would much rather be working in the garden, she told Clarrie, or in the orchard, than stuck indoors all day. Gerald had not bothered to consult her before buying the café. "I thought it was rather highhanded of him," she said, "but with your Uncle Gerald, it's his way or no way."

On Sunday, Trevor showed Clarrie around the village. They'd witnessed the steady traffic of planes going over and heard the noise of the raids in the distance and seen the fires from London lighting up the sky, but the only thing that had happened in the village was that a German fighter pilot had been shot down. He took her to the churchyard to show her where the pilot was buried. The villagers had collected money to put up a headstone engraved with the German pilot's name and rank, exhorting him to Rest in Peace.

"It was pretty nice of them, don't you think?"

Remembering the shattered tombstones, the broken coffins, and the matted skull in Weaste cemetery, Clarrie did not answer.

Trevor seemed surprised. "Don't you think it was the right thing to do? What if it was one of our men shot down over Germany?"

"I suppose we can be thankful they didn't carve a swastika on the gravestone," she said.

The buzz bombs flew over the village without warning, night and day. During the day, everyone carried on as usual, but at night, the sound of a buzz bomb overhead made Molly, the red setter, howl so loudly she woke everyone up, and sent the family trooping out to the shelter. Clarrie wished Uncle Gerald had let Arthur pour the concrete floor. As it was, the corrugated tin roof was too low for anyone other than Nicholas to stand upright. When it rained, they were obliged to wade to their bunks through three or four inches of muddy water.

Clarrie couldn't bear being unable to stand upright. She begged permission to stay in the house, pointing out that since the buzz bombs were so unpredictable, arriving at any hour of the day or night, it was futile trying to avoid them. To her surprise, Uncle Gerald agreed, and said that from now on, she could stay in bed until it was time to go to work.

The meals were sparse. Aunt Ruth threw everything together in the cooking pot to save on fuel. Clarrie had told the truth about not caring for meat, but she found herself regretting giving up her ration.

After a dinner consisting of a boiled potato, a spoonful of carrots, and a slice of bread, she excused herself and left the table to get an apple from a tray in the hall. She had just bitten into it when Uncle Gerald emerged from the dining room.

"Those apples are for the market, not for home consumption. We only eat the windfalls."

"Sorry," Clarrie said. "I didn't know." She stood there, holding the bitten apple, not sure what to do with it. When Uncle Gerald had gone she ran upstairs, and after one or two guilty bites, flushed the core down the lavatory

Working at the café, she found no opportunity to look for another job. Several months went by and still she received no wages from her uncle. From time to time, she brought up the need to look for work, but Uncle Gerald discouraged her. There was little opportunity in the village, he said, which seemed true enough; he added that he was working on it and hoped to find something for her very soon.

One evening, after she'd gone up to her room, Clarrie overheard her aunt and uncle talking about her.

"She's getting her room and board," Uncle Gerald said. "What more does she need?"

"She needs pocket money," Aunt Ruth said. "I gave her a few stamps and some writing paper so she can send letters home, but she needs personal items, and a girl of her age might like to go to the pictures now and then."

Uncle Gerald said something Clarrie could not hear, but the next day, Aunt Ruth told her that from now on she could keep her tips.

Christmas passed with little in the way of celebration, and even less in the way of gifts. At home, despite the shortages and the lack of money, her mother would manage, against all odds, to set a festive table. Afterwards, a neighbor or two might drop in and there'd be joking and laughter and singsongs around the fire. Clarrie was swept by a wave of homesickness. She missed everyone, even Annie.

At the end of January, Uncle Gerald's mother, Granny Morgan, arrived at her new home. Clarrie moved her few belongings out of the small upper room, with its piled-high feather bed, and went to sleep on the sofa in the drawing room.

"Did you air out my room, young woman, and remember to turn the mattress?" Granny Morgan asked as Clarrie and the boys were helping her upstairs with her luggage.

Clarrie answered with a nod. She was put off by the old woman's sharp glance, hatchet jaw, and severely scraped-back grey hair.

"My mother will be helping at the café as soon as she's settled in," Uncle Gerald told Clarrie. "I've found a nice job for you. You start next Monday at Fort Brasted as a learner-tracer."

"A learner-tracer, what is that? Don't I have to fill in an application—go for an interview?"

"No need for an interview. Everything's taken care of. They'll show you what you're supposed to do." He handed her a card. "This pass gets you into the fort. Don't lose it." She wouldn't be expected to work on weekends, which was good, Uncle Gerald said, because they could still use her help at the café on Saturdays. He cautioned her not to discuss her education or her former employment with any of her coworkers. Someone at the fort was giving her the job as a favor to him, but that person wanted it kept quiet.

Clarrie wondered uneasily what he might have told them. Had her uncle made false claims about her experience in order to get her the job?

Chapter Fifty-three

Early Monday morning, she walked the mile-long lane to the High Street and boarded a bus that took her to the outskirts of Orpington where another bus, this one camouflaged by swirling khaki-colored paint, waited to transport employees to the fort. Clarrie showed the pass Uncle Gerald had procured for her. The bus gradually filled with other passholders, then took off, rattling and shaking, down a winding road that led deep into the woods. The ground was white with hoar frost, the trees black and bare. The bus squealed to a stop outside a barbed wire enclosure. A military policeman waved them through the gates into a clearing where they disembarked.

Clarrie had expected a fort to be something like a castle and was disappointed to find a cluster of cement buildings surrounded by paths lined with corrugated tin huts. She asked directions and was told she must walk a half-mile along one of the paths to the hut where she was to work.

A thin, harassed-looking woman introduced herself as Miss Chapman, the department supervisor. After a cursory glance at Clarrie's pass, she said, "Yes, we've been expecting you. Follow me." She led the way down the center aisle past rows of drawing tables to one that was not occupied. From under the table she brought out a box containing several double-nibbed pens, a ruler, a set of compasses, and a bottle of black ink.

In answer to the supervisor's questions, Clarrie admitted she had not done this sort of work before. The supervisor raised her eyebrows.

"I see. Unfortunately we're dreadfully busy right now. I have little time to spare breaking you in." With brisk, sure movements, she demonstrated the correct way to fill a double-nibbed pen and turn a draftsman's compass; telling Clarrie to practice, she hurried away.

It was bitterly cold inside the hut. Most of the other women were wearing jackets and woolen mittens with the fingertips cut out. The only sounds were the scratching of pens, and the hissing of a small paraffin heater in the center aisle. From time to time an office boy came in, his arms laden with rolls of paper, which he dropped on various desks. Clarrie chafed her fingers and practiced filling the nibs and covering a sheet of paper with different sized circles.

At noon, the women put down their pens, produced paper bags and thermos bottles, and ate at their desks. Clarrie asked the woman behind her if there was a café within walking distance. "There's a small cafeteria, but it's a couple of miles away on the other side of the fort. Lunchtime would be over before you even got there, but you're welcome to share my sandwich." She opened her lunch bag and unwrapped a dainty sandwich, offering it to Clarrie with stubby, ink-stained fingers.

"Thank you, but I can manage. I'm not really hungry," Clarrie lied. She took her poetry book out of her pocket.

"Have some tea at least." The woman poured milky tea into the thermos cup and handed it to Clarrie. "It will help warm you up. I have plenty."

"Thanks, I believe I will." Clarrie took the cup, gulped the warm, sweet tea.

The woman offered her hand. "Martha Pratt," she said. "What are you reading?"

"Poetry. W.H. Auden." Clarrie held out the book.

Martha glanced at the book. "Never heard of him." She showed Clarrie a paperback book with a shiny blue cover, decorated with planets. "Astronomy. Fascinating stuff. It gives a scientific explanation for how the universe began. None of that rubbish about God."

"Did the universe create itself, then?" Clarrie asked.

Martha grew animated. Behind the thick lenses, her myopic eyes lit up. "Yes, yes, exactly. It created itself. It's quite clear. It started with what we call spiral nebulae."

"Where did the spiral nebulae come from?"

"It was just there."

"Just where?"

"In space. Don't you understand?"

"But how did space get there?"

Martha looked a little flustered. "Everything is explained in the book. You'll understand better when you read it. I'll lend it to you when I'm finished."

At the end of the day, everyone was obliged to file through a checkpoint where their handbags, briefcases, and pockets were searched before they boarded the bus, and when the bus dropped Clarrie off in Orpington, she discovered that the connecting bus to the village did not run after five. She would have to walk back. Her tiredness vanished when she found a letter from her mother waiting on the mantelpiece. They'd heard from Arthur again, and he sent his love. Billy had passed his exams for the grammar school with flying colors. She was enclosing a snapshot of him in his school uniform. The sad news was that Cousin Clifford had been reported missing in action—they were all hoping he had been taken prisoner.

Clarrie sent up a silent prayer for his safety. She propped Billy's photograph against the clock on the parlor mantelpiece. He looked self-conscious, but very happy in his school cap and blazer. The memory of her own failure brought a bitter taste to her mouth. Still, she was proud of Billy. At least one member of the family had a chance to succeed!

She spent the rest of that week at the fort drawing circles and lines of varying thickness and practicing the prescribed method of block lettering. At the end of her second week, an office boy dropped a rolled blueprint on her desk, and darted away before she could ask any questions. She unrolled the blueprint. An engineer's drawing—squares, circles, broken lines, dots, arrows—and at the bottom, some cryptic scrawls. She rolled the blueprint up, tucked it under her arm, and went in search of the supervisor.

"It's a modification for a bomb bay door," the supervisor said. "It's important to follow the instructions exactly, and then make the necessary adjustments."

"But . . ."

"I can't spend more time with you," the supervisor said. "I'm late for a meeting."

Clarrie stared at the blueprint. The other tracers were hard at work. She did not dare interrupt them to ask for help. She went back to her desk and spread out the blueprint again. Follow the instructions? There were no instructions—only meaningless squiggles and scrawls. She felt as though she were ten years old, back in the examination room, confronted by symbols and signs that she must, but could not, decipher. She wasn't thinking clearly. Perhaps the fumes from the paraffin heater were making her sick. Modification of a bomb bay door? Somebody's life might depend on the accuracy of this blueprint, but she had no idea where to find the engineer who had drawn it. She copied what she could, and when the courier came back for the drawing, she told him to ask the engineer for clearer instructions. An hour later, the drawing came back covered with more cryptic scrawls and squiggles. Clarrie studied it with growing panic.

"Martha . . ."

"What is it?" Martha did not raise her eyes from her own blueprint.

"Can you decipher this scrawl . . . tell me what I'm supposed to do?"

Martha studied Clarrie's blue print. "Carry the line to the end, like so. Complete the circle. Trace a double line wherever you see these marks . . ."

By the end of her third week, she had mastered the art of block printing, and was comfortable with the various compasses and pens, but she found it almost impossible to decipher the engineer's instructions. When desperate, she had to ask Martha for help.

Martha, and the other women, all obviously well-educated, were older than she, and treated her kindly. She would have liked to join in their lunchtime chats, but was afraid they'd ask what she'd done before coming to the fort and how she'd got the job. It was best she kept to herself.

Martha dropped the astronomy book on Clarrie's desk. "You'll find it really interesting. I couldn't put it down."

Clarrie read the book without enthusiasm, grasping the gist of the matter, but skipping over anything that required detailed knowledge of astronomy and mathematics. She struggled through to the end only because she wanted to tell Martha she had done so.

"And are you convinced?" Martha asked, when Clarrie returned the book.

Clarrie hesitated. She wanted Martha to like her. "I'm afraid that the idea that the material universe somehow made itself strikes me as harder to believe than . . ."

"The man who wrote the book didn't think so and he's a highly respected scientist, brilliant in fact."

"I'm sure he is." Clarrie said. A phrase from the Bible sprang to mind, "The fool hath said in his heart, there is no God." She could hardly quote it to Martha without insulting her, and anyway, it was an opinion, not a valid argument.

Martha was saying something about an outing that she and some of the others were planning. ". . . a debate by some members of the Brains Trust. Would you like to join us?"

"The Brains Trust?"

"A group of scholars—intellectuals—philosophers—who discuss various issues on the B.B.C. You must have heard of them."

"I believe I have," Clarrie said, "And thank you, yes, I'd love to go." She would pay attention to where they caught the London train, and where they got off, in case she ever got the chance to go by herself.

London seemed to be the hub of the world, the very air made her tingle with excitement. The streets swarmed with men and women in every conceivable uniform—British, American, and Canadian; there were Polish airmen, French sailors with red pom-poms on their hats, dashing, sunburned Australians—and, she thought, with a sudden intake of breath, somewhere in the midst of this teeming city, no doubt still striding around in his paint-stained corduroy suit, there was Griff.

Outside the lecture hall, an attractive, well-dressed woman was urging people to sign a petition to release Sir Oswald Mosley, the leader of the British Fascist party.

Clarrie stopped to examine the petition. "But aren't we at war with the fascists?"

"We are at war with Germany and Italy and Japan—not with the British Fascist Party," the woman said. "Sir Oswald is British. He has done nothing to warrant imprisonment. He has been incarcerated simply because of his political views."

"Innocent people are dying because of those views," Clarrie said. "What about them?"

Martha pulled her away. "Don't get into an argument, Clarrie, we'll miss the debate." Clarrie allowed herself to be led away.

Several distinguished, scholarly-looking gentlemen were already on stage, seated in a semicircle facing the audience; the debate was apparently well under way—a lively exchange of views, interspersed with humorous anecdotes, all having reference to the desirability of a classical education. After an hour or so, a man with a snowy Van Dyke beard and charming smile summed up. The state of culture in wartime Britain was nothing short of deplorable. He had traveled this very day, he said, from Oxford to London in a railway carriage packed with soldiers. Only one man was reading a book, and the title of that book, he noted with a twinkle in his eye, was *No Orchids for Miss Blandish.* Could anything, he wondered, more eloquently bespeak the intellectual and cultural mediocrity of the average British soldier?

When Arthur was last home on leave, Clarrie had noticed a copy of that same book in his duffle bag.

She was suddenly flooded with anger at these smug, self-satisfied old men. She remembered how bone-tired Arthur used to be when he came home from work, and how, when he was fourteen and working as an armature winder, his hands and arms had been cut to pieces by glass fibers. And in spite of all the cards stacked against him, he and his shipmates were out there on the ocean at this very moment, ready to give their lives for their country.

When the time came for questions, she stood up. "I have not read *No Orchids for Miss Blandish*," she said, "so I don't know what you consider to be so bad about it, but I can guess that the soldier on the train had worked in a factory, or perhaps a coal mine, since he was fourteen years old with no opportunity to . . ."

A white-haired man from the row in front turned to her and in a loud voice said, "Sit down!" Whereupon one of the women from work tugged at Clarrie's skirt. "Sit down Clarrie, you're embarrassing us."

Clarrie brushed the hand away. She no longer cared what they thought. "Why speak so contemptuously of men who are fighting and dying for us?" she asked. "Why not save your scorn for people like Sir Oswald Mosley? He's cultured isn't he? He probably had the finest education money could buy, but what good did . . ."

"For shame!" The man in front turned to glare at her through his monocle. "She's a Communist. Tell her to sit down!"

"I'm not a Communist," Clarrie said hotly. "I'm not any sort of 'ist'."

Other voices joined in the cry, demanding that she sit down. Clarrie ignored them.

"That soldier on the train—almost any working-class English person in fact—would have more common sense than to fall for the ravings of a man like Hitler."

The master of ceremonies banged his gavel for order. "Do you have a question for the panel, Miss, or are you delivering a lecture?"

The distinguished gentleman with the Van Dyke beard nodded graciously in her direction. "If the young lady wishes to remain behind after the debate, I'll be happy to discuss the matter with her."

"I'm finished," Clarrie said. She sat down with her cheeks burning.

"If there are no more questions, then . . ." The master of ceremonies thanked the Brains Trust for a stimulating discussion, and the debate was over.

Clarrie kept her eyes down as she followed the rest of her party down the steps. She was surprised when three Indian women, their saris shimmering beneath flimsy coats, stepped forward and barred her path. One of them laid a small brown hand on her arm.

"We want you to know that we agree with you—with what you were saying in there. We are on our way to a café and would like you to join us and discuss these matters further."

Clarrie hesitated. The women from work were waiting at the corner. It occurred to her that the Indian women might have some sort of political axe to grind. Perhaps they were Communists trying to recruit her.

Martha called to her. "Clarrie, we'll miss our train if we don't hurry."

Clarrie smiled apologetically at the Indian women. "I'm afraid I can't," she said, "I'm with some people."

Her companions said little on the walk back to the station. She'd spoiled their outing. While they were boarding the train, she slipped down the corridor to a separate compartment and rode back to Orpington alone.

Chapter Fifty-four

Clarrie shuffled forward in the queue. The prospect of facing the women at the fort after making such a spectacle of herself in London made her break into a cold sweat. When she reached the door of the bus she stopped, unable to make herself climb aboard.

"Move along, please." The man behind her sounded annoyed.

"Sorry," she mumbled, "I just remembered something."

Keeping her head down, she walked swiftly back in the direction of the railway station. Now that she knew how to get to London, she'd go there and look for another job—in Chelsea, perhaps, where Griff had his flat. Chelsea was a place frequented by artists and all manner of bohemians. She ought to be able to find work there, something she could handle without putting anyone's life in jeopardy—as an artist's model perhaps. Judging by the models they'd used at the college, it wasn't necessary to be beautiful, all you had to do was sit still. Even she should be able to manage that.

By the time she'd found her way to Chelsea, it had started to rain, and she had left the house without a raincoat or an umbrella. She wanted to ask someone where to find a public library; it would be a good place to wait out the rain, and a librarian might know the whereabouts of Slade, or some other art school. But people passing on the street were hurrying to get out of the rain; they wouldn't thank her for stopping them.

She turned off the main road into a narrow alley. In spite of boarded-up windows and other signs of bomb damage, the alley had a certain charm—window boxes filled with flowers, brass lamps above gaily painted doors. Over one doorway someone had hung a faded tapestry. Clarrie was examining the woven pattern of knights on horseback, when a black cat crawled from underneath the hanging. The cat was followed by another. Clarrie peeped around the curtain. In a cosily jumbled living room, a plump little woman in a long nightgown sat stroking yet another cat—a fat white angora.

"Oh, sorry!" Clarrie said. "I saw the cats . . ."

The woman rose from her chair. "Have you lost a cat? This one adopted me just yesterday, but I really have no room for him."

"He's lovely." Clarrie stepped forward and stroked the damp fur. ". . . there was no door. I didn't think anyone was living here."

The woman smiled. "Bomb blast knocked it down. I decided to leave it that way. The curtain makes it easier for my cats to get in and out." She thrust the cat into Clarrie's arms. "Hold him for me a moment while I pour him some milk."

"This is Chelsea, isn't it, where the artists live?"

"Some are artists. Are you looking for one in particular?"

It was unlikely that this little cat lady would know Griff. "I'm hoping to find work as a model," she said, "but I have no idea how to go about it."

"It's dangerous to be wandering about London alone at your age."

"I'll be careful. Do you know of anyone who might need a model?"

The woman took the cat out of Clarrie's arms, set him down by the saucer of milk. "No, but I can give you the name of someone who might be able to help you." She wrote something on a scrap of paper and handed it to Clarrie. "He is a friend of mine. He lives just a short walk from here." She directed Clarrie to the address on the paper.

Clarrie thanked the woman and, after a short walk, found the house with no difficulty—a tall row house that had obviously seen better days, with a flight of crumbling stone steps leading up to a front door. A brass nameplate on the wall was inscribed "Desmond Drake."

She rang the bell twice, waited, and rang again. She was about to walk away when she heard a high-pitched male voice.

"Hold on a moment, whoever you are. I'm just getting out of the bath." Minutes later, the door swung open. A man stood on the threshold. Steam rose from his head, and from under his moth-eaten brown dressing gown. Clarrie introduced herself and held out the note.

"This lady says you might know of someone who is looking for a model."

He took the note and read it. His nails were polished like a woman's. "Do come in, darling," he said. "Forgive my dishabille."

He led the way up an uncarpeted staircase. The plaster walls on either side were pitted with holes, but the banister, evidently a relic from days of grandeur, was highly polished, the lintel post richly carved to resemble a pineapple.

They stepped off the landing into a bleak, high-ceilinged room where canvases of various sizes were stacked facing the whitewashed walls. A white telephone was attached to a wall and, in the middle of the room, a white typewriter sat on a small table. She wondered whether they'd come from the factory like that, or if someone had covered the normally black instruments with white enamel.

"Excuse me for a moment." He picked a silver-backed hairbrush from a dresser littered with hairpins and bottles of nail polish. He waved to a straight-backed wooden chair. "Have a seat, darling," he said as he disappeared through an archway at the other end of the room. Through the arch, Clarrie could see a chipped enamel stove and a narrow, lumpy bed under a white coverlet.

The floorboards of the room she was in were bare, splintery; the dresser had been jammed into the window bay, blocking the view of the street below. Why would an artist want to block out the light? And why had he turned his canvases to the wall? Dare she ask if she might see the paintings? Better not. He was perhaps unhappy with his work and didn't want anyone judging it. She could understand that. It was why she hid her poems.

Desmond Drake returned wearing black trousers, a lavender shirt, and felt slippers. Clarrie was suddenly conscious of her clumsy lace-up shoes, her scratchy woolen frock and commonplace, navy blue serge coat.

"Well, now." He sat down at the typewriter and switched on a white-shaded floor lamp. In the sudden brightness, Clarrie noticed a dark purple bruise below his left eye.

"I'll need a moment to gather my thoughts," he said. "You've caught me at rather a bad time, I'm afraid. I have just had the most disastrous quarrel with a friend—at least I thought he was my friend. One takes people in, doesn't one? Gives them a home and then . . . poof! It's so difficult to judge people these days don't you think? One trusts too easily, to one's sorrow. This one . . . frankly, my dear, I should have been warned—he was tattooed to the hilt—a big bruiser. He betrayed me shamelessly, hurt me terribly—they all do in the end. I had no choice but to throw him out. I told him off in no uncertain terms. 'You're an ungrateful beast!' I said, 'a brute!' He just knocked me aside and left . . . owes me money too . . . left me without a sou to my name. I don't expect I'll see him again."

"Some people are like that," Clarrie said. "They mistake kindness for weakness."

"Exactly. You understand perfectly." He inserted a sheet of paper into the typewriter. His tapering, manicured fingers were graceful as any woman's.

"By the way," Clarrie tried to keep her voice casual. "I wonder if you happen to know a man named Griff Williams? He's an old friend of mine. He lives here in Chelsea, but I've lost his address."

"Williams . . . Williams . . ." He shook his head. "I'm afraid not."

"Do you mind if I eat my lunch while I'm waiting?" She had left the house without breakfast and had been walking all morning without finding anywhere to sit and eat her sandwich.

He was momentarily taken aback. "Please . . . Oh . . . by all means." He nodded towards the alcove. "I can brew a pot of tea if you like, but I'm afraid I'm fresh out of milk."

"No. I can manage, thank you."

He resumed typing while Clarrie pulled a paper bag from her pocket and unwrapped her cheese sandwich. It looked rather worse for wear after being squashed in her wet pocket all morning, but remembering that her host hadn't a sou to his name, she held it out to him. "Would you care for half a sandwich?"

He veered his head ever so slightly away. "Oh, you dear girl . . . so very kind of you, but I think not. I must watch my figure." He pulled the paper from the typewriter. "This is the best I can do, I'm afraid. I don't use models myself—can't afford them. Most of these people are safe, I think. One or two might be inclined to—er—chase women. I've put question marks next to their names."

"Thank you." She accepted the paper. "It was good of you to go to so much trouble." She would have liked to stay and talk to him, to get to know more about his strange, bohemian life, but he seemed to be waiting for her to leave. She put out her hand.

"Oh, my pleasure." His handshake was surprisingly firm. "Can you find your own way down?"

"Yes. Thank you again. I'll be fine."

The rain had slowed to a drizzle. A ghostly sun drifted through the clouds, bathing the street in watery light. Clarrie studied the list Desmond Drake had given her. In which direction should she walk? She had no way of knowing which address was closest. Stupid of her not to have asked—he might have drawn her a quick map.

She turned right and right again, stopping from time to time to check the list of street names from the rain-spattered paper. Nothing. She walked up one street, down another. The rain had picked up speed again, stinging her face, drenching the front of her coat. She stopped a woman with a shopping bag and held out the list of addresses. "Excuse me, I wonder if you could direct me . . ."

The woman glanced at the list and shook her head. "Sorry. I don't know Chelsea very well, and I'm in an awful hurry. Perhaps you can find a policeman."

Clarrie stepped into a shallow doorway. The paper was now sopping wet, and so was she. Could she really, drenched and bedraggled as she was, go knocking on doors, offering herself to some strange men as a model? She tried to picture herself stepping into a high-ceilinged, art-cluttered room and taking off her clothes. Impossible! The whole idea was preposterous. She crumpled the damp paper into a ball, shoved it in her pocket, and turned back in what she hoped was the direction of the underground station.

As she crossed the square, she noticed two men walking towards her. Heads down, they were deep in conversation under a black umbrella. One of them walked with a familiar bouncing gait. He had a reddish beard, a wrinkled brown corduroy suit. Her heart set up a clamoring in her chest. She stepped directly in front of the men as they came abreast.

"Hello, Griff."

For a moment, he stared at her, puzzled, and then his expression cleared. "Clarrie! How wonderful to see you! What on earth are you doing in London?"

"Just wandering around."

"But what a surprise. Imagine running into you here. I thought you'd gone back home to Manchester."

His companion, a stooped, emaciated young man wearing a long muffler over his leather jacket, cleared his throat.

"Oh, forgive me, Toby," Griff said. "This is Clarrie—a friend of mine from the college." He turned to Clarrie. "But what are you doing in London?"

"I'm staying with my aunt in Kent. Actually, I've found a job there, but I'm playing truant from work today."

"Toby and I are about to go for coffee. Why don't you join us?"

They walked through a maze of narrow streets and down a flight of stone steps into a small café. When they were seated, the waitress approached. "Coffee and cake?" Griff asked. Clarrie and Toby nodded. When the waitress had gone, Griff asked Clarrie why she had left the college so abruptly.

"Stephen's death upset everyone, of course, but you seemed to take it so much harder than the rest of us. There was a great deal of speculation about it." A dark flush suffused his cheeks. "Some people were convinced that you were in love with him."

"No. I liked Stephen, very much, but I wasn't in love with him. I wasn't in love with anyone."

Griff looked up quickly. "I rather thought you might be in love with Alan."

"Alan?" Across the table, Toby was watching them with sharp, quizzical eyes.

"I saw you out walking with him one evening—your arms were full of lilacs."

"Oh, yes. We picked those for Jennie—to welcome her when she came back from Morecambe."

"Ah!" He smiled. There was a brief silence. "She and Alan are married, you know."

"I knew they were making plans."

"Speaking of marriage—" Toby stroked his dark moustache, and darted a probing glance at Clarrie. "Griff here is about to be married, too."

"Married?" Clarrie repeated. The clatter of dishes and the hum of conversation were drowned by a roaring in her ears.

"Aren't you going to congratulate me?" Griff said.

"Yes . . . yes, I do." Her hand shook as she sipped her coffee. "Who's the lucky woman?"

"Why, Margot, of course. You remember Margot?"

"But how can you be sure she's the right one?" she blurted,

Toby raised his eyebrows and looked at Griff.

Griff gave a nervous laugh. "Do you have some reason for thinking that Margot and I are not suited to each other?"

"No. No, I—that is . . . it's just that . . . marriage is so . . . irrevocable." Clarrie broke off a fragment of cake and popped it in her mouth. She must stop babbling.

Griff touched the edge of a fork lying beside her plate. "It's customary to use a cake fork," he said quietly.

Clarrie felt the blood rush to her face. She remembered, suddenly, a spectacular food fight in the common room. She and Nora had had to stay until almost eleven that evening cleaning tea-soaked bread and fragments of greasy rissoles from floors and tables and walls.

The cake crumbs stuck in her throat, and she went into a paroxysm of coughing. Griff handed her a glass of water. Water dribbled down her chin. She blotted her mouth with the table napkin. Damn him. Damn the lot of them.

Toby got to his feet. "I must be off." He reached over to pick up the bill. Griff snatched it away.

"Until next week, then," Toby said. He nodded to Clarrie and left.

"Is Toby an artist, too?" Clarrie asked.

"No. He's Margot's half-brother. He'll be the best man at the wedding. He came down from Cambridge for the weekend to talk it over."

"I hope I didn't say anything . . ."

"You didn't. I was a little on edge. Margot's people are terribly posh and rather . . . intimidating. Marrying into the upper class has its drawbacks."

"I thought you were already upper class?"

Griff laughed. "Middle class, perhaps, if you want to be generous about it. My father is a postmaster."

"A postmaster?"

"As you may imagine, Margot's people are not too happy about the match, but they dote on Margot, and she always gets what she wants. I spent the week at their house in Hampshire—an incredible place. They're having a problem keeping it up . . . finding servants and so on."

"Yes," Clarrie said, "Margot told me."

Griff sipped his coffee, watching her over the rim of his cup. "What sort of work are you doing in Kent?"

"I'm learning to be a tracer—copying drawings onto wax from engineers' blueprints."

Griff frowned. "How did someone like you get a job like that? I've been trying to find work along those lines myself."

"I did what you'd expect someone like me to do. I told them I'd spent two years at the College of Art." The lie was out before she could stop it.

There was an embarrassed silence. Griff stared into his coffee cup. He was obviously displeased. Clarrie dug her nails into her palms. He would never believe her, now, if she were to tell him the truth.

"Shall we?" Griff picked up the bill and dropped a few coins on the table. Clarrie fumbled in her handbag. He put his hand over hers. "Please."

As she stood up, she caught sight of herself in a mirror. She should never have worn this burgundy dress. The color was all wrong.

Griff helped her into her coat. Clarrie put her hand back to loosen the hair trapped beneath her collar and felt his hand touch hers. "Your hands are like ice," he said.

"Sorry," she said. She rummaged in her pocket for her gloves.

"Where do you go from here?"

"Back to Orpington, I suppose."

"I'll walk you to the station."

They walked through the streets in silence. When they reached the station, he bent swiftly and brushed her cheek with his lips. "It was really wonderful seeing you again."

Clarrie did not trust herself to speak. She was on the verge of doing something desperate—of throwing her arms around his neck and blurting out that she loved him. She was stopped by the shriek of a whistle as the train pulled in. "Here's my train," she said.

Griff held her elbow as she climbed aboard. "Can you manage?"

"I'll be all right."

She found a seat by the window and with her gloved hand wiped away a film of grime. Griff was walking up and down, looking in the wrong windows. Catching sight of her, he smiled and hurried to her. Clarrie tried to let him know, through her eyes, that she loved him, would always love him. He gazed into her eyes with a faintly puzzled frown. They stayed like that, their eyes locked in silent communication, until the train pulled away.

Chapter Fifty-five

It was nearing the lunch hour on Saturday. Clarrie had spent the morning peeling potatoes and washing cabbages under the cold-water tap at the back of the café. Her fingers were blue and so numb she could barely hold the tub.

"You look absolutely perished," Aunt Ruth said when Clarrie went back into the café with the cabbages. "Why were you working outside in weather like this, for heaven's sake?"

"Granny Morgan needed to use the inside sinks."

"Did she indeed. I can't imagine why. She's been sitting in the pantry for the past hour, drinking tea and filling up the cruets. Never mind. I'll take the cabbages. You can wash the breakfast things—it will warm your hands. When you've finished you can change your apron before the lunch rush starts. I'd like to close early and get back to the house in time to dress for the dance. You'll be able to wear that nice skirt your mother sent for your birthday."

The dance was to be held at the church hall, and since Aunt Ruth was on the planning committee, the whole family was expected to go. It would do Clarrie the world of good, Aunt Ruth told her, to get out and meet other young people. Her aunt was probably right, Clarrie thought. She ought to meet some people her own age. Griff was getting married. He was not for her. She must find a way to put him out of her mind.

Clarrie plucked a blue flower from one of the pots in the kitchen window, snapped off the stem, and pinned it to her hair.

"You look very nice," Aunt Ruth said as she came down the stairs. "But I wouldn't wear that flower in my hair if I were you,"

"Why? What's wrong with it?'

"This is not Hollywood, my dear. We're a bit old fashioned here in the village."

Clarrie stared at her image in the hall mirror. "Perhaps I shouldn't go to the dance at all if I embarrass you."

"Let's not be silly, now," Aunt Ruth said.

Clarrie pulled the flower from her hair, her eyes clouding with tears. She was about to crush the petals, when, swept by an unexpected surge of anger, she pinned the flower back in her hair.

Women, mostly middle-aged, thronged the entrance to the church hall greeting one another. From inside the hall, came the crooning voice of Bing Crosby singing "Don't Fence Me In." Clarrie followed her aunt and the rest of the family into a long room hung with paper streamers. Straight-backed chairs, occupied by elderly men and women, were lined up around the room. A mousy woman stepped forward, smelling of lavender. "I can't find a suitable cloth, Ruth, dear, for the refreshment table."

"It's in that basket. I took it home to wash."

Clarrie followed the two women into the kitchen. "If you tell me what to do, I'll be glad to help." It would be better to keep busy than to stand about looking uncomfortable.

"You might slice more bread for the sandwiches," the mousy woman said.

Aunt Ruth took the bread knife out of Clarrie's hands. "I can do that. Go . . . go and enjoy yourself. Everything's under control here." She smiled at the woman. "It's her seventeenth birthday."

Clarrie found a chair and sat watching the dancers. When the dance stopped, a young man with a small moustache came up to her.

"You're new here. I don't believe we've met." The band struck up a foxtrot. "Would you like to dance?" Clarrie got up and followed him onto the dance floor. They danced in silence for a while, and then he asked her name and why he had never seen her at the village dances. Before she could reply, another man cut in and whirled her away. The first man quickly reclaimed her.

"You were about to tell me who you are—where you've been hiding yourself." His hands were warm, his accent upper class.

"My name's Clarrie. I'm visiting relations," Clarrie said.

The music changed to a jitterbug. Several couples left the floor.

"Shall we try?" the man with the moustache said.

"Why not?" Remembering the lively antics of the students at the college hops, Clarrie was struck by the stiff, embarrassed movements of the dancers. We're all dancing as if we're half dead, she thought, and was suddenly filled with scorn at the lifeless festivities, and her own timidity.

"If we're going to jitterbug," she said, "let's jitterbug!"

She threw herself into the dance with abandon, copying the steps she had seen in American films. The young man stopped, astonished, then with a laugh, joined in. Clarrie's hairpins flew out.

"Your flower is falling," he said.

She tossed her hair back. "Let it fall, I don't care." When the music stopped she was panting and exhilarated.

"I have to run to the bog after that," the man said. "Don't go away."

Gasping for breath, Clarrie walked off the dance floor. Her hair was in disarray, her palms and underarms wet. People were looking at her. A dark-haired girl with a pinched mouth was sitting on one of the straight-backed chairs talking to a young man in a home guard uniform. She stared pointedly at Clarrie. The expression in her yellow brown eyes was unmistakably hostile. She leaned over and whispered something in her companion's ear. He glanced over at Clarrie and whispered back. They laughed. The girl reminded Clarrie of her old enemy, Myra Tarrant.

Aunt Ruth laid a work-roughened hand on Clarrie's arm and drew her aside. "Clarrie, don't fling yourself about like that," she whispered. "Everyone's looking at you."

Clarrie's face blazed. "It's the jitterbug. You're supposed to fling yourself about."

"But you looked so wild. It wouldn't be so bad if you'd smile. This is a small village and people aren't used to it; everyone will be talking."

Hatred flared in Clarrie's heart—long simmering hatred for all the spiteful, mean-minded people she had ever met. Shaking, she turned away. The doorway was packed. She pushed her way through the crowd and ran to the cloakroom to splash her face with cold water. Without bothering to comb her hair, or repair her make-up, she extricated her coat from a pile on the hall table and made her way to the door.

The young man came up behind her. "Whoa! You're not leaving already? I've been looking high and low for you."

"I have to get out of here."

"Me too. How about a stroll in the garden?"

Cold air hit her face as she opened the door. Stars glittered like shards of ice in the black sky. The man put his arm around her waist and led her down the stone path through the churchyard. The moon broke through the tangled branches of the trees, lighting up tombstones that leaned drunkenly on either side. The young man said his name was Nigel, and that he was an intern at St. Mary's Hospital. He began telling her of his experiences in medical school—of the fun he and his friends had cutting up a cadaver.

"An old woman . . . ghastly sight . . . almost made me puke." He squeezed Clarrie's waist. "Did you know that when women get really old, they lose their pubic hair? This old girl was bald as a billiard ball."

Clarrie removed his hand from around her waist. She regretted that she'd agreed to walk with this crude man. Ahead, a gnarled yew tree marked a turn in the path. Clarrie stopped. "I think we'd better turn back. It's too cold out here."

"I'll soon warm you up." He gripped her shoulders and pushed her back against the tree, pressing his body against hers, kissing her, thrusting his tongue deep into her mouth. Clarrie could smell whisky. She turned her head from side to side, pushing him with the heels of her hands.

He caught her hands in his. "Bit of a tease, aren't you?" She kept her lips clamped shut as he tried to kiss her again.

"Don't pretend you don't want it," he said. "You've been asking for this all evening."

"I'm not pretending. Let me go."

He released one of her hands, and fumbled inside her coat, trying to undo the buttons of her blouse. Clarrie clenched her free hand and swung wildly, hitting him hard against the side of his face. She broke free and ran to the side door of the church, catching her skirt on a nail as she darted through the lych gate. She fastened the buttons of her blouse, and wiped the smeared lipstick from around her mouth.

It was not yet ten o'clock, but already the dance was breaking up. People were calling to each other, saying goodnight in the doorway. Clarrie's cousins were playing tag with some young girls. Aunt Ruth and Uncle Gerald were chatting with another couple.

"Who was the nice young man you were dancing with?" Aunt Ruth asked as they climbed into the car. "I saw you go outside with him. Did you go for a walk?"

"He wasn't so nice," Clarrie said. "I think he'd been drinking."

"Well, he certainly didn't get any alcohol at the dance." Aunt Ruth reddened. "You can hardly blame him, I suppose, if he got the wrong impression . . . the way you were dancing."

"You fling yourself about like that, it gets the young chaps all hot and bothered," Uncle Gerald said. "They think you're an easy mark."

"Well, they're mistaken," Clarrie said coldly. She stared out the window in silence as they rode back to the house.

"Would you like a cup of tea?" Aunt Ruth asked when they got indoors. "It's what we usually have when we come home from one of these do's."

Pleading tiredness, Clarrie bade them goodnight and went straight to her room. She put on her nightgown and sat on the edge of the sofa bed, thinking miserably of the events of the evening. That man thought she'd been asking for it. If she had been asking for anything, it was certainly not for what had happened tonight. What had she done to make him pounce on her so roughly . . . sneer at her so contemptuously? It was almost as if he hated her.

On the mantelpiece was the smiling snapshot of Billy in his school uniform, and above the mantle, a large oval portrait of her grandmother as a young woman. Grandmother Waters had the same dark curls, the same firm, sweet mouth and level gaze as her mother and Aunt Ruth. She looked down sternly, a woman whose virtue would never have been called into question.

"Grandmother," Clarrie whispered. "Please help me. I don't know what to do . . . how to live." The eyes looked back at her without recognition. The mouth stayed firmly closed. The face was that of a woman long dead—a woman who had never known her and probably wouldn't have liked her if she had.

She fell to her knees by the side of her makeshift bed, pressed her face into the chenille coverlet and tried to pray. Her mind refused. She couldn't remember the Lord's Prayer. "Dear God," she said. "Help me. Please help me."

If God was there, he had no intention of making his presence known. Numb from cold, she abandoned her efforts and crawled into bed.

Chapter Fifty-six

Summoning her last shred of courage, on the following Monday, Clarrie returned to work. She was relieved when nobody mentioned the trip to London or asked why she'd taken a day off from work. She'd expected no less—these women were nothing if not polite—nevertheless, she detected a certain coolness in their manner. Why was it that whenever she spoke or acted honestly, she managed to offend someone?

She unrolled her latest blueprint. This drawing was more complicated than anything she had tackled so far. As usual, the supervisor was nowhere in sight. There was nothing for it but to swallow her pride and turn to Martha for help.

Martha patiently explained what it was the engineer wanted, and by mid-afternoon the blueprint was finished. Clarrie stepped back to admire her handiwork.

"I believe I'm finished," she said, turning to Martha. She flung out her arm to the drawing. Her hand hit the open inkpot. A stream of black ink shot across the drawing as the inkpot rolled down and fell with a crash to the floor.

"Oh, Lord!" Martha sprang to her feet and rummaged in her handbag. "I haven't even got a hankie!"

Clarrie stared, appalled, as Martha dabbed ineffectually at the blueprint with a small wad of pen wipers. Two or three other women stood up, craning their necks to see what had happened. "What a shame," they murmured. "What rotten luck!"

Martha dropped the pen wipers. "This is not good enough. We need a rag or something."

Clarrie came out of her trance. "Go back to work, Martha," she said. "I'll take care of it." She ran to the washroom and stood trembling in front of the mirror. A pair of green and glassy eyes looked back at her. "I hate you," she whispered. "I hate you, you stupid bitch."

On the counter was a jar filled with discarded razor blades used for scraping wax off the linen. She lifted out one of the razor blades and drew the edge gingerly across her left wrist. A thin line of blood bubbled to the surface. She'd need to cut deeper if she really intended to . . . but someone had opened the door. Quickly, she ran the cold water, rinsed off the blade and dropped it back in the jar.

Martha poked her head around the corner. "Have you found anything?"

"Yes. I'll be out in a minute."

Martha nodded and closed the door. In the cleaning cupboard, Clarrie found a first-aid box and a few rags. She wrapped her wrist in a gauze bandage. Concealing the bandaged wrist as best she could beneath the sleeve of her cardigan, she returned to her desk and began wiping up the spill.

The supervisor came down the aisle, a grim expression on her face. "Unpin your drawing and give it to me with the original." She rolled up the stained linen and strode back down the aisle. In a few moments she was back. She set a fresh bottle of ink and another drawing on Clarrie's desk. "See what you can do with this."

Clarrie's hands were shaking as she pinned the new drawing into place. She had difficulty unscrewing the cap off the inkbottle because her fingers were stiff with cold. Except for an occasional cough and the scratching of pens, all was quiet. Fumes from the paraffin stove filled her nostrils. Her head was pounding. She stared at the new drawing. What was this all about? The engineer's instructions might as well be written in Sanskrit. A drop of blood seeped from under the bandage and splashed on the drawing. She smeared it with her thumb, leaving a pink stain. She jumped to her feet and with a loud scream, threw her pen across the room.

Chairs scraped, people rose. The supervisor ran back down the aisle.

"Whatever is the matter?" Her eyes widened as she caught sight of the bandage. "Good heavens, child, what have you done?" She took Clarrie by the arm, and telling the others to get back to work, led her down a connecting passage to a first-aid station and left her in the care of a stout nurse.

The nurse thrust a thermometer in Clarrie's mouth, read the thermometer without comment, and examined her wrist. "What did you do here?" she asked.

"It was an accident," Clarrie said.

The nurse asked her name and address. When Clarrie didn't answer, she repeated the question. "We have to notify someone."

"I'm on my own. I'll be all right. There's no need to let anyone know."

"On your own? How old are you?"

"I just turned seventeen."

The nurse pointed to a folding cot and told her to lie down and rest. Clarrie pulled the hairy khaki blanket over her face and closed her eyes. She was aware of pain, but the pain didn't seem to be located in her body, or even in her mind. Whatever the source, she wanted it to stop. She pressed her face into the blanket. She would like to sleep forever, to feel nothing ever again. She clamped her mouth shut. Perhaps, if she could hold her breath long enough, she could make herself lose consciousness. As a child she'd often tried holding her breath in order to placate Annie, but she'd never been able to do it for more than a minute at a time. She took a deep breath and clamped her mouth shut until her lungs seemed about to burst. She sat up, gulping, desperate for air. Her body did not care what she wanted. Apparently it had a will of its own.

The nurse came over to tell her to put on her coat. She was to take the rest of the day off; there was a bus leaving for Orpington in fifteen minutes.

Clarrie stared bleakly out the bus window as the almost empty vehicle rattled and jolted over the wheel-rutted snow. A white vapor hung over the woods, shrouding the trees. The banks and ditches were littered with broken twigs and blackened branches. A few strange-looking toadstools had poked through the frozen leaf mould, their caps splotched with red.

At Orpington she got off the bus and walked unseeing along the High Street. There'd be nobody at the house yet, and if she went to the café, Aunt Ruth would want to know why she'd left work early. She stepped into Woolworth's and spent the last of her pocket money on a cup of tea and a bath-bun. She sat, sipping tea and picking absently at the bun, until it was time to start the long walk back to the house.

Chapter Fifty-seven

The next morning, Clarrie left the house at her usual time and headed toward the bus stop as though she were going to work. At the corner she doubled back, and crouched behind the chicken coops, waiting for everyone to leave the house. The sun appeared—a flat pink disk—but the next time she looked, it was gone. Everything in the garden was dead, the ground sealed by frost. Back toward the apple orchard, the blackened stalks of the scarlet runner beans still clung to their poles.

She was shivering, silently willing her aunt and uncle and the boys to come out of the house and pile into the van. She'd said nothing to them about what had happened at work and had been careful to keep her cardigan on so they wouldn't see the bandaged wrist. The boys were always dropped off at school before her aunt and uncle went on to the café, and they wouldn't be back before five. She would have the house to herself—plenty of time to do whatever it was she was going to do. She had no plan. She only knew that she could never go back to that icy hut with the smell of the paraffin burner and the sound of scratching pens.

The kitchen door opened, and the boys emerged with their school satchels, followed by Aunt Ruth and Uncle Gerald carrying crates of eggs for the café. Clarrie pressed herself flat against the wooden slats of the chicken coop.

"And what about all the hot water she uses?" Uncle Gerald was saying. "Does she have to wash her hair every day? Nobody washes their hair every day."

Aunt Ruth said something Clarrie couldn't hear. Then the van doors slammed shut, the engine started up, the wheels spun in the gravel, and the van took off down the drive.

They had never seen fit to give her a key, but the bathroom window was always left slightly open to let in fresh air. By climbing up the log pile she managed to reach the ledge and push the window open wide enough to crawl through.

The house smelled of wet ashes—Uncle Gerald had damped the fire down. Aunt Ruth's Chinese kimono was hanging on the bathroom door, its red, black, and gold dragons greasy and soiled. "You need a bath," Clarrie said out loud. She threw the kimono into the bathtub, and ran the hot water. Red dye swirled into the water. "Now I've ruined that, too," she said. She turned off the tap, plunged her hand into the scalding water, and pulled out the plug. She sat on the edge of the bathtub until the last of the red water had gurgled down the drain. She wiped the steam from the mirror with a towel. Had her eyes always looked so crazy and glittery? She dropped the towel and clawed at her face, leaving three red scratch marks down each cheek.

In the kitchen she switched on the wireless. A plaintive female voice filled the room singing, "They asked me how I knew, that my love was true . . ." A sharp serrated knife was lying exposed across the breadboard. Clarrie quickly thrust the knife into a drawer. She closed her eyes in an effort to shut out the violent and disturbing images that flashed before her:

a bread knife plunging into her heart, piercing her belly, slicing across her throat. If she were to squeeze that knife handle into the doorjamb and get it to stay put, she might be able to walk into it . . .

She hadn't been able to cut her wrist with the razor blade, let alone to plunge a knife into her belly. Mr. Hutchins had hanged himself. So had that woman in the park lavatory. She hadn't the nerve to do any of those things. There was always the gas, of course. She would just go to sleep, and it would all be over.

She walked into the kitchen, blew out the pilot light and turned on the gas oven. It was next to impossible to get her head in properly, because the door opened downward, like a flap. Feeling foolish, she knelt with her head as close as she could get it, breathing deeply, listening to the hissing of the gas. How ridiculous she must look, kneeling like this with her head on the oven door! What if a spark from the fire should ignite the gas and blow the house to smithereens? She got up, turned off the gas, struck a kitchen match and relit the pilot light. It caught with a loud whoosh that made her jump.

Stephen Wentworth had used a gun. That was the best way. One squeeze of a trigger . . . Why hadn't she thought of that before? Uncle Gerald had a home-guard pistol. He kept it on top of the wardrobe in the hall.

She carried a kitchen chair into the hall, climbed up and took the gun and a box of bullets back into the dining room. Six chambers; a six-shooter, like Billy's old cowboy gun. She put one bullet in the chamber next in line to fire and closed it again.

She ought to leave a note—some explanation for what she was about to do—but what could she say? Nothing terrible had happened. Her pain was not physical, but it was unbearable. She could not endure even one more day.

She went into the drawing room. Next to her bed was one of the little paperback poetry books she had bought at the Bramblebeck bookshop. W H. Auden. There was a poem about death . . . Yes, this was the one. With a red pencil she underlined the passage:

Has not your long affair with death
Of late become increasingly more serious;
Do you not find
Him growing more attractive every day?
You shall go under and help him with the crops,
Be faithful to him, and to your friends,
Remain indifferent.

She imagined Death as a pale, handsome man, dressed in a dark cape and a slouch hat. He would greet her with a sardonic smile, with penetrating, merciless eyes . . . Or was she confusing him with the devil? She put the book face down on the side table, picked up the gun and put it to her temple. No. Not there. Not her brain. She pressed the barrel to her chest—the left side, where her heart ought to be—and squeezed the trigger.

There was a loud blast and a faint smell of gunpowder. She sat for a while, feeling nothing. Perhaps I'm already dead, she thought, and my brain has not yet registered the fact. Gingerly, she inserted a finger into the hole in her chest. Blood. She brought the finger to her mouth. It was certainly blood.

A man on the wireless was singing, "If you were the only girl in the world . . ." Clarrie giggled. "If I were the only girl in the world, I'd kill myself anyway," she said. She got up and went to look in the hall mirror to make sure she was still there. "You are not fit to live," she said.

Apparently she was not fit to die, either. She had botched everything, even her suicide. In a little while, Uncle Gerald and Aunt Ruth would come home. What could she say to them? Uncle Gerald would be furious. She walked outside with the gun still in her hand. All around the rubbish bin curled and blackened potato peelings were embedded in the dirty snow. She sat on a fallen log and examined her wound. The wool around the hole was black with powder and sticky with blood.

"Oh, God," she whispered. "What have I done?" Was this the end? Was she never to marry, never to have a wedding night, never to bear children? What was it her father had said when Mr. Hutchins hanged himself? It was a coward's way out. Her father was right.

She got up, gun in hand, crossed the lane to the house opposite and rang the doorbell. A plump hand moved the lace curtain at the window, and dropped the curtain back in place. Clarrie rang again. When nobody came to the door, she went back across the road and sat on the log. Tinny music drifted from the house. Clarrie closed her eyes. She felt very sleepy. Perhaps she should go back in and turn the wireless off ? She heard footsteps crunching in the lane. A man wearing a bowler hat and carrying a rolled umbrella approached her. She got to her feet, thinking, for a fleeting moment, that it was her father come to save her.

The man nodded, "Good day." Then he stopped, his eyes on the gun. "What has happened to you?" he asked. "Are you hurt?"

"I shot myself, and I don't know what to do next."

He held out his hand. "You'd better give me that gun." Clarrie handed it to him. "Stay right there," he said, "I'm going for help."

She was being lifted onto a stretcher and into the back of an ambulance.

"I think I left the wireless on," she muttered.

"Don't worry about the wireless." The man who spoke pushed up the sleeve of her cardigan and plunged a needle into her arm. ". . . to help you relax," he said. Clarrie lapsed into silence and darkness.

She awoke shivering from the cold. Judging by the disinfectant smell she was in a hospital. Someone had taken off all her clothes and was urging her to stand up, to climb up on a small platform.

"Turn that way," a nurse said. "Face the fluoroscope."

A doctor with a shock of white hair approached, put a hand on her arm, and asked if she would mind if he brought in some interns to watch his examination—this was a God-sent opportunity for them to observe a bullet removal, and it would help prepare them for working with the wounded soldiers.

"You'll be making a valuable contribution to the war effort," he said.

Clarrie, standing naked and confused on the small platform, nodded her consent. The doctor beckoned, and six or seven young men in white jackets filed into the room from a door somewhere behind her.

The young men jostled for position and craned their necks for a better view of the image on the fluoroscope.

"The bullet, as you see, is lodged near the spine . . ." As the doctor lectured, he marked Clarrie's chest and back with green chalk. The interns pressed closer. One of them caught her eye, reddened and quickly stepped back. It was the man who had pushed her against the tree and rammed his tongue into her mouth at the village dance. Clarrie closed her eyes, pretending she hadn't seen him. When the lecture ended, the interns left the room, and a nurse, her dazzling white uniform stiff with starch, helped her back onto a stretcher, covered her with a starched sheet, and wheeled her into the hallway.

"Where are we going?" Clarrie asked.

"To the operating room," the nurse said. She pushed the gurney into a large room reeking of some sort of chemicals—perhaps it was chloroform—Clarrie wasn't sure.

Another nurse pierced her arm with a needle and told her to count backwards from a hundred.

"Is she out?" the doctor asked.

"Dead to the world."

Clarrie could neither move nor speak, but she could hear them clearly.

"She's starting to menstruate," the nurse said.

"Fetch a sanitary towel then." The doctor lifted one of Clarrie's eyelids for a moment. She glimpsed a ruddy clean-shaven cheek, felt warm breath on her face. Someone stuffed a pad between her legs. A bright light seemed to be burning into her brain. Her mouth was forced open and some sort of gag shoved between her teeth. The voices remained clear but distant. Clarrie couldn't quite understand what was being said. Something sharp pierced her chest. The light behind her eyelids burned red. There was a raw, tearing sensation, as though rusty scissors were slicing her in two.

She was swirling in darkness on the outer rim of a pit where a great fire burned, being drawn helplessly along a circular path towards the roaring flames. Shadowy figures shuffled forward, descending in an endless trek before vanishing into the white-hot pit. All was confusion; shrieks rent the air; arms, legs, flailed about as people struggled to escape the flames. She caught a glimpse of Stephen and Mr. Hutchins. She opened her mouth to call to them but could make no sound. A medicinal smell burned her nostrils, dried her mouth. From that other world, where her body lay open like a gutted fish, the doctor was calling to someone to do something, fetch someone. The screams, rising from the bottomless abyss, went on and on.

When she opened her eyes, a plump little woman was sitting by the bed, knitting something with blue wool. The woman smiled.

"Well, hello. I'd begun to think you'd never wake up."

"Who are you?" Clarrie asked.

"I'm a volunteer. I've been sitting here with you all night. You've been calling for someone named Riff, or Cliff—something like that. Your auntie doesn't know who he is. Is he a friend of yours? Is he on the telephone? Do you want me to call him for you?"

"No, thank you. I'm all right," Clarrie said. Her chest and left shoulder hurt. Her mouth was sore, and when she tried to move her whole body felt sore, but miraculously that other, deeper pain, had gone.

The plump little woman thrust her knitting into a bag. "You've been out for a long time. They told me to let them know the minute you came to. I'd better tell the nurse."

"You're very kind," Clarrie murmured. Her heart ached with love and gratitude for this little woman who had sat by her side all night. She closed her eyes.

Someone was tapping her on the cheek. "Wake up, Clara, you have to take some medicine." Two sapphire blue eyes, rimmed with black, spiky lashes, smiled down at her. Lovely, everything was lovely.

Clarrie smiled up at the nurse. "You are beautiful," she murmured drowsily.

When she awoke the second time, her parents were sitting one on either side of her bed. "Mam?" A dull pain throbbed in her left shoulder.

"Shh!" Her mother patted her gently. "Don't cry, love."

"I'm sorry, Mam," Clarrie said. She turned her head. "I'm sorry, Dad."

"You gave us a right bloody shock," her father said. "Two bobbies came to the house. Why didn't you let us know there was something wrong?"

"Why did you do it, love?" her mother said.

"I don't know. It was nothing in particular. I was just miserable."

"You're lucky to be alive," her father said. "Your Uncle Gerald said there were two kinds of bullets in that box. If you'd picked the other kind, you'd have blown yourself to smithereens.

Stephen hadn't been so lucky, Clarrie thought, remembering the slumped figure, the dark puddle on the carpet. "He's blown his head off," Griff had said.

Her mother stroked Clarrie's cheek. "She'll never do anything like that again, will you love?"

Clarrie's tears overflowed. She was unable to speak.

"We'd better leave you in peace, then." Her mother got to her feet. As they were leaving, her father bent and kissed Clarrie's cheek. "I have to go back tonight. Your mam's staying with Aunt Ruth 'til the end of the week, then she'll have to go back too."

"I'll be all right," Clarrie assured them.

Her parents had dropped everything and come all the way to Kent because of her. If she had died, they'd have been plunged into lifelong grief, and she might have spent eternity in hell—for it must have been hell—that terrible fiery place she'd gone to while the doctors were operating. God had given her another chance—a chance to live, and a chance to make amends to all the people she'd hurt. Through a high window opposite her bed, a patch of clear blue sky shimmered; robin's egg blue. So beautiful. She'd like a coat of that color.

The next day, her mother returned with Aunt Ruth, but the visit was brief. Aunt Ruth had driven Uncle Gerald's car, and she must have it back early to pick him up from the café.

"I brought your suitcase and all your things," Aunt Ruth said. "They're keeping them for you in the almoner's office. This way, you can go straight home from the hospital when they discharge you."

"Your Uncle Gerald's furious," her mother said. "He thinks people are blaming him for what you did."

"What makes him think that?" Clarrie asked. But she knew he had a right to be angry.

With every day that passed, she felt better. The fog of misery that had enveloped her for so long had gone, replaced by what could only be described as euphoria. The world was miraculous and beautiful; she must have been mad to want to leave it. She felt as carefree as a little girl again. Towards the end of her stay, she made a friend of the girl in the next bed, who was recovering from an appendix operation. The two of them joked and sang popular songs, accompanying themselves by banging on the tin lids that covered their dinner plates until the matron came out of her office and told them to stop.

Three weeks had passed in the hospital and, although the wound in Clarrie's chest was still draining, the doctor declared her recovered enough to go home. The nurse showed her how to change her own dressings.

The next day, her mother arrived to take her back to Salford. A nurse handed Clarrie's suitcase to her mother and asked her to please wait in the hall. She led Clarrie into a small office, where a doctor sat behind a desk talking to a ruddy-faced policeman. The doctor motioned her to a chair and told her that the constable had some questions to ask her.

Why had she done it, the policeman wanted to know. Had she misbehaved with someone?

Clarrie shook her head.

The policeman wrote something in a small notebook. "Then why?" he asked.

Clarrie was silent.

"You must understand that attempted suicide is a serious matter," the doctor said. The policeman and I are here to help you. Whatever is troubling you, we'll understand."

Clarrie told them that she didn't know why she had done it.

"Well, then." The doctor flicked a cigarette lighter with his thumb and lit a cigarette. He offered a cigarette to the policeman, who declined. The doctor blew out a stream of smoke.

"Will you promise never to do anything like that again?" he said. Clarrie promised. The doctor glanced at the policeman and nodded.

"Very well, Miss," the policeman said. "You're free to go."

A beam of light, streaming obliquely from a window overhead, danced on the green linoleum as she stepped into the hall. Her mother was sitting on a bench holding Clarrie's coat. Her eyes were closed, her lips clamped together. Two deep furrows creased the space above her nose. Clarrie touched her mother's arm. "Are you all right Mam?"

Her mother jumped at the touch, her eyes flew open, the furrows above her nose vanished, teeth and dimples flashed. "I'm fine, love," she said. "Are they all finished with you?"

"They told me I was free to leave."

Her mother got to her feet and helped Clarrie into her coat. "Do you want to stop for something to eat, love, or shall we go straight to the station?"

"Let's go home," Clarrie said.

Chapter Fifty-eight

Clarrie had been home for more than a week and so far they hadn't left her alone for a minute. Annie had stayed home from work today, on the pretext of having a cold. She was sitting by the fire, flipping through an old magazine with an air of exaggerated boredom. Clarrie rose from her chair. Annie lowered the magazine.

"Where are you going?'

"Upstairs," Clarrie said. "Don't worry, I'm not about to run amok. You needn't watch me every minute."

In the bedroom she unbuttoned her blouse and pulled away the gauze dressing and the square of bloodstained lint from her wound. Hearing Annie on the stairs, she quickly covered herself.

Annie came in the room. "Let's have a look at it."

Clarrie started to protest.

"Don't be such a prude," Annie said.

"I'm not a prude."

"Yes, you are. You always have been. Even when you were little you couldn't pee if anyone else was in the room."

Clarrie opened her blouse. Annie pushed up her glasses with one finger as she stared at Clarrie's chest.

"Why did you do a stupid thing like that?"

Clarrie examined the damage in the wardrobe mirror. The incision from the operation had healed, leaving a red, lumpy line from sternum to navel. The jagged wound under her left breast was still draining.

"You've ruined yourself for life," Annie said. "What if you want to get married?"

"If some man wants me, he'll have to put up with it"

"Aye, you're right. Button your blouse, and don't worry about it. Most men are lucky to get any woman if you ask me."

It was Saturday morning, the end of Clarrie's first week home, and by the look of things, it was her father's turn to keep an eye on her.

"I'll be going into Manchester this afternoon," he said gruffly. "I'm thinking of dropping in at the roller rink for an hour or two. You can come and watch me skate, if you like."

Clarrie looked up from her book in surprise. As far as she could remember, her father and she had never been out alone together. She had never seen him skate.

"I'd love to," she said.

But when they reached the rink they found it closed for repairs. "It looks as though I'm never going to get a chance to see you skate, Dad."

"You're not missing much. I'm not a patch on what I used to be." He leaned forward to examine a peeling, outdated poster advertising an exhibition of trick skating. There was a similar poster in her father's trunk—a rather garish picture of him dressed in a red and black Cossack outfit, leaping over a stack of barrels. The caption read, "Professor Hancock defies gravity." She'd been disappointed to learn that her father was not a real professor; music-hall entertainers were in the habit of dubbing themselves with a title of some sort—Doctor, Professor, Swami, Maestro—but nobody took such titles seriously.

"That's that, then," her father said. "I suppose we'd best go back home."

Clarrie was not ready to go home. "Can't we go somewhere else, as long as we're out?"

Her father suggested they walk down Oxford Street to the Ritz ballroom and see if anything was doing. The afternoon dance session was about to start and people were queuing up at the ticket office. He paid for the tickets and led her into the foyer and up a carpeted staircase to the balcony, where they found seats at a small table overlooking the dance floor.

The ballroom was swarming with girls and servicemen—Canadians, Australians, Poles, free French, American G.I's, but hardly any Englishmen. The dancing couples, pressed together hip to hip, moved slowly around the floor illuminated by red, blue, green, and yellow revolving lights.

Her father got up. "I'll fetch us something to drink." He went to the refreshment bar and came back with two glasses of poisonous-looking orange squash.

"I had no idca this place existed," she told father. "How did you know about it?"

"I won a clog dancing competition here once."

"Did you ever take Mam dancing?" she asked him.

"We were doing three shows a day on tour, so there was no time for dancing. She liked watching me skate, though." He lit a cigarette. "She was in the WAACs when I first met her. New Year's Eve, it was. Some of us chaps wanted to go out to celebrate, but there'd been a spot of trouble in town, and we were confined to barracks. For a lark we climbed the barbed wire fence into the women's camp."

Clarrie smiled. "Mam told me about that. You're lucky you weren't caught." There'd been five or six soldiers, all a bit tipsy. They'd carried with them several bottles of stout and a baked ham someone had filched from the cook-house.

"Most of the women were huddled by the stove, talking," her father went on. "But one lass was in her cot. She jumped out and wrapped herself in a blanket. Her hair was tousled, her eyes blazing. You should have seen the look she gave me. I backed away, fast, I can tell you. I mumbled something about bringing in the New Year, then tripped over a couple of kitbags and landed on my backside. She gave me her hand to help me up and asked me if I was hurt.

" 'I've only bruised my pride,' says I. 'Oh,' says she, 'you carry it in your back pocket then, do you?'

"I saw those dimples flash, and I was a goner. She was the loveliest creature I'd ever clapped eyes on."

"Like her photograph in the album?"

"Aye." He looked down at the dancers. "There isn't a woman here who could hold a candle to her. She was like a breath of fresh air . . . no paint, no powder, and she needed none. She wasn't the sort of lass you could just flirt with. I knew right there and then that I was going to marry her."

"Didn't she have anything to say about it?"

"I wouldn't take no for an answer." His voice broke. "I wanted to give her the best of everything."

Clarrie studied her father's profile. His nose, misshapen from repeated injuries, seemed to be veering to the left; his neck, against his stiff white collar, looked yellow and scrawny. He was worn out. He'd grown old waiting for a ship that would never come in.

Through a blur of tears, she looked down at the dancers. If she could turn back the clock, she would endure anything—any degree of pain—rather than add one iota to his troubles.

The family had either tired of their constant vigilance, or decided it was safe to leave her to her own devices. Clarrie, for her part, was engaged in a monumental struggle to rid herself of her obsession with Griff.

Over and over she relived their meetings—the kiss on the snowy bank of Rydal Water—the husky note in his voice when he'd held her at the dance—his eyes locked with hers through the train window in London. Running into him like that—it was as though fate had conspired with desire to bring them together, to offer them a chance. A chance not taken. Griff had made his choice. She must root him out of her mind, out of her heart.

She kept herself busy around the house, cleaning, helping with the laundry and the daily food shopping. She'd been home about a month when her mother gave her two shillings and told her to go out and enjoy herself.

"Go to the pictures or something," she said. Clarrie accepted the money and took a bus into Manchester, but instead of going to the cinema, she returned to the Ritz Ballroom.

The ladies' room was jam-packed with girls gossiping and giggling as they primped. The air reeked of perfume and face powder. Many of the girls were in ATS uniform. They seemed so sturdy, so full of health and energy and purpose. Clarrie caught a glimpse of her own reflection. She was standing apart, her eyes guarded and watchful—observing, not participating. What is my purpose, she asked herself, why am I always on the outside?

"How does Eric like your new jive frock?" one of the women said to her friend.

"Oh, he loves it." Her eyes sparkled with excitement. "He's sick of seeing me in my uniform, especially these ugly drawers." She stepped away from the mirror and lifted her skirt to straighten the seams of her thick lisle stockings, revealing plump thighs and khaki knickers.

Clarrie powdered her nose and ran a comb through her hair. The feverish excitement around her, the beat of the music coming from the dance floor, were proving irresistible. She took a last glance in the mirror, then made her way down the stairs to the dance floor. Weaving her way through the crowd of onlookers, she took her place near one of the poles that supported the balcony, and looked around, pretending to be searching for someone.

An American sergeant caught her eye and smiled at her. Clarrie smiled back politely. The sergeant made his way towards her. He was only an inch or so taller than she, five-seven or -eight, and his dark hair was thinning at the temples, but his brown eyes, behind rimless spectacles, had a warm, humorous glint. He cleared his throat.

"Are you waiting for someone, or would you like to dance?"

"I'm afraid I don't dance very well," she said.

He grinned. "I'm willing to take my chances. I'm no Fred Astaire, myself."

The band struck up a new tune. "Ah, Duke Ellington!" he said.

"Duke Ellington?" She remembered her short-lived American pen pal mentioning that name in one of her letters.

"He wrote this song. It's called "Don't get around much anymore." The sergeant's hand on hers was warm and firm as he led her onto the dance floor. He drew her close, the brass buttons on his uniform pressing against her chest. She caught a pleasant whiff of shaving soap.

He danced simply, making no sudden moves, attempting no fancy steps, and she had no difficulty following his lead. When the music stopped, there was a scattering of applause. Several couples left the floor as the band began a tango. "Jealousy." She and Griff had danced to this same tune at that last dance. She mustn't think of that.

The American was holding her hand. "What d'y say? Shall we give it a try?"

"Yes." Clarrie said. "I'm game if you are."

He stumbled once or twice, but managed to avoid stepping on her foot. "I do a mean tango," he said.

"What do you mean, 'mean'?"

"What do you mean, what do I mean?" His smile animated his whole face. Lines radiated from the corners of his eyes. Against his olive-skin, his teeth were white and even.

"You said you do a mean tango."

"That means I do a great tango. But I'm being sarcastic. In Brooklyn we turn everything around to mean its opposite."

Clarrie shook her head. "The word 'mean' already means poor. You've turned the word around to mean its opposite—great—then flipped it back to its original meaning."

"Come again?"

"Never mind," Clarrie said. "Actually, you dance rather well. I'm afraid it's your partner who needs lessons."

He asked her name and told her his was Sonny, "Sonny Paradiso."

"Sunny," she said. "As in sunshine?"

"No. Sonny with an O. My real name is Luke—I was named after my grandfather, but everyone calls me Sonny."

"Why?"

"Because I'm my parent's first son, I guess. We call my brother 'Junior', but that's not his real name, either."

Clarrie laughed. "Is his name Luke, too?"

"Anthony, same as my father. Where I come from, there's nothing unusual about calling a kid Sonny or Junior. I guess you don't do that over here."

"No. In an English public school, your brother would be Paradiso Minor and you'd be Paradiso Major."

He grinned. "Thanks for promoting me." He pointed to the three stripes on his khaki jacket. "I'm only Paradiso Sergeant."

"Well, English public schools are really private schools, so you'd still be two stripes ahead."

"Are we speaking the same language?"

"I'm speaking English," Clarrie said. "I'm not sure what language you're speaking."

When the dance was over, they emerged from the artificial light of the dance hall into the grey street. Sonny told her he had to get back to camp, but if she was willing, he'd like to see her again.

"I'll pick you up at your home, if you'll tell me where you live."

Clarrie hesitated. After five years of war, the house was terribly shabby—damp wallpaper peeling in the scullery, and that ugly shelter taking up all the room in the kitchen. She would be ashamed to bring anyone home.

"Salford's a bit out of the way. It would be easier to meet somewhere in town."

"Whatever you say."

They agreed to meet the following evening in front of Manchester's Central Library.

"I thought we'd take in a movie, if that's okay with you," Sonny said next evening.

Clarrie pointed to a poster at the library entrance, advertising a sculpture exhibit. "It's early. I'd like to look at the exhibit before we go."

"Okay."

They walked noiselessly across the white rubber floor and came to a halt before a sculpture—the torso of a man whose lower parts were hidden in a block of granite.

"Consummatum Est," Sonny read. "What do you suppose that means?"

"I think it means 'It is finished'."

"It sure doesn't look finished."

Clarrie giggled. "You ought to show more respect. Epstein is a famous sculptor. I believe this is meant to be Jesus."

"He looks more like Charles Atlas," Sonny said. He flexed his muscles. "You too can have a chest like mine."

Laughing, they left the library and stopped at a café for tea and cake. A Canadian soldier, entering as they were leaving, cast an admiring glance at Clarrie.

"How come you Yanks get all the good-looking girls?" he asked Sonny.

"It's the uniform," Sonny said. He put a protective arm around Clarrie, and steered her across the street to the Odeon Cinema to see Casablanca. After the show, they walked to the bus station shelter arguing the merits of the film. Clarrie was surprised that Sonny was more enthusiastic than she.

"It was too sentimental for my taste," Clarrie said

"You Limeys have no sense of romance."

"Romance and sentimentality are not the same. If he really loved her, he wouldn't have let her go. I don't think they knew how to end it."

"He was trying to do the honorable thing—trying to protect her. What about the music? Didn't you like the music?" He began to sing "As Time Goes By."

They had entered the dim, green-glass bus shelter, and were facing each other, close enough for her to breathe his clean, soapy scent.

"You have a nice singing voice," Clarrie said, "but you've changed the subject. The song is not what we were talking about. "

"In other words, you want me to shut up."

"That's not what I mean. We seem to be having difficulty communicating. We're always at cross purposes."

"Let's not talk then." He pulled her closer and kissed her firmly on the mouth. The kiss was unexpectedly sweet.

"I think we're communicating very well," he said when they came up for air.

Chapter Fifty-nine

They began meeting regularly at the library to catch a film, or to go dancing in one of Manchester's crowded dance halls. Sonny's easy American confidence, his buoyant optimism, seemed to rub off on her. Clarrie found herself laughing more readily, and brooding less over her inadequacies and failures. He gave her small gifts from America—marshmallows covered in toasted coconut, Baby Ruth candy bars, bags of the small, pale, hard-shelled nuts he called chichis. Clarrie, uncomfortably aware of the widespread belief among the G.I.'s that English girls could be bought with a few chocolate bars or a pair of silk stockings, and anxious to dispel any illusions Sonny might have on that score, reciprocated by packing sandwiches and apples and a bottle of ginger beer for a Sunday picnic in the park.

She hated having to borrow her parents' hard-earned money for something as simple as a picnic. Telling herself that it was high time she stopped leaning on them and earned some money of her own, she applied for a job in the recently opened Manchester News Theatre and was hired on the spot as an usherette.

The job, alternating between matinee and evening shifts, required few skills. She was to lead people to their seats with an electric torch, sell ice cream and cigarettes during the intermissions, and open the side doors to let people out when the show ended.

It was enough for now. She was marking time, licking her wounds, waiting for she knew not what.

With her new wages, she splurged on two tickets to a performance of *Hamlet* at the Palace Theatre. Sonny seemed pleased when she gave them to him, but during the second act he dozed off. Clarrie nudged him awake.

"Sorry," he whispered. "I've been on my feet since five this morning."

While they were strolling to the bus stop after the play, Clarrie spoke of her love for poetry. Sonny confessed that he'd never taken much interest in it.

"Ask me about music," he said. "I do know a little something about that." He told her that before joining the Army Air Force, while he was still in high school, he'd played saxophone and clarinet in a small dance band.

"You went to high school?" She'd seen films about American high school students. There didn't appear to be much studying going on. Andy Hardy and his friends seemed to spend a lot of time putting on shows and eating banana splits in the malt shop.

"Everyone in America goes to high school. I wasn't a good student. I used to play hooky from school and stand in line for hours to catch Glenn Miller or Harry James or Benny Goodman at the New York Paramount. The place was always mobbed. Some of the kids got so worked up, they jumped out of their seats and danced in the aisles."

"But not you?"

"I'm not the type to let myself go like that. I was happy just to sit and listen."

"You should try being a little more spontaneous."

"If I have to try, it won't be spontaneous."

"Just do or say whatever pops into your head."

"Okay. When are you going to bring me home to meet your folks?"

"My folks?" Why did he want to meet her family? She'd assumed that as soon as the war ended, Sonny and she would go their separate ways.

"Don't you want to bring me home?"

"I believe that should be 'take me'."

Sonny grinned. "Right here, on the street, in broad daylight?" He slipped an arm around her waist, pulled her closer and kissed her cheek.

Clarrie removed his arm. "Now you're being a little too spontaneous."

"Just how spontaneous do you want me to be? Should I dance on the table with a lampshade on my head?"

"If you're thinking of doing that at my house, you'll have to bring your own lampshade—we haven't got any."

"Is that an invitation?"

"If you're free, you can come to dinner on Sunday, but I warn you, our house is old and shabby—five years of war haven't helped."

"I don't care about the house, I want to meet your family."

"You'll find us a bit rough, I'm afraid. Lancashire folk have a reputation for bluntness."

Sonny grinned. "I'm from Brooklyn, honey. They don't come any blunter than that."

That evening, over supper, Clarrie broached the subject of Sonny's visit.

"Why must it be an American?" her father asked, "what's wrong with a nice English chap?"

"Well, for one thing, no nice English chap has bothered to ask me out."

"That's because they're all fighting on foreign soil," Annie said.

"The G.I.'s are on foreign soil too."

Her father snorted contemptuously. "You'd never know it, the way those military policemen carry on down at the docks—you'd think they owned the place—chewing gum, swinging their bloody truncheons, throwing their weight around."

"Sonny's not like that. Anyway, I've already invited him."

"And what are we supposed to feed the poor bugger?"

"We'll manage," her mother said. "We can kill one of the chickens. And if we drink our tea without sugar for a few days there'll be enough for an apple pie."

Clarrie cast a critical eye over the room. "Can't we get the shelter out of here? I hate to bring Sonny home with that eyesore looming over everything." "Sonny?" her father said. "What kind of a name is that for a grown man?"

"His name is Luke, actually."

Her mother opened the cupboard door and pulled out a half-empty bottle of Camp Coffee. "Americans like coffee, don't they?"

"They don't drink that bottled stuff," Clarrie said. "It's got chicory in it."

"If the bottled stuff is good enough for us, it's good enough for him," her father said.

"Sonny says they cook coffee in something called a percolator. It's got a tube down the middle that keeps the water bubbling up over the coffee grinds."

"They had one of those in that picture with Katherine Hepburn," Annie said. "She didn't know how to work it, and she let it boil all over the place."

Her mother put the bottled coffee back. "Where am I going to find a thing like that in Salford?"

"Can't you boil it in a pan?" Clarrie asked.

"Aye, that's what I'll do. I read in one of those books about pioneers that the trick is to let it boil up three times. I think they put an eggshell in it, too, and a pinch of salt. I've always wanted to try it. I'll go into Manchester tomorrow and see if I can find some coffee. I've got to take Billy in anyway. He's lost his new cap; I'll have to buy him another."

"See if you can find some fresh flowers for the table while you're at it, Mam," Clarrie said.

"Flowers? Coffee?" William blew out a cloud of smoke. "Is President Roosevelt coming to dinner?"

"I suspect that this young man means more to our Clarrie than she's letting on," her mother said.

Clarrie reddened. "I just want him to feel welcome. Our Arthur said the Americans were very nice to him when he was on leave in New York."

On Saturday as she was leaving to do the shopping, Sally asked William to kill one of the chickens. "Put it in the sink and I'll pluck it when I come back."

William put down his paper with a sigh. "I wish you'd stop trying to turn me into a bloody farmer. You know I don't know the first damn thing about killing a chicken."

"Well, it's time you learned. You have to stun it first, then chop its head off with the axe. Choose a nice fat one, but not the one with the dark patch on its wing. Clarrie and Annie can do the cleaning up afterwards."

Annie switched on the wireless. "You brush the stairs down, our Clarrie, while I tackle the windows."

Clarrie wrapped a kerchief around her hair and went to fetch a brush and dustpan from the cellar-head. Her father was standing in the open door of the scullery gazing into the yard at the chickens. "Courage, Dad," she said.

"Bloody chickens," he muttered. "I hope you're not expecting me to be here when this Yankee chap comes tomorrow, because I'm going out."

"He's expecting to meet you, Dad. He'll think it strange if you're not here."

"You can tell him I had to see a man about a dog. Fetch me the axe. I'd better get this chicken business over with."

Clarrie brought the axe up from the cellar and went back into the kitchen. "I believe he's actually going to do it," she said to Annie.

She was on her knees, brushing the stair carpet when she heard a loud squawking coming from the scullery. The squawking was accompanied by a string of oaths. Clarrie dropped the brush and ran downstairs.

Annie came down from the ladder with a bucket in her hand. "This I've got to see."

The scullery door opened. Their father stood in the doorway trembling, his face white, his glasses and woolen undershirt splattered with blood. There was blood on the axe in his shaking hand. "Run quick! Fetch your mother," he croaked. "The bloody chicken is running around with its head hanging off."

Clarrie dashed out to the corner bus stop, but there was no sign of her mother or Billy. She ran back to the house. Annie and her father were standing in the middle of the scullery, where the expiring chicken lay on its side in a pool of blood. Feathers were drifting soft as thistledown about their heads. Blood was smeared over the sink, the meat safe, the draining board, and the walls.

"Dad's gone and killed the wrong one," Annie said. "This is Chirpy, Billy's pet."

"How the hell was I supposed to know? Your mother said something about the fat one with the dark patch. I thought it was the one she wanted me to kill." He picked up the chicken by the feet, and threw it on the draining board. "I've got to get washed and changed. I'm going out. You two better take care of this mess before your mother comes back."

Clarrie and Annie worked quickly and soon cleaned up the scullery. Back in the kitchen, Clarrie looked balefully at the Morrison shelter.

"What's the use of trying to make the house look nice with this monstrosity taking up all the space?"

"Mam's asked them a couple of times to come and take it away," Annie said. "They told her it would take four or five men to move it, and they can't spare them right now. I bet we could do it ourselves if we took it apart first."

Clarrie pulled aside the cloth and crawled underneath to see how the shelter was put together. Billy had adopted the shelter as his private cave. Among the blankets and cushions and old coats was a heap of dog-eared magazines—*Hotspurs*, *Wizards*, and *Beanos*—and lined up against the wall, a row of jam jars holding Billy's shrapnel collection. Clarrie examined each corner. "The nuts and bolts are easy to reach," she said to Annie. "Nothing seems to have been soldered." She crawled out. "Let's do it."

Annie began pulling out the blankets and pillows.

"Be careful," Clarrie said, "they're full of crumbs." She took the bedclothes to the scullery to be washed, and came back with her father's toolbox. "Irresistible force meets immovable object," she said.

They were carrying the old table in from the front room when their mother came in, her arms full of Michaelmas daisies. "What're you doing?" she asked.

"We're moving the old table back," Annie said. "We shifted the shelter into the back yard."

"Just the two of you?"

"Aye. Looks as if two women are equal to four or five men."

"You girls shouldn't be lifting things like that. Our Clarrie's not got her full strength back, yet. Where's your dad? Did he kill that chicken?"

"Where's Billy?" Clarrie asked

"He's gone to his pal's . . . why?"

"Dad killed Chirpy by mistake."

"Oh, Lord! That child's going to be heartbroken. Still, it can't be helped. We'd have had to kill Chirpy sooner or later—the poor old thing had stopped laying."

"You should have seen Dad, " Annie said. She did an imitation of her father, dithering in the doorway with the axe, calling for them to run and fetch their mother. The three women laughed until tears ran down their cheeks.

"Poor Billy," Clarrie said when they had calmed down. "Not only did we chop Chirpy's head off, we've taken apart his cave, too."

"It's a relief to have it gone," their mother said. "The room looks almost spacious without it." She went into the scullery to pluck the chicken, while Clarrie and Annie cleaned the kitchen. When they'd finished, Clarrie surveyed the room. The fireplace gleamed, the windows sparkled, and the house looked as fresh and cheerful as it was possible to make it.

Sonny arrived early on Sunday afternoon, just as William was about to make his escape. Through the open lobby door, Clarrie saw the two men shake hands. Her father took Sonny's hat, hesitated for a moment, then took off his own hat, and walked back with Sonny into the kitchen. Billy, who'd been waiting on the corner with several friends, followed them in. The boys crowded around Sonny, admiring his uniform, asking questions about America and about the different airplanes he worked on. "Got any gum, chum?" they asked him.

"You lads ought to remember your manners and not be so cheeky," William said. "Don't you have any homes to go to?"

"It's all right," Sonny said. He handed out sticks of gum, and the boys, except for Billy, beat a hasty retreat.

"I expected someone a bit taller," Annie said, eyeing Sonny critically. "I thought they grew everything bigger in America, but my Walter would make two of you."

Sonny grinned good-naturedly. "It's out West where they grow 'em big."

"Pay no attention to our Annie," Clarrie said. "She thinks she's being funny."

Her mother lifted the roast chicken out of the oven and carried it to the table. "Dinner's ready!"

"This is one of the chickens we raised ourselves," Clarrie said.

"We?" Annie said. "You mean Mam, don't you? I've never seen you go anywhere near them."

William picked up the carving knife. "And you couldn't leave them alone," he said to Annie. He turned to Sonny. "One day she gave all the chickens a bath and set them shivering on the windowsill to dry—freezing cold it was, too—it's a miracle they didn't perish from pneumonia."

"They looked better when they dried." Annie passed her plate to her mother. "And poor old Chirpy looks a lot better now than she did when she was running round the scullery with her head half off."

Sally flashed Annie a warning glance.

Billy looked up. "Did she say Chirpy?" His face had suddenly become stained with red blotches.

Sally glared at Annie. "You couldn't keep your mouth shut."

Billy jumped up. "You've killed Chirpy!"

"It was an accident, love, your dad made a mistake."

"How could anyone make a mistake like that?"

William took a sip of water to stop his coughing. "I'm not a farmer, am I?" he said when he recovered. "I can't tell one bloody chicken from another."

Billy headed for the stairs. "I'm not eating Chirpy!"

"Get back here young man, and eat your vegetables," Sally said. "I made a nice apple pie for dessert. You love apple pie."

"You didn't even notice Chirpy was gone," Annie said. "She couldn't have been all that important to you."

"I don't want any dinner!" Billy ran upstairs. A moment of silence descended on the table.

"Well," Clarrie said to Sonny. "You asked for it. You've only yourself to blame."

"It's a lot like home," he said.

"I thought everything ran like clockwork in America." Annie said.

Sonny grinned. "Some of us have a tendency to brag."

William was reminded of a drunken G.I. in the pub, who was bragging about America's superiority:

"'Cricket?' The G.I. spoke loudly enough for everyone in the pub to hear. 'What kinda fancy-pants game is that? You wanna real man's game, yous ought to switch to baseball, and while you're at it, youz ought to get rid of your King and Queen. They got no place in the modern world.'

"A chap at the next table, spoke up. 'Thanks for the advice, Yank, but we happen to like cricket. We happen to like our King, too.'

"The American took another gulp of beer. 'Oh, yeah? Well, I say the hell with cricket, and the hell with King George.'

"'Well,' the English chap says, 'I say to hell with baseball . . . and I say to hell with . . . with . . .' He apparently couldn't bring himself to say anything derogatory about President Roosevelt, so after hesitating for a minute, he ended triumphantly with, 'I say to hell with Babe Ruth!'"

"We all love your President Roosevelt, over here, you know," Annie said when everyone had stopped laughing. "But we don't understand why it took America so long to get into the war."

"Pay no attention to our Annie," Sally said. "He must have had a good reason."

William wanted to know about American politics. "Now, as I understand it," he said to Sonny, "your senate is like our House of Lords, and your congress is like our House of Commons."

"Not exactly." Sonny looked uncomfortable. "I can't say I understand how your government works either."

"Leave the poor lad alone, Will," her mother said. "Let him eat his pie." She hovered anxiously over Sonny. "Is your coffee all right, love?"

Sonny looked up, surprised. "Oh, is this coffee?"

There was a shriek of laughter around the table.

Sonny's ears reddened. "I mean . . . I thought that . . . well . . . this being England, I assumed . . ." He stopped. "I guess I'm up the creek without a paddle," he said sheepishly.

Sally took his cup. "Let me make you a cup of tea," she said. "That's something I do know how to do."

"Well, what did you think of him?" Clarrie asked after Sonny had gone.

"He's a nice chap, Sonny," her mother said. "He seems down to earth. I liked him right from the start."

"I've seen worse," her father said.

Clarrie smiled. Coming from her father, this was praise indeed.

Chapter Sixty

After that first visit, Sonny came regularly to the house. He presented William with several large cans of grapefruit juice.

"Clarrie tells me you don't get any citrus fruit. I thought maybe you could use these. It's very sour—the guys at the base call it battery acid—but it might help clear your bronchitis."

"It's good stuff, that grapefruit juice," William told Sonny. "Battery acid or not, it does the trick. I thank you for it."

And when Sonny arrived at the house one day flushed and shivering, Sally took his temperature and made him sit by the fire with a blanket around his shoulders while she went out to get some patent medicine. She came back with a small bottle of brandy.

"Brandy?" Clarrie said. She'd never known her mother to bring alcohol into the house.

Her mother's rosy face grew redder. "The poor lad's caught a chill. He ought to be in bed." She poured a jigger of the brandy into a cup of hot tea and sweetened it with black currant jam. "It's better with a squeeze of lemon," she said, "but it's been years since we've seen a fresh lemon."

Sonny sipped his drink. "This is great. It's like being home. The army doesn't believe you're sick unless your temperature's over a hundred and two."

Seeing Sonny huddled by the fire, basking in her mother's warm ministrations, Clarrie thought how young he looked—much younger than when she'd first met him. He was only three years older than she, and yet so protective of her. She felt a rush of tenderness—for Sonny, for her mother, for both of them together.

Clarrie, with Billy in tow, showed Sonny some of her old haunts—the barren open place where her school had once stood, and the tip. While Billy hunted for shrapnel, she told Sonny stories of her childhood—how she'd been lost at the fair, how she and Gladys had discovered her grandfather dead in his allotment shed.

She and Sonny walked down to Weaste Cemetery, where Clarrie bought a bunch of blue scabious from a flower seller. She told Sonny how she'd slipped down into the bomb crater and seen the skeleton. The craters had been filled in, and the shattered stones cleared away, but with so many headstones gone, she couldn't get her bearings. As they passed an overgrown grave, edged with white marble, a white headstone and the name "Hutchins," caught her eye. She read the inscription: Marjorie Jean Hutchins, infant, born September 11th, 1930; died, November 27th, 1930. "Suffer the Little Children to Come Unto Me." Underneath was a second inscription: "Albert Hutchins, born April 3, 1892; died, November 27th, 1934. Rest in Peace."

"He was our butcher," Clarrie told Sonny. "My mother used to work for him. He was such a kind man. He hanged himself on a meat hook."

"Same day of the month as his daughter died," Sonny said.

"So it is. I hadn't noticed." Clarrie's eyes filled with tears. It was starting to rain, and there seemed little hope of ever finding where Granny Hancock and Janet were buried. "God bless them, anyway," Clarrie said. She laid the blue scabious on Mr. Hutchins's grave.

Walking around Manchester one afternoon, she and Sonny stopped to watch a number of war prisoners at work refilling a bomb crater. She told Sonny how she had crawled under the barrier to dodge past the bomb.

"Not a live bomb, I hope?"

"Of course it was live. It was right after a raid. I was late for work and all the streets were roped off. It was a bit of a lark, actually."

"A lark. Like playing Russian roulette? Plain stupid it seems to me. I don't admire stuff like that."

Clarrie fell silent. She hadn't told him about her suicide attempt. This was the first time he had said anything critical of her.

"These guys don't look like Germans," Sonny said, indicating the war prisoners.

"No. They're eyeties," she said.

"Eyeties?"

"Italians. That's what everybody calls them."

"Eyeties. I suppose it's better than being called wops, but it still sounds like an insult."

"Well, they're the enemy—were, that is, before they switched sides."

"I'm an eyetie too, you know. These guys all look like my relatives in Brooklyn."

Clarrie blushed. She had forgotten about his Italian background. She studied the prisoners. They were a ragged bunch; dark, scrawny, unshaven. Bent over their shovels, they appeared to be very much defeated. She looked at Sonny, at his smooth-shaven face, his smart uniform, his confident bearing. "You're an American," she said, "there's a world of difference."

"I'd be in their shoes if my grandparents hadn't emigrated to the States," he said. "If we were to get married and have children, they'd be part eyetie, too. How would you feel about that?"

Clarrie laughed nervously. "Children? Aren't you jumping ahead a little?"

One of the prisoners had paused in his work and was leaning on his shovel, gazing at her with frank admiration. Sonny put a possessive arm around her waist. "That poor guy's drooling over you. Let's get out of here."

Fine needles of rain pricked their faces as they crossed the square. They walked down Princess Street in the growing dusk and stood side-by-side looking over the bridge into the canal.

"When I worked at the factory, I sometimes spent my lunch hour down there," she said. "It was the only place I could read in peace." She described how Grimsby's factory had buckled and fallen into the canal. "Let's go down and walk along the bank," she said.

Sonny held her hand, and with the help of his flashlight they made their way down the mossy steps.

She was not wearing stockings, and the walk had made blisters on her heels. On the bottom step, she sat to unlace her shoes.

"What are you doing?" Sonny asked.

"I want to go barefoot."

"Don't do that."

"Nobody can see us. You needn't be embarrassed."

"It's too cold, and you might step on broken glass or something."

"Shine your torch on the ground, then."

The stones felt cold and slippery under her feet as they walked along the towpath. "Let's sit for a while," she said.

They'd reached her old reading nook at the corner of a low brick wall near the lock. She told him about the barge people, about the way they tied the barges to the capstan while they raised or lowered the water level.

"Right now," Sonny said, "I'm not interested in the water level. I want to know how you feel about me—about us."

A brackish smell rose from the canal. Water slapped gently against the wooden lock. Clarrie shivered. Sonny pulled her to his side, and chafed her hands. His hands were strong, warm and dry.

"Why don't you answer me?"

"I don't know what to say. I'm not sure how I feel."

"Now who's being cautious?"

"We're very different," she said. "Different nationalities, different interests, different religions . . ."

"Different sexes," he said.

"I don't think that's quite enough for . . ." She hesitated. "Whatever you have in mind," she said lamely.

"You know what I have in mind. They'll be shipping us back to the States any day now, and I'm afraid I may not get a chance to see you again."

"I'm sure there'll be lots of glamorous American girls to help you get over me."

"I'm not interested in any glamorous American girls."

"Why, what's wrong with them?"

"They're not you."

"Ah, the poor, unfortunate creatures."

"You have all the qualities I admire in a woman."

"Such as?"

"Gentleness, intelligence, a sense of humor—"

"For a moment there I thought you might be interested in my body."

He kissed her. "I was coming to that," he said. "I was about to tell you that I love your soft skin, your silky hair, your shapely hands, your sweet kissable mouth . . ." He kissed her lightly. His mouth was warm and firm. She caught a whiff of shaving soap.

"You've forgotten my eyes, like limpid pools," she said.

"I didn't forget them. You interrupted."

"Don't stop," Clarrie said.

"What I love most of all is your finesse."

"My what?"

"Finesse. You know—refinement, class."

"Class?" Clarrie laughed. "You're laboring under a misapprehension—I'm a common working girl—one of the rabble—the great unwashed."

He kissed her again. "I know class when I see it. You are perfect."

"Please don't say that. You don't know me."

"What don't I know? Tell me."

The blood rushed to her face. She unbuttoned her blouse. "I'll show you."

"Oh, Clarrie, don't do this to me now. I have to walk back to the station in a few minutes."

She removed the gauze pad from under her breast.

"Look."

"What? What arc you doing? I can't see anything."

"Use your flashlight."

He flicked on the light. "Jesus. What happened?"

"I shot myself."

There was a long silence.

"You're shocked and disgusted. I don't blame you."

"I'm not disgusted. I am shocked, though. When did this happen?"

"I'd just been released from the hospital when I met you."

"What made you do it? Was it over some guy?"

"There was somebody I thought I was in love with, but . . ."

"What did he do to you? Did he take advantage of you?"

"He kissed me once, that's all."

"Why, then?"

"I don't know why."

"How could you do this to yourself ?" He stroked the injured breast with one finger. Your breasts are just the way I imagined them . . . like Venus de Milo."

"Except for the rather ugly wound," Clarrie said.

A beam of light came bobbing towards them over the cobblestones. Sonny swung his light in the other direction. Clarrie caught the gleam of a badge on a policeman's helmet. "It's a bobby," she whispered. She hastily buttoned her blouse.

"What's going on here?" The policeman shone his torch into Clarrie's face. His voice softened. "Are you all right, miss?"

"Yes, thank you."

"Right." He shone the torch in Sonny's face. "I think you'd better get this young lady home before her mam starts to worry."

"We're just talking," Sonny said. "We're trying to decide whether or not to get married."

"Oh, aye?" The policeman sounded skeptical. "We have an old saying round here my lad, 'If you don't want the goods, don't maul 'em'."

Clarrie began putting her shoes on. "We were just about to leave, Constable."

"What was eating that cop?" Sonny said, as they climbed back up the steps and into the street. "Is it against the law to neck with your girl in this country?"

"Perhaps he saw my blouse open and assumed you were trying to take advantage of my innocence."

"Shooting yourself. You must have been crazy to do a thing like that."

She released his hand. The rain was stinging her face, bedraggling her hair.

"You always seem so happy," Sonny said.

"Obviously, I'm not." There was a rumble of thunder, and a flash of lightning illuminated a display of trusses and artificial limbs in a plate glass window. The rain came pelting down. Sonny put his hand on her back, steered her into a dark doorway, drew her close and kissed her. Clarrie pushed him away.

"You're going to miss your train," she said. "There's no need to see me to the bus."

"I'm taking you to the bus stop," Sonny said.

"I think we ought to break this off before we get in any deeper," she said when they reached the bus shelter. "We really have little in common. It's all happening too fast."

"I admit you've thrown me a curve ball."

"And you need time to think it over—to decide if you really want to marry someone with a screw loose?" She kept her voice light, thankful for the cover of darkness.

"Don't talk like that." He tried again to kiss her, but she swerved her head away.

"I need time to think, too," she said. "We should stay away from each other for a while."

"Stay away? For how long?" Dimmed headlights shone through the green glass shelter as the bus pulled in.

"At least a month. You can write to me when the month is up—if you still wish to see me, that is."

"Clarrie!" Sonny caught her by the sleeve and brushed her lips with his as she stepped aboard the bus.

"One month," she said.

Chapter Sixty-one

The Manchester News Theatre was a miracle of modern design. Its curved bucket seats, shaped to conform to the contours of the human body and tastefully upholstered in a nubby indigo fabric, were set in a semicircle that sloped gradually down toward the screen. Heavy draperies of the same indigo fabric lined the walls, muffling the sounds of the outside world.

Clarrie finished showing people to their seats for the matinee and took up her post under the glowing red exit sign above the side door. Music swelled; the blue draperies concealing the screen parted; the shimmering transparent curtains rippled back and the all-news program began. British forces in Germany had liberated a prison camp at a place called Belsen.

A line of dazed, starving prisoners shambled past a barbed wire fence, their striped garments filthy, their faces devoid of expression. It was as if they neither understood nor cared that their captivity was ended. The faces of the British soldiers registered horror and disbelief.

One of the soldiers, his nose and mouth covered by a handkerchief, was operating a sort of bulldozer above a heap of human corpses. The shovel moved forward, scooping up bodies as though they were so much rubbish; churning bodies tumbled, flinging out skeletal arms, stick legs, knees and ankles knobby as tree roots. A gasp went up from the audience.

Clarrie looked away, blinded by tears. When she looked back at the screen, the driver of the bulldozer had climbed down, and was doubled over, retching.

The newsreel continued, revealing horror upon horror, until the curtain rippled back, signifying that the news from Europe had ended. Several people got up to leave. "Those Germans must have gone insane," a woman said as she passed by Clarrie. An old man half-rose from his seat. "Is it over, love?" he asked.

"Not yet, sir," Clarrie said. He sat down again. A portentous male voice announced the "March of Time" and a row of American beauty contestants, in bathing suits and high-heeled shoes, paraded across the screen, their teeth, skin, and hair glowing with preternatural health. One by one, they paused to smile for the camera as the announcer read out the bust, waist, and hip measurements. When the beauty contest ended, a pretty housewife in a frilly apron stepped into a gleaming, antiseptic kitchen to demonstrate a new electric dishwashing machine.

The opening strains of "God Save the King" brought the remaining audience to its feet. Clarrie pushed open the exit door. A veil of blue cigarette smoke swirled for a moment in the open doorway and then the light flooded in. Across the street, an American G.I. was leaning against the wall reading. Sonny! Less than a week had passed since their last meeting, but there he was. He folded his newspaper and threaded his way through the crowd towards her.

"I thought we had an agreement," Clarrie said as he approached.

"I know. I'm not supposed to be here. I came out without a pass. I had to crawl out under barbed wire behind the firing range."

"Well, you shouldn't have."

He stroked her cheek. "You've been crying. What's happened?"

She stepped aside to let somebody by. "I'm through for the day. Wait here while I close my section and get my coat."

"Where shall we go?" he asked when she returned. "I haven't got much time."

At the corner of the street, they caught a bus to Platt Fields, where they sat on the grassy bank by the duck pond.

"Why were you crying?"

"It was the newsreel . . . a concentration camp . . . Oh, it was so horrible . . ."

Sonny put an arm around her shoulder. "The Germans are animals."

"They're human beings, Sonny, just like us. Given the same conditions, who knows what we'd be capable of ?" The tears spilled over.

He stroked her back, kissed her cheek. "I can't imagine you ever hurting anyone."

A family of white ducks drifted into view. A small bespectacled boy, wearing a cap, ran to the edge of the pond and threw scraps of bread to them. Sonny took a fresh handkerchief from his pocket and wiped her face.

"I've already hurt a lot of people," Clarrie said. "I hurt my parents cruelly when I tried to kill myself. I very nearly destroyed their lives as well as my own."

"You weren't trying to hurt anyone but yourself."

"But I did. I was so self-absorbed, I didn't even consider how it would affect my family. As a child, I always imagined evil spirits—demons with horrible faces lurking in the curtains and in the wallpaper. They seemed to be watching me, waiting their chance to suck me into their world. I think they almost got me."

Sonny hugged her, kissed her on the mouth. "Maybe you should wear a clove of garlic around your neck."

"Garlic?"

He grinned. "An old Italian superstition. Garlic is supposed to protect you from the evil eye."

"Witchcraft?"

"I guess. I was kinda puny as a kid—wouldn't eat my pastina. I was sick all the time with colds, earaches, sore throats—you name it. The doctor came to the house and took out my tonsils—on the kitchen table, if you can believe it—but it didn't help. My mother got a bug in her head that someone had given me the evil eye." Sonny gave an embarrassed shrug. "She took me to the neighborhood medicine woman to have the curse removed. I was about four or five at the time. I remember being stretched out on a table with candles around me, like a corpse at a wake. The witch, or whatever she was, muttered some prayers, and then put garlic around my neck and on my navel."

"Did it work?"

"In a way. After that, if I refused to eat, Ma only had to threaten to take me back to the witch woman and I'd choke down my dinner in a hurry. And as you can see, I grew up strong and sassy. By the way, if you ever get to meet her, don't mention it. My mother doesn't like to talk about it. She prides herself on being a modern, enlightened woman—she belongs to the League of Women Voters—but as she says, when your kid is sick, you'll try anything."

He glanced at his watch. "I need to get back, and we haven't even talked about . . . what I wanted to talk about."

"I thought we'd agreed to separate for a month."

"But this is urgent. Now that the war's over in Europe, I expect to be shipping out soon."

"Where will they send you?

"I'll probably wind up in the Pacific. I don't want to take the chance of losing you." Sonny's voice broke. "When the war's all over, I want you to come with me, back to the States." They fell silent, watching the ducklings squabble over a crust of bread.

"Do you think you could take me on?" Sonny said at last.

"Take you on? Are you suggesting a wrestling match?"

"I'm trying to propose marriage," Sonny said. "I've never done anything like this before. You're not making it any easier."

"What about my crazy suicide attempt, and my ugly scars?"

"You took me by surprise, that's all. It doesn't change the way I feel about you. I thought you felt something for me, too. Was I wrong?" The ducks had finished the bread and were drifting away.

"I'm not sure how I feel. We hardly know one another, Sonny, and you're asking me to leave my family, my country, everything I love."

"But we'll be together. You'll like it in the States."

A jumble of scenes from American films flashed through her mind—Indians riding bareback across the prairie, the Joad family driving from the dust bowl in their overloaded jalopy, Jimmy Cagney rattling his prison bars with a tin cup, Jimmy Stewart filibustering congress . . .

"I can't imagine what it's like over there. Where would we live?"

"My parents own a house in Brooklyn. We'd have to stay with them until we find our own place."

He described his parents' house: two six-room apartments, one above the other. His family lived on the ground floor and rented out the apartment upstairs. The walls were painted, not wallpapered. There were tiles halfway up in the kitchen and bathroom. The rooms were warmed by radiators.

"No fireplaces?"

"There's a coal furnace in the basement."

"But . . . when you're home in the evenings, where do you sit? I mean, what do you look at?"

He shrugged. "I've never really thought about it—at each other, I guess, or at the radio."

A vivid picture flashed into Clarrie's mind—she and Sonny, sitting side by side in a bare, white room, staring at a radio. "What would we do?" she asked him, "How would we spend our time?"

He'd take her to Chinatown, he said, to Greenwich Village and to Coney Island. They'd see all the shows in the New York theatres, take moonlight boat trips up the Hudson, ice skate at Rockefeller Center, feast on lobsters at Sheepshead Bay . . .

"Sounds wonderful. What would we use for money?"

"I know sheet-metal work; I've taken courses in electronics—and there's my music. I'm pretty good on the sax and the clarinet. My father thinks I'm good enough to play with one of the big bands, but there's a lot of stiff competition."

"I'd love to hear you."

"Come with me to New York and you will." He looked at his watch. "I've got to get back to base before they miss me. Be thinking about what I said. I'll meet you outside the library tomorrow." He kissed her.

Through the window of the bus, Clarrie watched the twilight shrouding the streets. People were hurrying home from work, heads down, past gutted buildings, boarded-up shop windows. An old woman in clogs and shawl clumped along, shaking her head, muttering to herself. It was only the old women now, Clarrie thought, who wore clogs and shawls. Soon, there'd be none of their generation left to keep up, or even remember, the old customs. She was filled with a sense of grief and loss. Nothing lasted. Everything was shifting, changing, disappearing before her eyes. The future was a closed door to which she had no key.

That night she dreamed that she and Sonny were walking along a street when the earth suddenly split in two, opening a deep jagged chasm between them. From opposite sides of a widening rift, they reached out and grasped each other's hands.

The dream seemed to be telling her that she and Sonny must hold on to each other. But how could she be sure he was the right man for her? She hadn't had a chance to get over that business in Kent, to get over Griff, and here she was contemplating marriage. It was all happening so fast: she felt she was being drawn into marriage by a force more powerful and compelling than her own will.

Chapter Sixty-two

"Next month, you say?" William reached for the poker and thrust it between the bars of the grate.

"Yes, sir," Sonny said. "We're hoping for your approval."

When William failed to respond, Sonny cast a questioning glance at Clarrie.

"So what do you think, then, Dad?" she asked. Her father balanced the poker handle against the fender, thrust two tobacco-stained fingers into the breast pocket of his waistcoat and brought out a half-smoked cigarette. With the stub between his lips he leaned forward, took the poker from the fire and lit the cigarette. He turned to Sonny. The milky ball of his bad eye quivered as it shot to the side and back. "A bit sudden, isn't it? What's your hurry, lad?"

"There's a rumor we'll be shipping out soon. I figure I'll be sent home, back to the States."

William released a ring of blue smoke. "All the more reason to wait—give yourselves time to think it over."

Sally came in from the scullery. "Think what over? What're you talking about?"

William sat down in his chair and took a puff of his cigarette. "They're thinking of getting married next month. Sonny wants our Clarrie to go with him to America."

Sally looked from Clarrie to Sonny. She set the teacups on their saucers. "Marriage is a big step, love."

"I know." Sonny glanced at Clarrie. "Normally, we'd wait, but these aren't normal times. If we get married while I'm still in the service, the Army will pay Clarrie's passage to the United States."

"I see." William rose from his chair again and began jabbing at the coal.

"If I'm out of the service, it will be a while before I can get the money together and send for her."

"What are you planning to do then lad, when you're demobbed?"

Sonny shot a questioning look at Clarrie.

"When you're out of the service," she said.

"I'm not worried about that. I'll soon find something."

"He knows how to repair airplanes, and he's a musician," Clarrie said.

William nodded. "I've no doubt you're a capable sort of chap, but it might be harder than you think. There'll be a lot of other chaps getting out, looking for work—that's what happened after the last war."

"I guess we'll have to take our chances, along with everyone else."

William sighed. "I hope you know what you're doing, the pair of you."

"You'll have to excuse us, love," Sally said. "America's a long way away, and we can't help worrying. I was hoping our Annie would get married first—she's the eldest, you know. Have you thought about where you'll be getting married?"

Sonny shrugged. "I'll leave that up to Clarrie."

"Her dad and I were married in a registry office. We didn't want any fuss."

"I want to be married in church," Clarrie said quickly, "if that's all right with you, Sonny."

"Whatever you say."

"If it's to be only a month from now, you'd better get down to the church and make the arrangements," Sally said. "The rector will need time to call the banns. You can have your tea when you get back."

"Call the what?" Sonny said.

"The banns," Clarrie said. "In church they make a public announcement of a couple's intention to marry. They do it for three or four Sundays before the wedding. It gives people time to come forward if they know of any obstacle to the marriage."

"What do they consider an obstacle?" Sonny asked as they walked to the rectory.

"I don't know—a wife or a husband one of the parties might have forgotten to mention, perhaps."

"Like Orson Welles in that movie we saw."

"Jane Eyre. Yes. The novel is better than the film—Charlotte Bronte. You don't happen to have a demented wife back there in America, do you, locked up in your attic?"

"I don't even have an attic, so unless you've got something to hide, I think we're in the clear."

"I believe I've told you all my secrets."

"What if this priest, or whatever he is, won't agree to marry us?"

"He's called a rector. Why should he refuse?"

Sonny shrugged. "Because I'm a Catholic, sort of."

"Would you rather we got married in the Roman Catholic Church?"

Clarrie had from time to time broached the subject of religion, but in this matter, Sonny, like everyone else she knew, didn't like to talk about it.

"Not particularly. I went to church mostly to keep peace with my mother. If we got married in the Catholic

Church, we'd have to promise to raise the children Catholic, and . . ."

"And what?"

"Catholics aren't supposed to practice artificial birth control. We'd wind up with a houseful of kids, and we haven't even got the house yet."

Clarrie laughed. "Looks as if those hypothetical little eyeties of ours are causing trouble already!"

Sonny slipped an arm around her waist. "They take after their mother."

On the way back from the rectory, Clarrie stopped to make an appointment at the hairdresser's. A plump young woman with bleached hair was sweeping up clippings from the floor. Clarrie recognized her old classmate, Muriel Monk.

"Muriel?"

"Clarrie? I didn't recognize you. What have you been up to?"

"Muriel and I went to school together," she told Sonny "But we haven't seen each other for ages. How long have you been a hairdresser, Muriel?"

"I'm actually a trained beautician. I'll be giving it up soon though, to get married."

"Is it anyone I know? Richard Beaumont, perhaps?"

"Richard Beaumont?" Muriel frowned. "The name's familiar, but I can't place him."

"He used to be sweet on you. You signed his autograph book."

"Oh. That red-haired kid from Sunday school. I haven't seen him for years. No, I'm engaged to Herbert Wardle. He's in the navy, but he'll be getting out soon."

"You're marrying Herbert?" Clarrie couldn't hide her astonishment. Muriel Monk—everyone's little darling, the very spit and image of Shirley Temple—engaged to chubby Herbert Wardle!

"I'm getting married, too," Clarrie said. "This is—" She hesitated. The word "fiancé" did not fall readily from her lips, and "my intended" sounded common. Too bad the good old English word "betrothed" had fallen out of favor. "—my fiancé," she said, capitulating. "We've just come from the rectory. The wedding's set for the second week in August. I want to make arrangements to have a permanent wave. I'm told it might take a few weeks before it's at its best."

Muriel put down her broom and felt Clarrie's hair. "Yes. A perm's the only thing for hair like this. It's very limp isn't it? A bit drabbish, too. You could use a touch-up." She brought out an appointment book. "You'll need to have it done right away. I'm booked for the rest of the fortnight, but I've nothing on tonight. I'm going home for my tea, now, but I can take you around seven, if that's all right."

Clarrie shot a questioning looked at Sonny.

"I'm due back at the base by nine, anyway."

"Very well." Clarrie smiled at Muriel. "I'll come back later."

On the way home, she told Sonny how Muriel had got the doll meant for her. "She got the boy I wanted, too."

"The kid with the red hair?"

"The same. Muriel was very pretty and well-dressed. I was a bit jealous of her. I can't picture her marrying Herbert."

She told him how Herbert used to march home from the Boys' Brigade, beating his drum and bellowing "Onward Christian Soldiers." "I wore a pair of his baggy pajamas once, for a Sunday school play. He seemed to think that made me his girl."

"You wear a guy's pajamas, what can you expect?"

"Well, it looks as though I've lost my admirer. You men can't be trusted around blondes. Those bouncing yellow curls get you every time."

"Not necessarily," Sonny said. "Some guys prefer limp and drabbish."

When they got back to the house, it was Arthur, looking handsome and fit in his Royal Marine uniform, who opened the front door.

Clarrie flung herself into his arms and burst into tears.

Arthur patted her back. "There you go again with the old waterworks."

Sonny handed her a handkerchief. "Thanks." Clarrie wiped her eyes. "This is my brother, Arthur," she said.

Sonny grinned. "I kinda figured . . ."

"We didn't know where he was. I was about to write and tell him our news."

"Mam has already told me." Arthur turned to Sonny. "You must be the . . ."

"Yeah, I'm it. Sonny Paradiso." The two men shook hands.

"How long are you home for?" Clarrie asked. "I want you to be here for the wedding."

"Sorry, love. I wish I could, but I have to be back in Portsmouth in a couple of days."

"It's not fair," Clarrie said.

"Tell it to the Marines."

They walked into the kitchen. Sally had the green cloth folded back, and was chopping parsley on the bare wooden table.

"Where's Dad?" Clarrie asked.

"He had to go back to work."

"When will tea be ready?"

"Annie won't be home for another hour."

Arthur put his hand on Sonny's shoulder. He was a good head taller. "What say you and me go over to the pub for a quick one?"

Sonny looked at Clarrie.

"Fine with me," she said, following them back into the lobby.

"Not you, love," Arthur said. "This is man to man."

Sonny squeezed her hand. "We won't be long."

"How did it go at the rectory?" her mother asked when they'd gone.

"Fine. They'll start calling the banns this Sunday."

"We'll be sure to go to church then. I don't know about your dad. I suppose he ought to go since he'll be giving you away."

"Giving me away?" Clarrie said. "I'm not sure I like . . ." Before she could finish the thought, the front door opened and her father came in smoking and coughing.

"Bloody cigarettes," he said. "I'm going to give 'em up one of these days."

After tea, Clarrie walked Sonny to the bus stop. "How did you and Arthur get along in the pub?" she asked him.

"I was wondering how long it would be before you asked."

"So tell me."

"We played a couple of games of darts, and drank some warm beer."

"Room temperature. What did you talk about?"

"He wanted to make sure I'd take good care of you. He told me you were very sensitive and easily hurt. I told him I was aware of that."

"Is that all?"

"That's about it. Seems like a decent guy."

"You'd think I was a helpless infant, talking about me like that, the pair of you." She was pleased, though, that Arthur was concerned for her welfare, and had let Sonny know it. As soon as Sonny's bus pulled away, she crossed the road to the hairdresser's.

"Your hair is thicker than it looks," Muriel said.

Clarrie stared into the glass at her crimson, overheated face, at the mass of tight curls that smelled like burnt rubber.

Muriel held up a mirror for Clarrie to view the back. "It needs a lot of loosening up. If you come back the day before your wedding, I'll thin it out for you and do a nice shampoo and set."

"Oh, dear," her mother said, when Clarrie stepped into the kitchen.

"Exactly," Clarrie said grimly.

"Never mind, love. You'll have plenty of time to work on it."

Next morning, Clarrie was awakened by a frantic knocking at the front door. She stumbled out of bed and ran to the landing. Mr. Timson was standing in the lobby talking to her mother. He had left his shop unattended, he said, in order to dash over with an urgent message. Sonny had called on the telephone to say he was shipping out in a couple of days, but he'd managed to get a special pass for tomorrow—Saturday—in order to marry her. He was depending on Clarrie to have the wedding moved forward.

None of his friends could get away, but he'd be waiting for her at the church tomorrow morning at eleven o'clock.

"I'll be glad to stand in as best man if you need me," Mr. Timson said. "The wife can mind the shop for a bit."

Clarrie's mother thanked him, and said that since Arthur had just come home on leave, it would not be necessary, but he was welcome to come over for a glass of port after the wedding. When Mr. Timson had gone, she called up the stairwell. "You better get dressed, Clarrie love. Sonny called Timson's. He's being shipped out. The wedding has to be tomorrow. You'll have to go back to the church and talk to the rector."

"He's waived the calling of the banns," Clarrie told her mother when she came back from the rectory. "Now I have to find something to wear."

"I'll gather up all the clothing coupons I can find, and you can take the bus into Manchester," her mother said. "You won't find much in Salford."

"What about this mess?" she asked touching her hair.

"You can wear that black straw hat you wore when you went to the Lake District."

"I wish you'd come with me, Mam." It was the first time in her life she'd had to shop for a new frock, and she had no idea how one went about it.

"We'll have to hurry, then," her mother said. "I have a million things to do."

Chapter Sixty-three

Clarrie had been feigning sleep for the past hour in order to comply with tradition. Her mother had told her to sleep late, because Annie, acting as her maid of honor, was planning to bring up her breakfast tray.

"She's given us our orders," her mother said. "She wants us all washed and dressed and out of the scullery before you get up, so she can get your bath ready. She's bought Yardley's bath salts for you."

Annie came bustling through the doorway bearing a tray laden with tea and toast. "Wake up. I've brought your breakfast." She set the tray in front of her. "It's just tea and toast. I was going to scramble a couple of eggs, but Mam used them all to make a wedding cake." Annie sat on the edge of the bed. "Aren't you excited?"

Clarrie sipped her tea. "I haven't had time to think about it."

"I've put the water on for your bath, but it won't be ready just yet."

"Thanks."

Annie helped herself to a toast triangle. "Did you and Mam have one of those mother and daughter talks?"

"About what?"

"About the facts of life—you know—like they do in the pictures—the birds and the bees."

"You know Mam better than that."

"Aye." Annie stuffed the rest of her toast into her mouth. "She does get a bit flustered." She reddened. "If you have any questions, I'll be glad to . . . I mean, I'm older than you and I've had a bit more experience."

Clarrie felt her own face growing hot. She wondered just how much experience Annie had. "I doubt if you know any more about it than I do," she said. The words were intended as a bit of friendly banter, but they came out sounding dismissive and brusque. "Thanks anyway," she added. "If I think of anything, I'll let you know."

"You seem to be taking it all in stride," Annie said. "I should think you'd be scared silly, not knowing what you're getting into."

"I'll be around for a while yet," Clarrie said. "I probably won't be leaving until the war's over."

"Aye, well, just remember, we're your family, us lot, right here. Nobody else."

"What's that supposed to mean?"

"It means you'll be three thousand miles away among a lot of strangers, and there won't be anyone to fight your battles for you."

"It seems to me that most of my battles have been with you."

"I'm not talking about family squabbles. What if they don't like you? Who are you going to turn to? Who's going to be there to keep an eye on you?"

"I don't need anyone to keep an eye on me. And anyway, I'll have Sonny."

"Blood is thicker than water."

"Porridge is thicker than water, too," Clarrie said. "I can think of a lot of things thicker than water."

Annie put the last bit of toast in her mouth and got up from the bed. "I'll get your bath ready." Something about the set of Annie's shoulders as she walked away, pierced Clarrie to the quick. In her way, she loves me, Clarrie thought. I must love her, too. Why else would I feel this queer pain in my heart whenever I think about her?

She carried the tray downstairs. Her mother was sitting at the kitchen table, sewing a button on Billy's blazer.

"Morning," Clarrie said. Her mother looked up smiling. "It's a beautiful day for your wedding," she said.

"Happy is the bride that the sun shines on," Billy said.

Annie came in from the scullery. "Your bath's ready."

Clarrie thanked her. "I'm certainly getting the royal treatment."

"Don't get too used to it," Annie said.

Clarrie paused by the sideboard to admire a golden fruitcake tied with a white ribbon. "Looks wonderful, Mam," she said. "When did you find time to bake?"

"Your mam's been working all night," her father said.

"It's an austerity cake, I'm afraid—no icing, no almond paste."

"I like it better this way," Clarrie said.

"Billy was standing in front of the mirror, adjusting his school tie, his blonde hair carefully parted. "I polished your shoes for you," he said.

"Not the suede, I hope?"

"Give me credit for some brains. I know you don't put polish on suede. I only polished the leather parts."

"Thanks, love." Clarrie ruffled his hair.

"Now you've messed it up," he said, pretending to be annoyed.

"You look like Little Lord Fauntleroy," Annie told him.

"I think he looks smashing," Clarrie said.

"Aye, so does he."

The bath was ready, fragrant and steaming on the scullery floor, with two clean towels and a pink satin dressing gown—one of Mrs. Perlman's hand-me-downs—draped over the wooden maiden. Sunlight pierced the steam cloud, dancing on the stone flags of the scullery floor, painting a lacy pattern on the walls.

Clarrie removed her pajamas and stepped into the bath. She examined the lumpy red operation scar, the ragged bullet wound scar under her breast. A few months ago she'd been ready to die for love of Griff Williams, and now she was about to marry someone she hardly knew. What if she was about to make an irreversible mistake?

"This is my wedding day," she whispered. She glanced down at her white body, at the concave belly with its round navel, the triangle of crisp curls, and the long, well-shaped legs. Would Sonny like what he saw?

Annie was knocking on the scullery door. "Hurry up in there," she called. "Dad's got to shave."

"I'm almost done," Clarrie said. She stepped out of the bath, rubbed herself dry with the harsh towel, slipped on the pink dressing gown and went into the kitchen.

"Watch it!" Her father brushed past her carrying a steaming kettle. The rest of the family was dressed and ready to leave for the church.

"Do you want me to stay and help you with anything?" Annie asked. "Do your nails or anything?"

"I can manage," Clarrie said. "You go on ahead. I'll come later with Dad."

She ran upstairs. Annie had laid out her clothes on the bed: clean underwear, a new garter belt, her two-piece linen suit, the stockings Sonny's mother had sent from America. Through the open window came the clear voices of children playing a song and dance game—one she had played as a child.

There came three dukes a riding, riding, riding.
Pray what are you riding here for, here for, here for?
We're riding here to marry, marry, marry . . .

She walked over to the window. Nobody in sight. They must be playing in the next street. Before the war, before the air-raid shelters, on any Saturday all the back streets would have been swarming with children playing, climbing, stoning steps, and jumping off walls. She'd been good at jumping from high places. She could climb out of this window right now onto the lavatory roof and jump over the wall. She'd get on a bus to somewhere—a place where nobody would think of looking for her. She could find a job, rent a room, make a whole new life for herself . . .

But Sonny was waiting for her in front of the brass eagle in the church. She could imagine how he'd look, with his straight back, his khaki uniform clean and pressed. He'd keep glancing towards the door. She remembered the song her mother sometimes sang when she was ironing.

There was I, waiting at the church.
Waiting at the church.
When I found, she'd left me in the lurch.
Lor' how it did upset me!

Sonny would be there as he'd promised. He'd move heaven and earth rather than let her down. She must not let him down.

She slid the silk stockings out of their cellophane envelope and pulled them on, taking care not to snag them. The luxurious feel of the silk and the smooth way the stockings clung to her legs surprised her. The lisle ones always twisted around her legs like corkscrews. In spite of the last minute adjustments, the skirt of her costume was still too big around the waist. She hunted frantically through her dresser drawer to find a safety pin to hold it up. She pinned a spray of pink carnations, already a trifle wilted, to her bodice, and applied a dusting of powder and a little lipstick. She dabbed attar of roses on her wrists and behind her ears and made a last-minute effort to subdue her frizzy hair. Her father called to her from the foot of the stairs.

"You'd better stop titivating, young woman, and get downstairs. Your mam and the others have already gone on ahead."

"Coming!" Clarrie shoved the offending frizz beneath her hat, pulled on her new net gloves, picked up a small white prayer book from the dresser, and went down to join him.

He was waiting in the lobby by the open door. In front of the house, its motor running, was a sleek black car with white satin ribbons stretched from bonnet to windscreen. She cast a questioning glance at her father. "I thought we were going to walk to church."

He cleared his throat. "Aye, well . . . it's not every day . . ."

A uniformed chauffeur moved quickly to open the door for her. Clarrie, clutching her prayer book, slid across the satin-covered seat to make room for her father. In the bright light of day, it was clear that the carnations were the wrong shade of pink. In spite of the warm sun, her hands, encased in net gloves, were icy cold. The closed car smelled strongly of flowers—her carnations perhaps.

"Smells like a funeral in here," her father said. "I'd better open the window."

"Just a crack, Dad. I don't want the wind blowing my hair about."

They rode the rest of the way without speaking, moving slowly along Eccles New Road, listening to the hiss of tires and the flap of the ribbons across the bonnet. Clarrie studied the back of the chauffeur's neck—turning bright red in the warm sun. The collar edge of his white shirt, though stiffly starched and clean, was frayed. She wondered if his wife had learned the trick of turning a collar.

When the wedding car pulled up at the church, the chauffeur alighted to open the door. Several passersby stopped to watch. Her father slipped something into the chauffeur's hand. "No need to wait," he said. "It's a nice day. I believe we'll walk back."

Annie, dressed in her best blue frock, with a velvet Juliet cap over her bronze curls, was waiting in the vestibule. "It's about time," she snapped. "Sonny's there waiting for you, like patience on a monument. He probably thinks he's been jilted."

"I couldn't find a pin to hold up my skirt . . ."

"Never mind that. Let's go in. I'm supposed to go first and then you and Dad follow."

Clarrie took her father's arm as they followed Annie down the aisle. The church was almost empty. Sonny in his Army Air Force dress uniform, and Arthur, in his Marine uniform, were standing by the brass eagle, just as she had imagined. As she walked forward on her well-polished, high-heeled shoes, she glanced to the right, half expecting to see the empty pews filled with phantom school children, and her own childhood ghost watching her with mild astonishment.

Sonny stepped forward, beaming, and took his place by her side. The rector whispered instructions to them, bound their hands together with an elaborately embroidered stole, told them when to kneel and when to move up the steps to the altar.

"Repeat after me," he said, "With my body, I thee worship . . ." When it came time to say, "and with all my worldly goods, I thee endow," Clarrie, thinking of the few clothes and books that were her "worldly goods," broke into a nervous giggle. Sonny looked up and winked at her.

Outside the church a small group had gathered to wait for the bride and groom. As Clarrie came out into the bright sunshine, a sudden breeze snatched her hat off and whipped her hair. Billy, his own blond hair blowing about, ran to retrieve it. A woman laughed. "Good Lord, isn't her hair a mess!" The whisper was loud enough for everyone to hear. Sonny put his arm around her waist.

"Hello, Mrs. Paradiso."

Back at the house, the table had been set with the things Sally had prepared during the night—cold chicken, tiny new potatoes boiled with a sprig of mint, watercress salad. Several neighbors came by to offer congratulations. Sally gave them each a slice of austerity wedding cake and a glass of port to toast the bride and groom.

"I've put you and Sonny in the front room tonight," she said after the neighbors had left. "Annie's changing the bedclothes and making everything nice and clean. It's the room you were born in, you know."

"But I have to go right back," Sonny said. "Didn't Mr. Timson tell you? We're shipping out early, and if I'm not back at the base by five, I'll be declared AWOL."

Clarrie groaned. "He didn't say anything about that . . . I assumed . . ."

"Everyone's been confined to barracks—they made an exception for me for the wedding."

"I'll tell Annie not to bother, then," Sally said. "You two still have a little time—why don't you go for a walk?

"It's not my idea of a wedding night either—sleeping in a hut with a bunch of snoring guys," Sonny said as they walked hand in hand to Buille Hill Park, "but these aren't normal times." He reddened and cleared his throat. "It's like

Thomas Paine said, 'These are the times that try men's souls'."

Clarrie, her eyes blurred by tears, giggled.

"What's so funny?"

"You," she said, "quoting the great men of history."

"I'll have you know I won the history medal at P.S.187 two years running."

"Thomas Paine. I'm afraid I don't know much about him. Wasn't he some sort of traitor?"

"Depends which side of the Atlantic you were on," Sonny said.

"We'll soon be on opposite sides, ourselves."

Sonny kissed her again. "Not for long, I hope."

Sonny's first letter revealed that he hadn't been sent back to the U.S.A, as they'd expected, but was in Germany with the Army of Occupation. "It's only fair," he wrote, "that the guys with battle experience get to go home first."

Letters flew back and forth, Sonny's filled with the events taking place at Nuremberg, where he was stationed. Clarrie reported the events taking place in her family—Clifford's release from a German prison camp, Arthur's engagement to the elder Rourke girl, Annie's impending marriage, and her mother's duodenal ulcer operation. She told him of things she'd seen in the newsreels, gave critiques of the books she was reading, and tried to amuse him with cartoons clipped from magazines and newspapers. In between letters, the time dragged interminably.

Through her job at the news theatre, Clarrie kept abreast of every new development in the Pacific. She and Sonny had been apart less than a month when the dropping of an atomic bomb on Hiroshima, and three days later, a second bomb on Nagasaki, brought about the unconditional surrender of the Japanese. The war was officially over.

Christmas came and went with Sonny still in Nuremberg and their marriage still unconsummated. Clarrie wrote a long letter to Sonny's parents, describing the wedding. And then came a letter from Sonny postmarked New York. He was back home, honorably discharged from the Army Air Force and anxiously awaiting her arrival. But it was not until the following March, after eight long months of separation, that Clarrie received an official letter from the U.S. Army telling her that she should go to Tidworth Army Camp, to be "processed" prior to transportation to the U.S.A. She had been assigned a berth on the HMS Queen Mary bound for New York.

"So you're off to America, then," her father said as he set down her suitcase in the railway station. His voice sounded husky, his glasses were so filmed with steam she couldn't see his eyes.

"You'll be sure to write to us, won't you, love," her mother said. "Let us know how you're getting along."

"Of course."

"If you don't like it, you can always come home," Annie said. "I'll be getting married soon, and I'll be moving out, so you can have the bed all to yourself."

Billy thrust a piece of twisted metal into her hand. "Shrapnel from my collection," he said. "It's my best piece. It has German writing on it."

"Thanks, love. I'll treasure it." She kissed his cheek. "You'll be all grown up by the time I . . ."

The porter was slamming doors shut. “You’d better get on board, then,” her father said.

She settled back in her seat and looked out the train window at her family. Her mother, father, Annie, and Billy stood in a small cluster looking self-conscious and uncomfortable. Suddenly, she was anxious for the parting to be over.

The train started with a jolt. Clarrie blew them a kiss and waved. Her father took two steps forward as though to remind her of some last thing, then stopped and for some reason removed his hat. As the train pulled out, she did her best to ignore a small insistent voice telling her she would never in this world see her father again.

Clarrie awoke to a change in the sound of the ships engines, and saw through the porthole a number of tugboats laden with uniformed men, chugging through the water. Voices sounded from the passageway as several women who’d ventured onto the deck were herded back to their cabins. A brusque male voice came over the loudspeaker, ordering them to stay in their cabins until cleared by customs. Clarrie sat on her bunk to wait.

Seven days ago, she, along with hundreds of war brides, many with babies, had been loaded onto army lorries, and driven to the Southampton docks, where the Queen Mary, her three huge smoke-stacks billowing grey clouds, her gangplank in place, awaited their arrival. The passengers were no sooner on deck, than there came a deafening blast from the ship’s horn, and the ship began to move. The women had crowded the rails, watching the English coastline fade away through tear-filled eyes. Some of them had their arms around each other’s waists and were singing, “White cliffs of Dover.”

As a child, she had often dreamed of traveling on an ocean liner, but the journey hadn't been anything like she'd imagined. The moment England's coastline faded from view, she'd lost her bearings, her sense of who and what she was. She'd spent the voyage—according to the stewards, one of the roughest crossings the Queen Mary had ever known—not seasick, like so many of the women, but in a kind of limbo, unable to think or write or take part in any of the ship's activities. She'd spent most of her time on deck, staring out at the grey, churning water.

At last, duly cleared by a surly customs man, Clarrie went up on deck to join the swarms of excited women crowding the rail. The women wrapped their arms around each other's waists as they had done leaving England, but now, instead of "White Cliffs of Dover," they were singing, "Kiss me once and kiss me twice and kiss me once again, its been a long, long, time . . ."

Clarrie stood a little apart, mesmerized by the New York skyline. Skyscrapers rose like a mirage into the grey March sky. The angular buildings, narrow as pencils, seemed to crowd against each other as though engaged in a grim struggle to escape the earth. Nothing she had read, nothing she had seen on film, had prepared her for this. It struck her that America was not, as she had fondly believed, merely a larger, more up-to-date version of England. There was something alien here; something harder, stranger, more powerful and more fantastic, than anything she could have imagined. She pulled her coat around her and braced herself against the cold salt air.

The End

www.ingramcontent.com/pod-product-compliance
Lightning Source LLC
Chambersburg PA
CBHW020602310726
48979CB00008B/1308/J

* 9 7 8 0 9 8 1 7 3 1 5 1 3 *